P9-CDH-647

Storm

Withdrawn *Clouds*

Rolling In

 # 1 in The Bregdan Chronicles Series

Ginny Dye

A Voice In The World Publishing
Bellingham, WA

Batavia Public Library
Batavia, Illinois

Storm Clouds Rolling In

Copyright © 2010 by Ginny Dye
Published by A Voice In The World Publishing
Bellingham, WA 98229

www.BregdanChronicles.net

www.GinnyDye.com

www.AVoiceInTheWorldPublishing.com

ISBN 1503326667

All rights reserved. No portion of this book may be reproduced in any form without the written permission of the publisher.

Printed in the United States of America.

Batavia Public Library
Batavia, Illinois

For my grandfather,
Wallace Lorrimer Gaffney
1893-1976
"Dandy"

Thank you for encouraging me
to follow my dreams
no matter what the cost.
My gift of writing
is yours - the Bregdan Chronicles
are for you.

A Note from the Author

There are times in the writing of history when we must use words we personally abhor. The use of the word "nigger" in *Storm Clouds Rolling In* is one of those times. Though I hate the word, its use is necessary to reveal and to challenge the prejudices of the time in order to bring change and healing. Stay with me until the end – I think you will agree.

My great hope is that *Storm Clouds Rolling In* will both entertain and challenge you. I hope you will learn as much as I did during the months of research it took to write this book. Though I now live in the Pacific Northwest, I grew up in the South and lived for 11 years in Richmond, VA. I spent countless hours exploring the plantations that still line the banks of the James River and became fascinated by the history.

But you know, it's not the events that fascinate me so much – it's the people. That's all history is, you know. History is the story of people's lives. History reflects the consequences of their choice and actions – both good and bad. History is what has given you the world you live in today – both good and bad.

This truth is why I named this series The Bregdan Chronicles. Bregdan is a Gaelic term for weaving. Braiding. Every life that has been lived until today is a part of the woven braid of life. It takes every person's story to create history. Your life will help determine the course of history. You may think you don't have much of an impact. You do. Every action you take will reflect in someone else's life. Someone else's decisions. Someone else's future. Both good and bad. That is the **Bregdan Principle**...

Every life that has been lived until today is a part of the woven braid of life. It takes every person's story to create history. Your life will help determine the course of history. You may think you don't have much of an impact. You do. Every action you take will reflect in someone else's life. Someone else's decisions. Someone else's future. Both good and bad.

My great hope as you read this book, and all that will follow, is that you will acknowledge the power you have, every day, to change the world around you by your decisions and actions. Then I will know the research & writing were all worthwhile.

Oh, and I hope you enjoy every moment of it, and learn to love the characters as much as I do!

I'm already being asked how many books will be in this series. I guess that depends on how long I live! My intention is to release two books a year, each covering one year of history – continuing to weave the lives of my characters into the times they lived. I hate to end a good book as much as anyone – always feeling so sad that I have to leave the characters. You shouldn't have to be sad for a long time!

Seven books are already written (January 2015), with many more on the way! If you like what you read, you'll want to make sure you're on our mailing list at www.BregdanChronicles.net. I'll let you know each time a new one comes out!

Sincerely,
Ginny Dye

PROLOGUE

1850

Moses had come to watch his daddy die.

Slinking back into the sheltering brush, he struggled to evade the probing fingers of light groping for him from the blazing fire. The two men coaxing the fire into a roaring mountain of flame had not heard him creep to where he could see into the clearing. His ebony skin and rough, dark clothes merged into the darkness. The only evidence of his presence was the glowing white of his eyes. He would take his chances. Nothing would keep him from this last glimpse of his daddy.

He knew his mama would thrash him good when she found out he had come. He could well imagine her fear when she discovered he was gone, but he'd had no choice. He had to. At eleven years of age he was now the man of the house. He couldn't live with himself if he didn't do this. He had to say goodbye to his daddy.

"Bring him on, boys!" A hoarse shout exploded into the still night.

Moses slunk back further into the darkness, every muscle tense with fear. They were coming!

"The rope's ready. There's soon to be one less nigger to bother us."

Moses shuddered at the hatred oozing from the unknown, and as yet unseen, man's voice. He knew if they found him they wouldn't hesitate to kill him as well. Killing was in the air tonight. He could feel it as surely as he could feel the velvety leaves brushing against him.

It had started the night before when the slaves on the Manson plantation revolted. Before the night was over they had killed Master Manson and set fire to his barns. Over fifty slaves had disappeared into the inky

Virginia night. News had spread fast to the other plantations. By the end of the night two hundred slaves had made their break for freedom. Moses's daddy, Sam, had been one of them. Most of them had not gotten far.

The slave owners and overseers had banded together and called their hunting dogs into service. Sam, along with a large group of slaves unfamiliar with the low-lying swampland northwest of Richmond, had gotten bogged down. Lost and confused, he had been easy prey for the diligent hounds. Word of mass captures had filtered back to the plantations. Everyone knew the one they called the *giant black* could only be Sam. Moses's mama, in from a long day in the fields, had slapped her hand over her mouth, screamed, and fainted dead away.

Moses was the only one who had overheard the overseer talking on the porch when he delivered some wood to the big house. Crouched behind a thick bush, risking a beating if he were caught, Moses had heard him say they were going to kill the giant black to teach the others a lesson. He had grabbed his chance, slipping away in the ruckus that followed word of the capture of at least a dozen slaves from their plantation.

"Daddy!" Moses slapped his hand over his mouth and looked around wildly. The excited voices of men surging into the clearing covered his mistake. Though Moses couldn't slink into the lush growth any further, he could feel his slender body almost pulling into itself. Fear knotted his stomach and made his teeth chatter in the stifling July heat.

Sam was at the head of the line of six slave men being led into the clearing. The towering oaks formed a mighty tunnel for the procession. The trees, like the air embracing them, were still and somber, reflecting back the light from the roaring flames. They seemed to know only sorrow would come from this night. Moses hardly recognized his own daddy. The chains holding the six together were a mockery. Their bashed and broken bodies could not have afforded them another escape attempt. His daddy was the worst. Moses figured that was because Sam had been a leader. It was the only way he could explain the open, bleeding cuts, the face swollen almost beyond recognition, the useless, broken dangle of both arms.

He wanted to call out and run to him. Fear kept him silent. Fear...and the understanding he would have to take care of his mama and three sisters now. They needed him. He feared what awaited him back at the plantation, but he feared what was playing out before his eyes even more.

Time seemed to stand still as the drama unfolded. The trees, the brush, even the air seemed to be holding its breath.

"Get the head nigger over here. It's time to even the score!"

Moses stared at the overseer from his own plantation. James Stewart was a large man, with coarse features and a vicious temper. More than once he had seen it turned on his fellow slaves. He had felt the lash himself. Now the big man was after his father. His trembling deepened to shuddering spasms as he fought to control the moans wanting to explode from his body.

Sam was prodded with vicious pitchforks like an animal, until he was below the waiting noose. Slowly it was lowered to where he quietly waited. At that moment, Moses felt a surge of pride for his Daddy. The man who had taught him from childhood to always be proud of who he was might be broken and battered, but he was not beaten. The glow of pride still burned in his eyes. In spite of the pain racking his body, he held his head high and stared defiantly at his killers. It seemed to enrage them more. They wanted this slave — the one they considered less than human — to cower before them.

"This one seems to think he's something more than the animal he is! I think he needs a little more education." One man, clothed immaculately in gentlemen's clothing, strode forward from the pack. "I'll consider it an honor to provide that education."

Moses felt sick at the hatred pulsing through the clearing. What else were they going to do to his daddy? He watched as the noose was pulled tight around his glistening neck and Sam was prodded up onto the wooden platform assembled in the clearing. He leaned in a little closer as the fancy-dressed man approached with an evil sneer on his lips and then gasped as a flash of light reflected off the huge knife the man pulled from his tunic. Moses's eyes flew back to his daddy. He couldn't take his eyes off him one more time. He had come to watch him die. Watch him he would.

"Think you're too good to be a slave, don't you, boy?"

Silence filled the night.

Moses finally recognized the voice. It belonged to Master Borden who owned the plantation two miles down the road. He had lost close to thirty slaves and two of his barns had been burned. Master Borden wasn't a large man, but his bearing spoke of authority as firelight glistened off his silver hair. His bronze face was set in harsh lines.

"I spoke to you, boy!" His deceptively gentle tone had sharpened with the obvious anger surging through his body. "Answer!"

Moses's eyes were glued to his daddy. He saw Sam's eyes glitter with hatred, but no words came. His shoulders squared a little more and his ebony eyes fixed on his attacker. Moses saw something else. He saw the lines of Sam's mouth tighten. He saw the brows come together. He knew that look. It meant his daddy was getting ready to do something important, but what? The rope, pulled snug around his neck, was holding him upright. Leaning forward against the protecting darkness, he held his breath.

Turning his back on Sam, Master Borden held the knife high in the flickering light and yelled to the other five slaves watching from the side. "Let this be a lesson. For you, and for whoever might be watching!" His evil laugh filled the night air as he waved his knife at the darkness pressing in around him.

Moses gasped and shrank back even further into the stifling night, ignoring the blackberry thorns tearing at his skin. Did they know he was there? Were they coming after him next? It seemed to the boy that even the giant oaks pulled back from the venom in Master Borden's voice. It was almost as if he could feel the brush draw him a little closer into its protective embrace.

"This creature standing before me is no more than an animal. His Master was good to him, and what did he do? He repaid him by running away. By setting fire to his barns!"

Moses barely kept from crying out. He knew his daddy hadn't done any fire setting. He had just wanted to be free. He had wanted to go north and make enough money to buy freedom for his family. He had overheard his daddy and mammy talking just days before the revolt. Daddy talked about the freedom available in the North, where a man could take care of his own family. There had been no mistaking the longing in his voice. He'd heard something else too. Hope. Hope that things might someday be better.

"He doesn't just deserve to die. I think maybe we should carve on him a little, so his body will be easier to bury!" Master Borden gave an evil smile as he shouted into the night. The madness of the night, the killing in the air, was reflected in his wild eyes. He waved the knife in the direction of the other plantation owners. "Loosen that rope a little. I don't want him to have an easy way out. He's going to get what's due him!" Waiting until his orders had been obeyed, he laughed triumphantly and moved forward, knife raised.

Moses couldn't stifle the groan that rose from his gut. For the first time he questioned the wisdom of his coming. Could he watch while these men cut his daddy? It was all he could do to not bolt and run. He had to know. He had to see. Afterwards he was never sure if the words he whispered were audible or if they only echoed in the empty fear of his heart. "Goodbye, Daddy..."

The men in the clearing, however, had made a mistake. They had assumed Sam's broken arms were useless and had not tied them behind his back. Moses watched as his daddy shifted his weight and tightened his face in concentration.

Sam made his move. Master Borden was holding the knife high in the air, waving it as he yelled wildly. Sam lunged and with a cry of pain managed to grab the knife with the hand of his broken right arm. The knife was pointing down when, no longer held by the rope and knocked off balance by the momentum of his lunge, he fell from the platform. All two hundred fifty muscular pounds of him came crashing down on the unsuspecting Master Borden.

Wild yelling and cries filled the clearing. When quiet reigned again, Master Borden lay dead, stabbed through the heart by his own knife.

Sam swung quietly from the end of the coarse rope.

Blinded by tears, Moses stumbled through the dark woods, running to escape the scent of death. He would never forget what he had seen that night.

He would never forget.

ONE

April 14, 1860

"Miss Carrie, if you don't sit still I'm never going to get this braid right! How do you expect me to get it straight with you bouncing around like a rabbit?" Rose, her black eyes flashing, stood back and laughed helplessly.

"I hate having braids! I wish I could just get my hair cut short and be done with it. It takes way too much time to have to fiddle with it!" Carrie Cromwell's brilliant green eyes snapped as she gazed with disgust at her long ebony hair. She knew people thought her wavy hair was one of her best features, but right now it was getting in her way. She laughed merrily. She could just imagine her mother's horror if she were to do such a thing. Not to mention the rest of her proper, southern Virginia neighbors. They already shook their heads when they talked of her to one another. "Couldn't you just see Mother? She would give up all hopes of ever raising a proper daughter." A feeling of mirth replaced the impatience she felt with her hair.

"What are you in such a hurry for anyway?" Rose teased, her hands flashing faster.

Carrie flashed her slave a look of exasperation. "Do you really need to ask? Look outside!" she demanded. "It's a day as perfect as a newborn baby. Spring is bursting out all over this land. Granite is waiting for me."

Rose nodded her head knowingly. "Now I understand." Her hands continued to flash. "You may not care how you look, but Missus Cromwell would skin me alive if I let you out of here without every hair in place."

Rose and Carrie had been friends from the time they were old enough to toddle around. Master Cromwell, the owner of Cromwell Plantation, had encouraged the friendship between his daughter and the slave child born just two weeks earlier. At the time, it had suited both of them just fine. Neither had thought to question the arrangement. It was simply the way things were. The two had spent countless hours wandering the plantation until Rose, at age ten, had become old enough to fill her role as Carrie's personal maid. At least they could continue to be together. Eight years later, they were both still satisfied, but beginning to question the restless stirrings they felt sometimes.

Giving a final tug, Rose secured the braid and then quickly twisted it into a bun. "There. Now get out of here. I think you have a horse waiting."

"Thanks Rose. You're wonderful." As Carrie leaped from her bench in front of the dressing mirror, she stopped long enough to give Rose an impulsive hug

"Carrie!"

Carrie halted in her flight and turned impatiently. "What now?"

"Dinner is in two hours. That doesn't give you much time."

Carrie waved her hand. "Dinner is dinner. As long as I get there on time everything will be fine." She knew that wasn't really true. Her mother expected her to appear for each meal looking like the wealthy plantation owner's daughter she was.

"There is company coming tonight," Rose reminded her.

"Oh bother!" Carrie groaned. "You're right. I had totally forgotten." Her face clouded for just a moment and then cleared. "I'll be back in time," she declared defiantly. "I've got to get out of here." The last words were thrown over her shoulder as she disappeared through the open door.

Drawing deep breaths of the fragrant spring air, Carrie strode to the stables. She knew her mother would disapprove of her hurried pace, but she couldn't be bothered with her mother's opinions right now. She didn't have much time. Then, just as she reached the stable corridor, she saw Granite being led out.

"You have him ready!" Carrie's voice was filled with childish delight as she gazed lovingly at her towering, gray thoroughbred gelding. Granite had been a gift from her father when she turned fourteen. They had been inseparable since then.

"Of course, Miss Carrie. You expected less?"

Carrie flashed a smile at the pretend hurt in Miles's voice. Miles had been in charge of her father's stables since before she was born. She had heard her father comment several times that Miles was one of his most valuable slaves. He managed Master Cromwell's stable of twenty horses with a skill unmatched by any in the area. Carrie knew her father had received several excellent offers to buy him but had turned down each one. "Of course not, Miles, but I know you have a mare in there about to foal. You don't ever get too far from them. Thank you for having Granite ready for me." She took hold of the reins and walked to the mounting block where she could gain access to the towering heights. Usually she enjoyed spending time talking with her friend. He had taught her many secrets about horses—and people, too. Not today, though.

"I ain't never lost a baby for yo' daddy yet, Miss Carrie."

Carrie smiled at the pride in his voice and leaned down just long enough to whisper confidingly to Miles. "Someday I'm going to ride like a man. This silly sidesaddle business is for the birds. No one is meant to ride a horse like this."

Miles nodded. "I believe you, Miss Carrie. You done always wanted to do things a better way. You be a round peg."

"A round peg?" Curiosity kept Carrie from dashing off. "What do you mean, a round peg?"

"People been making you square holes all yo' life. Can't put a round peg in a square hole, Miss Carrie. You still be tryin' to find where you fit."

Carrie stared into his open face for a long moment. How had he gotten inside her head? Then, straightening, she waved gaily and headed Granite for the open gate.

From her place by the bedroom window, Rose watched Carrie go. She shook her head with amusement and then turned to straighten the dressing table. She paused to gaze at her appearance in the ornate mirror gracing the cream-colored wall and examined her face critically. People told her she was beautiful. She didn't know if she was or not. Not that it made any difference. She was just a slave. Perfect caramel-colored skin set off with exquisite features did her no good because she was never going to fall in love and get married. Marriage meant nothing but pain. She had seen too many couples separated—one sold—while the other stayed. Her own father had been sold right after she was born. It was hard to watch her mother's pain all those years.

A noise down the hall startled Rose from her reverie. She couldn't be found staring into Carrie's mirror when there was so much work to be done. She didn't know who was coming to dinner tonight but it must be somebody important. Mistress Cromwell had called all the house slaves together that morning and instructed them to have the place shining before nightfall. Company was common around the Cromwell Plantation, as it was on all Virginia plantations, but not all of it warranted special instructions. Who could be coming? Rose shook her head at her questioning. There would be no answers until the carriage arrived at the door. Usually Carrie filled her in on what was going on. This time even she didn't know. Rose didn't know if it was because it was a big secret or because Carrie just didn't care and thus hadn't taken the time to find out. She suspected it was the latter.

Rose's first job was Carrie's room. She had already made the spacious four-poster canopy bed with its exquisite rose-bordered, white coverlet. The bed had been a gift from Carrie's doting father after his last trip to London for business. Moving easily about the room, which was familiar as her own, she straightened the floor-length, rose-colored drapes and readjusted the bows on the tiebacks. She grabbed the broom and made quick work of the gleaming hardwood floor, rearranging the white and rose rugs scattered about. Finally, she reached into the closet and pulled out the dress Carrie would wear that evening. Rose always selected Carrie's clothes. She had a natural eye for what would look best on her young mistress and what would be most appropriate for any occasion. Carrie simply didn't care. Her young mistress didn't consider herself beautiful, but those who saw her when she was excited about something couldn't take their eyes from her. She exuded a light that drew people to her—strangers and friends alike.

Rose allowed her hand to travel longingly down the gleaming, yellow satin gown. Then she shook her head firmly and snatched her hand back. Dreams were useless. She would never wear anything like this. Dreaming would only make her unhappy. She grabbed the water pitcher and washbowl and headed for the kitchen. She had work to do.

Carrie laughed as the cool, soft air enveloped her. She leaned forward and spoke softly into Granite's ear. He immediately burst into a smooth, ground-eating canter. She needed her place today. Even if it meant being late for dinner and incurring her mother's disapproval, she needed her place. No one else knew about it. It was Carrie and Granite's secret. Not even Rose knew where she went when her heart was burdened and she needed to figure out life.

As she rode, she gazed out over the twenty-five hundred acres that comprised Cromwell Plantation. She loved the land passionately. Carrie knew all its moods—all of its secrets and hidden places. When she was just eleven, in spite of her mother's protests, her father had set her free. She could still remember the conversation.

"Daddy, I want to ride alone." Even then, Carrie was determined when going after something she wanted.

"Alone?" Her father's expression was one of amused patience.

"Yes, alone! I don't want Miles to ride with me. I don't need him. I want to explore on my own. I want to find secret places. I can ride as good as him any day," she boasted.

Her mother, seated at the other end of the table, watched the interchange with a horrified expression. It deepened as silence stretched in the room. "Thomas! You aren't considering giving in to this latest crazy request are you? I simply won't hear of it. My daughter running around the countryside on her own? Preposterous," she snorted.

Carrie remained silent. She knew from long experience that saying anything would not further her cause. Pitting her mother and father against each other only thwarted her plans. She was hopeful however. Her father's extended silence meant he was thinking about it.

Her mother jumped in again. "Thomas, please tell me you're not considering this. Carrie is getting to the age where she should be spending more time around the house. It's bad enough that she spends hours on that crazy horse with Miles. Carrie is getting older. She needs to learn how to run the plantation. She needs to spend more time on her studies, more time practicing the piano. Heaven only knows how much practice she needs with her sewing."

It was all Carrie could do to control her groan. She forced herself to remain quiet with her eyes glued to her father. He turned to look at her. His eyes challenged and gave her confidence at the same time. She knew her father believed in her. She returned his gaze with a confident one of her own.

Thomas Cromwell looked down the table at her mother. "Her studies are fine, Abigail, and there is still plenty of time for her to learn to run the plantation. She's young, and she needs her freedom. All of our people adore her. They'll look out for her."

Carrie could have shouted with joy. Somehow she maintained her composure. The only evidence of her *excitement was the slight excited wiggle of her body in the velvet chair.*

Her father turned to look at her sternly. "You and I will talk later about where you are allowed to go. If you do anything foolish, it will be the only time. With freedom goes responsibility. You can't have one without the other."

Carrie pulled herself back to the present. That had been seven years ago. Since then she had covered every square inch of the plantation. She knew it better than her father himself. Would her intimate knowledge of the land come in handy someday? Carrie pulled up, surprised by the thought that had just crossed her mind. Where had that come from? She shook her head. Sometimes her vivid imagination made her laugh even at herself.

She took a few minutes to look around her now. To her, Cromwell Plantation was the most beautiful place on earth. The gentle rolling fields, the embracing woods, the undulating pastures that were home to their horses. She had stopped her mad dash in the middle of one of Father's tobacco fields. The tiny sprigs of plants had just begun to force their way through the rich soil. Their brilliant green reached for the sunlight that sank into the dark earth, beckoning them to life. The even rows spread out before her spoke of the abundant harvest that would be theirs in several months. They had Edmund Ruffin to thank for that. Carrie could remember the worried look on her father's face as he had watched the yield from his tobacco harvest become less and less. Master Ruffin, from nearby Evelynton Plantation, had been her father's salvation. His many experiments in agriculture had revealed the secret of marl. The fertilizer, applied to their fields, had worked a miracle, restoring the calcium that years of tobacco growing had leached from the soil. Declining crops had been reversed. Prosperity was once more a commonality of life. Tobacco was still the primary crop, but many fields were now sprouting the new growth of corn and wheat as well.

Carrie's father had made sure she knew about the workings of the plantation. Most fathers would have hidden their struggles, but he wanted to make sure she understood what they were up against and what it took to make it all happen. Carrie knew her father saw her as the son he never had. Her mother had almost died during her birth and had never conceived again. As hard as her mother tried to conform her into the perfect southern lady, her father fought even harder to give her freedom and let her learn in the direction her interests lay. While she could have cared less about her sewing skills, she was deeply dedicated to understanding crops and fertilizer. The mystery of growth—the magic of death necessary to cause renewal in spring—was one she never grew tired of. She loved to ride over the cold, barren fields during the winter months. It always amazed her that underneath the hard, unyielding ground lay everything needed to produce abundant growth. She would sit for long minutes contemplating how the harshness of winter was necessary to bring about the beauty of spring.

"Miss Carrie! What you doin' here?"

Startled, Carrie looked around. Only then did she realize she had stopped less than one hundred yards from a group of slaves at work in the fields. "Sadie! You shouldn't be asking me that question, I should. What are *you* doing here? I told you not to start back to work until day after tomorrow."

Sadie ducked her head and spoke softly. "I'm fine, Miss Carrie. I just came over to say howdy. You look mighty fine up on dat horse." She looked back over her shoulder and her next words came out in a rush. "I got's to be goin' Miss Carrie. Have a nice day." She hurried back over to the group and bent to her work of weeding the fledgling plants.

Carrie returned the wave the rest of the slaves sent her way. Her eyes, however, were fixed on the horizon. What made Sadie leave so fast? The dust in the distance told her two more horses were on the way. As the pair drew closer, Carrie recognized their overseer, Mr. Adams, and his bay mare, Ginger. She stayed long enough to give him a casual wave, but she didn't want to get pulled into conversation. She had already wasted valuable time. She urged Granite back into a canter and then let her thoughts return to Sadie.

She would have to go down to the quarters to check on her tonight. Sadie really shouldn't be working today. Just two days ago she had spiked a high fever which took hours of cold compresses to bring down. The one area Carrie showed an interest in that sparked her mother's approval was her nursing in the quarters. Medicine fascinated her. She had started young, going with her mother on her rounds as she took care of the slaves. Owners were expected to take care of their own people. Carrie had watched, enthralled, as her mother doctored cuts and sprains, and ministered remedies to colds and other ailments. Mistress Cromwell helped deliver babies and she had even sewn up some nasty cuts. Carrie was determined to duplicate all her mother did. By the time she had turned seventeen, she had taken her mother's place at all but the most critical illnesses. The slaves had always loved her, but now they seemed to view her with adoration. Not only did she take care of them, she treated them with respect and caring. Still, she couldn't help but feel the restless resentment simmering in the air at times.

She would talk to Mr. Adams about Sadie later. Or maybe she would have her father do it. Mr. Adams always did what she told him to, but his mocking politeness unnerved her at times. It was hard to tell what he was really thinking behind his calculating gray eyes. All she knew was that at times he made her feel uncomfortable.

In retaliation against such serious thoughts, Carrie gave a very unladylike war whoop and leaned forward in the saddle. Responding to her light mood, Granite launched forward into a dead gallop. His strides devoured the last mile to the river. Carrie could feel her bun loosen and fall as the gushing wind tore at Rose's careful work. She smiled as the braid cascaded down her back. No matter. She would look proper again before dinner. For now she was free and she meant to make the most of it.

Granite's mad dash slowed as he entered the trail into the woods. He knew where they were headed.

Carrie allowed him to choose his own way as they wove through the thick trees. There was a trail, but you could see it only if you were on foot and moving slowly. Carrie had discovered it the same year her father set her free. She suspected the only other inhabitants were deer meandering their way to the river for a drink. It was perfect. No one could ever find Carrie here. She should know. There were times her father spent hours searching for her in a fruitless game of hide and seek. He was always frustrated in his attempts, but he understood her need for secret places. He actually seemed to take great pleasure in the fact that his spirited daughter knew his own land better than himself. Carrie was sure that even if he had suspected her hiding place he never would have tried to find it because he knew how special it was to her. Carrie loved both her parents dearly but her father understood her almost better than she did herself. Her brow creased as she thought of her father. He had changed lately. All he talked of was politics, and the look of worry on his face seemed to have become a permanent fixture.

Granite gave a soft nicker as he broke out into the clearing that was their destination. Carrie gave a soft gasp of delight.

"Oh, Granite. I knew it was time for them. I was right!"

Trailing vines of wisteria had turned the tiny clearing into a royal lavender palace. The fragrant blooms hung down in cascades that filled the air with a heady perfume. Fragments of sunlight seemed to dance diamonds through the flowers. Dogwood trees, lush with luminous white blossoms, mingled with red bud trees sporting their own purple blooms. The hum of bees busy in the wisteria mingled with birdsong, provided a background symphony as butterflies swirled and fluttered through trees. Carrie sat quietly for a few moments and then dismounted. Looping Granite's reins around a nearby branch, she circled the clearing slowly, breathing in deeply to fill every part of herself with the beauty.

Not a week went by—unless weather made it impossible—that she didn't come here. It was here she had pondered the deep process of growing up. Here she had retreated after misunderstandings with her mother. Here she had struggled with the complexities of understanding herself. Of course it was here she would come on a day like today.

She breathed deeply and moved to where the clearing perched on the side of the James River. Brushing off her favorite boulder, she settled down, smoothing the folds of her forest-green dress around her. Her eyes gazed into the distance. The river had always had the power to cast a spell over her. Its ever-changing personality seemed somehow to always match hers. Today was no exception. The surface seemed to be a contradiction. As the sun cast bright laughter into some spots, while fluffy clouds cast shadows on the water all around them. Was the river laughing or scowling? Indeed, it seemed to be doing both at the same time. Carrie understood. Tucking her feet underneath her, she rested her chin on her fist and allowed the play of light to pull her in. Maybe it would give her answers today. Maybe the river would help her understand the contradicting swirl of her own emotions.

Carrie loved Cromwell Plantation. She loved every inch of it—the fields, the woods, the river, the tiny meandering streams. She loved the horses and all the other animals. She especially loved the slaves. They were her friends. Her mother thought it proper to keep more distance, but Carrie had fostered relationships that were deep and bonding. She would just as soon spend a day in the slave quarters as she would with her friends on the neighboring plantations. More so if she were completely honest. Her friends were all proper young plantation mistresses. They were content with sewing and knowing the proper ways to run activities and functions. Carrie was bored with what she considered their silly talk. Which brought her to her dilemma. If she loved the plantation so much, why did she want to leave?

The question had been burning in her mind for months now. She could no longer ignore it. The future stretched before her, empty and boring. She loved many things about her life, but she was no longer satisfied.

She wanted something more. Long days of running a plantation, of duplicating her mother's life, caused her to feel as if she would be sick sometimes. Carrie knew her days of avoiding it would soon be over. She had turned eighteen just the week before. Even her father was going to expect her to give up her wild, carefree days in return for responsibility and duty.

Carrie could no more help the trapped feeling welling up inside of her then she could stop the flow of the mighty James River. She had tried but to no avail. All she knew was that she wanted more. *She wanted more!* She wanted her life to stand for something, but what? That's where she kept drawing a blank. She didn't know what she really wanted. But she was sure of what she didn't want. She didn't want to follow in her mother's footsteps. She didn't want to fill her days with plantation details. She didn't want to give orders about the condition of the house and the preparation of meals. She didn't want to select fabrics, make clothes, and order draperies.

Carrie laid her head down on her knee and groaned. Why couldn't she be like her other friends? They were excited about the prospect of someday running the plantations that had been in their families for more than a century. They simply took their position in life for granted. Why couldn't she do the same? Her life would be so much easier. Neighbors wouldn't look at her askance when she did something—like galloping down the main road—that didn't fit their mold of social acceptability. Why did she have to be so different? Maybe if she tried harder she could make herself be what everyone expected her to be.

For long minutes she allowed her despairing thoughts to sweep over her. This battle had raged in her heart for two months now. She had to come to some kind of resolution. The turmoil was eating at her heart and mind. She was tired of the flaming thoughts of discontent that kept her awake at night. Finally she raised her head, her eyes once more searching the depths of the river. The tossing waves seemed darker and higher. Her eyes moved to the east toward Richmond, where she saw a mass of boiling clouds coming closer. Another spring storm was on its way. In the short time she had sat there, the advancing cumulus had blotted out most of the sun. Only one bright spot tossed on the river. Carrie fastened her eyes on the defiant spot. It seemed to be enjoying its moment of rebelliousness. The clouds danced across the sky in a vain attempt to block it out. Just as it seemed they would succeed, the little spot swirled away to light on another tossing wave. Carrie watched carefully. If the little spot could have spoken she was sure it would have laughed and told her of the fun of defying the surrounding sameness. It brought her hope. She may be the only one of her kind, but she didn't want to change. The rest of the world could be clouds but she wanted to be a bright spot that defied the surrounding sameness. Of that she was sure.

Having made that decision, she leaned back against the tree that grew behind her boulder. She wasn't like everyone else. She would accept that. But what would it mean for her? Where would it take her? What price would she have to pay? What was she going to do? A low rumble of thunder drew her eyes back to the approaching storm and back toward Richmond. Did her future lie in the bustling city she loved so much? Would she find the answers to the questions she couldn't voice yet? The questions that created a churning and stirring she could not deny?

A distant bolt of lightning and the impatient stamp of Granite's hoof broke her from her reverie.

"Lands, Granite! We have to get out of here. I'm barely going to make it to dinner on time as it is. If I get home all wet I'll never be ready on time. Rose will have my skin!" She pulled Granite over to the boulder, mounted, and turned him quickly. "Let's get out of here, boy."

That was all Granite needed. It was his job to get them home. It was Carrie's job to dodge the flying limbs and leaves as the storm moved ever closer. Carrie cast a last, longing look at the clearing as they flew down the trail. She hadn't found the answers to her questions, but at least she was looking at them straight on. And she had reached one major milestone. She knew she wasn't content to just fit in. She was different and no one was going to force her to fulfill the status quo. She was still eighteen, carefree, the wealthy daughter of a plantation owner, and almost late for dinner.

All thoughts flew from her mind as Granite ate up the distance to home.

TWO

"Thomas! Where is Carrie? I sent Rose for her, but she came back and told me she hadn't returned yet. I demanded to know where she was, but Rose pretended ignorance. I'm sure it's *pretended* ignorance. I think she's hiding something from me and just doesn't want me to know. You really need to do something about it. Those two are just much too close. It's not right!"

Carrie stopped in her tracks as her mother's strident voice floated through the open door. Wrapping her arms around her drenched body to control her shivering, she stood still on the porch and listened. She hated to eavesdrop, but she was curious. Why was her mother so upset? This sounded like something more than the usual impatience with her wayward daughter.

"I doubt Rose is hiding anything from you, dear. It's very likely she doesn't know where Carrie is. She's probably gone to one of her secret places. She'll be back."

Carrie smiled at her father's calm response. He had few defenses against her beautiful mother. Abigail's soft blond hair and blue eyes still had the power to draw him in and he loved her fiercely. He had often tried to explain to Carrie that her mother couldn't help it that her whole life was the plantation house and its efficient management. She simply had no ability to understand her spirited daughter. It was obvious now that his attempt to calm his wife was a futile one.

"Secret places," she snorted. "Thomas, when are you going to realize our daughter is a woman now? She's eighteen for heaven's sake! It's high time she quit running off to *secret places*." The sarcasm dripping from her voice left no doubt as to the contempt she felt. "There's a lot of work to be done around here. I've worked hard all day to get ready for our company tonight. And where has Carrie been? Down in the slave quarters this morning visiting Sarah and now off gallivanting around the plantation somewhere. Robert Borden will be here in less than twenty minutes. Where is your daughter?" she asked in a decidedly exasperated voice.

Carrie watched, glad they had not yet seen her, as her father walked over to where her mother stood looking out the window at the sudden shower that had exploded minutes before. He laid his arm across her shoulder. "Carrie will be here, Abigail," he said soothingly. "She's never late when she knows we have company." He paused. "There is something else bothering you." His flat statement invited her to share whatever it was.

Carrie leaned in closer and held her breath. She knew she should be racing upstairs, but she had to know what was bothering her mother so much. Several moments passed before her mother spoke again.

"I had tea today with Lucy Blackwell," Abigail's voice was deeply troubled. "She thinks there is going to be a war." Her voice caught and then she whirled to stare up at Thomas. "I told her that was pure nonsense. I'm so tired of people and their crazy talk about the South seceding and there being war. It's spring. Why can't we just enjoy it?"

The demanding tone in her voice could not cover the desperation. Her mother had grown up on a plantation further up the James River in Goochland County. She had never known anything but wealth and ease. Even when their own fortunes had been in jeopardy, it was Carrie in whom her father had confided. He told her he didn't know how Abigail would have responded and he didn't want to alarm her. She had never known how close the plantation had been to real trouble.

"You know Lucy Blackwell is nothing but a gossip," Thomas said firmly. "She also overreacts to the smallest things. The Union is going to remain, Abigail. Virginia will never secede. Why, our country got its start just a few miles from here down in Jamestown. Richmond served as the capital of our country during the Revolution. We're Americans. We always will be."

Carrie could stand it no longer, even though the forced confidence in her father's voice made her want to listen longer. Her shivering was now uncontrollable and if she were to be ready in time for dinner, she must go in. She stomped her feet to make it seem as if she had just come onto the porch, swung the door open, and dashed inside. She immediately headed for the sweeping staircase that led to her room.

"Carrie Cromwell!" her mother gasped. "What in the world happened to you?"

Carrie tried to look remorseful. "Oh, I'm just a little wet, Mama. Granite and I didn't quite beat the storm." She couldn't help the smile that broke out on her face. "But what fun we had! We almost beat that old storm. The rain felt so good. It's quite warm you know." Barely taking a breath, she whirled and headed for the stairs. "I don't have much time, Mama. I have to go upstairs and get ready. Rose will be waiting." She cast an impish smile at her father and started to dash up the stairs.

"Carrie Elizabeth Cromwell!"

Her mother's strident voice stopped her flight. When she called her by her full name, it was best to pay attention. Carrie fought to control her impatience and turned to face her mother's wrath. "Yes, Mother?"

Abigail stood in silence for several moments, almost as if she was savoring this rare opportunity for control, however small it may be. She stared in blatant disapproval at her daughter's sodden condition. "I had tea with Lucy Blackwell today. Louisa sent her best to you."

Carrie stared at her mother. She had stopped her to tell her *that*? She didn't know what to say, so she simply nodded. The name Louisa Blackwell did not conjure up pleasant thoughts in her. She and Louisa, the same age, had grown up together but had never gotten along well. Carrie found the other girl petty and childish, with a nasty tendency toward temper tantrums if she didn't get her way. Her simpering ways were nauseating. The tension had grown between them as they matured.

"She couldn't join us for tea because she was working too hard, the dear thing." Carrie simply stared at her mother as she paused for what Carrie knew was theatrical effect. "She is quite looking forward to having us all over for the tournament and for the ball tomorrow. There was so much to be done today. She had been up since early in the morning, supervising all the house slaves in the preparations. Her mother told me that she is such a help, especially since dear Lucy hasn't been feeling well lately."

Carrie wanted to laugh and scream at the same time. Time was ticking away and her mother was chattering about the Blackwells. She caught a glimpse of Rose peering around the stairwell but didn't dare look up at her. When her mother paused, Carrie knew she had finally led up to where she wanted to be all along and was now ready to fling the final arrow.

"Lucy Blackwell told me how sorry she felt for me." Her mother's eyes tightened and began to glimmer with anger. "She told me how *sorry* she was that my own daughter wasn't more of a help—how distressed I must feel because you were determined to shirk your duties and responsibilities around the house." Her smooth voice had taken on a sharp edge.

Thomas attempted to break in. "Abigail—"

Carrie held up her hand to silence him. "I'm sorry I'm such a disappointment to you, Mother. But I really must get ready for dinner. I'll be down soon." With those cool words, she turned and walked sedately up the rest of the stairs.

Carrie felt her mother's eyes boring into her back and could imagine the flabbergasted look on her face. As she reached the top of the stairs, she heard her mother's voice.

"Thomas..." Abigail's voice trailed off helplessly. "What should I do about her?"

"Do about her?" Thomas asked casually. "You have quite a lovely daughter. She's bright and has wonderful manners. I don't think you need to *do* anything about her."

Carrie wanted to hug her father as she turned down the hallway to her room. Her mother's voice floated after her.

"We'll discuss our spoiled daughter later. Right now we have company coming and I have a few more things to check on. I only hope Rose can work another miracle."

Rose was indeed working another miracle. She had not been able to get Carrie's hair dry, but the ringlets escaping the bun she had created worked to make Carrie's flushed face even more becoming. The tangled heap of wet clothing in the middle of the floor could be taken care of later.

"Oh, Rose," Carrie laughed. "You should have seen Mama's face when I came in the front door." Then she sobered. "She looked so serious before she caught sight of me all wet—almost like she was scared. I hope everything is all right." She paused as she remembered what her mother had said. Now that she was not shivering on the porch she was remembering the fear in her mother's voice. "Father seemed to be okay, so it couldn't have been anything too serious."

Rose was obviously too busy to respond. Her hands flashed as she put the finishing touches on Carrie's hair.

Carrie's thoughts drifted toward the unpleasant confrontation in the hallway. She knew she was a disappointment to her mother. She had tried for so long to be what her mother wanted. Her honest heart examination at the river had simply revealed that she could never be someone she wasn't, no more than her mother could stop wanting her to be what she could not be. Carrie struggled to push down the hurt crowding for space in her heart and focused on the evening ahead.

"Who's Robert Borden, Rose?"

Rose stepped back and looked at Carrie in disbelief. "You're asking me that question? You're the one supposed to let *me* know what's going on."

"Oh, pooh," Carrie scoffed. "You know better than me what's going on most of the time. I know how the grapevine works." She smiled up at her friend. "Now come on. I know he's coming for dinner. Who is he?"

Rose just shook her head. "All I know is that I've got less than five minutes to get you in that dress and ready to appear as a proper young mistress. I aim to do my job. Stand up here and let me get this beautiful dress on you."

Carrie wanted to argue, but she knew Rose too well. Her friend wouldn't talk if she didn't feel like it. She stepped around her soggy riding garment on the floor and moved to where Rose was waiting. Obediently she lifted her arms while Rose slipped the yellow satin gown over her head, taking care not to disturb her hair. She stood still while Rose's flying fingers nimbly latched all the buttons, and then moved over to stand in front of the full-length mirror behind her vanity.

"You look beautiful, Miss Carrie. I think you look plenty good enough for that Robert Borden!"

Carrie laughed and whirled around. "I *knew* you knew who was coming. Robert Borden? I don't think I've ever heard of him."

"Maybe not, but your mama went to great pains to get him here. Seems she and his mama grew up real near each other, up there in Goochland County."

Carrie listened carefully. "Borden... Of course," she murmured. "Anna Borden. I've heard Mama talk about her. Not in years, though. When her husband died they seemed to drift apart. I never did know how her husband died. What else do you know?"

"I know you're going be in a heap of trouble if you don't get downstairs and be ready to receive your company. Now get going!"

Carrie nodded and began to move toward the door. "Wish me luck tonight. I'm going to do my best to not do anything to shock Mama. I don't think her heart can take another one today." Laughing merrily, Carrie ran down the steps into the welcoming foyer below.

"Quite the place isn't it, Manson?" Robert Borden was immediately taken by Cromwell Plantation. It was so different from his brick plantation home thirty miles up the river. He was entranced by the gleaming white of the three-story house surrounded by columned porches on all sides.

"Yes, sir. It's quite a place." Manson's voice was noncommittal. Robert didn't expect more. He was courteous to his slave, but the carriage driver knew he didn't expect him to carry on a conversation. He just wanted him to do his job. Manson did it well.

Robert Borden was glad to be here. As far as he knew, Mistress Cromwell had no idea he had finagled his mother into resuming communication with her old friend just so he would receive this invitation. The courteously written note he had received from Abigail Cromwell simply mentioned she would love to welcome the son of an old friend when he was passing through. He had managed to be passing through quite soon. Less than a week after hearing from Abigail Cromwell he had received the invitation from Louisa Blackwell inviting him to the tournament and ball at her plantation. He'd had no mind to accept until he realized the proximity to the Cromwell plantation. It was Thomas Cromwell he wanted to connect with. The growing madness in the country was causing him to seek out those he knew to be of like mind. All the information he had received told him Thomas Cromwell was a sensible, intelligent man who loved the United States.

As they drew closer to the main house, his attention was once more drawn to its beauty. The mansion seemed to be embraced by the towering oaks surrounding it. The fresh green of the early spring leaves made the gleaming white even brighter, and they offered added softness to the already graceful lines of the old house. Huge boxwoods lined the dirt drive leading to the house, their glistening wetness unmarred by dust because the earlier rain had washed them clean and settled the road. Smatterings of pink and white dogwood, along with brilliant purple lilacs, added their color to the beauty. Thomas took a deep breath and prayed he hadn't come all this way on a long goose chase.

Carrie arrived, breathless, in the foyer just as the sound of carriage wheels and hoof beats met her ears. Her mother's stern look was softened by her father's equally loving one.

"You look lovely, Carrie."

Abigail softened. "Your father is right. I can't believe there has been such a transformation from the wild child I saw just minutes ago."

Carrie grinned, relieved her mother was willing to put her anger behind her, even if it was just because their company was almost there. "You know Rose works magic."

The carriage pulled to a stop in front of the house. Together, the three moved out onto the porch to meet their guest. The rain had stopped and the sun was beginning to peek through. Carrie looked around in delight. She couldn't help wishing she could head out on Granite again. The world was always so incredibly beautiful after a storm. She glanced up, but quickly lowered her head so her mother couldn't accuse her of being inattentive of their guest. She had just needed to assure herself that the sky was the same brilliant blue it always was after a spring storm.

"Robert Borden! What a pleasure to have you at Cromwell Plantation. Welcome." Abigail moved forward graciously to greet him. "Please meet my husband, Thomas Cromwell. We're thrilled you could join us tonight," she said warmly.

Carrie lowered her eyes in time to catch Robert staring at her. Flushing, she smiled slightly and dropped her eyes just as Robert tore his own gaze away from her.

Bowing low over Abigail's hand, Robert spoke smoothly. "It's *my* pleasure indeed, Mr. and Mrs. Cromwell. It was so kind of you to offer me your hospitality while I make my way to Charleston."

Carrie's father looked at him more carefully. "You're on your way to Charleston, Robert?"

Robert nodded. "Yes, sir. The Democratic Convention is there in just nine days. When I'm not working my plantation, my interest is in politics. I want to be as close to the action of what is happening in our country as possible."

Thomas nodded, studying him thoughtfully. "How old are you, son?"

"Twenty-one, Mr. Cromwell."

Abigail laid a hand on her husband's arm. "You can have this conversation inside," she said graciously. "I'm sure Robert would like to get cleaned up and I imagine he's famished after traveling all day.

Robert laughed. "You're right, ma'am. Dinner sounds very inviting. It won't take me but a moment to freshen up."

Abigail nodded. "Before I have you shown to your room, I'd like you to meet my daughter, Carrie."

Robert turned eagerly. "How do you do, Miss Cromwell? It's a pleasure to meet you."

Carrie pulled her thoughts back from galloping Granite through the wet fields. Smiling, she extended her hand as he bowed over it. "Thank you, Mr. Borden. It's a pleasure to have you at Cromwell Plantation." She almost laughed at his bemused expression.

Robert turned to follow Abigail into the house.

Carrie watched them go and then reached for her father's arm, detaining him on the porch. Both stood silently while Abigail led their visitor into the hallway. They heard her clear voice giving directions to Sam, the butler, to take Robert upstairs. Shortly after, they heard her footsteps retiring to the kitchen to check on last minute preparations for dinner.

Carrie smiled up at her father. "I'm sorry about earlier. I never meant to be caught in the storm. I lost track of time. I'm truly sorry I upset mother."

Thomas smiled down at her fondly. "Your mother can't help being the way she is, Carrie."

"And I can't help being the way I am", Carrie said quietly, yet firmly.

Thomas looked at her thoughtfully. "You went to your place today." It wasn't a question.

"Yes. It was such a beautiful day. I had to get away." Carrie gazed at her father beseechingly. "I know I haven't tried very hard to be what mother wants me to be, but I can't. I've thought about trying to change, about being different." Her level voice took on a strained tone. "But I can't. I have to be me. I'm sorry it makes her so unhappy."

Thomas wrapped an arm around his daughter's shoulder. "Don't ever be sorry for who you are, Carrie. Your mother will be fine. It will take time though. Don't be too hard on her. The situation in the country is scaring her. She is afraid of losing all she has ever known. I'm afraid she takes it as an insult that her only daughter doesn't share her deep feelings about plantation life."

Carrie wheeled to look up into his eyes. "You know I love the plantation, Father. I just can't get excited about having my whole life revolve around running it."

Thomas nodded again, took her arm, and began to walk toward the front doors. "I know, Carrie. But right now we have company to entertain. I believe I heard the young fellow's footsteps on the stairway. We need to go in. We can talk more later if you would like." Then he smiled impishly. "I think, though, that there is a young man who will be very disappointed if he doesn't get to spend as much time as possible with one Carrie Cromwell." He put his hand on the doorknob and stopped to gaze down into her eyes. "It will take a special man to win your heart, Carrie. Someone who can love your free spirit and fiery independence." His sober tone caused Carrie to stare at him, but he continued with a gentle smile. "You will steal and break the hearts of many young men. Take compassion on them," he said softly. Without waiting for an answer, he opened the door and walked in.

Carrie had no time to respond, for as they entered the house Robert Borden appeared around the corner of the foyer.

"What a wonderful home, Mr. Cromwell! It's every bit as beautiful inside as it is outside." Robert's voice was sincerely enthusiastic.

"Thank you, Robert. This house is very special to my family. It dates back to the 1700s. My family were some of the first people to settle Virginia."

"You must be very proud of them, sir."

"I am. They have left me a legacy I sometimes struggle to live up to. Most importantly, they helped give me a country I am proud to be a part of."

Robert nodded eagerly. "I had heard you felt that way, sir. That's one reason I'm here. Do you think the Union will stand, sir?"

Thomas managed a dry laugh. "You certainly know how to get right to the point, young man."

Robert merely nodded. "The time for idle chatter seems to be long gone. I know there are still many in Virginia who long to see the Union stand firm, but I'm afraid we're becoming a minority in the South."

Thomas nodded but inclined his head toward the dining room. "Why don't we have this discussion at dinner, Robert? I know you're hungry."

Robert looked discomfited. "Will we not bore the women with talk of politics, sir? I don't wish to appear rude. We can talk after dinner if you wish."

Thomas smiled. "My wife has learned to accept my passion for politics lately. My daughter seems to thrive on it." With those words, he led the way into the dining room.

Carrie managed to stifle her laugh as she followed them. She loved the huge dining room with its mahogany table that would comfortably seat fourteen. When needed, there were panels to extend its length for special occasions. An impressive sideboard, two smaller tables, and old mahogany chairs in abundant supply lined the walls—with the exception of the wall that was mainly arched windows looking out over the horse pastures in the distance.

The next hour flew by as course after course of delicious Virginia victuals were placed before them. Servants standing by with peacock feathers made sure the first of the spring flies didn't land on the piles of sumptuous food laid before them. Conversation while they ate remained general and light, ranging from the weather, to horses, to planting conditions.

Finally, Thomas leaned back in his chair, lit the pipe handed to him by one of the table servants, and nodded toward his young visitor. "You asked me a very important question before dinner. It's one I hope with all my heart I have the right answer for. You asked me if I think the Union will stand. Robert, the Union *must* stand. I fear the consequences if the secessionists have their way."

"I too, sir," Robert responded quickly, obviously eager to talk politics. He leaned forward, his face tight with anticipation. "Yet their power seems to be growing, especially in the cotton states. I fear what their hotheaded passion will mean for those of us here in Virginia."

Abigail broke into the conversation, her voice soft and almost pleading. "Thomas, must we really talk of politics again? Mr. Borden surely does not want to fill his evening with this senseless ramble about what the North and South are going to do to each other." She smiled brightly at Robert. "Can't we just have a pleasant evening? He *is* our guest."

Robert turned his most charming smile on her. "Thank you for your concern, Mrs. Cromwell, but politics is exactly what I would love to spend my evening discussing. Especially with your husband. I have long admired him from a distance. I would love to know his thoughts on the issues besieging our country today." He reached out a hand to touch her arm. "I hope you will not find me an ungrateful guest for wanting some of his time."

Abigail relented gracefully. "Certainly not. We are glad to have you as our guest." Rising from the table, she beckoned to her daughter. "Carrie and I will leave you to your discussion."

"I believe I'll stay here, Mother." Carrie felt Robert's eyes on her but merely gazed steadily at her mother.

Abigail gave Carrie a despairing look but said nothing more before she left the room. Thomas winked at Carrie and turned back to his guest. "I understand your concern, Robert. Our country, North *and* South, seems to be full of hotheaded people who are allowing their passionate hearts to rule over their heads. Yet, in Virginia especially, there is still a large number who are allowing their heads to rule."

Robert nodded thoughtfully as he settled back into his chair. "Many of my neighbors in Goochland County think the only way for the South to maintain the life we have always known is to secede. Their arguments are impressive, sir."

Thomas gave Robert a penetrating stare. "And what do you think?"

Robert met his probing gaze with unflinching eyes. "I think I am very confused, sir. My allegiance has always been to the Union. I'm a Southerner, but my years of schooling in the North have given me many Yankee friends and a love for the country as a whole. Yet, the North seems to want to destroy the only way of life many of us have ever known. I'm not sure how I feel about standing by and letting them do that. I, too, am afraid of what secession might mean, but daily I grow just as afraid of what remaining in the Union will mean. That, I suppose, is my main reason for making the trip all the way to Charleston. What happens at the Democratic Convention will have much to do with what happens in our country in the next year or so. There is already much division among the Democratic Party. I fear things could become more heated in Charleston."

"The problem with the secessionists is that they don't understand what secession would really do to the South."

Robert turned his eyes toward Carrie. "What do you mean, Miss Cromwell?" His voice was courteous but slightly flustered.

Carrie hid a smile. It was obvious he had never had a political discussion with a female before. "Our strength as a country lies in the very *unity* of our country. Secessionists fear such a union will mean the loss of their lifestyle. I think secession will *guarantee* the loss of that lifestyle. The North needs our agricultural strength. We need their industrial strength. But most importantly, I don't think the founders of this country—my ancestors—gave their blood and such a mighty effort for freedom just to see it tossed away when we can't agree. There must be a way to keep our country together." Her eyes flashed as she finished, her napkin twisted in her fist. Her mother's obvious fear earlier that evening had given a fresh spark to all she had learned in her conversations with her father and from her reading.

Thomas spoke again as Robert continued to gaze at Carrie. "My daughter speaks my heart as well. Secession is not the answer for the South. I'm afraid if the secessionists in this country are allowed to win this battle, all I have lived and struggled for will cease to exist. I do not believe a peaceable secession is possible. No liquid but blood has ever filled the baptismal fount of nations."

Robert frowned and looked back at Thomas. "So you believe, sir, that secession will mean war?"

"I'm afraid so." Thomas nodded sadly. "And war of any kind is always horrible and destructive. It would mean nothing but tragedy for our country."

Silence reigned at the table for several minutes as the three of them looked forward into the future, saddened by what could occur if the hotheads of the country had their way.

Robert broke the silence. "The abolitionists of the North are becoming more strident. That is one reason I have returned home from college, in spite of having just a few months left before I would have earned my degree. People from the South are becoming very unpopular in the North these days. Several of my classmates returned with me. I intend to finish my degree somewhere in the South."

"Ah, yes..." Thomas tapped his pipe, anger flitting across his face and sharpening his voice. "The abolitionists. I wonder if they really know the troubles they are stirring up down here? I wonder if they are ready to deal with the true consequences if they get their way."

"They demand total emancipation of the slaves, sir."

"Yes," Thomas acknowledged tersely. "It would mean the end of our civilization as we know it."

"Why, Father?" The question slipped from Carrie's mouth before she realized she had spoken. She wasn't even sure where the question had come from. But it was spoken. She waited for her father to answer.

"Slavery is the cornerstone of the South. I don't believe freedom for the South is possible without slavery. It is the basis for our entire civilization." Thomas drew deeply on his pipe and settled back into his chair, warming to his subject.

Carrie was surprised by the immediate reaction that surged through her. She did not for the life of her know why her heart was rebelling at her father's words. She had heard them plenty of times before and had simply accepted them as truth. Why was she questioning them now? Fastening her eyes on her beloved parent, she listened.

"The abolitionists in the North simply don't understand the way of life in the South. Oh, I know they ramble on about the desire of the slaves to be free and I know they even help some of them obtain that freedom, but they aren't looking at the long-range consequences of their thoughtless and reckless actions. Our Negroes are quite simply fulfilling their destiny. And I, as a slave owner, am fulfilling *my* destiny. My destiny is to take care of the Negroes God has given to me. My Negroes are quite simply a part of my family. It is my responsibility to provide for their protection, happiness, and welfare. It is their job to fulfill the responsibilities they hold."

"I quite agree with you, sir," Robert broke in, "but the abolitionists are stirring up people in the North with wild tales of abuse and mistreatment of the slaves."

Thomas nodded. "Unfortunately, there are a few rare cases where the slaves are not treated as they should be. Much of that comes from the rising class of slave owners. Unlike those of us who view our position as masters as a somber responsibility, there are those who view the slave only as a profit center. The new owners work hard at some profession until they have money to obtain land and slaves. Then they hire an overseer and remain in town while the Negroes do their work and are sometimes abused. But that doesn't make slavery a bad thing. It simply means there are people in the system who abuse the power God has given them." He paused to dump the ashes from his pipe and then carefully repack it. He seemed lost in thought. Robert and Carrie waited for him to continue. "The truth is, the slaves quite simply couldn't exist outside the world of slavery. They need us. Left to their own devices, they have neither the mental ability nor the motivation to survive. That's why it is part of my destiny to care for them. I freely acknowledge that all I have is due to the work and effort they give me, but that is simply the fulfillment of their part of the plan of destiny."

Unbidden, vivid images crowded into Carrie's mind. The intelligent shine of Rose's eyes. The eager thirst for knowledge as they studied together. Old Sarah bent over the fire in her cabin reading her Bible. Miles carefully crafting new shoes for a tiny foal born with a twisted leg. Were these people of mental inferiority? Were they incapable of taking care of themselves? Somehow she knew the images crowding her mind were the source of her most recent questions.

Carrie's father continued, pulling her thoughts back to the table. "Take the load of slaves I purchased yesterday—"

"You've purchased more slaves, Father?" Carrie didn't know why the idea bothered her. It never had before.

"Yes, Carrie. There are several owners in Virginia who are afraid war may be coming, so they are selling their slaves to large plantations farther south in order to recoup some of their investment. I think differently. I hope with all my heart that war will not come, and I will fight with everything I have to keep that from happening. But if war does come, the South will be victorious. Of that I am certain. It makes sense to buy as many slaves as possible for that time. There was a fine lot being offered today. I purchased ten—six women and four men."

Carrie merely nodded, her face impassive.

Robert, however, grew enthusiastic as Thomas talked. "I'd never thought about it that way before, sir. When I return from Charleston I intend to strengthen the stock I have. My brother and I have both been in school lately and have not been able to attend to crop planting as much as we would desire. We have kept my mother very comfortable with breeding."

"Breeding?" Carrie had never heard of such a thing. She noticed her father open his mouth as if to stop Robert's explanation and then he shut it again, sitting back in his chair to listen.

"Yes," Robert responded casually with a touch of pride in his voice. "My brother and I buy mostly female slaves. They usually prove to be quite prolific in their production of children. The market for young slaves is quite strong. We do quite well selling off our stock on a yearly basis."

Carrie couldn't stop the feeling of bile rising in her throat. Robert raised black children simply to sell them away from their mothers? She had developed a genuine liking for Robert as she had listened to his conversation with her father. Confusion rose to choke her as she stared at him. How could anyone do such a thing?

Thomas seemed to sense her disgust and spoke quickly, his voice soft but firm. "It is necessary to do what we must. All of us. Destiny is a hard taskmaster, even when quietly and philosophically obeyed." His voice deepened. "Resisting our destiny would cause destruction and mayhem. Some say we should set the slaves free to flounder in their very freedom. I think not. Our destiny is linked with theirs. We are bound to them and wisdom teaches us not to cut them loose. It is in this way that we truly show our respect for the Negro."

Carrie, under his watchful eye, nodded once more but the fire of controversy in her heart was raging. Why was she suddenly so uncomfortable with what she had accepted all her life?

Just then, Robert, seemingly oblivious to her turmoil, turned to her with his most charming smile. "We seem to have eaten up the entire night with politics. I had hoped you would be able to show me the beautiful horses you have here."

Carrie, eager to leave the current conversation behind, shook off her somber mood and turned to him with a smile. "We have the best in Virginia," she stated quietly.

"Is that the truth?" Robert laughed. "With that being the case, would you consent to my riding one of them in the tournament tomorrow? I received an invitation to participate in the Blackwell's event, but my trip to Charleston made it impossible to bring my horse along. I hadn't planned to ride, but suddenly I feel the desire."

Carrie nodded eagerly, her thoughts now focused on Robert's request. "You may ride Granite. There is none better." Carrie saw her father's surprised look but kept her eyes on Robert. Her decision to let him ride Granite was as unusual as all the other thoughts rampaging through her mind, but she had spoken and couldn't take it back now.

"And who is Granite?" Robert asked.

"He is my horse. The finest in the state. He will give you a smooth ride and he is fast as lightning." She spoke with confidence and felt only a twinge of remorse at the vindictive feelings rising in her. A Blackwell horse always won the annual event, but only because Carrie could not ride Granite in the competition. Females were not allowed to compete in the tournament. Even if she couldn't be the rider, it would do her heart good to see a Cromwell horse win. As long as Robert was a good competitor—which, without any reason, she somehow suspected he was— Granite would do his part.

Robert nodded. "Can I meet him?"

"Certainly. Father?" Carrie placed her balled-up napkin on the table and rose from her chair.

"By all means." Thomas smiled and stood as well. "Robert, Carrie isn't exaggerating when she says he's the best in the state. I've yet to see a finer Thoroughbred than this gelding." He walked with them to the front door. "I'll be in the parlor with your mother when you two return. Take your time. It's a nice evening."

The air was soft and fragrant when the two left the porch and ventured out onto the lawn. Carrie's thoughts were occupied with the competition the following day. She turned to smile up at Robert. "Granite should still be in the stables. I told Miles I was going to bring him a treat before he put him out for the night." Holding up a carrot, she said, "He deserves a reward for getting me home in time for dinner. I was rather a wet mess, but we made it in time." She laughed merrily.

"A wet mess?" Robert looked bemused.

"Yes." Briefly, Carrie told him of her rather wild ride back to the plantation. She finished with, "I haven't had so much fun in a long time." Then her face clouded. "I'm afraid my mother finds me rather a helpless case." She looked thoughtful for a moment and then shrugged and looked up at him with an impish grin. "We can't all be what we're expected to be though, can we?" With those words she disappeared into the shadowy barn.

Carrie stared into the mirror as Rose brushed her hair with long, sweeping strokes.

Finally Rose broke the long silence. "You okay, Miss Carrie? You've been mighty thoughtful since you came upstairs." The quiet question invited one of the heart-to-heart conversations they often had.

Carrie shook her head, obviously not willing to talk about what she was feeling. "I guess I just have a lot on my mind."

Rose continued to brush Carrie's hair until the ebony mass shined in the lantern light. Soft spring air flowed in through the window, billowing the edges of the curtains and causing the lantern light to cast swirling shadows on the floor.

Finally Carrie broke from her reverie. "Thanks Rose. I'm very tired. You can go now."

Rose sensed her friend and mistress was deeply troubled about something but knew Carrie would talk to her about it when she was ready. Rose nodded, patted her shoulder, and turned to leave.

Carrie's voice stopped her. "We'll finish our reading on Monday. I'm sorry I'm so distracted. Do you mind terribly?"

Rose shook her head. "I'm tired too, Miss Carrie. Finishing on Monday will be just fine." She patted Carrie's shoulder again, walked to the door, eased it open, and closed it quietly behind her. The great house had grown very quiet. Rose moved noiselessly down the gleaming hallway toward her room at the rear of the house. No one knew about the lessons her mistress gave her on a regular basis. Master Cromwell knew only that she could read, and only at the most basic level. The Cromwells would have demanded the lessons cease if they knew Carrie was teaching her all that she herself was learning. Rose had a quenchless thirst for knowledge and soaked up all she could learn, and she had discovered ways to learn even more. Slipping into her room, she quickly lit the stubby candle on her windowsill. She had managed to slip it out of the kitchen that day. It would give her maybe twenty minutes of light. Reaching under her thin horsehair mattress, she pulled out the book she had slipped from Master Cromwell's library earlier that week. She knew she would be beaten—even by her kindly master if it was discovered, but she was willing to take the risk. She had her reasons.

Carrie continued to stare into the gilded mirror gracing her wall. Tonight the reflective depths seemed to pull her into their shimmering waves. As she stared into the glass, it seemed to echo back all of her troubling thoughts and emotions. The creaking night noises of the house seemed to be swallowed by its embrace. Carrie's mind traveled back as she let it pull her in. Back to the time when the mirror first landed on American shores. Back to the time when her European ancestors, having left everything they knew, had arrived to start a new life.

She knew the story. Her great-grandmother had left a life of comfort and luxury in England to travel to the wild American colonies with her husband, who was convinced America was the land of opportunity and riches. She had left everything behind. Everything but the grand mirror. It had arrived in America boxed carefully in a wooden crate to protect it from the rigors of sea travel. It had remained in the box for almost ten years, mocking her ancestor for thinking America would offer it a home grand enough for its beauty. Yet, finally, her great-grandfather had indeed carved a home from the wilderness fine enough to be a home for the ornately sculpted mirror. Almost six feet tall, it commanded admiration from all who saw it. Abigail Cromwell had wanted it moved from Carrie's room and taken downstairs to grace the majestic hallway. Her husband, usually bending to her demands, had remained adamant that the mirror stay in Carrie's room.

"The mirror has always been there, and there it will remain." When Thomas Cromwell spoke in that tone of voice, no one argued with him. The matter was already settled.

The mirror had become Carrie's confidant. Tonight was no exception. She felt its depths probe her own, asking if she were equal to her ancestors. Asking if she had the same courage, the same strength of heart her great-grandmother Natalie had possessed. Carrie could only stare into its murky shadows that reflected the light of the lantern, praying with all her heart that she did, and questioning the sudden need for the mirror to know.

Her reverie was broken by the sudden clatter of wheels on the cobblestones out in front of the house. Moving to her window, she watched as the overseer, Mr. Adams, joined her father on the front porch to meet the wagon pulling up to the house. Huddled in the back of the wagon against the early spring air were the ten slaves her father had purchased the day before in Richmond. The conversation between the three men was brief. Her father nodded and turned back into the house. Mr. Adams joined the other man on the seat of the wagon and indicated with a nod of his head the direction of the slave quarters.

Carrie watched as the wagon rumbled away into the darkness and then crawled into bed to ponder the restless stirrings in her heart, wishing she could be in the quarters to witness what was happening.

THREE

Moses gritted his teeth as he fought to still the rage rising in his throat, threatening to choke him. Gripping the small square of material that held his few belongings, he cast his eyes around the small clearing as the wagon rumbled to a stop.

Dark shapes appeared in the doorways of tiny cabins, dim lamplight offering no more identity than gender. Soft conversation faded into silence as compassionate, understanding eyes followed the huddled forms in the back of the wagon. Many Cromwell slaves had never been further than the fields of Master Cromwell. There were plenty more, however, who were far too familiar with the upheaval and heartbreak of leaving family and home because of the auction block.

"This is far enough!" Adams yelled into the silent darkness. "Unload them here."

He jumped from the wagon, released the pegs that held its gate closed, and let it fall to the ground. "This is your new home. You might as well start getting used to it." His mocking laugh rang out into the night air as he jumped back on the wagon seat. The last huddled shape spilled onto the ground and he waved the driver on.

No one had moved from their doorways. As if in honor of their grief, no one wished to break the silence. Moses shifted, wondering where he was supposed to go. Surely someone was in charge around here. At his home plantation, there had always been someone in charge of the new slaves. The thought of home, of his family, caused a mixture of rage and grief to struggle for control of his body. Silently he fought off the weakness engulfing him.

The rest of his group seemed just as bewildered. It had been a long two days. Herded onto the auction block early the morning before, they had been sold and then moved to a holding area to await transportation to their new owner. Their holding area had been the back of the wagon. They had been left to sit in the bright sunshine until the sun was high in the sky, with neither food nor drink. Finally the driver had ambled up and, without a word, begun the seemingly endless drive that deposited them here long after the sun had gone down.

No one moved until the rumble of the wagon wheels faded in the distance. Then the soft rustle of a long dress broke the stillness. "I 'magine y'all be right thirsty and hungry."

Moses strained his eyes to determine where the mellow, smooth tones were coming from. Finally the owner of the voice moved close enough to see. Gliding toward them was a tiny woman clothed simply in a white cotton dress. Her hair, gilded with silver, reflected the dim light shining through the cabin doors. It was her eyes, though, that held Moses's attention. The ebony eyes shone with a light that came from somewhere deep within. He fastened his own weary eyes on her as she glided to a stop in front of them.

"Welcome to Cromwell Plantation. My name be Sarah. I know y'all must be mighty tuckered out. And none of y'all look as if you've et at all today. We're fixin' to fix dat problem."

Her words were a signal to all the other watchers. Nameless shapes turned to disappear into their cabins. Moments later, they reappeared with corn cakes and large mugs of cold water. As Moses watched, two more women appeared with a basket full of fresh baked sweet potatoes. One man set up a primitive wooden table near the bewildered arrivals. The women deposited their bounty on the table and stood back with gentle smiles.

It was all Moses could do to keep from bolting to the table. His last food had been a piece of bread early that morning, but he waited along with the rest of the new slaves.

"Let's pray," Sarah said, lowering her still beautiful lined face.

Moses watched in astonishment as others bowed their heads. Finally he allowed his head to bend down toward his massive chest in a gesture of respect.

"Father, thanks for this her' food. Thank you too, for the safety you done given our new friends here. Amen." Sarah raised her head. "Y'all can eat now."

Moses didn't need to hear anything else. With one giant stride he was at the side of the table, his towering frame dwarfing the tiny woman standing next to it. His eyes devoured the table, but he forced himself to look down at Sarah. "Thank ya, ma'am." His duty taken care of, his work-worn hands reached down to grab several corn cakes and a couple of sweet potatoes from the piles waiting for them. He spotted a tall oak tree on the edge of the clearing and sank down next to it, allowing his long legs to stretch out for the first time that day. He had been careful to make eye contact with no one, save for his brief thank you to Sarah. He just wanted to be left alone. He wanted to eat, and he wanted to be left alone.

"Hello, boy."

Moses jerked his head around. He had not heard Sarah's approach. He looked up at her in confused anger and then lowered his head again. Taking a huge bite of a corn cake, he stared bitterly at the ground.

Without a word, Sarah sank down beside him. Muted conversation floated through the air as newcomers conversed with the slaves of Cromwell Plantation. But beside the tall oak, silence reigned. Sarah said not a word until he had finished his meal.

"What be yo name, boy?"

Moses glanced up to meet her glowing eyes. He stared, wondering at the source of light in the old slave's eyes. Then he looked back down.

"Moses." The silence stretched between them once again. Maybe she would catch the hint that he just wanted to be left alone. But she seemed content to sit there beside him.

Finally she spoke again. "Where ya come from, Moses?"

"Smith Plantation." He recognized the look of sorrow that shadowed her face. She knew. In spite of the efforts to keep slaves from communicating with each other, the grapevine worked.

Sarah placed a work-hardened hand on his shoulder gently. Moses flinched but didn't pull away. The caring touch felt like balm to his battered spirit, but it also brought up too many memories. His own mama... Catching his breath, he jerked his eyes back down to the ground.

"This here place ain't like de Smith place, Moses."

Moses shrugged his shoulders. He had heard that slaves were treated better at Cromwell Plantation, but what difference did it make to him? His whole world had been torn from him just that morning. It didn't matter how anyone treated him now. He had lost his reason to live.

The dimly lit clearing seemed to fade before his eyes as his mind traveled back to the auction house. They had all been brought together from the Smith place, all of them to be sold at one time. That is what gave Moses hope—they were all still together. *Maybe someone will...* His hopes were short-lived. Who really wanted a whole family? Especially when the mother was old and bent from too much hard work and too much abuse, and the one sister would never walk right. But still Moses hoped. It had been his job for so many years to care for his family.

It took but the fall of the gavel on the auctioneer's stand to end all of that. His mother and sisters were the first on the block. It didn't take long to auction them off. At least his mama and Sadie were together.

"I know this old woman doesn't look like a very fine specimen, but gentlemen, looks can be deceiving. You won't find a finer cook anywhere in Virginia. For twenty long years she has set the table at the Smith Plantation with wonderful home-cooked food. She can do the same for the lucky gentleman who is the highest bidder." The auctioneer paused and scanned the crowded room. Now was the time for his best salesmanship. He knew he would have to sell Sadie as a package deal with her mammy. How else would he unload a twelve-year-old cripple? "And with her, gentlemen, goes a fine girl, twelve years old. Don't let her crippled condition turn you away. She works hard in the kitchen with her mammy and never lets her problem keep her from the work she has to do. Look at it this way boys—you'll never have to worry about her running away. She'll stay where she's put!" Laughter swept the crowd and he threw in one final shot. "Her crippled condition has not been since birth. She still has the capacity to bear many fine young specimens for the highest bidder!" One look told him he had done his job. Men were leaning forward in anticipation. "Where will the bidding begin? "

Moses watched in sullen silence as the voice of buyers rang through the room. Mama and Sadie went to a man named Johnson. All Moses was able to find out was that he lived almost one hundred miles north of Richmond on the river at the base of the mountains.

June went on the block next with three other young girls.

"Look at this fine young girl, gentlemen. At only fifteen years of age she is already a skilled housekeeper. She can sew and even does lacework."

Moses wanted to cry at the terror stamped on his little sister's face. She had clung to Moses's hope that they would all stay together. He watched as she gazed beseechingly at Mr. Johnson, begging him silently to purchase her as well. Johnson indeed joined in the bidding but dropped out when June's price went higher than what he already paid for the combination of her mother and sister. Shaking his head, he turned away from her beseeching eyes. His little sister went for a price of eight hundred dollars to a man named Saunders who owned one of the plantations farther south down the river. It was all Moses could do to not jump on the block and grab her. The tears running down her face and the fear that caused her to tremble were like a knife in his heart. He had promised his daddy, and he had failed. He could only watch in helpless agony as they led his mama and sisters away.

The thought of it caused him to want to break something. Anything. There must be a way to ease the war raging in his body.

His turn came shortly thereafter.

"You won't find a strong buck like him every day, gentlemen. He stands at six feet four inches, and is solid muscle. He puts in a hard day's work and doesn't ever give any trouble. He's only twenty years old. You'll get plenty years of good work out of this fine specimen. And think what he could do for your breeding program."

The bidding began. Most bidders dropped out when the price went above fifteen hundred dollars. Only two bidders battled it out to the end. Cromwell seemed satisfied with the price of two thousand dollars. When the gavel dropped, he merely nodded and turned away to talk to the man standing next to him. Moses regarded his new owner stoically before he was marched from the stage and out to the wagon. There he had sat all day imagining his mama and sisters' pain and terror, and being eaten from the inside with grief and guilt.

Sarah sat quietly beside him all this time, but she had not moved her hand. The soft touch seemed to have given him the courage to allow his thoughts to travel over the events of that day.

Raising his head, Moses repeated, "Thank ya, ma'am."

Sarah nodded. "You need ta git some rest, boy. Morning comes mighty early aroun' dis here place. But at least tomorrow be Sunday. We don't got ta do no work."

"That's a mighty fine looking lot of slaves, Adams."

Adams looked over at the driver, Crutchins, and nodded with a smirk. "They're a fine looking lot, but as far as I'm concerned they just mean trouble."

"Whatcha mean?"

"Oh come on, man!" Adams's craggy features flushed as his pale blue eyes gleamed balefully. "Surely you see what's going on all around us here. Didn't you here about the fire down at the Morgan place last week? And the barn that burned at the Simpsons' place a few days before? That's nigger work. There's trouble coming, Crutchins. The niggers are smelling their freedom and it ain't going to mean nothing but trouble." Adams despised the slight sound of panic in his voice but his fear had been growing daily—along with his hatred.

Crutchins regarded him thoughtfully. "Yeah, I heard about the trouble. It ain't nothing but those fanatics in the North. They're down here trying to stir up trouble just like they did with John Brown up in Harper's Ferry last year. Our niggers aren't coming up with these ideas on their own."

Adams shrugged. "Don't matter much if they are. The results are the same. I don't mind admitting it makes my blood run cold to think of all these niggers free. All this secession talk has gotten me to thinking. I've heard some people talk about the possibility of a war if the South was to split off from the North. I don't think the North has the guts to come down here and fight us Southern men. It wouldn't be much of a fight anyway. They'd tuck their tails between their legs and run back up to their soft factory jobs before we'd had time to hurt them much, but it might be fun to have a shot at them. Maybe that would teach them to leave us alone down here. Those people just don't understand what would happen if all these niggers suddenly got free. There wouldn't be a safe place to live in the South. We might as well change the name of this part of our country to *Little Africa*. It wouldn't take long before they would turn it into the same wildness they came from. What would happen to all of us?"

Crutchins's response was a fearful silence, his eyes darting wildly as Adams's somber question hung in the stillness of the spring night. Hovering above the wagon, it followed the two men as they rode the last piece down the road. Both were lost in the murky depths of their own thoughts. Neither took notice of the fragrant air that reached out welcoming arms to embrace him. Their fear kept any comfort at bay.

Adams fought to control the dark thoughts crowding his mind. It would never do to give in to fear. He knew if he did that he would lose control over the seventy-five slaves Cromwell paid him to oversee. It was hard sometimes, though. Especially like today when he was forced to stand next to Moses. The young giant made him feel like a peon. His wiry body seemed diminutive next to the young buck's strength. He knew he wouldn't stand a chance if Moses, or one of the other powerful men hardened by hours of hard work, were to turn against him. He knew he ruled because of fear. Cromwell didn't like him to use the whip he carried with him at all times. Most of the time he complied with his wishes, but there were times when the slaves needed to know where they stood. They needed to be reminded who was the boss. What Cromwell didn't know wouldn't hurt him. And then there was the pistol. Even his wife, Eulalia, didn't know he carried one with him all the time now. He aimed to be ready if the Cromwell slaves decided to stir up the same trouble as some of the other niggers in the area.

"He's too soft on them, you know."

"Huh?" Crutchins looked confused.

"Cromwell," Adams snapped. "He's too soft on his slaves. Someday it's going to spell trouble. I can feel it coming." He wanted to sneer as Crutchins looked at him quizzically. The portly, middle-aged man owned no slaves himself. He was content to make a living for his wife and two children by being a driver for area plantation owners. Adams knew the complacent man had no desire for the burdens that went with the responsibility of plantation wealth. Adams own desire burned in his gut. Losing his farm and five slaves several years ago had lit a raging fire of bitterness in him. He knew it would only be stilled when he was once again in the position he craved. He felt nothing but contempt for men like Crutchins.

"Take that Moses fellow," Adams continued. "He's going to be trouble."

"What makes you think that?"

Crutchins's tone said he didn't care, but Adams chose to ignore it. He just wanted to talk. "I know where he came from," Adams continued. "The fellow up at the Smith Plantation knew how to get a good day's work out of the slaves there. He knew being too soft wasn't any good. Mr. Smith put him in charge and left him in charge. Smith lived in town and only came out a few times a year to check on things. That's the way it should be done."

"I hear tell he lost that plantation. That's why all the slaves were up for sale." Adams spun around, fire spitting from his hardened eyes. "It had nothing to do with how the plantation was run! My brother did a damn good job—"

"Your brother?" Crutchins's eyes narrowed.

"That's right! My brother." Adams hadn't meant to let that slip, but it didn't really matter now. "It's the Yankees who are causing all of our problems down here. Them, and all this fool talk of secession. It's causing our economy to suffer. The little farmer is having a hard time keeping up." The Smith Plantation, with over eight hundred acres, could hardly be called little, but it didn't matter. Crutchins didn't have to know everything.

Crutchins remained silent but lifted the reins a little to hurry up his team. Adams was lost in his bitter thoughts when they rounded the curve and he spotted his house.

"Here you go, Adams. My missus is waiting for me so I've got to go."

Adams wasn't done, however. "This is just another example of what I'm talking about."

"What's that?" Crutchins said, sounding bored and tired.

"My house shouldn't be a half mile down the road." He chose to ignore the fact he would live in constant fear if his house were any closer. "How does Cromwell expect me to keep things under control when I'm this far away? Those niggers are probably hatching up some evil plans right now."

Crutchins just nodded and pulled the team to a halt. "Goodnight, Adams."

Adams climbed wearily from the wagon and turned to continue his bitter tirade. But with a gentle cluck, Crutchins had his team rolling away before he could speak. Closing his mouth again, he wiped a grimy hand across bleary eyes and turned toward his cottage. He couldn't blame the driver for wanting to get home. He had heard Missus Crutchins laid a fine meal. The thought sped his steps. His own wife wasn't that great a cook, but he knew there would be hot food waiting for him. His two boys should be in bed by now. He could sit by the fire and eat in peace. The idea was a welcome one.

FOUR

Abigail Cromwell looked over from where she was seated at her dressing table.

"Robert Borden seems like a very nice young man."

"He does indeed," Thomas agreed. He was tired and ready to call it a night, but he remembered the question he had seen appear in his wife's eyes earlier. Something was obviously still troubling her. He turned and watched her from his position on the bed. She looked lovely in her pale yellow dressing gown. "Come here, Abigail."

She smiled softly, and rose to join him. They sat in silence for a few minutes as the cool spring air swirled in around them.

"What's wrong, Abby?"

"You always know, don't you?" Abigail managed a smile as she laid her head on his shoulder.

"Well, I do tonight."

"Lucy Blackwell told me something else today." Thomas waited patiently as she searched for the right words. "Several of their slaves ran away last week."

Thomas nodded. Unfortunately, slaves running away was becoming a much more common occurrence. The Underground Railroad was becoming bolder in its efforts to free the slaves. "None of our slaves have run away, Abby. We treat them well. Why would they want to leave?" He chose his next words carefully. "I've heard that the Blackwell overseer can be a little rough."

"But that's not all." Her voice sharpened with fear. "They were discovered gone after Giles, the stable keeper, discovered a fire in the main barn. He caught it in time, but what if he hadn't?" Quickly, she made the switch from Blackwell Plantation. "What if it had been our barn, Thomas? What if our slaves decided to kill all our beautiful horses? Think how horrible it would be.

Think what it would do to Carrie!" Her voice rose to a hysterical pitch.

Thomas wrapped his arm around her shoulder. "It didn't happen here, Abby," he responded softly, "and it won't. You'll have to trust me. Our slaves know we're good to them. They know that without us they couldn't survive. Nothing is going to happen."

Abigail took several deep breaths, seeming to be comforted by his words. He knew it was more because she *wanted* to believe he spoke the truth than because she really believed him. She wouldn't have even that small comfort if she could see into her husband's mind. Thomas could only hope and pray that what he spoke was the truth. There were so many factions at work in their country. So many people determined to free the slaves. So much nonsensical talk about emancipation. The fools didn't know what they were talking about, but Thomas was afraid their passion would create a situation that would mean tragedy for everyone. Determinedly, he shoved his thoughts aside. He had always protected Abigail from the hard things of life. He would continue to do so for as long as it was possible. "Tomorrow should be a wonderful time."

The tactic worked. The idea of the tournament and the ball seemed to erase dark thoughts from his wife's mind. "Oh, yes, Thomas! *Everybody* is going to be there!

"You mean everybody who is *somebody*," he responded teasingly, happy to see her focused on something pleasant.

"Well, of course. You don't think Lucy would invite any of the wrong people do you, dear? I'm so glad to hear she invited Robert Borden to join the festivities."

"I am too, dear. I quite enjoyed the young man."

"And he seemed to be quite taken with your daughter, sir."

Thomas stifled a laugh. So she had noticed too. "Really?"

"Don't pretend innocence with me. It was written all over his face!"

Thomas laughed and nodded. "I'm afraid he is rather smitten."

Abigail had turned to look out the window. Now she spun to face him again. "Why are you afraid? It's high time our daughter found a suitable young man. It's time she grew up."

Thomas controlled his sigh. He knew it was too much to hope that Abigail would understand Carrie. Thomas, too, wished for Carrie to find someone to care about her deeply, but he sensed his daughter was anxious to spread her wings. He didn't think she was considering marriage. He wisely chose to say none of that, however. "Well, we'll just let things take their course. When the time is right, Carrie will find that special person. Until then, I am going to enjoy having her at home. I'm not anxious to see her leave us yet."

Abigail fell silent. When he put it that way, there was really nothing she could say.

Thomas smiled and blew out the light. He had scored a victory.

Moses pulled his wool blanket closer to his chin and snuggled down against the early spring chill. At least Sarah had been right about some of the things she had said. The slaves at Cromwell were at least treated a little better. His bed back at the Smith Plantation had consisted of a few hard boards nailed to a support coming off the wall. Here there was actually a rough horsehair mattress to soften the familiar boards.

The sweet potatoes had been another surprise. He could still taste them. He could hardly believe they still had some this time of the year and had been amazed when one of his cabin mates told him Cromwell allowed them to store vast quantities to take them through the months in between harvests.

"You all right, Moses?"

Moses recognized the rough tones of Jupiter, one of his cabin mates. Jupiter wasn't much older than Moses and had lived all his life on Cromwell Plantation.

"Yeah. I be all right." He was not about to tell Jupiter of the tears choking his throat and the pain that seemed to be pulling his heart in two. Where were his mama and Sadie? How were they being treated? Would their new overseer beat them? What about June? What was going to happen to him? Stifling the groan that rose to his lips, Moses rolled to face the wall.

"It's better here you know," Jupiter said quietly. Silence stretched for several moments before he continued, almost as if he was speaking to himself. "We're still owned like animals—and treated like animals—but at least we get treated pretty good."

FIVE

Carrie glanced up at Robert Borden shyly as he looked out over the early morning mist hovering over the fields. Normally, she would have been focused on the beauty of fresh green trees glimmering in the mist but not today. Robert looked incredibly handsome astride Granite. The Thoroughbred's gleaming iron coat was the perfect background for his dark good looks. She let her eyes drink in the sight before she cast them back down to the carriage where she sat waiting with her mother for her father to join them. She was uncomfortably aware of her mother's speculative gaze and could only hope her cheeks weren't as red as she feared they were.

The early morning air was crisp, but the lap rugs Miles had carefully placed over them kept them warm. Miles had then given his assistant, Charles, a stern lecture about being careful with the carriage and horses. Carrie was glad they were getting an early start. She didn't want to miss a minute of the festivities and it would also give Granite a rest before the tournament began.

"You look quite handsome this morning, Mr. Borden."

Robert turned to smile down at his hostess. "Thank you, Mrs. Cromwell. You are looking quite lovely yourself. The blue of your gown brings out the beauty of your eyes, ma'am."

Abigail smiled graciously. "Thank you. I hope you do well in the tournament today, Mr. Borden. There is quite stiff competition I understand."

Robert inclined his head modestly. "I will do my best. The wonder of it is that I have such a fine animal to ride. Your daughter has been quite generous. I'm afraid, though, that she may have been too generous.

The offer of one's horse is no small matter. I'm afraid I may have been remiss in accepting such an offer."

Carrie raised her head quickly. "Oh no, Mr. Borden. I truly wish you to ride Granite." She met his eyes briefly and then looked back down quickly, but not before she caught his warm smile. Carrie felt her cheeks flush even hotter but kept her eyes resolutely fixed on her white gloved hands. She knew she was behaving in a silly manner, but she simply didn't understand the confusion she was feeling. Last night had been fine. Robert Borden had been just another houseguest. Somewhere in the night her feelings had changed. She had planned on meeting him in the barn this morning but couldn't bring herself to do it. All her casual confidence had vanished. Her fists clenched of their own accord. It was that silly dream! Never before had she had such a dream.

She had been in her secret place, dressed in a flowing, simple white gown, and seated on her boulder with Granite munching grass behind her. Suddenly Robert was there, appearing out of a fine mist bordering the opening. She rose to meet him. Neither spoke, but held each other in a warm embrace. They stood there for what seemed like forever, locked in each other's arms. Slowly, Robert held her away and gazed down into her face. Then he lowered his head, his lips drawn near to hers...

A stirring in the room had startled her awake. Carrie kept her eyes squeezed shut until the servant ignited a blazing fire in her fireplace and then slipped from the room. Spring was here, but the mornings were still chilly. The blaze would feel good as Rose got her ready for the day. Carrie only opened her eyes when her room was once more empty, but then fixed her stare on the filmy canopy over her bed and didn't move. What could such a dream mean? She had never dreamed such a thing about a man before. In fact, she couldn't remember *ever* dreaming about a man. Confused by the sudden tangle of her emotions, Carrie lay still as her face flooded with color and her heart beat a faster rhythm. She talked sternly to herself until her feelings and thoughts were once more under control.

Rose had not suspected a thing as she hurried to get her mistress ready. There was no time for their usual small talk. There was just enough time to get Carrie ready for the tournament, and check to make sure she had everything she needed for the ball and for an evening away from home.

Carrie felt composed when Sam arrived at her door to collect her trunk. She even managed to act natural through breakfast. It was seeing Robert astride Granite that threw her into such a state of confusion. Every detail of the dream had come flooding back. How on earth could she act natural with someone that she had dreamed about kissing just the night before? *Almost kissing*, she told herself sternly. *He didn't actually do it.* Carrie knew she was behaving badly, but the only thing she knew to do was keep her eyes hidden. Rose always told her that her eyes spoke everything going on inside of her. It would *not* do for Robert to suspect what she was thinking.

"Are my lovely ladies ready to depart?"

Carrie could have cried with relief when she heard her father's cheerful voice. Suddenly all she wanted was for the carriage to start moving. Anything would be better than sitting here in awkward silence while her mother and Robert struggled to carry on conversation.

Carrie felt much more like herself when their shiny, green carriage turned into the drive leading to the Blackwell Plantation. Whatever her feelings toward Louisa Blackwell, it most certainly did not extend to the plantation. Carrie had loved Blackwell Plantation from the time she was very young. She had often longed for a corridor of cedar trees to line the road to Cromwell. Louisa's home had been one of the very first pieces of land developed in the New World. When she was younger, Carrie had wandered among the mighty cedars, listening quietly, hoping they would tell some of the secrets they must surely hold. Their silence had never diminished her joy. Oftentimes she would pick sprigs of the fragrant greenery and take it home to simmer in a pot of water on the wood stove. The heady aroma had always delighted her.

This morning was no different. The storm from the previous night had released a wonderful cedar fragrance into the morning air. The day was warming nicely, but there was still just enough coolness to trap the aroma close to the ground. Carrie felt as if she were riding through a cedar-lined closet. Closing her eyes, she inhaled deeply.

"We couldn't have a more perfect day for the tournament." Abigail's eyes sparkled with anticipation and her smooth skin was flushed with excitement.

Carrie smiled. "I think you love parties more than anyone I know."

Thomas laughed. "Don't ever expect her to change, Carrie. Her enjoyment of them seems to simply increase as the years pass." He looked at his wife fondly. "You look beautiful, Abigail. You're simply glowing with life. No wonder people sometimes have trouble telling who is mother and who is daughter."

"We're here, father!" Carrie exclaimed, allowing herself one small wriggle on the carriage seat to express her excitement. Sometimes growing up was so tedious. She preferred her younger days when it was perfectly acceptable to bounce all over the carriage.

"So we are, dear."

Carrie knew her father was not immune to the pleasure of these occasions. Plantation life, however wonderful, was also one of isolation. It was occasions like these that brought him into contact with his neighbors and gave him the chance to share opinions and ideas with other men of his kind. She knew he had been looking forward to the Blackwell festivities for weeks now. With so much going on in the world, he longed for the opportunity to discuss it with other Virginian men.

There were two other carriages in front when Miles eased the Cromwell carriage in to join them. At two stories tall, the Blackwell House was not as high as her beloved home, but it sprawled further, and the aged, red bricks gave a stately look to the distinguished mansion. The spacious circular drive surrounding a beautiful boxwood garden offered plenty of space for the fleet of carriages that would be arriving soon. Off in the distance, Carrie could see more of the tournament horses being led into the freshly painted, red barn. Many of them had already been here for several days. Carrie knew that many of the competitors had gotten here up to a week early to practice their skill and make sure their horses were familiar with the course.

Carrie looked up at Robert and smiled. It was the first time she had looked directly at him since they'd left home. "You can take Granite to the barn over there, Mr. Borden. Charles, Miles's assistant, will take charge of him until you need him."

Robert returned her smile. "Thanks, Miss Cromwell. I will do my best to bring honor to your horse and to your plantation."

"I'm sure you will, Mr. Borden. I hope Granite gives you a good ride," Carrie said demurely. Carrie saw her father struggling to choke back his laughter as he turned away. If anyone else would have dared suggest Granite wouldn't give Robert the best ride of any horse there, she would have responded with fiery indignation. Her own attitude startled her. She saw her father watching Robert with heightened interest. What was he thinking?

"It's good to see you, Cromwell!"

Thomas turned with a forced smile toward his greeter. "Good morning, Ruffin. It's good to see you as well. Perfect day for the festivities, isn't it?"

"That it is, indeed. I'm glad to see you could make it. Tension seems to be growing on our Southern plantations. Not all owners feel it is wise or even possible to leave their homes for such festivities."

Carrie watched her father smile through gritted teeth. She knew he was in no mood to tangle with his neighbor today, however, he maintained his pleasant demeanor and refused to rise to the bait. "Wouldn't have missed it for the world, Ruffin."

Just then a reprieve arrived in the form of Alfred Blackwell. Within minutes, a group of men formed and headed for the large wraparound porch and the spittoon—a centerpiece at all parties.

Carrie watched with amusement as her father escaped Edmund Ruffin. The two had at one time been close friends. It was Ruffin's agricultural expertise that saved the Cromwell plantation from ruin. But now they were both solidly entrenched on opposite sides in the controversy embroiling their country. Father was a staunch Union man. Edmund Ruffin was a fire-eating secessionist. Many times they had butted heads and hearts over the issues. Carrie knew her father wished to escape any nasty confrontations today. She wasn't sure it was possible.

"Oh, Carrie! You're here! Let me show you upstairs to my room. We'll be sharing it with Natalie Heyward and Sally Hampton tonight."

Carrie turned with a smile to meet her lifelong friend. She was determined to be as pleasant as possible in spite of the differences between them. "Hello, Louisa. It's wonderful to be here. It's such a beautiful day."

Chatting easily, the two girls made their way into the house. Carrie knew Miles would bring her trunk up when he was done with Granite in the barn. As they passed through the entrance of the elegant, old brick mansion, she paused to smile a greeting at Polly, the Blackwell's cook. Louisa barely cast a look in the direction of her faithful slave.

"Didn't I recognize Granite out there earlier?" asked Louisa as they made their way up the spacious staircase to her second-floor bedroom.

"Yes."

"And wasn't there an absolutely divine-looking gentleman riding him?" Louisa cast an eagerly questioning look in Carrie's direction.

"That was Robert Borden." Carrie didn't care to address whether she considered him absolutely divine. Louisa found many men absolutely divine. Yet, she had to admit that Louisa never suffered a lack of young men flocking around her. Louisa was beautiful, with glowing blond hair setting off her dainty features and startling blue eyes. It had never bothered Carrie before, but now she suddenly felt a desire not to have Robert in that flock.

"Robert Borden..." Louisa paused on the stairs. "That must be the young man from Goochland County mother invited. I'm not really sure how he wound up on the guest list. I don't really know anything about him."

Carrie continued her steady walk up the staircase. She wouldn't be the one to enlighten her friend.

"I wonder if he means to ride in the tournament?" Louisa continued her questions as she moved to catch up with Carrie.

Carrie remained silent. She had learned it was best not to antagonize her hostess.

Louisa wasn't easily deterred, however. "Is that why he's on Granite, Carrie? I believe he had written back to mother, telling her he wouldn't be able to ride because he wouldn't have his horse with him. Is he actually going to attempt the tournament on *your* horse?" The tone of her voice indicated she found the idea simply ludicrous.

Carrie turned to glare at Louisa just as they reached the door to her room. With great control, she managed to keep her voice even. "Yes, he's riding Granite in the tournament. And he's going to win." The last words were delivered in a quiet tone. She opened the door and strode into the room, all the while silently praying that Charles would arrive soon with her bags.

Louisa laughed merrily as they moved into her sunny bedroom. She leaned against one of the four-poster beds. "Have you forgotten, Carrie? There has been no one to beat a Blackwell horse in ten years. My brother Nathan will be riding Comet again this year. The two have never been beaten. Surely you don't think your gray gelding and that unknown man can vanquish them?"

Carrie did indeed think they could, but she didn't really know why she was so certain. Granite, she had confidence in. Robert Borden was a complete unknown to her.

"Oh, Louisa, we're here! We're coming up."

Carrie breathed a deep sigh of relief as a familiar voice drifted up the stairway. She knew she was close to losing her temper. Louisa's arrogant haughtiness was sometimes more than she could take. At times she could be merry and amusing but that was usually only in the presence of young men.

Seconds later, Natalie Heyward and Sally Hampton swept through the door, resplendent in their silk hoop dresses. Carrie glanced down at her own lime-green gown, thankful Rose had picked this one for her. She knew it set off her features well. In the company of other girls who put so much stock in their appearance, she was glad to know she had nothing to be ashamed of.

"Why, Carrie. You're here already. It's so wonderful to see you." Natalie finished off her exuberant greeting with a big hug. Carrie returned the hug and smiled at the large-boned redhead. Natalie was not beautiful, but she had an open, friendly nature that drew people to her. Sally Hampton was a slender blonde with even, pretty features and a smile like sunshine. Carrie, in truth, was happy to see both the girls. Though they lived on nearby plantations, she hadn't seen much of either one of them for quite some time. They had always had good times together. She looked forward to this day in their company.

More than that, she looked forward to what would happen in the tournament.

SIX

House slaves moved quickly to clear away the remnants of the dinner feast. Carrie, her blood coursing with excitement, joined the stream of people flowing toward the tournament arena. The competition was due to begin in just forty-five minutes. Robert had excused himself fifteen minutes earlier from the meal in order to collect Granite and make sure he was warm and loose before the tournament began. He had paused at the door to cast a warm smile in Carrie's direction and then moved quickly to join the other young men going after their horses. Carrie had looked up just in time to see Louisa's calculated look.

Carrie joined her throng of friends at the side of the arena, eager not to miss any of the opening ceremonies. She smiled as she looked around. It was indeed a perfect day for the tournament. The storm the night before had cleared the air, the sky was a crystal blue, and the air sparkled with freshness. The fresh spring green of the trees swayed gently in the breeze and the fragrance of early spring blooms lent their own unique perfume.

Close to one hundred friends and neighbors lined the rails of the arena. The men looked elegant in their suits, while the women were resplendent in their brightly colored gowns and hats, many holding frilly parasols to ward off the mid-day sun. Carrie turned her face eagerly toward the sun. She could seldom be bothered with a parasol, opting instead for the healthy glow the sun gave her and not caring one fig that many of her friends shook their heads over yet another one of her oddities.

She heard the drum of hoof beats and looked up to watch the line of young men galloping toward the platform erected especially for the day's activities.

Carrie quickly singled out Robert Borden racing toward her. Already he looked at home on Granite. The two made a dashing pair. Within seconds the cavalcade of young riders and horses surrounded the platform. A mighty horn was blown and the master of ceremonies, Colonel James Benton from a neighboring plantation, raised his voice to carry through the now quiet throng.

"Ladies and gentlemen, it is now time for the *charge of the knights*." His steely gaze swept over the crowd before he turned his attention to the competitors. "Gentlemen, you are gathered here today to participate in the most chivalrous and gallant sport known. It has been called the sport of kings, and well it should. It has come down to us from the Crusades, being at that time a very hazardous undertaking. You probably know, but I intend to tell you once more..." He allowed his voice to trail off as laughter rippled through the crowd. Every year he said the same thing. It was now part of the tradition everyone loved and expected.

"The knights of that day rode in full armor, charging down the lists at each other with the intent that the best man would knock his opponent from his horse. It was a rough and dangerous pastime. Many were seriously hurt. Some were killed. But we, in this day, have gotten soft and tender—as well as much smarter, I believe—and have eliminated the danger and roughness of the sport." Again, laughter riffled through the crowd, but no one spoke up to mar the seriousness of the charge.

All levity left the colonel's voice as he leaned forward to address the young men. "But with all that, it is still a manly and fascinating sport.; One that tests the horsemanship, dexterity, skill, quickness of eye, steadiness, and control of the rider, and the speed, smoothness of gait, and training of the horse. It is an honorable sport and I do not need to mention that a knight taking any undue advantage of his opponents will be ruled out of the tournament." Having pressed his point home to the competitors, the colonel continued on with the instructions.

Carrie knew the rules by heart, but still she listened attentively.

"The three ring hangers are spaced twenty yards apart. The start is twenty yards from the first ring—making the total length of the list sixty yards. Any rider taking more than seven seconds from the start to the last ring will be ruled out. Should anything untoward happen during the tilt that would prevent the rider from having a fair try at the rings, he will so indicate by lowering his lance and making no try at the rings. The judges will decide whether he is entitled to another tilt. All rings must be taken off the lances by the judges. No others will be counted. The rings on the first tilt will be two inches in diameter; on the second tilt, one and a half; on the third tilt, one; on the fourth tilt, three quarters; and on the fifth ,and last, tilt—if there are competitors left—one half inch."

Having dispensed with the rules, the colonel smiled and regarded the young men warmly. "All of you are riding not only to win, but to gain the coveted honor of crowning the lady of your choice the Queen of Love and Beauty at the ball later tonight. The next seven riders will have the privilege of honoring the lady of their choice as lady-in-waiting for the queen. Only the members of the court will participate in the opening figures at the ball tonight. Good luck to you. May the best man win and the fairest lady be crowned."

Another mighty blow on the horn announced the beginning of the competition. A rousing cheer rose from the crowd, along with a whoop from the riders as they galloped their horses in the direction of the starting line.

Robert held Granite back.

Carrie, from her position in the crowd, wondered what was holding him back. She saw his eyes casting about through the crowd. Then, out of the corner of her eye, she saw Louisa making her way in Robert's direction.

"Oh, Mr. Borden!" Louisa's voice rang out over the crowd loud enough for Carrie to hear.

Robert spun Granite. Carrie watched as the two exchanged greetings and then Robert scanned the crowd one more time. Carrie saw a flash of anger and a look of determination in Louisa's eyes. She knew Louisa had met men like Robert before. She was always able to conquer their proud ways. Carrie feared Robert Borden would be no exception. Then she immediately wondered why she feared it.

Moving forward now, Louisa held a dainty lace handkerchief up to Robert.

Carrie stifled a groan. She had forgotten. In the midst of her excitement about Granite competing in the race, she had forgotten the tradition of the knight's token, and Louisa was giving Robert her handkerchief. Carrie's eyes narrowed. What *was* Louisa thinking? Her own brother was riding in competition against Robert. Why would Louisa give her handkerchief to a rival?

Robert took the proffered token and with a courtly bow tucked it into the pocket next to his heart. Smiling, he turned and headed Granite toward the starting line. Louisa, turning away after Robert rode off, caught Carrie watching the exchange. She gave a satisfied smile before she swished away to join a group of her male admirers.

Carrie, disgusted with herself, bit her lip and turned away. She was furious with Louisa but knew she didn't really have a right to be. She should have already given Robert a token, though heaven knows what she would have given him. Louisa had simply done what Carrie already should have. She turned back and gazed at Robert astride Granite. A sudden thought hit her like a bolt of spring lightning. Who was to say Robert couldn't have more than one token? She had never heard of it being done before, but what did that matter. Robert was riding *her* horse. Carrie cast in her mind for an adequate token. Suddenly she knew. Eyes alight with determination, she edged through the crowd until she reached the starting line.

"Mr. Borden," she called. The crowd and the milling of the horses drowned out her voice. "Mr. Borden!" she called again, louder this time.

Robert turned Granite to meet her, his face instantly wreathed in smiles. Moving over to where she stood, he vaulted from the Thoroughbred and looked down at her. "What can I do for you, Miss Cromwell?"

"I thought..." Carrie hesitated.

"Yes?"

Chiding herself for her childishness, she forced herself to continue. "Well, I thought you might...I mean..." Firmly she brought herself under control. This was ridiculous. He would either accept it or turn it down. Gathering all the dignity she could muster, she curtsied and spoke calmly. "You are riding a Cromwell horse and I thought it only proper that I give you a token from the Cromwell household. I apologize for being remiss and not doing it sooner."

Robert smiled. "I would be honored, Miss Cromwell."

"May I borrow your knife, sir?"

"Excuse me?" Robert made no effort to hide his confusion.

"Surely you carry a knife."

"Well, yes, but what need do you have for a knife?"

"A knife, please?" Carrie's voice was soft, but determined.

Robert, obviously mystified, reached behind to pull a small knife from its sheath on his belt.

"Thank you, sir. I'm afraid I didn't come prepared for the tournament, so I'm rather limited with what I can give you. I hope this will suffice." Reaching up, Carrie took hold of a curly lock that had escaped from her bun. Swiftly she cut her hair and handed it to Robert. "I trust you will win, Mr. Borden."

Robert, watching in amazement, slowly reached out to accept the extended token. "Thank you, Miss Cromwell. I will indeed win. You may count on it." Bowing low, he turned and swung back into the saddle. He smiled at her upturned face and rode away to join the others.

"Ladies and gentlemen, our first contestant is the Knight of Granville." The crowd hushed as the determined young man steadied his horse and gripped his sword tightly. With a wave of the flag, he was off.

Carrie watched closely as the young man thundered down the list on his black mare. Leaning slightly forward in the saddle, all of his concentration was focused on the job at hand. He got the first ring! A mighty cheer rang from the crowd. The second ring! And the third! With a triumphant whoop he brought his horse down to a trot and returned to the judges' stand to relinquish his rings. Before he was even there, the flag dropped and the next contestant was off.

After the initial clapping had worn down, the crowd began to melt away toward the refreshment tent. The tournament would go on for quite a while. Few were willing to watch it in its entirety. They would wait until the last couple of tilts when the field was narrowed to a handful of determined, talented young men who were intent on winning all.

Carrie edged closer to the finish line where she would be sure to have a good view of the list. She intended to watch the entire competition. She wanted to know how Granite was handling the course and she was curious about the competition. She had always enjoyed the tournament, but never before had her heart been so engaged.

Robert was number ten in the initial field of thirty. Carrie watched carefully as the first nine knights went through the course. Only four of them were able to collect all three rings. Robert was talking quietly to Granite. The well-muscled Thoroughbred knew something was coming. He seemed to be watching the tournament just as closely as his rider. Granite needed to be ready but loose when his time came. Carrie had seen the result of horses strung too tightly.

"The Knight of Borden."

Robert moved forward as his name was called. Carrie tensed as he gripped Granite's reins and leaned forward slightly. Out of the corner of her eye, she saw the flag flash down. They were off! Granite seemed to float across the ground as he thundered toward the first ring. Robert eyed the circular prize carefully and steadied his arm. The first ring was his! The second and the third both followed quickly.

Carrie clapped enthusiastically as Robert brought Granite down to a trot and circled around to the judges' stand. He would be in the second tilt, and he had ridden Granite beautifully. They seemed to fit each other perfectly. Carrie's belief that the two could win the entire tournament skyrocketed. She watched, smiling, as Robert rode over to her.

"This is quite a horse you have here!" His eyes snapped with excitement, making him even more handsome.

"And you are quite a rider, Knight Borden!" Carrie's excitement had chased away any reticence, and she smiled up at him radiantly. Suddenly she realized he was staring at her with open admiration. Discomfited, she flushed and looked down.

"Thank you for your vote of confidence," Robert replied gravely. He waved casually and rode off to join the rest of the knights who had won the right to ride in the second tilt.

"Ladies and gentlemen, we have fifteen young knights who will compete in the second tilt. Remember, the rings have been reduced in size from two inches to an inch and a half."

Robert and Granite again claimed three rings, as did eight other riders.

"Ladies and gentlemen, nine young knights will compete in the third tilt for the one-inch rings."

Carrie knew Robert's main competition was Nathan Blackwell. Nathan's mare Comet was a veteran of the tournaments, as was Nathan, who hadn't been defeated in ten years. Carrie allowed herself a small smile at the thought of dethroning the young knight. She had nothing against him personally. In fact, she had always liked Louisa's friendly brother. She found Nathan to be quite different from his sister—direct and to the point.

Once again Robert and Granite were off. Again they captured all three rings, narrowing the field to only five young knights.

Carrie, excitement bursting in her veins, gave him a brilliant smile as he rode back to join the other four knights for the fourth tilt. The next tilt, with rings only three quarters of an inch in diameter, would require all of his concentration.

The first two knights thundered down the tilt. The first succeeded in capturing two rings but was disqualified because his time had been greater than seven seconds. The second had captured only one. Number three, the Knight of Bradenton, had failed to capture even one. Nathan Blackwell was next. Nathan sat astride his horse calmly, awaiting his turn. The Knight of Blackwell knew he was good.

The flag dropped and Nathan released Comet into a smooth gallop. He missed the first! Carrie leaned forward to watch. Maintaining his composure, Nathan captured the remaining two rings.

The crowd broke out into loud cheering. The final tilts of the competition had lured everyone back to the sidelines and Carrie was glad she had staked out her place earlier. From where she stood she had a clear view of the entire tilt. Watching Robert closely, she saw him single her out from the crowd. Carrie gave him a wide smile of encouragement, nodding to let him know she believed he could do it. She noted with approval his steadying hand on Granite's neck. The gray gelding was handling the excitement well—now was no time for him to get tense. Robert would have to capture at least two rings for the tournament to continue to the final tilt. If he got three rings, the competition would be over.

The flag flashed once more and they were off. Granite moved as smoothly as ever, while Robert's body was held in readiness. The first ring was his, but the second ring remained where it had been. Carrie held her breath as they thundered toward the third and final ring. It was his!

The crowd broke into a roar once more. It had been years since the Knight of Blackwell faced such stiff competition. All eyes were glued to the list.

"Ladies and gentlemen, we will give the Knight of Blackwell and the Knight of Borden a five-minute break, and then we will resume with the final tilt to determine the winner—and the man who will crown the Queen of Love and Beauty tonight!"

The murmur of the crowd swelled to a muffled roar as wagers were placed on who would win the tournament. Few Virginia gentlemen could refuse an opportunity for a friendly bet.

"Your Robert seems to be doing quite well."

Carrie turned to look into Louisa's eyes. She didn't particularly like what she saw but had no intention of inviting a confrontation. "Mr. Borden is not *my Robert,*

Louisa. But yes, he is doing quite well. So is Nathan." She kept her voice casual.

Louisa narrowed her eyes. "Even if your Mr. Borden should win the tournament, you needn't think he will crown you Queen tonight."

Carrie's eyes widened in surprise. "I haven't given that a thought, Louisa." In truth, all her energy was focused on the possibility of Granite winning the tournament and finally showing his superiority to a Blackwell horse.

"Well," sniffed Louisa, her expression making it obvious she didn't believe what Carrie was saying, "I saw you give Mr. Borden that silly lock of your hair."

Carrie reddened as she struggled to control her anger. She had known Louisa too long and knew exactly what she was thinking. This was *her* ball tonight, and Louisa intended it to go the way she wanted. Evidently what she wanted was Robert Borden.

Louisa broke into Carrie's thoughts. "I know he took it. Of course, he's too much of a gentleman not to. But he received my token first." She paused with a wicked smile. "And really, Carrie, he'll want someone much more polished in the social graces—someone who could honor his family name should he someday choose to take a wife."

Carrie's lips parted in surprise. Was this what growing up was doing for Louisa? "Really, Louisa. I hardly think—" An announcement from the master of ceremonies cut off what she thought.

"Ladies and gentlemen. The final tilt will now begin."

Carrie snapped her lips shut and turned toward the competition. Louisa, flashing a haughty, satisfied look, turned with a swish and moved back in the direction of her friends.

"I'd say Granite stands a mighty fine chance of winning this thing, beautiful daughter."

Carrie, thoughts of Louisa's nasty comments floating from her mind, turned toward her father with a brilliant smile. "Oh, Father! I'm so glad you came to join me. I believe they can do it. I believe Granite and Robert can win."

"I certainly hope so," her father rejoined dryly, "or I'm out quite a bit of money."

Carrie laughed and swung her eyes back to the course just as the flag waved and Granite charged once more down the course. Robert was riding beautifully. Carrie knew how difficult the final tilt was. A half-inch ring was already a tiny thing, but when it became something you were trying to snag from a charging animal, it seemed to be almost not there.

Carrie stifled a groan when Robert just missed the first ring. Steadying himself once more, he zeroed in on the second. He was just feet from the ring when it happened.

A sudden puff of wind caught a handkerchief being held lightly on the sidelines and blew it directly in front of Granite. Startled by the flying square of white, Granite broke stride and stumbled sideways into the post. The agile Thoroughbred managed to regain his footing, but Robert, leaning forward in the saddle to spear the ring, had no chance to recover his balance. The ground rose hard to meet him.

A hush fell over the crowd as Granite thundered on to the end of the tilt, and then slowed and looked around in surprise at the absence of his rider.

"Robert!" Carrie's voice was the first to break the shocked silence. She tore away from the crowd and ran to where he was struggling to stand.

Her father was right behind her. Putting his strong arms under Robert's, he helped lift him to his feet. "You all right, son? That was a pretty nasty fall you took. Are you sure you don't want to sit for a while?"

Robert shook his head and managed a rueful smile. "I'm okay, Mr. Cromwell. Just my pride is a little battered. What happened?"

Carrie explained quickly, aware of the sympathetic murmurs sweeping the crowd. "What a shame. You could have won. I know you could have!"

"What do you mean *could have*?" Robert asked. "Surely such a thing qualifies me for another chance."

"It certainly does, young man." Colonel Benton had walked up while they were talking. "If you feel like riding again, you certainly are entitled to another tilt."

"How's Granite? Did he hurt himself on the post?" Robert asked.

Someone led Granite up and Carrie hurried over to examine him. After several moments she turned to Robert. "He's fine. He has a little scrape, but it doesn't seem to be bothering him. He's a little excited, but he'll calm down."

Just then Nathan rode up on Comet. "Say old man, I'm really sorry. That's a rotten piece of luck. You might have vanquished me."

Robert looked up with a grin. "I'd say that is still a distinct possibility, Knight Blackwell. Give it your best shot, Nathan. I'm going to try and beat it!"

Nathan laughed, "You're going to ride again? On this horse?"

Carrie's eyes flashed. "Certainly. And he will win!" She was aware others shared his feeling that Granite would be too tense after his experience to give Robert a good ride. She knew differently.

Nathan made no effort to hide his dubious expression. He thought for a moment and then leaned forward to regard Robert. "If you're so determined to ride, why don't we share Comet? That way the end will be the result of our spearing skill. I'd hate to take unfair advantage of you."

Robert looked at him in surprise. "That's quite a generous offer."

Carrie held her breath as Robert's brow creased in consideration. Comet was a fine horse and she would probably give him as good a ride as she would give Nathan. Granite was still rolling his eyes and moving nervously. She knew Robert wanted to win, but it was important to her that Granite win as well.

Robert turned to her and asked quietly, "Do you think Granite will be okay?"

Carrie never hesitated. "He will be fine. He's gotten you this far. Let him take you all the way."

Robert gazed at her for a moment and then nodded. "I'll ride Granite, Nathan. Thank you for your quite generous offer, however. Good luck."

"Good luck to you too, Borden. You're going to need it." Smiling, Nathan turned away and rode to the starting line.

Carrie put her hand on Robert's arm. "Talk to him and stroke his left shoulder. He loves it and it always works to calm him down."

Robert nodded and leaped back into the saddle. Then, leaning down, he gazed into Carrie's sparkling emerald eyes. "This one's for you."

Carrie watched as he returned to the starting line. She couldn't help the flush that rose on her face or the thrill his words had given her, but now was not the time to analyze her feelings.

With a flash of the flag, Nathan was off. Thundering down the tilt, he missed the first ring. He missed the second. He grazed, but missed the third. Shaking his head, he turned at the end of the tilt and rode back to the starting line.

Robert moved Granite toward the line. The big gelding had responded beautifully to Carrie's remedy. Granite was relaxed and ready. The crowd applauded as they approached the line, and then fell silent.

The flag flashed and they were off. Granite was steady as they flew toward the first ring. Missed. Carrie could almost feel Granite tense as they approached the second ring. Leaning forward, Robert focused on the ring. At the last second, Granite shifted and veered just slightly. Carrie groaned as Robert focused on the last ring. She clasped her hands tightly, all her wishing directed toward the pair, and groaned again when they missed it. Releasing her breath in a sigh of disappointment, she prepared for another tilt, but realized the crowd was suddenly cheering wildly. Puzzled, Carrie looked around.

"The victory goes to the Knight of Borden—by one ring!"

Carrie's eyes flashed to Robert and Granite. Robert held the sword up to his face, seemingly as surprised as she was. Suddenly she understood. She had been so intent on Granite's misstep that she had missed seeing the ring slide onto Robert's sword. He obviously had not realized it until just now either.

Grinning, Robert held up his trophy and then leaned down to give Granite a big hug. "You did it, old man. I don't know how, but you did it." Granite swung his head proudly as Robert guided him toward the platform.

Carrie was there waiting. "I knew the two of you could do it. Congratulations!"

Robert grinned. "Thanks, but you have only Granite to congratulate."

"Oh, Mr. Borden, you were quite the chivalrous knight out there. I was so proud it was *my* token you were carrying close to your heart."

Carrie stepped aside as Louisa swept passed her to gaze up at Robert.

"Thank you, Miss Blackwell. Most of the credit goes to Granite, however. He is quite a horse."

"Yes, I'm sure he is," she responded dismissively.

"All knights move forward to the judging platform please, for the awards." Colonel Benton's voice boomed out over the excited chatter of the crowd.

Robert nodded pleasantly. "I must be going, ma'am."

Louisa allowed a pretty pout to form on her well-shaped lips. "If you must. I'll be looking forward to the ball tonight, kind knight."

Robert looked after her thoughtfully as she swept away.

Carrie turned away into the crowd. She had gotten the victory she wanted. She must be content with that.

SEVEN

Rose moved gracefully down the dirt road toward the slave quarters, whistling quietly to herself as she walked. Sunday nights were her favorite time of the week. After six long days under the watchful eye of Master and Mistress Cromwell, it was good to have a free night. Gazing around, she took a deep breath. The sun had just started to dip behind the towering oaks lining the road she now walked on. The crystal clear air seemed to shimmer with the golden glow the sun was leaving in its wake. The sky, still a brilliant blue, was beginning to take on the purplish hues of dusk. The evening swirled around her with all its delicious freshness as she strode the last few yards to her mama's house.

"Hello, Mama." Rose smiled as she moved forward to plant a soft kiss on Sarah's wrinkled, leathery skin. She peered into her eyes, until, satisfied with what she saw, she stepped back. She was always afraid of what she would find. Her mama was old. At fifty, she had already lived far beyond the average lifespan of a slave. Rose didn't know what she would do when her mama went home *ta be wid de Lawd*, as Sarah put it. Her mama was her rock.

Sarah returned her smile and reached up to pat Rose's cheek. "We be havin' comp'ny t'night."

Rose nodded and settled down on one of three crude chairs in Sarah's tiny clapboard cabin. She wasn't surprised. Sarah was known as the whole slave quarters' mama. She was too old to work the fields anymore. Every day, when the men and women departed to work the tobacco, they left their children in a central area of the quarters. Sarah's job was to watch over and supervise the *chillun*, as she called them. The children adored her, and the other slaves had learned to respect the old woman.

"Who's coming, Mama?"

"His name be Moses. He be one o' de marse's new ones." Sarah turned back to poke the glowing coals baking her sweet potatoes. "He be needin' a friend t'night."

Again Rose just nodded. "What can I do to help, Mama?" She asked every time. She knew the answer by heart.

"Not a thin'. I have every thin' ready. Just waitin' for these taters to be done cookin'."

"I brought you something, Mama." Rose reached into the deep pocket of her brightly colored calico dress and pulled out a carefully folded linen napkin. She pulled the corners back to reveal a half dozen freshly baked rolls. Laying them out on the rough table, she dug into the other pocket. "Miss Carrie sent these to you. She said to tell you she hopes you're doing well." Her second digging movement brought forth a small jar of plum preserves. She smiled and deposited it next to the rolls. Everyone knew how much her mama loved rolls and preserves.

"Bless her." Sarah's response was quick and fervent. "She be a good chilc'. You tell her thanky fer me." Her eyes rested with pleasure on the gifts laid out before her, but she didn't move from her place at the fire. Moving her hand deftly, she flipped the taters one last time, and poked them to pull them from the coals. "Dey be just right now."

Rose smiled. "Everything is always just right, Mama. There isn't anyone that can cook like you. I may eat fancier food up at the big house, but it's never as good as yours." Rose gave her mama a quick hug and kissed the top of her head tenderly.

Just then a tentative knock came at the door. Rose swung the door open and took a startled step backward. She had never seen anyone the size of the young giant who filled the doorway. For a moment she was speechless, and a little frightened. His huge form blocked out all sunlight trying to squeeze through the door.

"Welcome, Moses. Come on in, boy."

Still silent, Rose stepped aside to let him enter. Rose watched him carefully as he moved gracefully into the cabin. She liked the tender way he looked at her mama. She recognized the pain in his eyes. She had seen it many times in the faces of new slaves. Moses might be a giant, but his heart was just like theirs. She felt her heart begin to calm.

Sarah took control. "Sit over dere, Moses. Like you to meet my girl. This be Rose."

Rose smiled gently as Moses nodded his head in her direction. "Howdy."

"Hello, Moses. It's good to meet you. I'm glad you could join us for dinner."

She almost smiled when his friendly gaze faded and was replaced with dark suspicion. Rose understood. She didn't talk like the rest of the slaves. Her speech distinguished her as being one of the house slaves and as such, she was open to suspicion. It was not uncommon for house slaves to spy and tell on the lower field slaves.

Sarah read his look and moved closer to put a hand on his shoulder. "Moses come from de Smith place."

Rose felt compassion but understood when Moses looked down. He didn't want their pity.

Sarah's leathery hand tightened its grip on his shoulder. "She be alright, Moses. She can be trusted." Her words, soft and tender, hung in the air for just a moment, warring with the fear and doubt that was an everyday part of plantation life.

Rose watched closely as the final bright rays of sun streamed through the still-open door of the cabin. Her mama had the magic that could always find a crack in the walls people put around their hearts. She smiled as Moses relaxed under her soothing touch.

It was enough to satisfy Sarah, who clapped her hands together in delight and moved back toward the fire. "Food be ready. I'se sho nuff hungry."

Moses smiled then—a big smile that lit his face and brought his pain-filled eyes to life. "My mama used to say de same thing. Ever' time it be time to eat." For a moment the pain welled in his eyes and cracked his voice.

Rose, watching from the fireplace, didn't know what to say. She was too busy feeling something, but what? When the big man smiled it seemed to explode right into her heart. She wanted to make him smile again. She wanted to make him laugh with enough joy to squeeze the unbearable pain from his eyes, and she wanted to cradle his head close to her bosom. Suddenly the room was too small. She could do nothing but stand still as the confusion of feelings swept over her like a sudden spring squall. Where were these feelings coming from? Was she going crazy?

"Rose? You all right, girl?" Sarah's concerned voice broke in on her thoughts.

Rose shook her head slightly and tried to bring the room back into focus. "I'm fine, Mama." Forcing herself to smile lightly, she moved to where Sarah was laying supper on the table. "I'm hungry enough to eat half of this myself!"

"Moses might hab sumpin to say bout dat, girl!"

Roses glanced up into the big dark eyes regarding her just as a deep chuckle rumbled from his throat. Confusion gripped her once more as she looked quickly back at the table. What in the world was going on? She had never responded this way to someone before. Taking several deep breaths, she forced herself to regain control. She managed to keep her hand from shaking as she reached for the rolls laid out on the napkin. "Care for some rolls, Moses?" She was relieved that her voice sounded natural.

Gradually the tension in the cabin subsided. The warmth of the fire cast a soft glow over the room that seemed to bring a spell of peace as well. No one spoke as the food rapidly disappeared. Outside, day retreated as night staked its claim. The songs of birds abated and were replaced by a chorus of tree frogs heralding the newly arrived spring. Even when the last crumb of food was gone, no one spoke. All were loath to break the spell.

Moses stared deeply into the flames of the fire. Where was his family? Were they eating tonight? Had his sisters found any friends? Was his mama okay? Not knowing was tearing at his soul, yet he was aware of a strange peace soothing the raw pain. He didn't understand it, but he welcomed it. He needed it.

"You need ta be careful here, Moses." Sarah's gentle voice finally reached out to break the spell. Moses said nothing, just turned his dark eyes to question her. "Dat Adams be a mean one."

Moses just nodded. He'd known that from the moment the overseer's calculating gray eyes had fixed on him. "Meanness ain't nothin' new ta me."

Sarah had more to say. "Dis place ain't like where you come from. Marse Cromwell be a good man. We be slaves, dat be fo sho, but we get treated good. We eat good. There ain't be no beatings around here either. Least, not many…" Her voice trailed away.

"Then why you be telling me to be careful?"

Sarah stood up to poke the coals of her fire and add another log. She seemed to be choosing her words while her back was turned to them. Finally she swung around. "De overseer at Smith. His name be Joe Adams?"

Moses nodded, sudden understanding making his stomach clinch.

"Our Adams be his brother."

Moses closed his eyes and groaned.

Roses turned to her mama in protest. "But it's different here, Mama. They don't do things the same way the Smith Plantation does. It's better here."

Sarah nodded. "Yeah, girl, it be better, but men be men. And pride be a right powerful thing. Joe Adams was a big man what wid all dem slaves he controlled. He done lost all dat. Lot of people gonna figure it ta be his fault. Blood and hate be a mighty strong link. Dem two brothers share that link. So far the marse has kept Adams here under control. De hate be growing in his heart tho. One day it gonna spill on over. You can be sho he knows where Moses done come from. Just be careful, boy. You done had too much hate spill out on ya."

Moses nodded wearily. He was used to hate spilling out into his life. He had known little else. He certainly didn't know what he could do to stop it. It was just part of being a slave. It would never change.

"There has to be a way to make sure nothing happens, Mama. I can talk to Miss Carrie. We'll figure out something." Rose's voice held a hint of panic.

"Miss Carrie ain't found her own self 'nuff yet to take on de likes of Adams. Someday, if I don't miss my guess, she will. But she ain't ready yet." She turned to Moses. "You just be careful. Ya needed to know."

Somber silence filled the room until Rose began to tell him about life on the plantation. He pushed aside thoughts of Adams and listened closely. The more he knew, the easier it would be to adjust to his new existence.

It was almost time to put a new log on the fire when Moses broke into her recital. "You don't talk like de rest of us. Don't much talk like a house servant either."

Rose shook her head shyly. "I don't guess I do." She hesitated. "I can read and write."

Moses couldn't hide his surprise. "But...but...dat be—" He stopped, not sure how to continue.

"Illegal?" Rose asked with a smile.

"Well, ain't it?"

"Yes." Rose allowed the silence to linger for a moment and then leaned forward to talk in a conspiratorial tone. "I learned with Miss Carrie. The marse thought I quit learning a long time ago. I still feel like I've just begun." The glow in her eyes was not a mere reflection of the fire. Moses watched quietly as her heart and soul came to life, aflame with the heat of her passion. "It didn't always used to be illegal, Moses. There was a time when most slave owners made sure their slaves could read and write." Rose read the look of disbelief on Moses's face. "It's true! It all stopped, though, when the North started sending down literature about setting us free. The white people were afraid that if all of us started reading that material, we would all run away or fight for our freedom. So they made it against the law to teach your slaves how to read and write. And they made it against the law for slaves to have anything written."

Moses felt a bit of admiration, but he shrugged. "So what? Reading and writing ain't gonna do nothin' fer me. I ain't never gonna be nothin' but a slave. What reason I got to learn dat stuff?"

"You don't always have to be a slave, Moses."

Moses stared at her, wondering if she wasn't quite right in her mind. "What you be talkin' bout, girl?"

Silence filled the cabin as Rose hesitated. Was it his imagination or did he see fear in her eyes? The silence stretched into the deep corners of the cabin. Finally, Rose looked up at her mama. The calm, steady gaze and gentle nod was all she seemed to need.

"I have a school, Moses. A small school that meets secretly on Sunday nights. I can teach you how to read and write."

"Why fer? Why do I need to know that stuff fer? You ain't answered dat question yet."

Rose hesitated again. "I can't answer that question yet, Moses. I trust you enough to tell you about the school. You're going to have to trust me when I say you don't always have to be a slave. When that day comes you're going to have to be ready. Being able to read and write will mean everything to you."

Moses stared into her flashing eyes. What he saw there reassured him. She wasn't crazy. And she believed what she was saying. "I don't know if I can learn dat readin' and writin'."

Sarah spoke from the shadows. "I didn' think I could learn either, boy."

Moses swung to stare at the wrinkled old lady in wonder. "You know how ta read and write?"

The light in her eyes was answer enough. Sarah rose from her chair, moved to a shelf by her bed, and reached up into the shadows. She pulled down a large book and made her way back to the fire. Then, laying her find on the table, she added two more logs to the fire. She settled back into her chair and waited until the crackling flames added new light to the cabin. Only then did she reach for the book and break the silence. "I learned ta read just for this. I still don't talk good, but I sho 'nuff can read."

Moses watched as Sarah picked up the large book and leafed through the pages. Finally she found what she was looking for.

Sarah's soothing voice vibrated firmly throughout the cabin as she read.

> Who shall separate us from the love of Christ? Shall tribulation, or distress, or persecution, or famine, or nakedness, or peril, or sword? As it is written, for thy sake we are killed all the day long; we are accounted as sheep for the slaughter. Nay, in all these things we are more than conquerors through him that loved us. For I am persuaded, that neither death, nor life, nor angels, nor principalities, nor powers, nor things present, nor things to come, nor height, nor depth, nor any other creature, shall be able to separate us from the love of God which is in Christ Jesus our Lord.

Lovingly, Sarah closed the book and fixed her eyes on him. "I learned to read so I'se could read my Bible." Triumph and victory resonated in her voice.

"The Bible!" Scorn ripped through the air as Moses struggled with the anger threatening to consume him. "White man's religion." For a moment he had the wild thought of ripping the book from the old lady's hands and throwing it into the fire.

Sarah merely waited while Moses fixed his eyes on her. An almost palpable peace reached out to him from the old lady's face. Her very serenity offered him a place to deposit his anger. Slowly the rage dissipated and control returned. Taking a deep breath, Moses settled back into his chair.

Only then did Sarah speak again. "You've had a passel of hurt poured into yer life, boy. You been beat—both inside and out. You got a right ta be angry. But yer hurt been caused by men, Moses. God neber did hurt you. It be men who ripped your heart out. It be men who made you wish nothin' more den ta die and get it over with. It be *men* who sold yer family and left you all alone. God neber did that. He wants to help you, Moses. He wants to take all that dark bitterness out o' yo heart and pour in his mighty love. Ain't nothin' can take God from you, Moses."

Moses had heard all he could take. Just the mention of God made his blood boil.

Sarah had time for one more statement. "That dark bitterness ain't gonna hurt no one but you, Moses. One day it will eat all dat's left o' your heart. Then you won't be a man anymore. You be just a shell."

Moses struggled to fight the fury rising in his throat. If she only knew. Suddenly, it was important she *did* know. Only then would she understand. He jumped up from his chair and ripped off the plain muslin shirt covering his massive chest and back.

"Don't talk to me 'bout de white man's religion. This is what it do ta niggers," he cried.

Silence filled the tiny cabin as the crackling flames illuminated the crisscross of swollen scars and welts turning his back into a dried mud flat.

Moses continued, keeping his voice low and controlled. "My first master did dis ta me. I was eleven years old. I had just watched my daddy be hung in de woods after trying ta run ta freedom. They caught him, brung him back, and hung him from a tree while I be watching. Dey told him he would die the only way an animal deserved to die. Then they came after the rest of us. My mama was waitin'. She knew it wouldn't do no good ta run. She had to watch while all of us—my sisters, too—were strapped to the whippin' post. Den it was her turn. All of us had to watch while they beat my mama. She almost died dat day. I'm sho she wished she had."

Sarah waited, tears glistening in her shining eyes. Rose wept quietly.

Moses stared into the fire. "When they were done, they told us they'd done it for our own good. That the only way fer us ta make it ta heaven was to repent of our sins. They were helpin' us repent. If they punished us, God wouldn't have to punish us so much when it be his turn. One of my sisters died. Carmen was too little... She couldn't take it." His voice broke in a sob as his mighty shoulders slumped before the terrible memory. Broken, Moses sank into his chair.

Sarah was immediately at his side. Her work-worn hand gently stroked his bowed head. Time seemed to stand still as the pain of generations past marched through the cabin. It was as if the voices of all slaves who had ever lived and suffered were crying to be heard in Moses's words.

Softly, Sarah began to speak. "Thirty years ago, Africa was my home. I had a fine man and two little girl chil'un. One day our village was attacked by another tribe. My man and chil'un were killed in the fightin'. All in the village were killed 'cept the women. They tied leather thongs 'round our necks and connected us ta each other in long lines. We left what was left of our village and marched through the jungle for a lot of days. I lost track of time. We barely had food and water to keep us alive. Beatins were common..."

Moses looked up as Sarah took a breath. "Why?"

Sarah shook her head and continued. "Big boats was waitin' fer us, but first we had to pass de inspection. We had heard rumors in our village about white men stealing people away, but we didn't think it could be true. We figured we be safe in our village..." Her voice caught with the memory. "There were so many of us there dat day. We all had to strip naked and be examined—every part of us. Some didn't pass that 'spection. Dey were de lucky ones. I made it. Before they loaded us on dem big boats, they put a brand on us. We all had dem brands—to let folks know someone owned us now."

Sarah's voice deepened. "A lot of us didn't make it over on the boat. Them men on the ship figured we would try to get free so all of us got put in the bottom of the ship. There weren't much air and even less food and water. They had to carry the dead out ever' morning. There was hardly room to sit. Never did lie down for that whole trip across the big ocean." Sarah's voice wavered again as she relived the memories, and then strengthened. "Some people killed themselves. One woman had her baby on dat boat. Didn't want her baby to live through dat. When no one was watching she jumped overboard with her baby and drowned herself. Right then, I was sho wishing it could have been me."

Moses gazed into the old woman's face, feeling her pain because he so strongly felt his own.

Sarah forged on. "I didn't want to live. I figured if I didn't eat then I could be one of those dey carried out of the bottom in the morning. Dey figured out what I was doin', though. One of the men brung a shovel with hot coals on it. Another one held me while the hot coals were placed right up to my mouth. My lips blistered right up. Then dat man with the shovel, he tell me dat if I don't eat I'm going to have to swallow dem coals. I ate. And just kept hoping I would die. The pain all around was more than I could bear, and I kept seeing pictures in my head of my man and chil'un. I thought I would go plum crazy."

The fire crackling in the cabin was the only sound. Even the frogs had ceased their croaking as if to honor her pain. "That big boat finally crossed the water and dumped us here in Virginia. I was scared bad but firm ground felt mighty good under my feet. If I was goin' to have to live, I wanted to be off dat boat. Marse Cromwell bought me dat day. Well, Marse Cromwell's daddy, that is. Along with a whole passel of others. I be the only one left o' that group." Sarah sighed and continued. "I worked the tobacco fields along with ever'body else. There weren't no more beatins and we had 'nuff to eat. After hearing some o' the stories from surroundin' plantations, I decided I was pretty good off. Then Marse Cromwell bought a slave named John." Sarah's face softened with the memory. "Me and John fell in love lickety-split and got married after just a few months. It wasn't long after that that Rose came along. I thought I had me a new life. Not like the old one but good just the same." Sarah breathed in deeply to control her tears. "Rose was a bitty baby when Marse Cromwell sold John at some auction in Richmond. I never even found out where he be sent to. One day he was there—my fine man—the next he was gone. I gave up all hope that day. There didn't seem to be no end to the bad things waiting to happen in my life. I became a bitter, angry woman. Didn't see no reason to live."

Silence stretched into the cabin.

"What happened?" Moses couldn't keep from asking.

"I remembered that mama aboard the boat. How she had jumped overboard to free her and hers baby. I waited till late one night, got Rose wrapped up in a blanket, and walked down the road till I found de river. I had waded in up to my waist when God stopped me." Sarah smiled at the look of disbelief on Moses's face. "I know. I felt the same way you did. God was a bad man made up by white people to keep us willin' to be their slaves. I had cursed him over and over, but still, it be Him dat stopped me. I couldn't walk out no further. It was like a giant hand was holding me back. I tried, but I just couldn't get no further. Rose was cryin'. I was cursin'. Finally, I gave up and turned back around to sit on the shore. It be when I turned around dat de water started glowin'."

Moses stared as the old woman's face became radiant with wonder as she relived her experience.

"It was a dark night. But that water begin to glow with a white light. It turned that water into the purttiest blue you ever seen, but just the water right around me. And the water got warm. It was like God was giving me a bath. But the bath wasn't for my body. It be for my heart. Warm waves of love washed right through me. I don't know how long I stood there. I never wanted to leave that river. I wanted to feel dat love washin' through me forever. Finally, the light began to fade and I walked out o' dat river a new woman. I knew deep down where no one can't never take it away that I had been with God. Not the God the white men talk about— I'd been with the real God. He took all my pain and anger and he traded me back peace for it. He put a light in my heart dat can't nobody take away."

Sarah's voice faded away, swallowed by the deepening shadows in the room. The logs sputtered and hissed. Long minutes passed as the old woman gave Moses time to take in all her words. She wasn't done, however. "Moses, boy. I hate bein' a slave and I hate slavery. But I decided a long time ago that I weren't gonna hate the people who make me a slave. I'll do what I can to change it, but I won't hate." Sarah did nothing to hide the vehemence of her words.

Moses looked deeply into her eyes as she continued.

"I want to be free someday, boy, but I want my heart to be free now." Kneeling down in front of the hulking giant, Sarah wrapped her arms tightly around him. "They can destroy your body, Moses, but only you can let dem destroy your heart and your soul. Dat be your decision."

The fire had died down to little more than molten ashes when Rose stood and broke the spell. She didn't know how long the three of them had sat in silence, only that the silence was a good one. Her mama did that to people. Sarah liked to get people to be silent. She said that was the only time their thoughts could be loud enough to be heard over the daily demands of living. Rose could hear her mama's voice echoing in her mind. *You got ta be quiet girl. It be the only way to hear yo' heart. And yo' heart be the only thin' you can trust. God will speak to you in your heart. But ya got to be able to hear it.*

Sarah looked up and nodded at Rose. "I know ya got to go, girl. Hope you get a heap of learnin' done t'night."

Rose smiled. "Thanks, Mama." She looked over to see Moses's eyes fastened on her. "Think about what I said, Moses. If you decide you'd like to be part of our school, just let my mama know. You're welcome anytime." Moses nodded, but she couldn't read his expression. She gave her mama a warm hug and turned toward the door.

Moses's voice was barely audible. "I'll come tonight if that be okay wid you."

EIGHT

"Really, Carrie! I don't know why you didn't bring your girl. Whoever heard of getting their own self ready for a ball."

Carrie had to admit that she now doubted the wisdom of her earlier decision to let Rose stay home. Gritting her teeth, she struggled to tame her wild locks into some semblance of the elegant bun Rose could so effortlessly create. She was so absorbed in her efforts, she could ignore Louisa's caustic tone.

"Here, Carrie, let me help you with that."

Carrie knew Sally was trying to act as a buffer between her and Louisa. Their hostess was in high form tonight. She had been crossed and now her acid tongue was unleashed. Carrie preferred to fight her own battles, but she was grateful for her friend's help tonight. She had too much on her mind to bother with Louisa. "Thanks, Sally," she said. "Just when I think I have it under control, these curls seem to develop a mind of their own." Carrie's frustration from Saturday rose up to meet her again. "Oh, if I could just cut it all off!"

Sally's hand flew to her mouth in an effort to control her alarmed gasp. "You don't mean it!" Her blue eyes widened in shock.

Louisa gave a nasty laugh as she turned and swung from the room. "If you'd seen her earlier today, you'd know she means it well enough."

Carrie flushed a bright red as she remembered the token she presented to Robert Borden. She didn't regret it. She just wished that blasted Louisa hadn't seen her. She would never hear the end of it.

"Carrie?" Natalie's questioning voice broke into her thoughts.

Carrie had absolutely no intention of talking about her impulsive act. She shrugged and said lightly, "Oh, I'll keep my hair. My poor mama would drop in her tracks if I were to do such a thing. Sally, I do so appreciate your help. You're an absolute angel."

Sally smiled. "Your hair is beautiful. I only wish I had raven locks like you."

"But, Sally, your blond hair is so beautiful!"

Carrie allowed the mundane chatter to ebb and flow around her. She could take part without even thinking. Thank goodness! It gave her the freedom to pursue the other thoughts rampaging through her mind. The last rays of sunlight had long ago fled before the advancing tide of night. A soft breeze billowed the curtains and caused the voluminous folds of her ball dress to rustle gently from where it hung on the wardrobe door. Lantern light filled the room with a soft glow and the first flames of a newly laid fire cast their warmth to all parts of the room. The other girls were ready. Their servants had already been there to prepare them for the ball.

"Where is Rose? Is she ill?"

Carrie shook her head as Sally's question reached out to bring her thoughts back into the room with her two friends, pulling them from the tournament field. She wanted to hold tight to the picture of Robert winning the tournament on Granite. The sound of his words had rung in her heart all day. *This one's for you, Carrie!* She could still feel the warmth of his gaze upon her. She could also still feel the coldness of Louisa's stare when her friend had pushed her way past Carrie to smile up into Robert's face. She was sure no one had even noticed when she turned and slipped away into the crowd. She pushed the memory away now with effort.

"Where is she then?"

Sally's question reminded Carrie she hadn't answered the first. She shook her head and laughed. "Sorry." She forced herself to focus. "Rose isn't ill. It's just that Sunday is her day with her mama down in the quarters. I decided I could take care of myself." The only response from her two friends was an uncomprehending stare. The looks weren't unkind, just blank. Carrie tried again. "I am eighteen you know. If I can't get myself dressed for a ball, I'm pretty sad indeed."

"But, Carrie..." Sally's voice trailed off as she shook her head disbelievingly.   Natalie   lightened   the atmosphere by laughing. "You know our Miss Carrie. Anything to provide a stir. I'm sure there is no one else among my circle of friends who would care the least little bit if her slave wanted to have supper with her mama in the quarters. Sometimes Carrie, I'm not sure if you're kind or just a little slow in the head!"

Carrie laughed along with her. She was thankful for Natalie's   somewhat   humorous   acceptance   of   her decision. Louisa had not been so kind.

"All done, Carrie." Sally stepped away and allowed Carrie to turn her head toward the mirror.

Carrie smiled in delight. "Rose couldn't have done better. Thank you." With the help of her two friends, it took just moments for her to slip into her ball gown. Once it was securely fashioned, she stepped away and did a graceful curtsy to her reflection in the mirror.

"It's beautiful." Sally's admiration was genuine.

Carrie smiled as she realized with a sudden rush of pleasure that her friend was right. The dress had been a gift from her parents the Christmas before. This was the first chance she'd had to wear it. Fold after fold of ivory satin cascaded to the floor. Heavy emerald green silk outlined the demurely dipping neckline and lent a touch of elegance to the puffy quarter sleeves. A glistening emerald brooch, one of her father's many gifts, nestled in the creamy curve of her throat. Her eyes, not to be outdone by the emerald, shone in the soft light.

"Oh, Carrie. You'll be the perfect Queen of Love and Beauty tonight."

Carrie whirled around in confusion. "What do you mean?"

Natalie stared at her and then laughed merrily. "What do I mean? Why, any blind person could have seen how Robert Borden was looking at you today."

Carrie shook her head. "Louisa gave him her token—"

Just then the door opened and Louisa swept in. "You're right, Carrie. I *did* give him my token, didn't I? And who else would Robert choose to be Queen?"

As Louisa laughed in triumph, Carrie was glad she had not been there to hear Natalie's proclamation. Carrie sincerely hoped she would not be chosen the queen tonight. She still had to endure Louisa's hospitality until the following morning. She knew what it would be like if the girl was thwarted. It was enough to know Robert and Granite had won the race.

Robert cleared his throat and looked around the ballroom nervously. Virginia hospitality had mandated that everyone be cordial and pleasant to him, but he still felt like the outsider in this group of close friends and neighbors. As he looked around, he almost laughed aloud at his nervousness. Some conquering knight he was. It bothered him to admit that Carrie was the source of his nervousness. In an effort to calm himself, he deliberately took in every detail of the scene around him. It had been a habit of his since he was just a boy and was expected to act in the composed manner of a wealthy plantation owner's son.

The rich oak of the ballroom floor was awash with the light of hundreds of candles flickering and throwing light off each other. For this night, lanterns had been put aside. Great armfuls of spring flowers were artfully arranged in vases that lined the walls and rested on tables placed next to silk upholstered chairs. Windows had been left open to allow the warm spring breeze to drift in, bringing the heavy drapes to life. Even later, when the night grew chilly, the air would be welcomed by the avid dancers.

Robert couldn't help but wonder what would happen to this world if the worst happened. What if Thomas Cromwell were right? Would secession from the Union mean war? The confusion of his own thoughts rose to mock him. Surely life as he had known it would never cease to exist.

Yet, he could almost feel it. Storm clouds were gathering in the distance. Storm clouds that most wanted to turn away from. The very blackness of those clouds made men everywhere—both North and South— turn away in denial. It would never happen in their country. But while they shook their heads, were the clouds growing darker and more menacing?

Robert shook his head to clear away the disturbing thoughts and glanced around to see if anyone had noticed how troubled he was. He was determined to push the foreboding thoughts aside. This was a night for fun.

Couples had been filtering into the ballroom, announced by the Blackwell house servants. Music began to fill the room as band members coaxed notes from their instruments. A sudden flash of color drew Robert's attention, and when he turned his gaze toward the ballroom entrance, he saw Carrie move into the room. He took a quick, deep breath and locked his eyes on her. Never had he seen someone so alive, or so beautiful.

Carrie was mesmerized by the activity surrounding her. Wordlessly, she gazed around, taking it all in. She may not want to spend the rest of her days on a plantation, but she could definitely spend the rest of her life dancing. She loved all of it, from the formal ballroom waltzes, to the rousing Virginia reel. Her heart pumped harder as she envisioned it. She looked for her parents, smiling proudly when she spotted them. They were quite the elegant couple tonight. Her father looked dashing and her mother was the perfect southern belle in her light-blue gown. The whole room had transformed into a shimmering sea of satins and silks.

Her father looked up and caught her eye. His expression told her she looked lovely. She smiled back brilliantly and started toward them.

Just then, Alfred Blackwell, accompanied by Colonel Benton, moved to the center of the ballroom and held up his hand to gain attention. Everyone ceased talking and turned their eyes to him. Suddenly, Carrie noticed Louisa making her way toward Robert. Louisa stopped along with everyone else but glared daggers at her father. What was she doing?

"Welcome to the annual Blackwell Ball!" Alfred Blackwell shouted. He waited for the clapping to die down, and then continued. "As usual, we are blessed to have so many of our friends and neighbors here tonight. It's a privilege to have each one of you. Before we get started, there is a special ceremony yet to be performed. Our ball does not yet have its Queen of Love and Beauty, or its court of ladies-in-waiting. Our Colonel Benton here is going to take care of that for us."

"Not me, Blackwell," Colonel Benton protested. "There is a young man here who rode his heart out to earn that honor tonight." He smiled over at Robert. "Robert Borden, please join me here, sir."

Carrie watched with pride as he strode confidently to the center of the room.

"You have broken a long-held Blackwell tradition today," Colonel Benton proclaimed solemnly, his eyes twinkling. "I'd say it was about time Nathan Blackwell was dethroned!"

Nathan joined in the good-natured laughter filling the room. "You got me this time, Borden. It won't be so easy next time!"

Robert smiled at his new friend. Then he turned back to Colonel Benton just as the older man handed him a beautiful crown formed of wisteria and dogwood intricately woven together. The room grew completely silent as he accepted the crown. Raising his arms high, he held the crown aloft for the whole room to see.

Carrie, watching from her post next to the door, felt a thrill course through her body. Robert had ridden so magnificently today. He deserved to be the conquering knight. Her gaze swung to Louisa. Of course she would be crowned the queen. She had given Robert the first token and she expected to reign with him tonight.

Robert allowed his gaze to scan the entire room as he let the suspense build. "I am honored to be the conquering knight of the Blackwell Tournament. The competition was stiff. Admiration runs deep for my worthy opponents." He paused. "The honor of choosing the Queen of Love and Beauty is not one to be taken lightly. It is, at best, a very difficult decision. So many beautiful young ladies, all worthy of the honor. Most of you do not know that I did not attend with the intention of riding in the tournament. Because of extended travel plans, I was not able to bring my horse. Carrie Cromwell was kind enough to remedy that situation for me. It was her horse Granite that carried me to victory today."

Carrie was watching Louisa. She saw her face stiffen and take on an expression of disbelief. Confused, Carrie turned her attention to Robert.

Robert continued. "In honor of Miss Cromwell's supreme unselfishness and in honor of a magnificent Thoroughbred with a great heart, I crown Miss Carrie Cromwell the Queen of Love and Beauty." Robert moved toward the entranceway as he spoke these last words.

Carrie heard his words and saw him moving in her direction, but she couldn't believe her own eyes and ears. Surely he knew what an insult this would be to Louisa! She felt her cheeks flushing as Robert came to a stop in front of her. She settled her eyes on the proffered crown and fought to think clearly. When she glanced up, Robert's dark brown eyes probed her own. The message was unmistakable. *Trust me. This is what I want.* Carrie's heart jumped in response and she allowed her own indomitable spirit to rise to meet Robert's.

Carrie smiled as she curtsied deeply to her knight. Robert carefully placed the crown on her glimmering hair and reached for her hand. All around, she could hear the murmurs of approval. The sound of her friends' and neighbors' voices added to her joy. No one seemed angry that Robert had not chosen the beautiful daughter of their host. She would most definitely have to deal with Louisa later, but tonight—tonight was hers. She would make the most of it. She knew she and Robert would perform the first dance alone before the ladies-in-waiting were selected. Tucking her hand in Robert's arm, she allowed him to lead her to the middle of the dance floor. Only then did the music start. Turning to face him, she smiled joyously. "Thank you."

Robert's response was immediate. "Thank *you*, Miss Cromwell. You honor me by being my queen tonight. There has never been one lovelier."

The intensity of his eyes and voice caused Carrie to blush and look down. The next thing she knew, Robert had swung her into an elegant waltz. She quit thinking then. She would enjoy the night, the music, and the dancing. Music swirled around them, joining with the glowing lights and gentle breezes. It was a perfect night.

After leading his beautiful wife through several dances, and a rousing Virginia reel, Thomas Cromwell was ready for a drink.

"I hear that Borden lad has an interest in politics."

Thomas stifled a groan. Any conversation with Edmund Ruffin lately meant conflict. He supposed there was no avoiding it. "That's right. A fine lad he is."

"I hope he has more gumption than the rest of our so-called Virginia politicians. Our whole state seems to be full of gentlemen eager to bow in acquiescence to the almighty North."

Thomas was aware Ruffin's words linked him to this group. He considered walking off to find Abigail but caught sight of her in the midst of a gaggle of women and tossed that option aside. Just then, Alfred Blackwell and Colonel Benton strode up to join them. Stifling a sigh, he remained where he was. To walk away now would appear rude to his host.

Ruffin continued. "It grieves me deeply that fellow Virginians would be willing to sacrifice our southern civilization. It confounds me that once levelheaded men cannot see the danger of allowing things to continue as they are." He was obviously aware he was now speaking to a larger audience. "It will take brave men to turn the tide of current events. The North would come down and destroy all that we hold dear. The abolitionists continue to fire up sentiment against our way of life. Secession is the only answer. Only when we are free as a nation to determine our own destiny, apart from the heavy-handed meddling from the North, will this struggle be over."

Thomas sighed. He had heard it all before. Long before the cry of secession had become an accepted voice in the South, he had been hearing this type of rhetoric from his fire-eating neighbor. The voices were louder now, and there were more of them. Daily his heart grew heavier as he imagined the outcome if his hot-tempered neighbor and those of his kind were allowed to lead the way.

"I used to think you were a kind of mad man, Ruffin. Recent events have made me do a lot of thinking." Colonel Benton stuffed a plug of chewing tobacco in his jaw and began to work it thoughtfully. His usually jovial voice was heavy. "I used to think all that abolitionist talk was just a bunch of nonsense from people who had nothing better to do with their time than harass a way of life they didn't understand. John Brown made me think differently. Those abolitionists are crazy people who will kill and destroy to get their way. I've always been a Union man myself. I've always been proud to be an American. Now, I'm not so sure. If being an American means the North is going to control how I live and try to turn the South into another Africa by setting all the niggers free, well then—"

Thomas broke into the colonel's speech. "Now, Colonel, I think you may be overstating your case." Ruffin snorted as if to interrupt him, but Thomas forged ahead. "There are those in the South who would have us believe the only way to save our way of life is to secede from the Union. I believe the very opposite. I believe the only way to save our way of life is to *stay* in the Union. Our very strength lies in our unity. Secession will mean war. War has never brought anything but destruction and death. We need what the North has to offer, just as they need what we have to offer." His voice grew firmer as he cast aside any hope of averting conflict. "I'm afraid fire-eaters like Ruffin here may be leading the South into a time of great tragedy and heartache." Thomas believed his words with all his heart, but he well knew the lessening impact they were having. Strident voices everywhere were fighting to be heard and just as it so often happened in the past, the voices that shouted the loudest were the ones heard best. The voices that fed on fear and prejudices drowned out all else.

Ruffin again snorted his disdain. "We need nothing from the North. They are nothing but tyrants who want to control us. The only answer is secession. The idea that it would mean war is ludicrous. The North would never come down here to fight us. It would be pure folly." Rubbing his hands together, he warmed to his subject. "Our South is by far the superior civilization. No one can challenge the nobleness of our cause or question our outstanding character. It is true that the soil of the South has produced a better man. Why look at it! Slavery. The plantations. Our men have been bred and trained for command and leadership. Though it will never happen, I would welcome the contest between a lean, hard Southern man fighting for liberty, family, and property, and a soft, flabby Yankee mechanic waging an unconstitutional, utopian war of aggression and tyranny!" Waving his hands wildly, Ruffin had now attracted the attention of those around him.

Thomas listened to his neighbor with a sinking heart. He disagreed with all his heart, but he knew many of his friends and those listening agreed with Ruffin. He wished he could get them to see what folly this talk of secession was. Get them to think clearly with their heads instead of following the passion of their hearts.

Ruffin, aware he was drawing a crowd, continued with his tirade. "In just eight more days the die may be cast."

Just then, Carrie and Robert dropped out of the dancing to get refreshments. Robert turned to Ruffin. "Eight days, sir? Are you referring to the Democratic Convention in Charleston?"

"I am indeed."

Robert nodded. "I leave for there tomorrow."

Ruffin turned to eye Robert with renewed interest. "And what do you hope to see accomplished there, young man?"

"In truth, sir, I don't know. Northern Democrats seem assured of Douglas's nomination. I am not so sure. There are many Southerners unhappy with the compromising senator."

"And well they should be," Ruffin said caustically.

Robert continued. "I'm afraid, though, that a split at the convention will mean disaster for the Democratic Party. It could mean a victory for the Republican Party and I'm afraid of what that would mean for the South."

Thomas watched Robert carefully. The young man was genuinely expressing his views. Thomas knew what was coming next.

Ruffin pounced. "That would be the very best thing for our beloved South."

"Excuse me, sir?" Robert was obviously confused.

Thomas had correctly guessed that Robert had little exposure to rabid fire-eaters. His political experience had been among the more moderates of the party. Most of the fire-eaters resided in the cotton states farther south. Virginians, for the most part, did not share those intense feelings.

Ruffin continued to enlighten him. "Yes, young man, it would be the very best thing that could happen. Maybe then the South would cease all this kowtowing to the North. If the Democratic Party is divided in such a way as to ensure a *Black Republican* victory next year in the presidential election, maybe all Southern men will have the courage to unite under the banner of the South, disentangled from Northern alliances. Perhaps then the South will act for its defense and only salvation." Ruffin's face grew redder and his arms waved wildly as he became more passionate. "If not, submission to Northern oppression and aggression will be the set course of the South. Our fate will be sealed." His booming voice ground to a halt as he leaned in close to Robert.

Thomas watched Robert's face fill with doubt. He knew Ruffin had no qualms against using Robert to make a point to his audience as a whole. He would not feel one misgiving that he was bringing such discord to a social function meant for laughter and fun.

Ruffin wasn't done. "Robert Borden. You own a plantation up in Goochland?"

Robert nodded. "Yes, sir. With my brother and mother. My father is deceased."

"Own slaves?"

"Yes, sir. Close to seventy-five."

"How do you feel about someone coming down and setting all your slaves free?" He didn't give him time to answer. "How do you feel about all your former slaves living around here, having the same say as you about what goes on?" He pushed on. "How do you feel about the South turning into a little Africa if there were no white men to control things?" He seemed not to care if Robert answered or not. He was making a point. "How would you like to lose your means of make a living for your family? How would you like it if life as you know it were about to end?"

Alfred Blackwell stepped in to end the show before Robert could answer. "That's enough, friends. It's time for our real refreshment." His words were enough to break the spell Ruffin had cast over the crowd. Breaking off, small groups drifted into the main dining room.

Carrie stood quietly at Robert's side. She knew what one of Ruffin's tirades could do. Even the most clearheaded person could become confused by his elegant rhetoric. She knew how difficult it sometimes was to not allow the enflamed opinions of others to form one's own.

Robert looked down at her. "Feels rather strongly, doesn't he?" His expression was one of amused bewilderment.

Carrie laughed up at him. "Our Mr. Ruffin feels quite strongly about a lot of things. I applaud his passion, but I find I question many of his conclusions."

Robert nodded thoughtfully, looking at her with admiration. "My beautiful queen has a head full of brains to match her beauty."

Carrie just laughed again. "Please don't tell my mother. I'm afraid she despairs of me already. I think she would prefer that I quit thinking and simply enjoy being a plantation mistress."

"And that's not what you want?"

"Certainly not!" Carrie's response was immediate. She surprised herself with her openness, but she didn't regret it. She was being nothing but honest.

"And what is it you want?"

Carrie opened her mouth but then shut it again. She barely knew this man. What would possess her to think of sharing the secret only Granite knew?

Robert took her arm and steered her toward the table. "Excuse my intrusiveness."

Carrie hastened to apologize. "Oh! It's not that you're being intrusive. It's just that—"

"It's none of my business," he finished for her. "You're quite right, you know." Robert grinned down at her horrified expression. "It's quite all right, Miss Cromwell. But be sure of one thing." He paused for emphasis. "Someday, I hope to make it my business." Stepping aside, he said, "Now, what would you like to eat, my beautiful queen?"

Carrie could hardly focus her eyes on the sumptuous table. Robert's words swam through her mind and caused her to feel short of breath. She struggled to maintain a calm manner and made a show of inspecting the table. In truth, she was hungry. Lunch had been hours earlier and the light meal before the ball had worn off ages ago.

The traditional Blackwell Ball feast was spread out on a table more than twenty feet long. It fairly groaned under its load of hand-dipped chocolate fruits, cheesecakes, cookies, fresh fruits, and cheeses. The other end was piled high with savory meats, breads, and biscuits. Huge bowls of punch, cider, and harder brew for the men lay in wait.

Carrie smiled up at her escort brightly. "I'll eat because I'm hungry, but you have to promise me we can dance longer."

Robert laid his hand over his heart and bowed deeply. "Nothing would keep me from that honor, m' lady."

Carrie was exhausted. She smiled gratefully as Natalie and Sally lifted her ball gown over her head, and then released her hair and allowed it to tumble down her back. She reached for her brush, closed her eyes, and made big sweeping draws through the ebony mass. Her whole body cried of tiredness. It had been such a long day. That morning and the carriage ride seemed days ago. Even the tournament seemed as if it had happened in another age. It was the dancing that filled her mind—the swirling, gliding, and swinging that never lost its delight for her. She could still see Robert, so tall and handsome, gazing down at her. Laughing. Talking. She just wanted to go to bed and dream about it. Never had she felt this way before. She needed time to analyze it. To understand it. She looked with longing at her feathery mattress on the floor. A few more strokes...

"Carrie?"

"Yes, Sally?"

"What the men were talking about tonight? I couldn't help but overhear Mr. Ruffin. Is he right? Is the North really going to come down here and destroy our way of life?"

Carrie hesitated. She wished she knew the answer to that question. "I don't know, Sally. But I do believe the South needs to do all it can to stay within the Union."

"Oh, pooh! I hate all this talk about secession and slavery, states' rights against the Union... I'm sick of it."

Carrie looked at Louisa in surprise. She hadn't really thought the girl listened enough to what was said around her to even know what was going on. She watched as the blonde swung around on her dressing table bench and waved her brush in the air.

Louisa continued. "I tell you, I'm sick of all this talk and I won't hear any more of it. There are more important things to talk about."

Carrie wasn't surprised she felt that way. Louisa had always wanted to push away whatever wasn't pleasant. If she ignored it, she figured it would go away. From what Carrie could tell, that seemed to be the mentality of most plantation women. Focus on what was important and let the rest of the world spin on by. That was fine with her tonight. She didn't want to talk. She wanted to sleep.

Sally had other ideas. She was clearly troubled. "But what if he is right? What if the time comes when we're not safe with our people? It's happening you know. Just the other day I heard of some slaves' uprising. They killed their master and his wife. They even killed the little boy—only a few months old." Sally paused, the fear standing out against her creamy features. "I'm afraid. What if soon none of us are safe?"

Carrie tried to comfort her. "Sally, that's pure nonsense. You're good to your slaves. Why would they want to hurt you? Those slaves who killed their master were probably badly treated. That would never happen to you." She could only hope she was right. She knew her own mother was afraid of the same thing. Carrie had overheard her talking about it with a friend who had come to visit.

Louisa shook her head again. "I mean it! I don't want any more talk of that kind in my room. I'm sick to death of it." Her blue eyes flashed and she glared around the room until Sally nodded meekly. "If we're going to talk about something, we're going to talk about the wonderful ball tonight."

Louisa seemed to have gotten over her initial anger at being passed over as queen. Carrie gave a silent sigh of relief, but she looked up to see Louisa regarding her with a condescending smile.

"Robert really is quite noble, Carrie." Louisa laughed lightly. "Anyone could tell he wanted to choose me. What a perfect gentleman that he would select you just because you let him ride your horse. It really is a pity, though, that he felt so indebted. One should feel free to act from one's desire, not from a sense of obligation."

Carrie stared at her in astonishment but said nothing. She knew the truth. She had spent a few minutes alone with Natalie before Louisa came into the room. Nathan had saved the night. Nathan, knowing his sister and not wanting to see her spoil the evening for his new friend, had engineered things beautifully. He had seen to it that not one dance went by without an escort for Louisa. In truth, it hadn't been difficult. Louisa, when she wasn't angry over not getting her own way in some situation, was quite charming. Her beauty had long lured fellows to her side. It had not taken long for Louisa to fall into the spirit of the ball and even be overheard telling people she was so thankful *that Robert Borden fellow* hadn't felt obligated toward her.

Louisa continued, "I do believe that Graham Jackson was quite taken with me. Natalie, what do you know about him? He seems to be a friend of our neighbor, Clinton Fortson. Mr. Fortson is usually careful about the type of people he associates with. What can you tell me about him?"

Natalie shrugged and turned to Carrie. "Carrie, your father is awfully involved in politics. What does he really think is going to happen?"

Carrie hesitated. She knew how Louisa hated to be thwarted.

"Don't you answer that silly old question, Carrie Cromwell. I mean it! I will not have this talked about any longer."

Carrie turned to the angry girl. "I don't think they mean any harm, Louisa. Don't you know our whole world may be changing? Don't you care?"

"Oh, pooh!" Louisa cried. "These men and their little play fights don't mean anything. Things have always been this way—someone disagreeing with someone else over some petty thing. Nothing's going to change."

Carrie stared at her friend. She knew there was nothing she could say. Exchanging a meaningful look with Natalie and Sally, she laid her brush down and moved toward her bed. "Goodnight."

NINE

Rose put her finger to her lips in warning as she and Moses eased from Sarah's tiny cabin. She pulled her cloak tightly around her shoulders, patted her front pocket to make sure the forbidden paper was there, and looked carefully around. It would not do to be seen. She knew not everyone in the quarters was to be trusted. There were those who would sell out their own people in order to gain perceived favors. Rose grieved over those who were slaves not only in their bodies but also in their minds.

The furtiveness of her actions spoke a truth louder than words. Many were those who were enslaved by force, but there were just as many who had been taught to believe their own best interests would be served only by abiding the wish of their master. They believed the lie that they were inferior and could only rise to the level of the master through slavery. Rose knew that once the brainwashing was complete and the slave's mind destroyed, the slave would enslave himself. There would be no need to escape, for only through captivity could their dreams be achieved. She saw this in the eyes of many of the Cromwell slaves that had spent all their lives in slavery. That reality gave her the courage to do what she was doing. She was determined she would never be like them. She was willing to take the risks.

Moses followed Rose quietly as she headed for an unseen opening in the woods and slipped onto an almost invisible trail. Indeed, it was visible only to her, and she knew every dip and bend. Moses stayed close to her shadowy form as they melted into the dark forest.

The ebony night bent to embrace them, swallowing any evidence of their having been there. A soft wind whispered encouragement as they forged forward. The softness of the spring night wrapped itself around them, lending them courage to keep going. Every night sound seemed to whisper a refrain. *Break the bonds. You are more than you believe. Break the bonds. You are meant to be free...*

Rose continued to move forward gracefully, her thoughts on Moses. He walked as silently as she did, but she was aware of his powerful presence just behind her. She could imagine the fear he must be feeling. Her mama had told him to be careful, and here he was doing a thing that would certainly earn him a beating if he was discovered. He had made his choice, however, and she was glad to have him with her.

After several minutes, the trail took a plunging descent. Rose came to an abrupt halt and looked around carefully. Only blackness and the shadowy outlines of trees met her gaze. She felt Moses edge up next to her. She said nothing, just sank to the ground in a sitting position. Moses joined her, drawing his long legs up against his body. Still Rose made no sound. She knew a million questions must be rampaging through Moses's mind, but he stayed silent.

Suddenly, a rustle broke the night. Moses stiffened and moved his long legs slightly. Knowing he was scared, Rose reached over and put a hand on his leg. "It's okay." Her soft voice was a barely discernable whisper. Moses remained tense, but still. The rustling in the woods continued for long minutes.

Rose, sitting next to him quietly, was aware of the tension coiling his body. She knew this young giant could ruin everything for them if he was not trustworthy. She had taken a chance. But every night she crept out into these woods was a chance. Her position as Carrie's personal maid would not protect her if they were discovered. Every night the fear threatened to choke her. There had never been a beating on Cromwell Plantation. She didn't want to be the first, and yet, every night she taught her school made that a possibility.

Rose shook her head firmly, willing all such thoughts and pictures out of her mind. It would not do to let the fear take hold. That was the power, she knew. The white man ruled by fear. A people afraid were a people trapped in bondage. Break that fear and people would spring forward into freedom and liberty. That was why Rose was here. To help her people break the bondage of fear. When the time came for freedom, they needed to move forward with confidence. She would do what she could to make it possible.

"We're all here now."

Moses jerked as a strange voice whispered into the still night.

Rose pressed down on his leg once more and then moved her hand. Speaking in a low, controlled voice, she said, "Good. Did you bring the light?" Rose sensed rather than saw the shape that moved into the clearing to join them. Others emerged to join the first. A match flared and shattered the darkness. A shadowy shape moved forward with a handful of dry leaves. Another deposited an armful of tiny limbs and twigs. Gradually, a fire was created as offerings were brought. Only when there was a steady blaze illuminating the clearing did everyone move forward and sink onto the ground around Rose.

Rose was aware the rest of the group was watching Moses closely. The looks were not unkind, but neither were they welcoming. No one spoke. They just watched and waited.

Rose was the obvious leader of the group. "We're all here? Is William watching for us?"

"He sho is, Miss Rose." The response came from a slight girl who looked to be only fourteen or fifteen. "My brother will make sure we won't be caught."

"Thank you, Jasmine," Rose said absently as she looked around at the group filling the small clearing. "I'd like to introduce all of you to someone. This is Moses. He's new among us. He came in from Richmond yesterday."

Everyone nodded. They all knew that coming in from Richmond meant you had just been bought at auction. The curious stares continued, along with an increased tension. Rose understood. Never before had she brought someone so new to their little school. Usually they had to prove themselves. Rose knew she had to be careful. One wrong word spoken and all of them would pay the price. In her heart she knew it was okay, but she couldn't expect the other people to share the trust she felt for Moses— especially when she couldn't even say why she was so sure of it herself. It would take time.

Moses gazed around the circle. Rose smiled slightly at the surprised look on his face. What had he expected? He'd probably never known black folks who could read and write.

Seated next to him was Jasmine, the young girl who had spoken up for her brother. Her soft, young face glowed with eagerness in the firelight. Next to her was Sadie, a much older woman whose stooped shoulders and bent back spoke of long hours at the end of a tobacco hoe in the fields. Her eyes were fixed on Rose, impatient to get on with what they were here for. Next to her was Miles, the wise man who managed the stables for the Cromwell Plantation—quite a prestigious job by slave standards. There were young and old, field hands and house help. That was one of the beauties of her school. You didn't often see field hands mingling with house help. House help usually had a condescending attitude toward those slaves forced to labor in the fields. There was none of that here, as they were all working toward the same dream.

Rose reached deep into her cloak and pulled out a pointed stick, some pieces of paper, and what looked like a book. She caught Moses's look of amazement and smiled. Surely he had never seen a slave with a book. Those only belonged to white folks. Rose looked around. "We have a lot to do tonight. I figure we have about three hours. The first thing I want to do is go over all the letters again. Once you know all of those, reading is a lot easier." She leaned over to brush away the leaves that had fallen since their last meeting, picked up her pointed stick and held it poised above the ground.

"Miss Rose?" It was Miles's strong voice.

"Yes, Miles?"

"I got's somethin' yesterday in town I thought you might like to see." He reached into his pocket and pulled out a carefully folded piece of paper. "A fella slipped this into my pocket when nobody was lookin'. I can make out some of it, but the big words I ain't so good with yet." His voice caught with excitement.

Rose reached forward eagerly. It was always a special occasion to get something from the outside world. She managed, through careful listening and Carrie's generosity, to find out much about the world beyond the confines of Cromwell Plantation, but there was still so much she didn't know. Silence fell on the clearing as she grasped the offered paper. Then she looked at the headline and gasped. She took a deep breath and forced herself to read slowly, well aware everyone was watching her closely. She fought to control herself as the words poured into her mind. It existed! It really did exist! All the rumors were true. She had hoped and believed, but still she hadn't been sure. But if this paper told the truth...

"What is it?" Miles's insistent voice broke into her thoughts. "Is it what I think it be?"

Rose looked up, stared around at them, and looked back down at the paper. It was several moments before she began to read.

THE CONDUCTOR'S CALL

Welcome to all who want to come on board the Underground Railroad. There will be a conductor in your area soon. There are many trains running on a daily basis. Many are being carried to freedom in the North. Do you want to join your brothers and sisters who are now free?

Conductor Jamison will be visiting Cromwell Plantation. You must be on the watch for him. Let him know if you are interested in making a reservation. There are many who are working to free you.

Not a word was spoken after Rose finished reading. The whole group sat in stunned silence.

"It's true then, ain't it? We got a way to get out of here? Just like you said?"

Rose nodded slowly. "Yes, Sadie. It looks like it's true." All the while she was talking she was trying to control her spinning thoughts. She had hoped and prayed for so long— even when the hoping seemed to bring nothing but despair.

"What we gonna do, Miss Rose?" Miles asked in a hoarse whisper.

Rose wanted to laugh. She had been going to ask Miles the same question. She was only eighteen years old. Still, because she was their teacher, she knew they all looked up to her. Rose waited long minutes while her brain spun furiously. Finally, she spoke. "It's up to each of us to decide that. Assuming this Conductor Jamison actually shows up, I could have him come to our school to meet with us."

"How?" This question was from Moses. "I don't know nothin' 'bout no underground railroad, but how you gonna get a stranger through these here woods?" His voice clearly said that she must be crazy to even consider it.

Rose shrugged and smiled weakly. "I don't know. I'll have to figure something out."

Silence fell on the clearing once more. Visions of freedom floated through the air, tempting and tantalizing the hearts and minds that had recently awakened. Close on their heels were the voices of fear that had controlled them for so long. What if they were caught? What if these people who spoke of freedom were not really friends? And what if they ran away only to find their new lives were no better than their old?

"Rose?"

Rose turned to Moses and smiled up into his confused eyes. "It's the Underground Railroad!" She correctly interpreted his blank look. "They help slaves run away to freedom. I've heard about them for so long. There isn't really a railroad. The name just stands for a lot of people who give up their homes and their time to help slaves reach freedom in the North. I've heard there are people who want to help us, but it's just so hard to believe. I don't know much, Moses. Everything is kept very secret. But I've heard about slaves who run away.

And I don't hear about them being brought back. That means somewhere they're free!"

Visions of freedom pushed the dark specter of fear further from the dwelling.

"I kin hardly 'magine what it would be like to be free." Jasmine's voice was a mixture of disbelief and fervent longing. "Maybe I could get me hitched to a man and not have him sold off."

The visions grew stronger as each one there dreamed of what freedom could mean to them.

"We'd be in a heap o' trouble if we done get caught." Miles's words caused the fear to come charging back into the clearing. The visions began to fade. Fear crept closer.

Rose spoke firmly. "It's what all of you want isn't it? To be free?" She waited until all eyes were fixed on her—all heads nodding. "Our people have been controlled by fear for too long. Maybe this Conductor Jamison won't even come. But if he does, we can't let fear rob us of our dreams. All of us have had to fight fear every day of our lives. Fear of being beat. Fear of being sold. All of you have had to fight fear to meet here to learn how to read and write. I suppose all of life is fighting one fear after another." She paused and looked around. "But my mama says that the only way to live is to fight those fears and do what comes to you. She says if you're not fighting those fears, you're not living. You're just existing. That's why all of us are here. Because we want to live." She paused again to let her words sink in. Then she continued, "I say we hear this Conductor Jamison out. If he shows up. We'll know whether we can trust him or not. If we get in trouble for it, well, at least we'll have been doing something to fight our fears."

Rose's words pushed back the remaining fear until it faded into the dark shadows. With visions of freedom filling the hearts and minds of all present, it was agreed Conductor Jamison would be invited to their next secret school meeting.

With that taken care of, Rose forced herself to the business at hand. If freedom was indeed imminent for some of her friends, she wanted them to go forth as prepared as possible. With great effort, she forced down her own boiling emotions. Now was not the time to deal with them. She looked up and caught Moses watching her thoughtfully. Rose looked away quickly, but in just that one brief moment she realized Moses had the ability to read her heart—to see beyond the surface to what was boiling just underneath. The knowledge both unnerved and intrigued her.

"Let's see your alphabet, Jasmine." Rose sighed with relief when the eager girl produced a stick and began to draw her letters in the soft dirt. Activity was always her refuge when things became too overwhelming. She welcomed the distraction, especially now.

Moses leaned forward to watch Jasmine's intense features as she carefully drew. Rose knew the symbols she was drawing made no sense to him.

"Excellent, Jasmine. I can tell you've been practicing."

"Yes'um. At night when no one be watching. I do them only one at a time so I can scratch if out if anyone sees me."

Rose smiled her approval and the girl's face glowed. There were only three years separating the two, but the gap seemed much larger. Rose knew the gap would lessen as Jasmine fed her eager thirst for knowledge. She turned next to Miles. "How about you, Miles?"

The old man smiled proudly. "I 'bout got dem all. I tells you though, Miss Rose, I sho be tired of writing letters in the dirt. I want to be doin' some readin'!"

"And you will be soon, Miles. But reading isn't much different from training one of your young horses. I've watched you work with them. You have to lay a solid foundation before you can ride them. Isn't that right?"

"Yes'um. That's right."

"Well, reading is the same," Rose said seriously, staring around the circle at everyone. "If you don't lay a solid foundation, you'll never be able to do it right. Once you learn all those letters, you'll know how to move forward. You've got to get the basics right." Then she laughed. "I understand, though. I wanted to read the very first day Miss Carrie and I had a book set in front of us. I could hardly wait to know what all those shapes meant."

Rose lifted the sheets of paper she held in her hands and turned to Sadie. "Read this for us, Sadie." Sadie had been her first student and now she read beautifully.

Sadie smiled proudly as she reached out her hands for the papers. Edging closer to the firelight, she inspected the papers. "Why, this be a newspaper! The *Richmond Enquirer*." She gazed at Rose wide-eyed. "Where you get this paper, Rose?"

Rose just shrugged and smiled. "Read it, Sadie."

Sadie gave a short laugh. "You be somethin' else, girl. One o' these days, though..." She scanned the lines of the paper and her eyes sharpened. "Humph. There can't be no truth to this one!" Settling down she began to read. Her voice was halting and unsure when she encountered the big words, but she plowed on, determined to conquer this latest challenge.

PREFERS SLAVERY TO FREEDOM

Some four or five years since, William Burnett, of this county, by will, emancipated his slaves. The will was made by the testator in extremis, and its validity was strongly contested. Many of the people of the county and all the members of the bar will remember the interesting and exciting incidents of the trial. The Negroes succeeded in the contest and established their right to freedom. In pursuance of the testator's instructions, they were carried to the State of Ohio and there settled on a tract of land bought for their use and occupancy. It has been scarcely a year since they were snugly domiciled beyond the banks of the Ohio, in free territory.

On our return home from last Mecklenburg County Court, we met a Negro wending his way along the plank road in the direction of Boydton. He stopped us with a hearty and cordial salutation. It was the same Isaac Burnett who had been foremost in the struggle for freedom before the circuit court of the county only some 18 months before. He informed us that, abandoning his interest in the lands purchased for him and his associates in Ohio, he had deliberately returned to Virginia for the purpose of enslaving himself to a gentleman of Boydton, where it was his wish to spend the balance of his life. He is young and healthy, of decided intelligence, and better calculated for freedom than the majority of Negroes. But he had become thoroughly satisfied from a fair experiment that it was a curse rather than a blessing in his case, and consequently, he deliberately resolved to change his condition to that of a slave. He gave us a most deplorable account of the present state and future prospects of the little free colony he left behind him in Ohio. He said all were dissatisfied and would return if they could. That they had made little or nothing since their arrival in Ohio, and that their chances to make anything were next to nothing. In fact, that their condition was truly pitiable.

Sadie's voice ground to a halt. Then it rose indignantly. "Why, who ever heard of such nonsense!"

Rose lifted her voice against the murmur of agreement filling the clearing. "What if it's true?"

Miles turned toward her. "How could you say such a thing, Miss Rose?" he asked. "Who ever heard of a slave wanted to go back to slavery if he finally got hisself free?"

Rose looked at him thoughtfully. She had spent many hours thinking about this. "What do you think it would be like if you were free, Miles?"

Miles looked at her carefully now. "Well, I think it would be the greatest thin' in the world. I would be responsible only for myself. I could come and go as I please. I could have horses of my own—not have to just take care of Marse Cromwell's. I could have me a wife, maybe even find June." His eyes clouded over as he thought of his wife, who had been sold a few years before to parts unknown.

"What if you didn't have any money, Miles? What if you never owned a horse of your own? What if no one wanted to be your wife? What if you had to work all the time just to survive?"

"That ain't gonna happen, Miss Rose." Miles protested.

Rose persisted. "But what if it did? *What if it did?*"

Miles gave a frustrated sigh. Several long minutes passed while he stared into the fire. Finally, he looked up. "Then so be it. Even if I had nothing, I would have myself. I would have my freedom. That means more to me than anything. It would mean people would look at me and see another human being— not just a thing."

Rose smiled tenderly. "Hang on to that, Miles. You may need it someday." She gazed intently at the rest of the group. "All of you need to be asking yourself that question. You say you want to be free. Why? Being free doesn't necessarily mean all our troubles will be over. It just means we'll have the opportunity to handle them on our own. The man in that story didn't figure on freedom being hard. He thought it was the answer to all his problems. When he found out that it wasn't, he ran back to what he had always known. My mama says it's kind of like t Israel wanting to go back to Egypt. It was horrible, but at least they knew what to expect and they could always blame their misery on someone else." She paused and looked around again. "I can teach you how to read and write. You have to teach yourselves how to think. You have to ask questions. Lots of them. But my mama says it doesn't do any good to ask questions if you aren't going to look hard for the answers. We've all got to be doing that. The day may be coming soon for some of you to be free. Are you sure that's what you want? You'd better be."

Rose's little school stared at her in the darkness. Flickering firelight illuminated the confusion on their faces. They had never heard Rose talk like this before. She had challenged them plenty of times, but she had never been quite so harsh with them. Rose felt a slight twinge of sympathy for her students, but she pushed it down. The questions she had thrown at them were important ones—ones that demanded answers. Daily, she battled the frustration that she had come up with the answers for herself, only to realize the answers made no difference.

Moses, watching Rose closely, knew exactly what she was doing. His own mama had done the same for him. Even before his daddy had been killed, she had pestered him with questions. Nothing he ever said could be taken at face value. She had to know why he had said it, why he felt that way, and what he wanted to come from those feelings. He understood the group's frustration, but he also understood Rose's motive. His mama had told him that it was only when he stopped thinking for himself that he would be a slave. He could still hear her voice. *It's only when they own your mind that they really own you, boy. They never owned your daddy. And they'll never own me. I'm not a slave, boy. I'm a human being. I just happen to live in slavery.*

Moses thought back over the night. He had wanted to turn around and run when he and Rose were walking through the dark woods. He knew he was committing a crime deserving of a beating— at least in his master's eyes. His feet had kept him moving even though his heart screamed at him to run, to not do this thing that would guarantee enmity from the man Sarah had cautioned him about. Still, his feet had moved forward steadily, his heart pulling him toward a destiny that was murky darkness.

Moses wasn't sure when he had started to give up. He wasn't sure when he had started to feel like a slave. But tonight, Jasmine had changed all that for him. If that little thing of a girl could read, well then, so could he. Watching her draw her letters carefully in the dirt had fired a determination in him. It was just a small flicker, to be sure, but at least it was burning. He thought he would never feel again after seeing his family led away from the auction block. Now, he had a dream that was slowly taking shape.

The rest of the night flew by as each student worked hard on their letters or took turns reading from the paper Rose had brought to school. They didn't care that they had to share. Anything to read was considered a miracle.

Rose settled back against a tree as the last of her friends slipped into the cover of darkness. She knew they were all taking different paths through the woods and that they would all come out at a different place around the Quarters. They had become skilled at slipping undetected into their cabins. There may have been those who suspected what was going on, but so far none had revealed their secret.

Rose was tired. Each day in itself was exhausting. Her work was endless. She knew she had it easier than many of her friends who were field hands and for that she was grateful, but it did nothing to ease the exhaustion with which she ended each day. Her little midnight school was where her heart was, but in spite of the joy she felt when one of her students was suddenly reading, the energy it took was draining.

"That's a mighty big sigh."

Rose started at the sound of Moses's voice. She had almost forgotten he was there. He would come and go with her until he knew his way around in the woods at night.

Moses stared deeply into the waning flames. "You got a dream?" His strong voice was both thoughtful and serious.

Rose looked at him, wondering if she should take the risk of telling him. Would he make fun of her? She decided to be honest. "Yes, I have a dream." Closing her eyes, she allowed it to take shape in her mind. She could see it all as clearly as if she were actually living it. "I'm going to be a teacher. I'm going to live where I'm free and I'm going to have a whole school of free black children who are eager to learn and break the shackles that have held them for so long. I'm going to have all the books and writing material I can use. I'm going to raise all my children in freedom. And I'm going to travel." The dream continued to flood her mind. "I'm going to travel all over the North. I'm going to see New York. I'm going to Philadelphia and Boston. Maybe I'll go all the way out to the Oregon Territory!" Suddenly, she stopped and laughed. "You must think I'm a fool," she murmured, hoping against hope that he wouldn't.

Moses shook his head. "No. From where we be sittin' right now your dreams seem impossible. But my mama used to say that's what dreams were fer. To make the impossible seem possible. She believed dreams could come true. Somewhere's along the way I quit believin'. Maybe it was that night I saw my daddy hangin' from a tree. He died trying to make his dreams come true. I guess any I might have had died with him dat night. My mama tried to keep them goin' but it just didn't make no sense to me". He stopped and stared at Rose thoughtfully. "But you...you gots what it takes to make your dreams come true."

"What about you, Moses? What do you want? Even if you quit believing in your dreams, you must still have some."

"I wouldn't had no answer for that till t'night. But somethin' stirred in me while I be here." A deep silence fell as Moses struggled to put his feelings into words. "I'm gonna be free fo' my daddy. An' then I'm coming back. Comin' back to get my mama and sisters no matter what it takes. One day we's all gonna be free."

Rose's heart ached for him. His next question caught her by surprise.

"You gonna be running off on that Underground Railroad?"

"No." It hurt to even say the word and she caught her breath against the pain.

Moses looked at her in surprise. "But you said yourself that it was people willing to help slaves be free. How come you gonna pass up a chance like that? I figured you'd be the first one to go."

"Well, you figured wrong." Rose knew her voice was sharp. Moses's question had stirred up the turmoil that had boiled in her soul all night.

Moses said nothing else, but Rose knew he was watching her closely. She turned and looked into the deep eyes regarding her so carefully. Rose felt a slight sense of panic that those eyes could read her so well. Part of her wanted to turn and run as fast and as far as she could. Another part wanted him to see every part of her. "I can't go, Moses," she finally whispered. "I could never be free as long as my mama is a slave. I will never leave her. I will do what I can here to help my people, but I will never leave my mama."

Moses nodded. "I understand," he said simply. "I understand, Rose."

Rose took comfort in believing him. Somehow, it lessened the pain of her decision.

No more words were spoken as the two scattered the remains of the fire so as to not leave a trace of their presence, and traveled back along the path from which they had arrived. If anything, Rose was more careful. Anyone up and around in the quarters would be sure to hear the betraying crack of a limb. Breaking out onto the edge of the clearing above Sarah's cabin, Rose came to a standstill. She motioned with her hands to indicate Moses was to keep going. He touched her arm and then melted into the shadows along the edge of the woods. Rose watched only for a moment before she turned and disappeared back into the woods. It would never do to return on the road leading to the quarters. It would be too easy for someone to spot her.

Rose slipped from the woods just behind the big house. She glanced up at the window where she knew Sam was watching. Sam didn't care anything about learning to read, but he did care about taking care of her. The old butler had watched her grow up from a child. She edged carefully across the yard to the back door. Sam always made sure it was open for her. Under his careful tutelage, Rose had learned which boards to avoid so her steps would not create alarming creaks in the house. Not until he heard the soft closing of the door to her tiny room would Sam move away from the window where he watched so carefully. Rose was late. He would wonder what kept her out so long.

Eulalia Adams couldn't sleep. She didn't know how long she had tossed and turned in the darkness. Dread kept her awake. It was late and her husband wasn't home. She knew that meant trouble.

Just then, she heard the sound of horse hooves pounding on the road. *Oh God, let the children stay asleep*, she thought. She remembered the terror of her own childhood. She didn't want that for her own children, but the relentless cycle was continuing.

A muffled curse as her husband stumbled onto the porch confirmed her worst fears. He used to only get drunk on Saturday nights. Now, he would sometimes stay gone all day Sunday on drinking binges and return home late in the night.

Eulalia tried to control her trembling as she waited. Maybe he would just fall into a drunken stupor and pass out quietly on the bed. Oh, she knew there would be hell to pay for everyone who came in contact with him the next day, but perhaps she and the children could be spared this time.

"Woman!" Ike's slurred roar erupted from the main room of the clapboard house.

Abandoning all hope of a reprieve, Eulalia jumped up and hurried into the room, hoping to keep the children from being awakened.

"Why ain't my dinner done, woman?" Anger twisted Ike's face and caused his narrow gray eyes to become mere slits.

"Ike!" Eulalia exclaimed. "It must be after three in the morning. Dinner was put away a long time ago."

"Yeah?" he growled. "Well get it out again. How's a man to survive if his own woman don't get him food?"

Eulalia bit back the angry words that rose to her lips and turned toward the kitchen table.

"Those mingling Yankees are at it again."

Eulalia busied herself cutting fresh slabs of cornbread and pouring a large glass of milk. She was used to her husband's tirades.

Ike's bitter voice continued. "That bunch of niggers I brought to Cromwell yesterday? There was a big one in the batch. Moses is his name. He's going to be trouble. I know it. My brother told me to keep an eye on him. That nigger's daddy was a bad one. Killed a man up in those parts when they were trying to hang him. I heard that old nigger had the very devil himself in him. Said there was no other way he could have killed that man without there being a devil." He paused. "Woman," he roared. "Listen to me when I'm talking to you."

Eulalia choked back a bitter retort and turned to him. At least she had the cornbread cut. If she was lucky he would fall asleep before he wanted more. She moved across the kitchen briskly and placed the plate in front of him.

Ike reached up and grabbed her wrist in a cruel hold. Eulalia gasped but didn't utter a word or make a move. She knew it would only fuel his anger.

"You hear what I said about that nigger?"

"Yes, Ike." Eulalia had seen his anger and bitterness grow stronger and deeper each day. Ever since he had lost their farm and slaves, and gone to work for Cromwell. The bitterness ate at him like a blight. She was afraid of the hate growing in him. He had never been what one would call loving, but he had treated her and the children well before. Now they were nothing more than additional targets for his anger.

"That nigger came here to get me! That Moses fellow is after me."

Eulalia knew better than to tell him that was ridiculous. She knew those slaves had no choice about where they were sold when they stepped onto the auction block. She also knew there was no convincing Ike of that when he was drunk.

"He's a big one, he is, but I got me something bigger." Slurring his words, Ike suddenly reached down and whipped out the pistol he kept concealed in his waistband.

Eulalia gasped and shrank back in fear. Lantern light gleamed off the shiny metal and added an almost demonic glimmer to her husband's glowing eyes. "Ike! Put that thing away."

Ike laughed roughly and pulled her toward him. "You think I'm going to let that nigger get me?" Pressing the gun barrel into her temple, he continued his low, mean laugh. "I'll just be waiting till that nigger steps out of line. He'll get what's coming to him. I'll put a bullet right through his head. Cromwell will just have to deal with it."

Eulalia froze in fear. She knew if she moved that his unsteady hand might pull the trigger. *Oh, God...*Motionless, she held her breath as she prayed. And waited. Visions of five-year-old Matthew and eight-year-old Betty Ann asleep in their snug beds rose up both to haunt her and give her the strength to remain silent.

After what seemed an eternity, Ike sighed and lowered the gun. Rubbing his face as if suddenly confused, he released her wrist. Quickly, Eulalia stepped out of his reach. Watching him carefully, she knew the long binge of alcohol was taking its toll. Ike stared sightlessly at the food in front of him. His facial muscles seemed to droop along with the rest of his body. Eulalia watched as sleep overcame him. She made no effort to move his drunken body from its position at the table. Let him sleep it off there. She would make sure the children stayed in their rooms longer in the morning. Or maybe she would spirit them out the back door to play. She could bring them breakfast outside. They knew. They wouldn't even ask questions. They had learned a long time ago that the answers didn't make sense.

TEN

Carrie rose quietly just as the morning was casting its first rosy hues onto the horizon. She was careful not to make a smidgen of noise as she dressed and pulled her hair back into a loose braid. No one would see her. She would make sure she was back before the rest of the house began to stir. She had always loved to rise early. This morning especially, she needed the quiet solitude found when the rest of the world was still asleep.

She eased the door to the room open and looked back to see if any of her friends were stirring. Satisfied they were still deep in slumber, she moved down the hallway, descended the stairway quietly, and carefully closed the big door behind her. She had escaped detection and now turned to skip lightly down the stairs of the wide porch.

"Oh!" A delighted gasp escaped her lips. Motionless, she watched as the early morning sun, still lurking below the horizon, teased the wispy clouds into a mural of pink and orange flames that cast their light onto a purple canvas. Early morning mist from the river rolled through the trees and shrubs, beckoning her to come explore the mysteries of the world. Carrie smiled, flung her arms out to embrace the morning and then ran down the stairs and across the wide expanse of lawn. As she approached the edge of the lawn, she stopped and glanced back once more to make sure no one was watching.

What was that? Had she seen a drape fall? She stared hard at the house and then laughed at her imagination as she turned and headed down the wooded trail leading to the river.

The day promised to be a warm one. Still, Carrie was grateful for the warmth her cloak offered as she hugged it close to her body. It would take the sun a while to burn off the mist and warm the early spring air. For a moment, she considered going to the stables and claiming Granite for a ride but decided it would take too long. She needed time alone before she had to be back for breakfast. Fragrant odors of dirt and decaying leaves assailed her nostrils as she moved gracefully down the trail beneath the canopy of new spring foliage. Wildflowers raised their heads to catch the first rays of sun. She rounded a curve and surprised a deer just moving from the woods to cross the trail. Startled, they both stared at each other. Satisfied Carrie meant no harm, the tiny doe turned and stepped carefully back into the trees without issuing a snort of alarm. Enchanted, Carrie walked slower. She didn't want to miss a single treasure the woods had to offer. Already she felt her heart responding to the magic of the early morning.

When the trail emptied out onto a clearing along the river, she dropped down on a lichen-covered log and gazed out into the shrouded mist. Fingers of moist air surrounded her, causing tendrils of her curly hair to escape the confines of its braid. She tilted her head back and watched the last flaming clouds flicker and die as the sun slowly turned the purple dawn into a deep blue and the clouds transformed into puffy white cotton balls. Just as she felt that her heart would explode with anticipation, Carrie caught the first edge of the golden sun sneak its way onto the canvas of the morning. Mist swirled around her as it sought to escape the warming rays of the giant orb. Carrie laughed quietly knowing she would never tire of the miracle of God's world.

She leaned back on the log, listening as the tiny waves of the James River lapped against the shoreline, interrupted only by the occasional splash of a fish jumping in search of its breakfast. Gradually the sounds faded, replaced by the demands and questions of her heart. The events of the last two days rose in her mind to crowd out the reality of the world around her.

She allowed herself to be drawn in, closing her eyes to block out any distractions. It was why she had come. Why she had gotten up so early to escape the house and Louisa's acid tongue. Only when she was outside and alone could she really hear her heart.

Staring into the placid river, Carrie relived the day before— the tournament and the thrill of Granite and Robert winning, the fear Robert would choose her as the queen and then the thrill he actually had. Carrie frowned as she examined this feeling. Never before had she been so intrigued by a man. Vividly, she recalled the pleasure of dancing with him, the ease with which they moved together, the feel of his hand on hers, the swirl of the music sending her to heights she had never experienced. Her frown deepened. The feelings bothered her, but she didn't know why. They just did.

"You look much too serious for such a beautiful morning."

Carrie gasped and started at the sound of the voice behind her. She spun around but then lost her balance and began to fall off the log. As she grabbed at the slippery bark, she managed to regain her balance but knew she looked foolish. "Oh, my..." she started to say, but then lost her voice when she identified who had startled her. She was dimly aware that her blank stare made her look even more foolish.

Robert was immediately at her side, reaching out to steady her. "I'm sorry. I didn't mean to startle you."

Carrie could tell by the look in his eyes that he wasn't sorry at all. Laughter was pulling at them, and the edges of his mouth were twitching. Speechless, she stared at him for a moment. Then she laughed merrily.

Robert joined in her laughter and sank down on the log next to her. "What a surprise to find you here," he finally said.

Carrie heard something in his voice and looked at him closely. She didn't say anything—just looked.

Robert squirmed under her steady gaze. "Okay, it's not a surprise to find you here," he finally confessed after a few uncomfortable moments. "I saw you leave the house this morning and disappear down the trail to the river."

Carrie continued to look at him steadily. She had no idea what to say to this revelation.

Robert continued. "We've had so little time to talk since we met. And I have to leave today..." His voice drifted off. He shrugged and then smiled. "I simply wanted to spend more time with you, Miss Cromwell. I wanted to get to know you better. I'm afraid you may find me foolish. I hope you don't mind."

Carrie's eyes widened and she found her voice. "I don't mind at all," she said clearly, smiling warmly. "I'm glad you came." Robert's obvious discomfort had set her at ease. She would be herself. No more and no less. She was glad to see him. She saw no reason she shouldn't say so. There would be people in the Blackwell household that would be appalled at their lack of decorum in meeting at the river like this, but it would be easy to claim it an accident if they were discovered. The chance of that was slim. She almost laughed at Robert's visible relief that she wasn't angry or put out. She was glad he was a little unsure of himself. It made it easier for her as she tread these unknown waters.

Robert smiled in return. "Good. Because I still have yet to tell you how I actually won the tournament yesterday."

Carrie waited for him to continue. She knew Louisa would have immediately begun to pester him to tell, using her simpering ways and batting eyelashes to manipulate him. Carrie couldn't be bothered. She hated games and didn't want to play them with Robert.

Quickly, though without leaving out any details, Robert told the story of how Granite's slight swerve after he had been spooked had netted him the winning ring. "So you see," he concluded, "it wasn't I who won that tournament. It was actually Granite. I wasn't even aware I had the ring until everyone started cheering."

"He's the best horse there is," Carrie responded fervently. "Although," she added honestly, "I'm sure he had no idea what he was doing. I'm just glad he did it." She decided not to tell him she had guessed the truth already.

Robert nodded and continued. "Granite and I talked about it after the victory and knew that no one but you could be crowned the Queen of Love and Beauty."

Carrie looked at the handsome man seated next to her with the proud-little-boy look on his face and laughed loudly again. She was suddenly completely at ease. Robert was going to be a good friend. He was fun and surprisingly easy to talk to. She wasn't going to spend any more time trying to analyze her feelings toward him. She was just going to enjoy this new friend. She thought of what her other friends would say about how a proper plantation owner's daughter should conduct herself in the company of a possible suitor. Carelessly, she shrugged those thoughts away. She hadn't worried before what people thought about her unpredictable behavior. Why start now?

She laughed again, suddenly very glad Robert had found her. "I quite enjoyed being crowned the queen last night. Thank you."

Robert acknowledged her words with a nod and then turned to her with a serious expression. "So, Miss Carrie Cromwell. I still know so very little about you. Please remedy that."

"I don't know that there is much to know, Mr. Borden. You already know I'm a fanatic about my horse and that I love to dance." Then she smiled. "You may not care to know that in spite of the privileges of my position in society," Carrie drew the words out for emphasis, "I have absolutely no desire to spend the rest of my days as a plantation mistress. I can think of nothing more positively boring." She had mentioned it the night before, but suddenly it was important he know how she truly felt.

"Well then," Robert said as if he weren't surprised at all by her shocking revelation, "what is it that you want to do with yourself?" He smiled as he added, "I know it's still not really my business, but I would love to know."

"I—" Carrie fell abruptly silent and looked out over the water. What was she thinking? No one but Granite knew the true desire of her heart. She hadn't been willing to talk about it the night before. Why would she suddenly want to tell this almost complete stranger?

Robert waited quietly. Carrie was not a girl to be prodded or manipulated. If she confided in him, she wanted to do it out of her own heart and in her own time. She suddenly knew he would not push her, and her liking for Robert intensified. She realized now why she had almost told him. She wanted him to know. For some reason it was important that he know who she truly was. Not stopping to analyze her feelings, she raised her eyes to find his dark ones watching her steadily. "I want to be a doctor," she said firmly.

Robert looked into her suddenly flushed face and determined eyes. "What are you doing about it?"

Carrie's eyes widened in surprise. "You're not going to tell me I'm crazy?"

"Should I?"

Carrie groped for words. "Most people think I should just be content to be a wealthy plantation owner's daughter."

"I don't."

"But, why?"

Robert shrugged. "No one has the right to dictate another person's dreams."

Carrie looked at him with open curiosity. "Where did you learn to think like that? Was it going to school in the North?"

Robert smiled. "I'll answer that question, but only if you answer it for yourself as well."

"Fair enough."

"I suppose going to school in the North has made me change some of my ways of looking at things. The University of Pennsylvania is a fine school. They also have a highly respected medical school."

"I know," Carrie said quietly.

Robert looked at her and continued. "Education for women is much more accepted in the North. Or, maybe I should say, much more encouraged. I knew several women in the North who were excellent students." He paused and looked at Carrie questioningly. "I assume you have had tutors?"

"All my life."

"Good ones?"

Carrie wasn't offended by his probing questions. "The best. Mama would have been content for me to just learn how to read and write and do some figures. My father knew how much I loved learning, so he kept the tutors coming. When one was no longer a challenge to me, he would bring another one."

"A very unusual approach."

Carrie nodded. "Sometimes I wonder if Father regrets it. I'm not sure he likes being caught between his rebellious daughter and his traditional wife," she said ruefully. "It must be very difficult for him."

Robert laughed. "I imagine it might be."

Carrie leaned forward with an earnest look on her face. "Tell me about the University of Pennsylvania. About the medical school. Do they accept women there?"

Robert shook his head. "I have no idea." He looked at her thoughtfully. "You realize how difficult what you're proposing would be? There are very few women in medicine."

"Yes." Carrie's voice was steady, but then she hesitated. "I actually have no idea how to go about trying to achieve it. It's a dream. Perhaps a hopeless one."

"You have yet to tell me where this dream came from."

Carrie smiled. "It's the only thing about plantation life I have any interest in. I've been helping Mama in the quarters ever since I was very little. Finding someone very sick and then discovering a way to make them feel better—there is nothing more exciting than that." She paused. "But our methods are so simple. My father receives two medical journals. I read them from cover to cover every month. The things they talk about! The advances made in surgery! The new discoveries being made!" Her words flew from her mouth now as she grew more excited. "I want to be a part of all that. I want to help people." She suddenly stopped. "I just don't know how to go about doing it," she admitted softly.

"Why don't you go visit the University of Pennsylvania Medical College? Surely they would be able to give you information. The very least you could do is write them."

Carrie laughed. The idea of going to Pennsylvania was very appealing, but she had no idea how she would talk her parents into it. What reason could she give that would not throw her mother into hysteria over her unconventional daughter?

Robert's voice grew serious. "No one but you can make your dreams come true, Carrie. If you want them badly enough, you'll find a way to make them come true. But you have to want them badly enough."

Carrie's laughter died as she absorbed his words. "You're right," she said slowly. "Until today, they were little more than a fantasy in my head. But saying the words—actually telling someone—has made my fantasy seem more real. It's been something I've wanted all my life, but I suppose I never truly thought it could happen." She stopped, lost in thought. Suddenly she looked up with a brilliant smile. "Thank you, Mr. Borden. You listened to me. You didn't laugh. I'll never forget that."

Robert just nodded. "Dreams are not to be laughed at."

Carrie leaned forward. "Enough about me. What about you? What are *your* dreams?"

Robert settled back onto the log and swung his gaze to the river. "I love the South. The North is exciting and different. The cities are intoxicating. But nothing draws me like my home. The beauty of the fields. Watching things come to life under warm sunshine. But it's the river...The river pulls me. I seem to find myself in it." He turned to look at Carrie. "I wasn't surprised when you took the trail here this morning. Somehow I knew you were that way, too."

Carrie looked at him with full understanding.

Robert smiled and continued. "I want to expand Oak Meadows, my plantation. My brother wants to leave, I think. Abe wants to live in one of the bigger cities—probably Richmond— and build a business there. My mother and I want to stay. I want to see the plantation grow. I want to make all the improvements that have had to wait for so many years. I want to see the plantation thrive again the way it did when my daddy was alive. Now that I'm done with school I can make it happen."

"What happened to your father?" Carrie asked.

"He died."

Carrie was taken aback by the sudden flash of fury that tightened his face. She would ask no more. It was apparent he didn't want to talk about it. "I'm sorry."

Robert lapsed into silence, staring out over the water. Long minutes passed. Carrie wasn't uncomfortable with the silence. She didn't believe there always had to be words. Quietly she waited, until most of the tension drained from his face.

"What did you think of our elderly neighbor last night?" she finally asked.

"Ruffin?"

Carrie nodded.

"He hardly came across as being elderly," Robert said, smiling.

"He's sixty-seven."

Robert looked at Carrie in amazement. "I hope I have that much energy when I'm that old. He obviously felt strongly about the things he said."

"Our Mr. Ruffin can *only* feel strongly."

"A rather admirable quality, actually. One you seem to share with him."

Carrie laughed. "I guess you're right." She grew serious again. "The things he says scare me. He would push the whole South into secession if he could. I'm sure he intends to die trying..." Her troubled voice trailed off.

Robert leaned forward to look in her eyes. "Seeing the Union remain is the most important thing to me. I agree with your father that staying together is our greatest strength. I think ways can be found to deal with everything the country is struggling with." He paused. "But I agree with Ruffin on one thing. If there is war—if the North comes down here to force their beliefs on us—I won't stand idly by. It will be my land that is being threatened. My home. My way of life. If they come, I will fight."

Carrie's heart grew heavy as she imagined Robert going to war.

Robert's voice was strong and confident as he continued. "I pray it doesn't come, but if it does the South will be victorious. It will be a short struggle. The North has not a chance against us. We will fight and then we will build our country the way it needs to be built —on each man's right to decide his own destiny."

Carrie said nothing but her mind raced with one thought. *Why then has the South taken away a whole race's right to decide their own destiny? What about the black man?* Her thoughts remained just that— thoughts. She knew she felt them strongly, but they were still too new to understand, or deal with, or even know if she agreed with.

Carrie shook her head and forced herself to smile. "This is black talk for such a beautiful morning."

"You're right." Robert, too, shook his head slightly as if to rid himself of his intense thoughts. He turned to look deep into her emerald eyes. "I'd like to see you again, Miss Cromwell."

Protocol demanded she be coy. Carrie looked directly into his eyes. "I would like that, Mr. Borden."

Robert smiled broadly. "I'll be coming through here on my way back from Charleston. May I stop by? I'd like to see you on Granite. How about a tour of your plantation when I'm next here?"

"I would love that. And I would much rather you call me Carrie. If you don't mind," she added.

Robert shook his head "I didn't want to make assumptions, Carrie."

"You're my friend."

"Thank you. And please call me Robert." He looked like he wanted to say more, but turned to gaze at the river.

Carrie's own thoughts were spinning. She liked Robert more than any man she had ever met. She knew her mother was hoping she would find a wealthy plantation owner to marry and settle down with. Robert Borden would be the perfect answer. Yet, everything within her was rebelling. Not yet. There was still too much she wanted to do. She didn't want to get married.

Robert himself had encouraged her to follow her dreams. She didn't know how, but she was going to find out. She was going to do more with her life. Somehow. In the meantime, there was no reason she couldn't enjoy a friendship with Robert as she explored the new feelings springing up within her.

Slowly, they walked back up the trail, both loath to end their time together. "When do you leave for Charleston?" Carrie asked.

"Today. My driver is taking me straight to the train station." He paused. "I find myself even more eager to attend the Democratic Convention than before. After hearing Ruffin talk last night, I have a feeling it is going to be quite a show."

"I want to hear all about it when you return."

"I'm sure you do," Robert responded with a smile.

"You find it funny?"

"Not at all. I find it refreshing, for I believe you actually mean it."

Carrie stopped and stared at him. "Why wouldn't I mean it?"

"Carrie, you have no idea how different you are."

Carrie grinned ruefully. "You are wrong, kind sir. I know exactly how different I am. My mother tells me constantly that she wishes I could be more like her and the other girls my age who are becoming exactly what they were destined to be."

Robert shrugged. "How boring."

Carrie smiled at him brightly. "How right you are!"

Robert laughed loudly. "I like you just the way you are. Please don't change to fit what everyone wants. I would miss your refreshing honesty."

Carrie grimaced. "I shouldn't worry if I were you. I tried to change. I can't. I guess the world is stuck with me." Then she smiled and increased her pace up the trail. "In fact, the whole world is going to be awake soon. I want to be back before anyone knows I'm gone."

Robert suddenly grinned as they rounded the final curve. "You're too late. I think the world is already awake. Seems to be a lot of activity going on around here."

Carrie looked up and gasped. Gone were her illusions of slipping back into the house unnoticed. For the first time, she thought of her casual appearance. Her hand flew to her head and she gasped as she felt the riot of hair that had escaped her careless braid. Her face turned a crimson red.

"I can't go in like this!"

Robert laughed again, louder. Carrie noticed heads swivel toward them. "You're still the most beautiful woman here. Now go. And hold your head high."

Carrie gave him one despairing look. Then she turned and forced herself to walk slowly across the lawn. She bestowed a grave smile on the two carriages full of families leaving early to start the long drive home. She knew she would hear about this from her mother. Forcing herself to maintain a stately walk, she continued up the graveled path to the porch. Just as she reached the first step, she looked up to see Louisa glaring at her from the balcony off her room.

Carrie barely contained her moan of dismay. Louisa stared down at her with a look that could kill and then lifted her eyes. Carrie followed her gaze. She could have cried when she saw Robert still standing where she had left him. As she turned, he smiled broadly and lifted his hat in farewell. Then he turned back into the woods. She knew he was giving her time to go in. Steeling herself not to look up, Carrie lifted her skirts and slowly climbed the stairs. She smiled as the butler let her in, trying to control his look of surprise.

She held her head high.

ELEVEN

Carrie breathed a deep sigh of relief when the Cromwell carriage rolled away from Blackwell Plantation. It was just ten o'clock in the morning, but she felt like this day had already lasted forever. Thank heavens for the wonderful memory of spending time with Robert down by the river. She had surely been paying for it ever since.

Louisa had said not a word when Carrie had returned, flushed and disheveled, to her room. Her pointed silence and withering looks had needed no words to impart their message. Sally and Natalie's looks had been kinder, but they hadn't spoken either. They seemed to be too shocked. Carrie had wanted to laugh and explain what an innocent rendezvous it really was, but then she had grown angry, and her anger made her match their silence with her own. Let them think what they wanted. If they were all so eager to jump to such erroneous conclusions, then let them. She said not a word as she changed into a more suitable dress. She didn't even ask for help with her hair. Instead, she deftly braided and secured it into a bun every bit as good as one Rose could have done. *Well! At least I've proven I can do this.*

The silent treatment continued as she descended downstairs for breakfast. Good heavens! Had the whole world been watching when she emerged from the woods with Robert Borden? Did the whole world jump to horrible conclusions when they saw something they didn't understand? What was so terrible? All they had done was sit by the river and talk. Nothing improper had happened. What big difference did it make anyway if they weren't properly chaperoned? Carrie grew angry as her indignation grew.

She had seen Robert's carriage leave before she finished preparing for breakfast. Part of her was angry she had to face all this scathing disapproval alone. Another part was very glad he had escaped the ridiculous humiliation they had done nothing to deserve. Only her father seemed still in possession of some common sense. He had arrived downstairs and given her the same loving smile as always. He had even walked over to lay a supportive arm around her shoulder. Her mother's suffering silence said all it needed to.

Wasn't anyone going to even ask what had happened? Carrie was learning firsthand how many people care so little for the truth when the results of their imagination feed their thirst for scandal. Her desire to lash out in fury was intermingled with a need to laugh hysterically. The whole situation was so ridiculous. How had this happened?   Just then, she spied Louisa in the far corner, her head bent low in serious conversation with Mrs. Waterton, a neighbor who lived a few miles north. Carrie barely knew her, though she well knew her reputation for being a ruthless gossip. Mrs. Waterton looked up with a grim smile and locked her eyes on Carrie. The older lady observed her coolly for a few moments before she looked away haughtily. So that was it! This was Louisa's revenge for not being chosen Queen—for being thwarted in her attempt to add Robert to her list of suitors. Carrie had seen enough. She rose slowly from the table, raised her head high, and sailed from the room. Let these people say and think what they wanted. She, Carrie Cromwell, had done nothing to be ashamed of. Out of deference to her mother, she was not going to make a scene. But she most certainly was not going to continue to sit there like a lamb being led to slaughter.

Once upstairs, she dashed into Louisa's room, ripped off her traveling dress, and put back on the dress she had worn that morning. Back downstairs, she stopped only long enough on her way to whisper something to her father, and then escaped from the curious stares and whispers. She felt herself coming back under control as she took deep breaths of the fresh, morning air. By the time she got to the stables she could once again see the humor in the situation. Let them talk! In another few days someone else would do something not fitting in with proper plantation protocol and remove the attention from her. Gossip always had to have fresh meat on which to feed. Wagging tongues quickly tired of old news. This would pass.

Carrie was once more enjoying the day when she led Granite, fully tacked, from the barn. She was proud of the fact that she had declined all help from Charles. He had been mortified, sure he would be punished for letting her do it. "Oh, pooh, Charles," she had scoffed. "I made Miles teach me how to do it years ago. I'm just not in the mood to play the southern lady today. I need to do this." He had stepped aside with what looked like a glimmer of appreciation in his eyes and just watched quietly.

Thomas Cromwell was standing on the front porch of the plantation mansion when Carrie trotted smoothly up the driveway. He tried to suppress a smile but said nothing until she had pulled Granite to a halt. They both completely ignored the stares of the others on the porch.

"Good morning, Father."

"Good morning, daughter." He made no attempt to hide the laughter in his eyes.

Carrie smiled and leaned forward slightly. "I'll explain later."

Thomas agreed easily. "That's good enough for me."

Carrie's heart surged with love for her father. He knew that whatever had happened this morning must be quite innocent. She knew he trusted her. "I'm not riding home in the carriage," she said.

"I assumed as much."

"I don't think it would be a very good idea. Mother seems to be feeding at the gossip table."

Thomas frowned slightly. "She loves you, Carrie."

"Yes, and I love her. But I have no intention of bearing her silent disapproval all the way home." She knew her father hated being put between the two women he loved so much.

"You could always explain it to her."

Carrie tossed her head. "I will. But not now. She could have asked me this morning *before* she decided her wayward daughter had done something else scandalous." Then she softened. "I just need to be on Granite today, Father. I truly don't want to upset Mother."

Thomas nodded and gave her a gentle smile. "As long as you talk to her later. Your mother will be okay. I'll talk to her." He reached into his pocket for his watch and examined it. "Charles will be here in a few minutes. I plan on our leaving in twenty minutes. You need to go in and say goodbye to the Blackwells." He smiled at her mutinous look. "It won't make you feel any better to lower yourself to their standards. It takes great courage to continue being a lady in the face of gossip and misunderstanding. Go in there and show them you're a better person than they are."

Carrie stared into his eyes for a long moment, drawing on the strength she saw there. Her lips tightened for a moment before she dismounted lightly. She handed the reins to a nearby servant, ran lightly up the stairs, and gave her father a hug. "Thanks. I'll make you proud of me."

Thomas put his hand under her chin and tilted her eyes to meet his own. "I'm always proud of you, Carrie." Then he gave her a gentle shove. "Go make *yourself* proud."

Carrie forced a smile to her lips as she went in and told her host and his wife goodbye. "It's been quite lovely. Thank you so much for a wonderful time. I do hope I see you again soon." Alfred and Lucy Blackwell were both gracious. Carrie felt a flash of triumph when she saw the look of begrudging admiration in Lucy Blackwell's eyes. Her father had been right. The only way to meet gossip was head on. "Where is Louisa? I'd like to tell her goodbye."

Louisa's father shook his head slightly. "She left the house a few minutes ago. I have no idea where she went."

Lucy Blackwell turned to her husband and protested, "Why, I never saw her leave the house. I've been standing right here."

Her husband fixed his wife with a stern look. "I saw her leave, I tell you." She merely stared at him. He looked back at Carrie with a smile. "I'll tell her you asked after her. I would hate for you to be late leaving. I think I hear your mother coming downstairs."

Carrie smiled back at him. She knew what he was doing. Louisa's poison tongue was no secret to her father. "Thank you, Mr. Blackwell. Please do tell her I had a lovely time." She sailed out of the house and down the stairs to where Granite was waiting. Her father had been right. Facing up to it had made her feel much better. She could do nothing to stop the gossiping tongues of her neighbors, but she could indeed show herself she was above them. Her heart was light as she led Granite to the mounting block and sprung easily into the saddle.

On the way home, from her position on top of Granite moving at a steady trot slightly in front of the carriage, she could see her father's bent head as he talked to his wife. Carrie knew he was trying to ease the way for her. Poor Father! Surely he must grow tired of the tension between his wife and daughter.

The sun was barely above the horizon when Eulalia, dozing in the next room, heard Ike moving around. She had hoped he would sleep later, at least long enough to get the kids out of the house. She knew a pounding headache would add to his meanness this morning. She imagined him cradling his head in his hands as he tried to remember how he had gotten home last night. She heard him groan as he staggered to his feet. She jumped up from her bed and eased into the kitchen. Her presence would make her, not the children, the target for Ike's anger.

He turned to her, growling. "Where you been, woman? Where is my breakfast?"

"Your breakfast will be ready in a few minutes, Ike." She dashed to the fireplace and stirred the coals until she had a small blaze going. She longed to have a wood cookstove like some of her other friends, but as long as

Ike spent most of his wages on alcohol it would remain a dream. She poured water from a pitcher into the black kettle and hung it over the flames. Coffee would help her husband. She turned from the fire, cut a few slabs of bacon, and then sliced several thick pieces of bread. Eating would give him another channel for his anger. She wasn't afraid now. He woke up from his binges mad but not dangerous. The scars from his verbal tirades could not be seen by her children.

Ike cursed under his breath and headed into the bedroom. She heard water splashing as he performed his usual inadequate wash-up. Water was still dripping from his hair as he lurched out of the bedroom a few minutes later, still clad in the same clothes he had worn all weekend.

Cromwell would not be pleased. He set high standards for everyone, including his overseer. Keeping her voice light, she said, "I got you some clean clothes on the line. I'll bring them right in." Then she held her breath.

Ike's lips tightened in fury but the cold water splashed on his face had cleared his brain a little more. He looked down at his disheveled clothing. "Well, hurry up, woman. You'd think God could have given me a wife who cared a little more about her man. I work hard six days a week for you. The least you could do is have clothes ready when I need them."

Eulalia pressed her lips closed. She had deliberately not told him there was a clean set hanging on the wardrobe. He would only have thought she was belittling him for not seeing them. She poured a cup of hot coffee for him and hurried outside to get the clothes.

Ike gobbled down his food, slurped his coffee in silence, changed his clothes, and grunted before moving slowly out the door. Minutes later she heard him riding down the road. She had no use for niggers any more than her husband did, but she felt a small twinge of sympathy. Ike had had a mean look in his eyes when he rode off. She knew that anger would erupt on someone today. She only hoped it was gone before he got home.

"Hello, Sam," Carrie called gaily as she entered the house. Eager to see Rose, Carrie had released Granite to Miles and run into the house. The carriage was just now entering the drive. Impatient to get home, she had urged Granite into a gallop as soon as they entered the long road leading to Cromwell Plantation. She had laughed loudly as she imagined her mother shaking her head at another exhibition of her daughter's wild impulsiveness.

"Welcome home, Miss Carrie."

Carrie acknowledged his greeting with a wave of her hand and ran up the stairs. Just as she hoped, Rose was waiting in the room. "Rose! I missed you."

Rose smiled widely. "I missed you, too, Miss Carrie."

"Oh, Rose! It was glorious! Mr. Borden and Granite won the tournament." Excitedly, she spilled out the details. Rose moved forward to help her remove her dress. Carrie waved her away. "That can wait. I could hardly wait to get home and tell you about my time." Her face radiated as she told Rose of the ball. How Robert had chosen her for the queen. How angry Louisa had been. How much fun she'd had dancing. She told Rose everything, just like she always had.

Rose sat quietly.

Carrie finally grew silent. She leaned forward and looked closely into her friend's face. "You're so quiet, Rose. Is something wrong?"

Rose just shook her head and smiled slightly. "No, Miss Carrie. I'm fine. I was just listening to your story. It sounds like you had a wonderful time. I'm glad."

Carrie continued to gaze into the other girl's eyes. They had been friends for too long. She could read Rose's face too well. There was something...

Rose changed the subject. "Sadie is sick again. She's down with a high fever."

Carrie forgot everything when she heard that news. "Since when?" she asked sharply.

"She came in from the fields after a few hours this morning. Mama sent one of the children up from the quarters to tell me."

"I told her to stay out of the fields for a few days until she was well," Carrie said sternly, silently berating herself for not talking to Sadie when she saw her in the fields on Friday. Robert Borden and all the excitement had driven it from her mind.

Rose just shrugged.

Carrie looked down at her dress. "I don't need to change. This dress will do fine to wear down to the quarters. I'll check on Sadie and come back for Mama if I need her. "

"Would you like me to come with you?"

Carrie thought for a moment. "Yes, I would. You can unpack my trunk later. It's not going anywhere."

Carrie was quiet as she walked quickly down the trail to the quarters. Her mind worked furiously. Why had Sadie gone back to the fields? Why was her fever so high again? Carrie liked Sadie, with her quick, gentle smile and the way her eyes lit up when she was happy. She suddenly realized she hadn't seen that happen much lately. What was going on? Cromwell slaves had always seemed happy. As she walked, she saw now what she had been too blind to see before. The whole spirit in the quarters had changed. A heaviness seemed to hang over everything. Is that what was bothering Rose? But they were best friends. Why wouldn't Rose tell her? Carrie frowned and increased her speed. She intended to find out what was going on. The slaves trusted her. Surely Sadie would confide in her.

Carrie came to a stop in front of the cabin Sadie shared with several other women. Sadie's husband, Willie, had died from a strange disease a few years before. Carrie's mother had fought to save him, but nothing she did worked. Sadie had lived here ever since. Carrie had been coming down to these cabins almost every day for as long as she could remember. Why now did they seem dark and oppressive? She had never thought anything of them before. Why now did she shudder at the thought of living under these conditions herself? Her father's argument rose in her mind. *It is our destiny to be masters over the slaves. It is their destiny to be slaves. It is our responsibility to take care of them because they can't take care of themselves.* Carrie frowned. The argument sounded weak to her. She shook her head and pushed open the cabin door. She would have to think about it later.

The sight of Sadie shivering on the hard bed sent Carrie rushing to her side. "Sadie!"

"I be fine, Miss Carrie," Sadie whispered. "I just have me a little fever. It be gone in a little bit."

Carrie laid her hand on the older woman's head. "You're burning up, Sadie. How long has it been like this?"

Sadie shrugged her thin shoulders. "Just this morning, Miss Carrie. It ain't nothing."

Carrie pressed her lips together tightly. "I'll be the judge of that." She turned to Rose. "Go get a bucket of water from the well," she ordered. "I also need a pile of rags. We've got to get this fever down." As Rose turned to leave, Carrie called an additional order over her shoulder. "And bring Mama's bag from the house. I may need something in it."

"Do you want me to have your mama come down here?" Rose asked.

Carrie thought for a moment and then shook her head. "I think I can handle this." The truth was that she wanted to get to the bottom of what was really going on. She knew Sadie wouldn't talk if her mother were there.

Carrie turned back to Sadie as Rose disappeared. "This fever has to be coming from somewhere."

Sadie shrugged and turned her eyes away. Sweat beaded on her forehead as her shivering intensified. Carrie looked around the cabin and jumped up to grab several additional thin blankets. She looked with distaste at the barren dirt floor. How awful to be sick in conditions like these. Carefully, she tucked the blankets around the bony shoulders and watched as Sadie's shivering gradually subsided to an occasional shudder.

Carrie looked up as Rose entered the door. "Put the bucket here and give me the rags." Quickly she dipped the cloth into the cold water, wrung it out, and laid the compresses on Sadie's hot forehead. In less than a minute, it too was hot. Carrie quickly replaced it with another. She had no idea how long she sat there changing compresses before the fever began to subside. Sadie's eyes cleared a little and she smiled gratefully.

"Thank you, Miss Carrie. I be feeling a mite better."

Carrie nodded and continued her ministrations. "We need to talk, Sadie. You need to help me figure out where this fever is coming from. It's not like a regular fever. It goes away, but comes right back."

Sadie shrugged her shoulders again and looked away.

Carrie persisted, alarmed at the fear she saw lurking in her eyes. "You've got to tell me, Sadie. I can't make you better if I don't know what's going on." She kept her voice kind but firm.

Sadie finally turned her eyes toward Rose. She seemed to question her silently.

Carrie turned to look at Rose, her alarm increasing as she saw the hesitation on Sadie's face. "I can't help if I don't know."

Rose locked eyes with Carrie for a long moment before looking back to where Sadie lay on the bed. She nodded slowly. "Tell her, Sadie."

Sadie lay quietly for several moments. Then she pulled back the covers and struggled to sit up.

"You shouldn't be moving, Sadie." Carrie leaned forward to stop her.

"You want to know where the fever be coming from, Miss Carrie?"

"Of course I do." Carrie was confused.

"Then I be needing to sit up," Sadie said quietly. Carrie remained where she was, watching as Sadie reached down and pulled off her shoe with a slight grimace. She raised her leg to lay her foot across her knee where Carrie could see the bottom of it.

Carrie gasped at the sight of the ugly, infected gash across the bottom of the woman's foot. "No wonder you're so sick! How in the world have you been wearing your shoes?" The foot was swollen to almost twice its normal size and Carrie could see the swelling was extending up into the ankle. "Why didn't you tell me about this before?" Sadie averted her eyes once more, but not before Carrie saw the stark fear glimmering in their depths. "Sadie! How did this happen?" she asked sharply. Silence stretched into the shadows of the cabin. "I'm not leaving until you tell me."

"Go ahead and tell her, Sadie," Rose said softly.

Carrie took deep breaths to remain calm, a sick feeling in her stomach telling her that whatever Sadie had to say was going to be bad.

Sadie kept her eyes on the floor as she began to speak slowly. "Mr. Adams... He...he ..." Sadie shuddered as she tried to force out the words.

"Mr. Adams did this to you?" Carrie asked incredulously.

Sadie suddenly found strength from somewhere. She raised her eyes to meet Carrie's. "Yes, Miss Carrie. He cut me."

"He cut your foot?" Carrie demanded wildly. "Why?" She could feel the blood pounding in her head.

"I weren't working fast enough in the fields. He wanted me to work faster. He said this would make me remember. He tell me dat if I miss a day of work in the fields he'd cut the other one." Sadie's eyes filled with tears that she blinked quickly away.

Carrie felt sick to her stomach. How had this happened? Her father had always demanded his slaves be treated well. "Are other things like this happening?" The silence filling the cabin spoke louder than words. Carrie's horror mixed with a steadily building anger. She laid her hand on Sadie's shoulder and struggled to control her voice. "Sadie, I'm sorry. I will tell my father immediately. He will make sure this never happens again." She couldn't miss the terror filling Sadie's eyes. "My father will take care of it," she insisted.

"That might not do any good, Miss Carrie."

Carrie turned to Rose in astonishment. "Why not?"

Rose shrugged. "Mr. Adams is a bad one. The hate is growing in him every day. If your father talks to him, it may make it worse."

"*Not* talking to him is surely not going to do any good." Carrie was sure her father could fix the problem. She caught the deep look of concern the two black women exchanged but knew she had to do something.

She couldn't pretend ignorance now that she had the truth. "The thing now is to get this foot fixed," she said briskly, thankful for something to do. "We need plenty of hot water. Rose, give me some of the white powder out of the bag. Mama says it draws infection out." Carrie pushed down her anger and revulsion as she turned her attention to Sadie's foot. "Start a fire so we can boil plenty of water." Conversation ceased as she worked.

When Carrie and Rose emerged from the dark cabin, Carrie headed toward the stables. "I'll be back after a while, Rose. Please tell Mama I'm going for a ride. I need some time to think."

Rose was deep in thought when she entered the house a few minutes later. She had just enough time to unpack Carrie's trunk before she would be needed to help with dinner. Her mind spun furiously as she tried to imagine the results of Carrie's talk with her father. Had she been wrong to encourage Sadie to tell Carrie the truth? Would it just result in more trouble?

"We got more comp'ny." Sam's voice broke into her troubled thoughts.

"I didn't know anyone else was expected."

Sam shrugged. "I don't do no expecting. I just do what I be told."

Rose hid her smile. She knew Sam's compliance was all an act. He helped her get away with a lot of things. A desire for freedom burned deep in his heart and he dreamed of the day he could escape and be free from the plantation. "Who is it?"

"Somebody just passing through. Had hisself a letter of introduction from some fella Marse Cromwell knows in Richmond."

Rose nodded and turned to walk up the stairs. Then she stopped and turned back, nudged by a feeling she didn't understand. "What's his name, Sam?"

"Mr. Jamison."

Rose stared at him wide-eyed, suddenly speechless.

"Why you be staring at me like that, girl?"

Rose suddenly caught herself. It would never do to make anyone suspicious— especially Sam who was so protective of her. He covered for her with the school. But this. This was a different matter. She forced herself to shrug casually. "It's nothing, Sam. I just remembered something Miss Carrie asked me to do. I can't believe I almost forgot." She couldn't miss Sam's disbelieving stare. "I've got to go, Sam. Thank you for letting me know there is company here." She turned and escaped up the stairs, knowing Sam's eyes were boring into her back.

Within the confines of Carrie's room, Rose collapsed on the dressing table chair. Mr. Jamison! Here. Today. They had just gotten the note last night. She had never expected him to show up today. She wasn't ready for him. How was she to communicate with him? Her mind raced frantically as she tried to take in the fact that the conductor from the Underground Railroad was actually at Cromwell Plantation. She took deep breaths and tried to think calmly. After sitting quietly for several minutes, she rose and swiftly unpacked Carrie's trunk. Just as she expected, she found paper and a writing pen. She sat down at the dressing table and began to write.

Moses started his work in the fields that morning. So far, it was no different from anything he had known before. In fact, working in the fertile fields was almost pleasant. The ground on the plantation he had come from had been overworked and the plants it produced were yellow and sickly. The overseer said the slaves were to blame. The lash had flown freely, but still the plants came up with little to show for their existence. It was the reason the plantation had failed and been sold. This ground was different—the soil dark and rich, with a sweet odor. The tobacco plants springing forth from the earth were green and healthy. He would have to ask someone why. He dreamed of owning his own farm someday.

"Quit your daydreaming, boy!"

Moses looked up to see who Adams was yelling at. He had not ceased in his efforts with the hoe. His powerful shoulders kept up the rhythmic swinging easily. He was surprised to see Adams looming over him on his bay mare. He said nothing, just turned back to his work. He recognized the glazed eyes of a man who had tangled with too many bottles of whiskey. Adams had been angry ever since Sadie was removed from the fields. The sun beating down had done nothing to improve his temper.

"I'm talking to you, boy!"

Moses stared at the ground, wondering what he should do. Miss Sarah had told him to be careful. But how was he supposed to avoid this trouble? One look into Ike Adams wild, red-rimmed eyes had told him he was dealing with a man just like his brother. He looked up slowly. "Yes, suh?"

Adams grinned evilly, obviously relishing his power. "Ain't you used to working where you come from, nigger?"

Moses took a deep breath. "Yes, suh." He knew the look of a man who was in need of giving a beating. Men like Adams thrived on the feeling of power their position gave them. Adams had for too long experienced the kind of hatred that blotted out all reasonable thought. It was demanding an outlet. Moses sighed. He had hoped Cromwell Plantation was going to be different.

"It sure don't look that way, boy," Adams sneered. "I think you need a lesson to teach you how Cromwell niggers work. You didn't learn it too good where you came from."

TWELVE

Carrie cantered Granite down the road through the fields. She was on her way to her place, desperate to sort through what she had discovered today. She had hoped to be able to tell her father earlier than after supper, but he had left shortly after returning home to go meet someone. The thought of telling her mother never entered her mind. Mother would simply have told her to talk to her father. Carrie was confused and angry about what Sadie had confided today. It was bad enough that Ike Adams was mistreating the slaves, but there was another thought equally as troubling. Why hadn't their people told them what was happening? Didn't they know her father didn't allow abuse on his plantation?

Suddenly, a movement in the field to her right caught her attention. She squinted her eyes and watched the group of slaves working the tobacco, Adams looming over one of the men her father had just bought. She saw Adams reach to the back of his saddle but couldn't quite believe what she saw next. He was pulling out a whip. Fury choked her as she wheeled Granite and headed in their direction

"Take your shirt off, nigger," she heard Adams growl as she drew near. So far, no one had noticed her. All eyes were glued to the drama unfolding before them.

Jupiter was standing close beside Moses. "You ain't got to do that, Moses." His voice was low.

Moses just looked at him. "Won't do no good," he replied flatly. "He's a man needs to let loose some hate." Slowly, he peeled off his shirt.

Adams eyes gleamed as sunlight glinted off Moses's sweating, muscular back. "Good, boy!" he snarled and drew his arm back.

Carrie had seen all she needed to see. "What is going on here?" she demanded in a loud, commanding voice.

Ike Adams swore, dropped the whip, and whirled his mare around. "Miss Cromwell!"

Carrie made no attempt to hide her anger. "What exactly are you doing, Mr. Adams?" Gone was her anxiety about dealing directly with the overseer. She was eighteen years old. Her daddy had taught her everything about this plantation and instilled in her a respect for their slaves. Time, and her own heart, had instilled a deep love. She stared hard at the plantation overseer.

Adams blanched, his throat working nervously. "This nigger... He was giving me trouble."

"What kind of trouble, Mr. Adams?" Her words were clipped.

Adams shifted, his eyes darting. Then he straightened, obviously trying to regain some control. His voice was condescending. "This nigger don't seem to think he should work, Miss Carrie. He's been slow and lazy all day. I was thinking he needed some help to show him how Cromwell slaves work."

Sadie's wounds were fresh in Carrie's mind, fueling her anger. "So you're going to speed him up by beating him and hurting him?" She made no attempt to hide the contempt in her voice.

Adams squirmed.

Moses watched quietly.

Adams was still searching for a way out. "This nigger be a bad one, Miss Cromwell. If you don't allow me to get him under control now, he's going to mean big trouble later on. I wasn't going to hurt him. I was just aiming to scare him. I know your daddy don't like me to use the whip, but you got to show the new ones early on." There was a whine in his voice now.

"It is not your job to make those decisions," Carrie responded coldly. "My father has given explicit orders that none of his slaves are to be abused. I believe your responsibility is simply to follow his orders." She fixed him with a steely glare. "I will be taking it up with my father later. For now, I want you not to lay a hand on one of *our* slaves." As long as she remained on the plantation, she was going to fulfill her responsibility. There would be no abuse. She turned to leave, but quickly spun Granite around to face the furious overseer again. "One other thing, Mr. Adams. I am responsible for the medical care of all Cromwell Plantation slaves. I will be doing regular exams. If I find any signs of abuse, you will be quite sorry." Having delivered her final shot, Carrie turned and trotted Granite quickly away.

Only when she was out of earshot did she allow the tears to come—tears of anger and sorrow. She turned away from the river and headed home. She would be there when her father returned.

"Carrie, I would like to introduce you to Mr. Jamison. He will be staying with us for the night."

Carrie smiled, her manner gracious, though her fists were clinched with impatience. Her father had just arrived in the company of the man he was introducing. A conversation with him would have to wait. "Hello, Mr. Jamison. It is a pleasure to have you join us." She didn't remember ever having met him before. She was also sure she had never heard her father speak of him. And she was positive they had not been expecting company that day. Not that it made any difference. Hospitality was sacrosanct in the South.

Thomas answered her unspoken question. "Mr. Jamison came to us by way of my friend Mr. James Thomas."

"The tobacco manufacturer?" Carrie asked.

"The very same," Mr. Jamison agreed. "He and I grew up together as children in Caroline County. We were both equally poor back then."

Carrie laughed at the idea of James Thomas being poor. He was now the South's leading tobacco manufacturer, with one of the finest and most pretentious mansions in Richmond. Jamison laughed with her, a hearty laugh that spoke of enjoying life. Carrie liked the man instantly. His eyes shone clearly and the lines in his face revealed a kindness of heart. "How long will you be with us, Mr. Jamison?"

"Just until tomorrow, Miss Cromwell. I'm only here to check on the quality of the new crops. I represent Mr. Thomas in several concerns in the North."

"Oh, do you travel often to the North?" Carrie asked, thinking of her earlier conversation with Robert.

"I live there."

Thomas showed surprise. "I assumed you were a Southerner, sir."

"I am, Cromwell. A Southerner through and through. I just happen to have my current address in the North. I went to college at the University of Pennsylvania. A good business opportunity kept me there. James convinced me he needed me," he said modestly.

"You might find your Northern address uncomfortable soon, if my reports are accurate." Thomas's voice was cryptic.

Jamison nodded. "You've heard of the rising tension?"

"Yes."

"There does seem to be more than I have seen before, but so far it hasn't touched me. I believe my status as a businessman must offer me some protection."

Conversation flowed as the dishes were brought out to the table. Carrie found herself losing track of the talk as her mind drifted over the occurrences of the day. She was already planning what she would say to her father when they were alone.

Rose, from her station by the kitchen door, struggled to calm her pounding heart. She must think clearly. Too much depended on this. When she was sure no one was watching her, she had been casting covert glances at Mr. Jamison. Could he possibly be the conductor for the Underground Railroad? Everything about him spoke of a wealthy businessman. Why would he be involved in helping free slaves? What if he wasn't *the* Mr. Jamison? She had received the note only yesterday. Surely he couldn't have arrived so soon. What if it was all a setup? If she contacted him, would she discover it was all a giant hoax designed to capture slaves who had it in their minds to escape? She cast through her mind for a way to be sure, the questions colliding with each other in wild discord. Reluctantly, she came to the conclusion that there was no way to be absolutely certain. Yet, she had only this night to make the critical contact. With tremendous effort, she maintained her composure. It would not do to direct any attention her way. It would only arouse suspicion later. Her face remained impassive as she picked up the tray and moved back into the dining room. She had a job to do.

"What a wonderful dinner," Jamison said enthusiastically. "Your cook is marvelous."

Abigail smiled. "Thank you. She has been with us for as long as I have been married to Thomas."

Thomas nodded. "She was born here. My father always said she was the best cook in Virginia. She must be close to fifty years old now. I don't know what we would do without her."

"Slave or free?" Jamison asked casually.

Thomas shot his guest a sharp look. "There are no free servants on Cromwell Plantation, Mr. Jamison."

Jamison nodded pleasantly, but he could not completely hide the faint look of distaste as he lit his cigar. Rose was certain the sudden cloud of smoke from his cigar had veiled his expression from the others at the table but that look had done much to ease her fear. What had she told her students the night before? *We can't let fear rob us of our dreams. The only way to live is to fight those fears and do what comes to us.*

Jamison stretched his long legs and leaned back in his chair. "There is still daylight. Would you object to my taking a walk around your plantation? I fear my hours in the carriage have left me quite stiff."

"Of course," Thomas agreed instantly. "You are welcome to go anywhere you like. "I'm sorry I can't join you. There are some things I need to go over with my daughter. I'm afraid they can't wait till morning." He ignored the questioning look Abigail threw him, turned his head away, and winked at Carrie.

Rose quickly gathered up the remaining dishes, already casting in her mind for a way to connect with the conductor.

"What's on your mind, Carrie?"

Carrie turned to her father eagerly as they sat on the porch swing. Dogwoods in full bloom demanded attention, but Carrie hardly noticed them tonight. "Thank you for knowing something was wrong."

Thomas smiled gently. "How could I not know something was bothering my girl?

Carrie took a deep breath. "Mr. Adams is hurting the slaves," she said, her voice trembling slightly now that she was with her father.

Thomas leaned forward as his eyes narrowed. "How do you know? What is happening?" he demanded in a sharp voice.

In a voice ripe with indignation, Carrie told of Sadie's fever and her discovery of the gash on her foot. Her father listened intently. Then she told of finding Adams as he was about to whip Moses.

"You saw him do it?"

"No. I stopped him."

Thomas took a deep breath, his face becoming more grave. "Maybe you should tell me the whole story." Anger twisted his normally kind features as Carrie relived her experience. Concern darkened them as well. He sat for long moments after Carrie had finished speaking. When he spoke, it was slowly. "I'm not sure you should have involved yourself."

Carrie's eyes widened in disbelief. "Not get involved? You wanted me to do nothing while one of your slaves was beaten?" She couldn't comprehend what she was hearing.

"Of course I am furious that Adams was going to abuse one of my people. He has strict orders to never lay a hand on them. If they need discipline, he is to come to me. You can be sure I will deal with Adams before this day is over." He paused. "But that is my job, Carrie. It is best to not interfere with a man when he is doing his job. It can undermine his authority."

Carrie shook her head. "I can't believe what I'm hearing," she protested. "You've always told me this is *our* plantation. How could I stand by and watch one of our people be beaten? You wanted me to just ride away as if nothing was going on?"

"It's not that simple, Carrie." Thomas looked at his daughter and sighed. "Adams is a good overseer. He has worked hard for me, but he has a hard streak in him. I don't want to see that turned against you."

"I'm not scared of that cowardly man." Carrie made no effort to hide her anger and disgust.

In spite of himself, Thomas smiled. "Sometimes I don't know where you got your spirit."

"I got it from you," Carrie retorted. "You told me someday I would be responsible for Cromwell Plantation. You've always told me I could do whatever I had a mind to."

"Where has this sudden desire to be a plantation mistress come from?"

Carrie shook her head impatiently. "That has nothing to do with it. I still have no desire to live my life like Mama, but neither can I stand by and watch one of our people be hurt." Carrie had yet to stop and analyze all of her feelings. She just knew there was a passion rising in her heart that was growing stronger daily.

Thomas watched her carefully. Finally he shook his head. "Carrie, I'm proud of you. I'm proud you had the courage to stop what you thought was wrong."

"But..." Carrie prompted

"But, what?"

"I don't know. There just sounded like there was a but at the end of that."

Thomas laughed. "I'm used to verbal sparring with my beautiful daughter. I'm *not* so used to you catching me in my own game." Then he sobered. "You need to be careful."

"Careful?" Carrie echoed.

"Mr. Adams is a man who has had a great many blows to his pride. It has put a streak of meanness in him."

"Then get rid of him."

"It's not that simple." He struggled to explain as Carrie stared at him. "Our whole way of life is under attack from every direction. I'm afraid we may lose everything we've ever known. It's hard to find good overseers, Carrie. I don't know what I would do without him," he admitted. "I'll talk to him, though. I'll make sure this doesn't happen again. If it does, just let me know."

Carrie nodded as she tried to make sense of the conversation with her father. She wasn't afraid of Ike Adams. She would do whatever she had to, but she had enough sense to not say any of this to her father.

"I'm going to go see if your mother would like to take a walk. Maybe we can catch up with our Mr. Jamison." Thomas leaned over and gave his daughter a warm kiss on her cheek. "I'll take care of it, Carrie," he promised.

Carrie nodded half-heartedly as he moved off the porch. She stared into the lengthening shadows with a heavy heart. She had never seen her father like this. The man she thought she knew would have congratulated her and ridden off to upbraid Adams for his behavior. Instead, he had as much as told her to stay out of it and had gone to take her mother for a walk. What was happening? She had sensed fear in his voice when he had talked about losing their way of life. Was it really that bad? Was her father really afraid their way of life was going to be destroyed? Daily, she had watched the tiny lines around his eyes increase. She hadn't paid too much attention, but she would from now on. In the meantime, she had her own heart to figure out. She was changing, that much she knew. It bothered her that she couldn't define the changing, or even be comfortable with it.

Jamison walked slowly through the beautiful grounds. He wished he could enjoy the peace it afforded but his mind was too full. He was relieved at the ease with which he had gained access to Cromwell Plantation. Fellow conductors had told him the first assignment was always the hardest— and the scariest. He could only hope it got easier, but no matter. He would remain a conductor for the Underground Railroad. He had told Cromwell the truth. He was a Southerner through and through. He knew there were many Southerners who hated the idea of slavery. The gap between those who owned slaves and those who never would had broadened over the years. It was actually a tiny percent of landowners who could also afford slaves. The remaining Southerners had no particular reason to be loyal to the institution. Many of them provided way stations for escaping slaves on their way north. He would be counting on some of them for this assignment. If contact was made....

Jamison had received careful instruction from the Philadelphia Abolitionist Society, but hearing it and doing it were two different things. He had traveled all the way here on the hope that a hastily transferred piece of paper had found its way into the proper hands. At best, his efforts were wasted and another attempt would be made at a later date. At worst, the paper would fall into the wrong hands and he could end up in prison. Attitudes in the South toward participants in the Underground Railroad had intensified bitterly over the last several years as more and more slaves made use of the system. Jamison shook his head. It would do no good to imagine what could happen.

One question remained foremost in his mind. Would contact be made? He had no idea how it would happen. He had fabricated his need for a walk. At least it would give him time away from prying eyes. It might give someone a chance—

Just then a movement in the bushes caught his eye. He glanced around quickly to assure himself he was alone. His position was invisible to the house, so he stopped and waited. It might just be an animal.

Rose stepped quietly from the bushes. "Mr. Jamison?"

"Yes." He smiled in relief. "You're the girl who helped serve dinner?"

Rose nodded. "Mr. Jamison, I—"

"Jamison! I say, Jamison, where are you?"

Jamison jumped and whirled around. The shout was very close and he cursed under his breath. When would he find another opportunity? He groaned and turned back to the girl. She had disappeared.

Thomas smiled as he appeared from behind some bushes with Abigail. Jamison inspected him closely and assured himself his host had not seen anything. "Cromwell. Mrs. Cromwell. How are you? " He forced himself to breath normally. "You have a beautiful place here. You must be very proud of it."

"Thank you. I am. I'm sorry I had to neglect my duties as host for a time. I'm free now. Would you care to see the stables?"

"I would indeed," Jamison replied. He steeled himself not to peer into the trees as he walked by the place the girl had appeared. He shoved his hands into his pockets as he fell into place beside his host and hostess. He barely contained his smile as he felt the folded piece of paper that had not been there just minutes earlier.

"What you up to, girl?" Sam's voice was almost a growl as he stopped Rose on her way to the well.

"What do you mean, Sam? I'm just going after water." In all truth, Rose had no idea what he was talking about. She was too busy trying to hide the waves of disappointment and fear washing over her. Jamison had just driven off in his carriage. There had been no response to the letter she had slipped into his pocket last night. She had never known such fear as she felt last night when she held her breath and prayed the big oak she had chosen would hide her slender form. She had slumped down on the ground and sobbed silently when Jamison and the Cromwells disappeared down the road to the stables. She had been so close. And then to have her chance snatched away—it seemed too cruel. She had allowed hope to keep her going last night—hope there would be a response to her letter. That hope had been stolen from her with the departure of Jamison's carriage. Now she had nothing left but fear—fear that it had all been a hoax, and fear that she had revealed her desire for freedom. She had heard the stories of what owners were doing to runaway slaves.

Sam was regarding her with open suspicion. "You aiming to do somethin' stupid, Rose?"

Rose looked at him in surprise. "Sam! What in the world are you talking about?"

Sam just shook his head. "I promised your daddy I would take care of you after Marse Cromwell sold him off." Rose nodded impatiently. She had heard all of this plenty of times before. Sam peered at her closely as they walked behind the well wall. He looked around quickly and then shrugged his great shoulders. "You let me know if you'll be needing any help." Rose had no time to reply. Sam reached into his pocket, pulled out an envelope, and slipped it into her hand. He turned and walked quickly back to the house.

Rose leaned against the well to steady her trembling legs. She knew she shouldn't read it now, that she should wait until she was safely in her room. She sank down on the ground behind the protective covering of the well, unfolded the sheet of paper, and rapidly read its contents.

She was smiling when she entered the big house.

THIRTEEN

Robert leaned back in his seat and closed his eyes, grateful for a chance to unwind and relax. An axle had broken on his carriage on the way to the station. Manson had barely gotten him there in time to catch his train. He would have to send a letter of appreciation to the man who had stopped and helped him repair his axle. For now, he would get some much-needed rest.

"Robert Borden!"

Robert contemplated feigning a deep sleep. He had no desire to be bothered. He opened his eyes a mere slit to identify his intruder. "Matthew Justin!" All thoughts of sleep fled his mind as he jumped up and pumped the other man's hand. "What in the world are you doing here?"

"I could ask you the same question, old boy. The last I saw you, you were still a student in Philadelphia. I take it you finished?"

"Yes. They actually let me out of the place with a degree." Robert laughed, deciding not to tell him he had left with three classes to complete because of the rising tension. "I'm at home on my plantation in Virginia now. And what about you?" he asked. "Was some paper actually crazy enough to let you go to work for them?"

Matthew nodded, his long red hair bouncing off his shoulders as wildly as before. His bright blue eyes shone with excitement. "The editor of the *Philadelphia Inquirer* actually decided to give me a go at it. I've been there almost two years now."

Robert grinned at his old friend. He looked just like he always had—the angular face softened by a boyish grin, and the tall, muscular body that spoke of his farm heritage in the mountains of western Virginia. "I always knew you would make it."

Matthew shrugged. "I had to make it. There was no way I was going back to working in the tobacco fields.

My father loves it, but my heart was never in it. Journalism..." His voice almost caressed the word. "I love it as much as I thought I would." He paused. "Are you glad to be home, again?"

Robert nodded. "There is no place on earth like Oak Meadows. I have a lot of plans to expand the plantation."

"Does that have something to do with where you're headed now?"

Robert shook his head. "Not a thing. I'm headed to Charleston for the Democratic Convention."

"Really? Why? What draws you there?" Matthew was openly surprised.

Robert shrugged and smiled. "If my heart wasn't tied to Oak Meadows I might have followed my interest in politics. I've made my choice and I'm happy with it, but I still have a yearning to be in the center of things. At least enough to watch what happens." His tone grew suddenly serious. "I think this convention may be the most important one our country has seen. A lot is resting on in." He frowned and then looked at his friend. "What about you? Where are you headed?"

"Charleston," Matthew said with a grin. "Looks like we're going to relive some of those wild times we had in college. Besides being very important politically, I can guarantee you it's going to be one big party down there. When I'm not working," he hastened to add. "I'm going to be covering the convention for my newspaper, along with some other guys who are in the other car probably wondering if I fell off the train somewhere."

"Let them wonder." Robert moved his hat and coat to make room for his friend.

Matthew nodded and sat down. "They'll come looking for me if they get really worried. We have a lot to catch up on."

The first few hours passed quickly as they relived old memories of college days. Laughter rang freely between the two friends. Robert was thrilled to have run into Matthew. They had been suitemates for his first two years of college. When Matthew had graduated, they lost touch, but Robert had never stopped thinking about him. There were many times he had missed his friend's quiet understanding, mountain-grown wisdom, and common sense. As they sat at their table in the dinner car now, the conversation grew more serious.

"So, Robert, are you still a radical Democrat?" Matthew asked with a smile. Robert didn't answer immediately and the long pause caused Matthew to lean forward and look at him more closely. The silence stretched between them.

Finally, Robert answered. "I don't want to appear wishy-washy by not standing solidly somewhere, old friend, but at the risk of appearing that way, I have to admit I have some grave questions about my party. I never thought I would find myself feeling that way, but..." He shrugged his broad shoulders.

Matthew peered at him intently. "What has brought about this change?"

"All this wild talk of secession. From what I can tell, men on both sides are caught in the throes of passion. They are exchanging their reason for the passions of their heart. That can only mean trouble." Edmund Ruffin stood clearly in his thoughts. "I just spent an evening talking with a new friend. The man's name is Thomas Cromwell. He's a sensible man. I had heard much about him before I sought him out. He also is afraid the country is headed for big trouble, and is certain there will be war if the country splits. Cromwell was once a strong supporter and participant in the Whig Party, though he now aligns himself with the Democrats since the Whigs lost their political power. He is a strong Union man. I found him fascinating to talk to and took heart that there are still reasonable men to be found in the South." The thoughtful look on his face deepened. "There must be a way to heal the split trying to force this country apart."

Matthew sat silently. "There are extremists on both sides, Robert. How familiar are you with the Republican Party?"

"The Black Republicans?"

Matthew laughed. "Familiar enough, I take it."

Robert shrugged. "I know that everything my life is based on will be destroyed if the Republicans gain the presidency."

"Meaning slavery." It wasn't a question.

Robert nodded, suddenly realizing he had no idea where his friend stood on the issue. Suddenly he didn't want to know. He valued him as a friend too much. He wanted to enjoy their time together, not fight over the slavery issue. He was sure there would be plenty of opportunity for that in Charleston. "So tell me, Matthew. What's it going to be like in Charleston when we get there?"

Matthew let him change the subject and they continued to talk as the train rolled southward.

Robert gazed around at the chaos surrounding him. The Charleston train station was a madhouse.

"They're expecting at least four thousand visitors for the convention." Matthew had to shout to make himself heard over the din of the milling crowd. In the distance, they could hear a band playing. The clatter of carriage wheels on the cobblestone streets only added to the cacophony of sounds assaulting them from every direction.

Robert was intrigued. He had become accustomed to such madness during his years in Philadelphia. He had long wanted to visit Charleston and planned to make the most of this experience. He found himself wishing briefly that Carrie could be with him. He sensed she would love the stimulation of this atmosphere. Soon though, his attention was drawn by the men milling around him. There were delegates here from every state. Robert could almost pick them out from the hundreds of mere spectators descending on the city for what was certain to be a show. Politicians seemed to wear the mark of constantly being in the public eye. There were cold-eyed men who looked like professional gamblers— slicked-back hair topped eyes that glittered with the opportunities they hoped to find here. Everywhere there were stout, perspiring men dressed in solid black. Fine linen clothing, topped by stovepipe hats, spoke of their pompous self-importance. They leaned on their gold-headed canes, and carried on intense, whispered conversation with other men identical to themselves.

Robert felt a tug on his sleeve. "Let's get a carriage and get out of this madness," Matthew shouted.

Robert nodded, making no attempt to shout over the noise. He reached down, grabbed his bag, and followed his friend through the crowd. It wasn't much quieter by the street, but at least he didn't have to shout to make himself heard. "I'm assuming you have reservations in the city?"

"At some hotel in the middle of this madness. We have to be in the center of the action. Our editor would have a fit if we missed anything. What about you, old man? You manage to find a place to stay?"

Robert nodded. "I made reservations months ago. I wasn't going to miss this. I have a room at the Planters Hotel."

Matthew whistled, suitably impressed. "They sure didn't put us up in accommodations like those, I assure you. My editor told me to be thankful if I found a mattress on the floor."

Robert laughed. "You said you have to be in the center of things. Does that also mean you have to stay with the rest of your team of reporters?"

Matthew thought a moment. "I don't think it really matters where I stay," he said thoughtfully. "Not that I'll get much chance to lay down anyway," he added, laughing.

Robert nodded. "Then there is no reason you should not stay with me," he said firmly. "I have plenty of room and I would welcome the company." He was thrilled when Matthew enthusiastically agreed. He was glad to have reconnected with his old friend and he knew he might never find him again in this madhouse if they separated.

Matthew's attention was suddenly distracted. "The guys are waving me over." Within moments, Robert found himself in possession of Matthew's bags with a promise his friend would meet him for dinner in the hotel's restaurant.

After settling himself in the elegant hotel that was the meeting place for Charleston gentry, Robert set out to explore the city, turning down several offers from eager carriage drivers. He wanted to walk. The charm of the city captured him instantly. Evidence of a strong Huguenot tradition was reflected in its almost French appearance. Other parts looked as if they sprang straight from Georgian England. The mix was captivating.

Robert walked slowly through streets dominated by a myriad of slim, white church steeples. Richmond had its fair share of churches as well, but with Charleston's land and houses being so close to sea level, they seemed to be even taller and more elegant. The shops were quaint, and long rows of pastel dwellings boasted gateways and railings of delicate iron filigree. Everywhere were mansions with long piazzas and slim, white pillars. Robert was enchanted by occasional glimpses into the shaded, flower-strewn courtyards protected within their confines. Palmettos and live oaks dripping with Spanish moss lent an otherworldly air to the city.

Robert took deep breaths of the salt-laden air of the bustling port town as he strolled toward the Battery. Twisted live oaks provided a backdrop of beauty for the riotous flowers that splashed their colors onto the warm spring canvas. Carriages, carrying well-dressed Charlestonians with a distinctively disdainful air, clattered leisurely through the cobblestone streets. Elegantly dressed ladies sauntered along, eager not to miss any of the excitement descending on their town.

Robert's steps finally led him seaward. The gently lapping waters mesmerized him with their rhythmic motion. The very sameness with which they had caressed these shores for thousands of years was a fitting backdrop for this southern city. Just as he had been told, Charleston was, in every way, the past incarnate, forcing time to stand still and carefully preserving a cherished way of life that had a fragile and immutable pattern. It would listen to no demand for change and expected everyone who called it home to resist any change, to beat down anything that would even look like a concession to change. In the short time he had been here, he sensed the city was full of those eager to respond.

He stood quietly and allowed the lure of the water to sweep over him. A soft breeze filled his nostrils with the salty air and ruffled his hair. Once again he found himself thinking of Carrie. He stared almost unseeingly at Castle Pinckney on its low island and could barely make out unfinished Fort Sumter in the distance, where a few workmen unhurriedly put together bricks and stones in deep casements. None of it was of any interest to him. His mind was full of a vibrant girl with emerald-green eyes.

He had never met anyone like Carrie. He loved her animation and the fire of passion that lit her eyes when she felt intensely about something. Not only was she beautiful, she was intelligent and not embarrassed to show her feelings. He had met girls like her in the North, but the girls he knew in the South seemed concerned only with the daily affairs of life. As long as their social world continued to whirl, they were content. Carrie was obviously different. Surely, she was an enigma to her peers. A picture of her snipping a lock of hair at the tournament rose in his mind. She had won his heart with that one silly, lovable action. Grinning broadly, he moved on. He would get the chance to see Carrie again soon enough. A glance at his watch made him increase his pace. He had just enough time to make it back to the hotel to meet Matthew.

It was late that night before Matthew made his way back to the Planters Hotel. "I'm sorry, Robert. I trust you received my note?"

"I did, though I had no doubts you were in the midst of some journalistic drama." Robert laughed. "I managed to pass the evening quite pleasantly." He rambled on for a few minutes, telling Matthew about his day until he realized his friend wasn't listening. "Hey, old man, where are you? I don't believe you heard a word I'm saying!"

Matthew shook his head with a rueful grin that belied the look in his eyes. "You're right. You lost me at *journalistic drama.*" Robert watched him closely, and waited. Matthew finally continued in a heavy voice. "There's going to be trouble."

"Trouble?" Robert echoed after a long silence.

"There is a very dangerous game being played. The result can only be disastrous." Then Matthew fell silent again, deep in thought.

Robert restrained the impulse to grab him and shake out of him whatever he was thinking. He knew his friend. He wouldn't talk until he had his thoughts together. It was one of the things he had always admired— and one of the things that had always driven him to distraction. He sat back in his chair and waited.

Matthew finally leaned forward. Robert matched his action. "You ever heard of Phillip Yancey?"

Robert shrugged. "I know the name, but no more."

"You'll know more by the time you leave here. I've heard people in my circle call him the Prince of Fire-Eaters. He holds no hope that the South will do any justice to itself by remaining in the Union. Secession is the only thing that will satisfy him. Mark my words. He is here to destroy this convention."

Robert shook his head, not willing to accept his usually levelheaded friend's words. "I know there are fire-eaters here in Charleston. But they are a minority," he insisted, wondering who he was trying to convince. "There are still reasonable men in this country—both North and South. Compromise can be found."

"Do you want to see Douglas nominated, Robert?" Matthew asked directly.

Robert answered slowly, "I have grave doubts about Douglas. His position on slavery troubles me. If the South is not to be violated, we need a man who will take a stronger stand. I don't agree with his stand on Popular Sovereignty. But, having said that, I see no other man within the party who has a hope of beating Seward. The Republicans are almost certain to nominate him next month in Chicago. I fear what that would mean even more." He smiled. "I guess that is a long way to say, yes, I want to see Douglas nominated. Why?"

"It is going to take a great many men of reason to see Douglas nominated. I don't think there are enough of them here. There are many men here, led by the deceptively mild-mannered Yancey, who will fight Douglas without paying any heed to the cost of the fight. They have the advantage that any completely determined minority has in a meeting where the majority would like to have harmony. They are ready to go to any extremes. They will accept harmony if they can get it on their own terms. Otherwise, they are perfectly ready to accept discord. Phillip Yancey is here for only one reason. To create discord. It is the only possible way to meet his agenda."

Robert shook his head. "There are a great many men here who believe victory in November is critical. I must believe that men will lay their personal antagonisms aside and make the success of the party their first objective. If our party can hold its unity, it is almost certain we can gain enough electoral votes in the North to gain the majority we need to win the election."

"*If* can be a mighty big word. Consider this, Robert. How would most of these *reasonable men* react if the Republicans were to win the presidency this fall?"

Robert sighed. "It would be quite a shock. I, for one, do not want to see our country run by someone who has vowed not to support the values southern society rests upon. I'm afraid there will be trouble."

"Exactly. Trouble is exactly what the fire-eaters want. They believe they can get their way only if the Democrats lose the election. Most of the South is not yet ready to embrace secession. The shock of a Black Republican victory would almost certainly make them ready."

The convention opened at noon on a rainy April 23.

Robert hurried in to gain his seat in the gallery. His frustration mounted quickly. The acoustics of the great Institute Hall were horrible, due primarily to the stream of wagons and drays clattering over the cobblestoned streets just outside the doors. Try as he might, he could not make any sense of the garbled sounds rising to his straining ears. Things improved somewhat when massive loads of sawdust were dumped on the streets to deaden the noise. Once he could hear, Robert realized there was not much to listen to. Procedures were laid in place and speeches were made, but the real issues boiled just beneath the surface, not yet ready to emerge. When the long day ended, nothing had been accomplished.

"Ready for a little of the real action, old friend?"

Robert looked up, startled, as Matthew's hand clapped his shoulder. He had just settled down to a late dinner in the hotel's restaurant. He was tired after sitting in the gallery of the convention hall all day. Frankly, he just wanted to rest, but his curiosity made him ask, "What real action?"

"All the delegates of the cotton states are meeting tonight."

"Why?" Robert demanded. "The meetings are over for the day."

Matthew shrugged. "That's what I intend to find out. My journalistic nose says it's important. Want to go along?"

Ten minutes later the two men were striding quickly down the street. If possible, Charleston had gotten wilder. Liquor was flowing freely and the streets were full of milling, talking, speculating men, waving their arms and seeing who could shout their sentiments louder. Robert and Matthew were forced to sidestep several brawls that broke out on the sidewalks.

"How did you find out about this?" Robert shouted over the din.

"It's my job. I just keep my eyes and ears open. If you listen long enough and watch hard enough, it's amazing what you can learn. Besides, Yancey isn't trying to keep anything a big secret. His aim is to pull men over to his side."

Up ahead, a large contingent of men was entering a modest two-story building. He was surprised when Matthew took his arm to keep him from entering. "What are you doing?"

Matthew just shook his head and continued walking. Robert followed. Ducking into the shadows of the building, Matthew headed down the dark alley beside the building. Finally he came to rest next to a wrought iron staircase. He grinned in the darkness. "I didn't say we had been *invited* to this little get together. I just said I knew about it. This is our entrance."

Robert grinned in return. "Just like the old days."

"Yep. Just like the old days." Within minutes, the two had scaled the staircase, crawled into an open window, and quietly positioned themselves where they could see and hear the action going on below.

Robert's heart grew heavy as the night wore on. He listened intently as Yancey led most of the talking. When Alabama's Democratic convention had met in January, Yancey had put through a resolution that was basically an iron-clad demand for a slave code in regard to the territories that said the government had no power to abolish or legislate the existence or practice of slavery. The state convention had ordered this platform be submitted to the convention and had further ordered that the Alabama delegation was to withdraw if it was not adopted. The state had made no attempt to hide its definition of the battle lines.

"Gentlemen, we are in this battle together," Yancey challenged. "We either stand together, or fall together. What will it be?"

By the end of the night Yancey had done what he had set out to do. The delegations from Georgia, Florida, Louisiana, Texas, Arkansas, and Mississippi had agreed to go where Alabama went.

Robert and Matthew were silent as they wound their way back through the still bawdy streets. Men carried on, totally unaware that momentous decisions had been made within throwing distance of where they now stood. Matthew was the one to break the silence. "The convention is going to fall apart," he predicted heavily.

Robert disagreed. "I don't think that will happen." He was still looking for a happy ending, though hopes of it were waning. "It's true Douglas doesn't stand much of a chance now. His platform will never include the conditions Yancey laid out. But I believe Douglas will eventually withdraw. He will either see that it's for the good of the party or he'll just bow out of what is inevitable defeat. Surely an acceptable compromise candidate can be named. Once there is a candidate all of us can get behind, we can move forward and take the election in the fall." He tried to feel as confident as he sounded.

"You don't really believe that, Robert," Matthew broke in. "There is no one who can gain enough of the votes here to win the nomination. No, I'm afraid this act tonight has split the party irrevocably."

"Surely you recognize how critical the slavery issue is to the South. The party must stand together on this issue." There, Robert had said it. Even between old friends, the issue could not be ignored.

Matthew frowned, but answered honestly. "Slavery has never been an important part of life to those of us in western Virginia. We have carved out lives for ourselves without the aid of slavery."

"Yes, but surely you can see how life as I know it would be destroyed."

The silence stretched longer this time. Matthew, when he replied, was gentle but firm. "A life built on others being denied a life of freedom is not a life I would want. I don't stand with the ranks of the abolitionists, but neither can I support the institution of slavery."

Robert was thankful for the brawl that broke out right in front of him, saving him from having to respond. He didn't want to fight with his friend. Debate over current issues had always been a favorite part of their relationship, but this was different. He was not debating a distant current event. He felt as if he were being backed into a corner, forced to defend a way of life he had always taken for granted.

They walked the rest of the way back to the hotel in silence.

The Charleston convention went the way Matthew had predicted.

On April 27, the platform reports were presented. The Douglas platform attempted to push the slavery issue into the hands of the Supreme Court, stating that it was a judicial matter by nature and should be decided there.

Robert leaned forward in his gallery seat when Yancey walked to the podium. In a quiet, dignified voice he made clear the grounds on which he stood. There was only one stand the Democratic Party could make—that slavery was right. Neither he himself, nor the Alabama delegation for which he spoke, wanted a breakup of the Union, but someone had to make it clear to the democrats of the North that the Union would be dissolved unless constitutional principles protecting slavery triumphed at the polls.

"Ours is the property invaded," Yancey declared. "Ours are the institutions which are at stake; ours is the peace that is to be destroyed; ours is the property that is to be destroyed; ours is the honor at stake— the honor of children, the honor of families, the lives, perhaps, of all. All of this rests upon what your course may ultimately make out of a great heaving volcano of passion and crime, if you are enabled to consummate your designs. Bear with us then, if we stand sternly here upon what is yet that dormant volcano, and say we yield no position here until we are convinced we are wrong."

George A. Pugh, of Ohio, a Douglas supporter, jumped up to give an impassioned response. "The real root of the difficulty is that Northern Democrats have worn themselves out defending Southern interests. Now we are being ordered to hide our faces and eat dirt. Gentlemen of the South, you mistake us—you mistake us—we will not do it!"

Robert watched as the convention hall erupted in a giant uproar. All over the floor, delegates were on their feet, waving their arms, yelling for recognition. It resembled little more than a circus as chaos reigned supreme. Passion collided with passion, though none of it was recognizable. It ended with a slam of the gavel announcing that the convention had adjourned until morning.

Cold rain enveloped both the city and the hearts of those who were still hoping for reason to prevail. The numbers had dwindled as passion overruled lucid thought and the what-ifs dwindled before the importance of each man's need to promote his agenda. There would be no compromise because there were not enough men present who were willing to put their passions aside and choose clear thinking.

Monday morning, April 30, dawned fair and clear. Robert made his way to the convention hall. Not because he had any great hopes that things would change for the better, but simply because he had resolved to see it through to the end. Great trainloads of spectators, tired of the show, had departed the city. The galleries were now crowded with Charlestonians caught in the so-called *Yancey Spirit*. Robert sat quietly as his hopes for a united party died with each passing moment.

He leaned forward eagerly in his seat as the morning wore on. What was happening? Had the weekend worked some kind of magic? With a minimum of delay, the Douglas platform was accepted with a majority of the vote. Was there hope after all? Just as quickly his hopes were dashed as he realized it was a carefully orchestrated game.

One by one, the delegates of the cotton states stood quietly and announced their withdrawal from the convention. There were no threats, no denunciations, and no angry language. With a quiet, dignified finality, they simply withdrew.

Robert was unashamed of the tears running down his cheeks. His dismay deepened when Delegate Charles Russell of Virginia stood and declared that if a breakup was at hand, Virginia would go with the rest of the South.

Robert looked over to where Matthew was sitting. His friend exchanged a long, silent gaze deep with meaning and emotion. Matthew inclined his head and Robert looked in the direction he indicated. Yancey was leaning back in his chair, a broad smile enveloping his face. He had achieved what he wanted.

Robert stayed until May 3. He watched with a heavy heart as the cotton state delegates formed their own convention and developed their own platform. He watched from the gallery of Institution Hall as vote after vote was taken in an effort to win the two-thirds majority needed for Senator Douglas to gain the party nomination.

Finally, the convention threw in the towel. No one was getting anywhere. With a drop of his gavel, Caleb Cushing announced that the convention would meet again on June 18. They would try again later.

Robert waited quietly for the train that would carry him back to Richmond. The Democratic Convention was over. What the delegates had done in Charleston had been done in a hot twilight where nothing had been seen clearly. Action of any sort had been deemed desirable over the unendurable present. Robert knew they had acted under the shadow of acts committed in other places— in Congress, in Kansas, at Harper's Ferry. He realized with a heavy heart that the men given the responsibility of making decisions for all Americans had ceased to be free agents and had become men directed by the passions of their time.

"I'm sorry, Robert. Things may go differently in Baltimore on the eighteenth." Matthew tried to sound like he believed it.

Robert decided to play his game. "Maybe. There is time for change. The Douglas people may be able to win new Southern delegates who won't be as stiff-necked. Maybe Douglas will realize there is no hope for him and simply withdraw so someone less troublesome can be nominated." He didn't believe it for a minute. He had witnessed firsthand the passion ruling men's hearts and minds.

Matthew nodded. "It could happen." The sound of the train made them both realize their time together was almost over. "Look, Robert, I know we don't see eye to eye on everything, but I don't want our friendship to be infected with the same disease eating at the heart of this country. You are too important to me."

Robert turned to his friend with a relieved smile. "Thanks, Matthew. I share your feelings. We're friends. Friends we will remain." The two men clasped hands for a long moment before Robert turned and boarded the train.

FOURTEEN

Carrie leaned back against the carriage seat and smiled happily at her father. "Thank you for letting me come with you. It has been so long since I've been to Richmond. I can hardly wait to get there!"

Thomas gazed at her thoughtfully.

"Why are you staring at me like that?" Carrie demanded.

Her father smiled. "I was wondering where you came from." He laughed at her startled expression. "Oh, you are every inch my daughter, but I have no idea where you developed your love for the city. If duty were not calling me to Richmond, I would have preferred to stay on the plantation. I don't object to your enthusiasm for the city, but neither do I share it."

"But the city is so fascinating with all the buildings and the church steeples. I love looking at all the businesses and the people with so much to accomplish. It's been two years since I was last there. I can hardly wait to see all the changes. I'm sure many more buildings are there now. Richmond is growing very rapidly, you know."

"And how do you know that?" Thomas asked, amused.

"Why, I've read all about it," Carrie responded eagerly, her eyes shining with excitement. "I read all your magazines and newspapers."

Thomas shook his head. "My daughter's thirst for knowledge never ceases to amaze me," he said with a laugh. "Just one more way you are so different from your wonderful mother."

Carrie shrugged and continued on, eager to share what she had learned. "Do you know Richmond is the wealthiest city in the whole South? Why, I've read it's the wealthiest city of its size in all America— maybe in all the world! We are the largest manufacturer of tobacco in the nation, and half the tobacco grown in Virginia and North Carolina is marketed here as well. We are also the second largest flour milling center." Carrie's pride in the city was evident in the way she emphasized *we*. "We've also become the leading coffee port in the country. All those huge ships carrying flour to South America return with loads of fragrant coffee." She paused dramatically. "Richmond is a wonderful place."

Thomas laughed loudly. "You sound like a tour guide. Perhaps the city should hire you to promote it."

"No, thank you. I have other plans. I just intend to enjoy it."

"And what other plans do you have, daughter?"

Carrie grew suddenly evasive. The silence stretched between them and Thomas looked at her with concern. Carrie battled with whether to tell her secret dream to her father. Finally, she looked up. "Would you mind terribly if I kept my dream to myself a little while longer? It's very new and I find I'm not quite ready to talk about it."

Thomas managed a casual smile. "Not at all. You're becoming a young lady. It's not necessary for your old father to know all about you."

Carrie knew her father too well to miss the hurt he was trying to conceal. "That's not it at all, Father!" she cried. "It's just... Well, it's just that..."

Thomas leaned forward and held his finger against her lips. "Not another word. I know you'll tell me when you're ready. You've always had big dreams, Carrie. There's no reason for me to think that would change now. Hold on to them. I believe you can make them come true."

Carrie stared into his eyes for a long moment and then finally asked the question she had wanted to ask for a long time. "Why do you encourage my dreams, Father? Most other fathers I know would be appalled if their daughters had dreams other than the desire to be a proper plantation mistress. Why are you different?"

"Because *you're* so different," Thomas answered immediately. "I learned a long time ago that you're not going to be someone you're not." He shrugged. "I can't deny there have been times I felt it would be far simpler if you were like all the other girls around you."

"Simpler because of Mama?"

"That's a big reason, of course. I grieve the lack of understanding between the two women I love most." Then he hesitated.

"And because you have no son." Carrie spoke his thoughts, realizing they had never talked about this before.

Thomas nodded ruefully. "I can't deny that is true, Carrie. I've always promised to be nothing but honest with you. In so many ways, I suppose, I have treated you like a son. I have given you all the independence you ever wanted. You know as much about the farming operations of the plantation as I do."

"Do you regret it?"

"Not for a moment," he answered promptly. "I love you just the way you are. I suppose that's the real reason I'm so different. I wouldn't change you even if I could. I've watched you do things your own way from the time you were little. You are very special, Carrie, and I believe you are going to do special things. Things that require big dreams—and the ability to hang on to those dreams."

"Do the other men give you a hard time?"

Thomas looked at her quizzically. "Why all the questions?"

"I've had them a long time," Carrie admitted. "I just haven't asked."

"Why now?"

Carrie shrugged, not sure herself. "I seem to have questions about everything lately. I decided I should start finding answers to some of them. So, do they? Give you a hard time, that is?"

Thomas nodded. "I suppose they do. Our way of life is steeped in tradition and culture. It borders on heresy when someone breaks out of line to do something different. But," he continued firmly, "no one is going to tell me how to raise my daughter. Especially when my beautiful, spirited daughter is wonderful just the way she is."

Carrie leaned forward and gave her father a big hug. "Thanks. I love you."

"I love you, too," Thomas replied in a husky voice. "Sometimes I wonder if I've done you a disservice. If I should have insisted on shaping you into a proper plantation mistress. I fear I may have set you up for disappointment after disappointment as you battle against southern tradition." He laughed. "Not that I could have changed you, regardless. No, I would not go back and undo it if I could," he said strongly.

Carrie reached forward and took his hand but said nothing as she smiled lovingly. Silence fell between them for a while as the carriage rolled forward. Carrie knew Miles was giving all his attention to his driving, trying to miss the holes and ruts that early spring rains had pocketed the road with.

The rains had also produced one of the most beautiful springs Carrie could remember. She took in deep draughts of the fresh air as they surged forward. Warm sunshine bore testimony to the fact that the unpredictable days of vacillating weather were over. Just yesterday, Carrie had asked Rose to put away her winter cloak. It was one of her favorite traditions. Those rare times in the past when it had gotten chilly again, defiance kept her from taking it back out.

"Have you heard anything from the Democratic Convention, Father?" Carrie saw her father hide his smile. Of course, he would guess she was interested in more than politics. She blushed as she realized he knew she was fishing for information about Robert.

"I'm afraid I have, Carrie," he answered seriously, his smile fading. "I fear our neighbor, Edmund Ruffin, is quite a happy man today."

"What do you mean?" she asked, though she was certain she already knew.

"The last report I got was after the convention adjourned on April thirtieth, four days ago. Douglas had his platform selected, with a possibility of winning the two-thirds vote needed." He paused. "And then seven of our Southern states walked out," he finished heavily. He told Carrie as much as he knew about the events that brought it to pass. "There is a possibility things turned around down there since my last report," he said, though she could tell he didn't believe his own words.

"What will happen now?"

"I don't know. That's why I'm on my way to Richmond. I have a meeting with Governor Letcher. We are of like mind on the need to maintain the unity of our country and he will need all the support he can possibly get. Most of Virginia is not eager to see our country divided—though, there are many who would lead us in that direction—and too often the majority makes far less noise than a determined minority. Governor Letcher is a man of reason, but I fear he is about to fight an uphill battle."

"How are you going to help him?" Carrie asked curiously.

"I don't know," her father admitted. "That's why I'm going. I want to see exactly what I can do. There may be nothing, but I cannot rest with myself until I know. Landowners seem to be leading the drive to secession. I want to join my voice with those who are not being pulled in that direction."

"The real issue is slavery." Carrie was not asking a question.

Thomas nodded slowly. "Yes, and no. It seems to be slavery that has ignited the flame. It certainly is where the tension has become centered, but I believe it has expanded beyond that. Many of those raising their voice for secession have never owned a slave and never will. They are simply angered by the North deciding it can dictate our way of life down here. People don't like to be pushed into a corner. When they are, they lose sight of what they are fighting about. They simply fight to get out of the corner. At that point, reason loses all power to affect change. It becomes as futile an effort as trying to push back the tide."

Carrie listened thoughtfully but didn't respond.

"You seem troubled about something, Carrie."

She looked at her father but truly had no idea how to tell him what was on her mind. She couldn't remember ever feeling there was something she *couldn't* talk with her father about. Silence stretched between them. Carrie knew her father was waiting for her, and so, taking a deep breath, she plunged in. "I don't know what I feel about slavery anymore."

Thomas looked at her closely. "What do you mean?"

Once Carrie had started, it became easier to share her thoughts. "I know you believe owning slaves is our destiny and that the slaves, if left to their own devices, would be unable to care for themselves."

Thomas nodded. "That's true."

"But," Carrie protested, "I'm not so sure that is true."

"Why not?" Thomas asked carefully.

"I look at all the slaves at home. They do everything. They raise all of our crops. They make bricks, construct all of our buildings, take care of all our animals, and prepare all of our food. Those aren't the actions of people who cannot care for themselves."

Thomas nodded. "It is true they can do all those things but only because they have the leadership of the white people to guide them in those directions. Left to their own devices, they would revert this civilization back to what they came from in Africa."

Carrie glanced up at Miles's stiff back on the driver's seat. She was sure he could hear their conversation. What must he be thinking? But now that she had started the dialogue, she was loath to stop it. "There are many people who feel owning slaves is wrong."

"Yes, but those people simply don't understand the will of God in all this. The scriptures are quite clear about the basis for slavery. I know some would have us go against God's will, but they are simply ignorant."

Carrie couldn't miss the edge of anger in her father's voice as the silence built. She decided to avoid any further conversation about slavery as she was still too confused about where she stood herself. Her thoughts were as yet too unformed. She had no desire to argue with her father about it. "Where are we staying when we get to Richmond?" she asked brightly, wanting to leave the unpleasantness behind. "Are we going to stay with Mr. Thomas, your tobacco friend, like we did last time?"

Thomas allowed her to lead him away from the discussion. "No, we're staying at the Spotswood Hotel. I was keeping it as a surprise, but since you asked you might as well know," he said, smiling.

Carrie grinned with delight. "The Spotswood! How wonderful! It is such a beautiful hotel. I have dreamed of staying there since I was a child."

"It is indeed beautiful," Thomas agreed. "It is also the center of much of the political talk in Richmond right now. It seems to be the place where everyone is congregating to talk. I find I want to be in the thick of things during this trip to our capital city. I didn't think you would be adverse to the idea," he said slyly.

The rest of the trip passed easily as Carrie chattered about all the things she wanted to do while in Richmond.

"Miles will accompany you this afternoon, Carrie. If you don't mind, I'm going to stay here at the hotel and talk with some friends."

"Of course I don't mind. Miles and I will have a grand time exploring the city," Carrie assured her father. "I'm not at all hungry, so we don't even need to bother with a meal just now. You can eat with your friends. I'll find something if I want to eat later."

It had been just past noon when they arrived at the beautiful five-storied Spotswood Hotel. Its brick construction and iron facade gave it an air of quiet dignity. Richmond was both an old town and a booming, young city. Remnants of its patriarchal, agrarian society mingled easily with industry tycoons intent on bringing change and progress to the rapidly growing area. Spotswood reflected this spirit. Everywhere, you could hear conversations about the events capturing the minds and hearts of America as heated words mixed with voices of reason.

Carrie was intrigued by the Spotswood Hotel. She would explore it more thoroughly, but right now it was the city itself that beckoned her. The explosion of spring could be seen everywhere on the streets of the bustling city. The hotel's location on the corner of Main and Eighth was right in the center of the city she loved so much.

"Miles, I would love to go walk through the area around the Capitol again. It's been so long."

"Whatever you say, Miss Carrie," he said indulgently, falling into step beside her.

"Do you like Richmond, Miles?"

"I ain't got to see much of it, Miss Carrie. I can't rightly say whether I like it or not."

"But you come here so often," she protested.

"Yessum, I guess I do. But I mostly just be in one area."

"Where's that?"

Miles looked uncomfortable, and shifted his eyes away to avoid hers. "Down on Franklin Street, Miss Carrie."

"What takes you down there?" Suddenly, it was very important to know what was making her friend so uncomfortable.

Miles hesitated for a long moment before he spoke. "The auction buildings be down there."

Carrie looked at him sharply. She heard the pain in his voice but didn't know what to say. She thought about the wagonload of slaves that had come in a few weeks ago. She knew it bothered her, but she still couldn't find her own mind on it. She shook her head to force the clamor away.

Miles cleared his throat and asked, "Richmond be changed much from the last time you be here?"

Carrie was grateful for his change of subject. She was here to enjoy Richmond, and enjoy it she would. The bustle of Main Street thrilled her. "Miles, the city has grown so much! There are so many more people. And look at all the new businesses." Main Street was the business center of town. The streets were lined with storefronts topped with comfortable apartments and lodging. A steady flow of horses and carriages confined pedestrians to the sidewalks. Tall steeples of some of the city's forty churches reached for the sky, demanding attention over the bustling commercial area. Carrie stopped at the top of the street and allowed her gaze to sweep over the surrounding hills. Church spires dominated the skyline, with the columned splendor of the Capitol building proclaiming its importance.

Carrie allowed the Capitol building to pull her. She could almost feel its importance—knowing that within its walls men made decisions that could dictate the direction of her life. She couldn't put it into words; she was simply drawn to it. The park-like atmosphere of the wooded Capitol Square was enchanting. Everywhere, flowers were in full bloom, the canopy of trees providing the perfect setting.

A sudden sense of foreboding swept through her. She stopped suddenly and stared up at the sky. "What you looking at, Miss Carrie?" Miles asked, his eyes following her own.

She shook her head silently, pondering the sense of foreboding that had suddenly consumed her. Her former happiness was suddenly shadowed by the realization that, if her father was right, all she loved might soon be under attack. In spite of the bright sunshine, it was as if dark clouds were lowering onto the bright city, threatening to destroy the very ideals the country had been built on. What if there weren't enough men of reason to stop them?

"Carrie Cromwell!"

Startled, Carrie jumped and looked around. "Sally Hampton! Natalie Heyward! What a wonderful surprise. What are you two girls doing here?" She was delighted to see her friends, and relieved to see the sun shining brightly again. All the talk of secession must be affecting her more than she thought. She shook off her dark thoughts, glad to have something else to claim her attention.

"We're here with our mothers on a glorious shopping spree. Thalhimers has just gotten in a wonderful new shipment of dresses. We've been buying all day!" Sally's voice was euphoric.

"What about you, Carrie?" Natalie asked. "You didn't mention you were coming to Richmond when we saw you at Louisa's."

"No, my father decided rather suddenly to make the trip. I harassed him into letting me come along," Carrie said, laughing. "I do so love this city!" She laughed again at her own intensity. "Forgive me. I've just so looked forward to being here again."

The next hour passed quickly as the three girls continued their tour of the city, while Miles and Sally's driver, Tom, followed, chatting quietly. Carrie insisted they spend long moments in front of Washington's monument. As she gazed up at the impressive statue, she couldn't help wishing Washington would dismount from his horse and come back to save the country he had helped found. Surely he would be appalled that everything he and so many others had fought for was so close to being thrown to the winds. Surely he would have something to say to stop the madness. There was no movement, however. Washington, from his place in history, merely stared out over the multitudes, challenging them to find their way through this dark time.

"I'm starving, girls," Natalie announced.

Carrie laughed. "You're always hungry, Natalie."

"Not true!" she retorted. "But what does it matter? I'm hungry now, and I intend to do something about it. Does anyone care to join me?"

A short time later, the girls were seated at a cozy little restaurant on Main Street with bowls of hearty soup and thick slices of bread in front of them. Tall, cool glasses of iced tea promised to soothe their burning thirsts. Their two attendants were given lunch and permission to go off as long as they were back within an hour.

"So, have you heard anything from Robert Borden?"

"Sally Hampton!" Natalie exclaimed. "Have you no manners at all?"

"Oh, pooh," Sally scoffed. "Don't bother to look all proper and shocked, Miss Natalie Heyward. You know you're as curious as I am. You were just waiting for me to do the dirty work."

Carrie laughed as the two friends sparred. "There is no news here worth fighting over. I have not heard from Mr. Borden since he departed Blackwell Plantation for Charleston." She wanted nothing more than to discuss the Democratic Convention with her two friends, but she knew they would laugh at her and tell her to concentrate on things more important.

"Oh, yes, that Democratic Convention." Sally's tone left no doubt how little she thought of it. "I say those Northerners got what they deserved. It will show them how useless it is to try and push things over on the South!"

Carrie gazed at Sally, a little shocked. "You know what's going on in Charleston?"

"Why, of course, silly. Every proper southern lady had best be aware of the attempts of Northern aggression to destroy our way of life down here."

Carrie didn't like where the conversation seemed to be going. "Surely you have no desire to see the Union destroyed?"

Sally sniffed. "There is no reason to stay loyal to a government that wishes to abolish slavery. Why, in no time there would be all manner of uprisings and killings. No respectable white person would be safe if all the slaves were set free. It's plain craziness."

Carrie thought the sparkle in Sally's eyes reflected a certain craziness of its own, but she decided not to say so.

Sally rattled on. "I was talking with some other girls last week. We've decided it might be *fun* to have a war."

"Sally!" Carrie could force out no more than a shocked whisper.

Sally ignored her. "I've watched all those men marching with the Virginia Militia. They look positively divine in their uniforms. Can you imagine anything more romantic than a whole army of such stunning good looks?"

Carrie found her tongue. "People get killed in war, Sally."

"Oh, pooh! There won't be a *real* war, silly girl. The North may be pushy, but they're not silly enough to come down here and fight our boys. Why, we would send them running back with their tails between their legs." She laughed as she envisioned it. "It would be fun to have them give it a try."

Carrie felt sick. She couldn't believe this was her lifelong friend talking. Had the whole country fallen into this crazy way of thinking? She couldn't define where her deep-seated horror of war came from, since she had never experienced it firsthand. Yet, from somewhere deep within, she felt it— the pain, the suffering, the utter futility of men fighting one another.

Natalie, striving for peace, changed the subject. "I'm going to take a trip in June," she said brightly.

Wearily, Carrie turned to her. "Where are you going?" she asked as she was expected to. She couldn't have cared less right then.

"I'm going to visit my Aunt Abby in Philadelphia." She had Carrie's attention now, so she pressed on. "Aunt Abby is my mother's oldest sister. She went to Philadelphia to a girls' boarding school and just never came back. She fell in love with the city and then married one of its leading businessmen. He died several years ago, but she has chosen to stay there. I received an invitation last year asking me to visit and my parents have given their permission for me to go." She paused and leaned forward to take Carrie's hand. "My mother said I could take along a couple of friends for the month. Sally has already accepted. I would love for you join us. Would you like to come?"

Carrie was delighted. "Oh, Natalie, that would be wonderful!" She had always longed to visit Philadelphia. Robert's accounts of the city, along with his information about the medical college there, had intensified her longing. "I'll speak with my father about it as soon as possible. How soon must you know?"

"Oh, in a week or so," Natalie replied casually. "I do hope you'll be able to join us."

"So do I," Carrie murmured. "So do I."

Carrie was concerned by the drawn look on her father's face as they sat across from each other in the Spotswood's elegant dinner room. "I take it you haven't heard much good news today?"

"You're right," Thomas said heavily. "I'm afraid I heard nothing to encourage me and much to cause grave concern."

"Things didn't improve in Charleston?" Carrie guessed, already sure she was right.

Thomas shook his head. "They gave up yesterday. The delegates that walked out formed their own convention, developed their own platform, and then sat back to wait and see what the rest of the party— which they nicknamed the Rump Convention— would do. The remaining delegates, after countless numbers of attempts to garner enough votes to nominate a candidate, finally threw up their hands and left town. They are going to try again in Baltimore on June eighteenth."

"Well, isn't that a good sign?" Carrie asked hopefully. "Maybe things will change by then."

"I have no real hope of that. The madness affecting our country is not going to change substantially in the next few weeks. Unless it just gets worse," he predicted morosely, his face lined with fatigue.

Carrie looked at her usually optimistic father with surprise, casting around in her mind for something to say, while also seeing Sally's face, euphoric with the thought of war.

Thomas rubbed his forehead wearily. "No, I'm afraid the end result of all of this will be war. I fear there are not virtue and patriotism, nor sense enough left in this country to avoid it." He paused for a long moment. "I will do everything within my rather weak power to stop it, but in less than one year I predict this country will be in the midst of a bloody war. What is to become of us then, only God knows."

Carrie stared at him with a sinking heart. She had no words to ease her father's pain. She knew how much he loved the South and how beloved his way of life was to him. She could only imagine the agony in his heart. It still all seemed so unreal to her, but suddenly it was more real, and scarier, than it had been before.

Thomas forced a smile and raised his glass to take a long drink. "Enough dark talk. Tell me what you discovered in Richmond today, daughter."

Carrie hesitated to talk of such light matters but decided the distraction might do her father good. Detail by detail, she invited him into her afternoon. She painted the city in glowing terms, gratified to realize her storytelling was lifting some of the gloom from her father's countenance.

He was surprised to hear Sally and Natalie were in town. "Are their fathers with them?"

"No, this is a women's expedition." Carrie laughed. "They are here to empty Thalhimers of their stock of spring and summer dresses."

Thomas looked thoughtful. "Do you need dresses, Carrie? I hadn't even thought of that when we came. Your mother is probably expecting me to make sure you return with an adequate wardrobe."

Carrie shrugged. "I have plenty of clothes, Father." She loved pretty clothes as much as any girl, but she had plenty, and somehow she sensed even now that it was frivolous to focus on such trivial issues. "There is something I *would* like, though." Now was as good a time as any to ask.

"What is it?"

"Natalie has invited me to go with Philadelphia with her. I would dearly love to go."

Her father leaned back in his chair and regarded her with surprise. "Philadelphia? That's quite an invitation. How long would you be gone? Who else is going along, and where would you be staying?"

"We would be gone a month." She filled him in on as many details as she knew.

Thomas fell silent. Long moments passed, but Carrie was content to wait. "This is a wonderful opportunity," he finally said. Then his voice deepened with concern. "We are not living in normal times, however. I fear you will not find a warm welcome in the North."

Carrie held her breath. Surely he was not about to say no.

Thomas stared at her and then smiled. "If I were you...It's fine with me if you go," he finally agreed. "I simply cannot bring myself to say no."

"Thank you!" Carrie jumped up from the table and wrapped her arms around her father.

FIFTEEN

The next morning dawned bright and beautiful. Carrie's spirits matched the weather. The country might be falling apart, but she was in Richmond and soon she would be headed to Philadelphia. She had a whole day free to explore the city, and she intended to make the most of it.

Miles was waiting for her when she walked out of the Spotswood after breakfast with her father. "Good morning, Miss Carrie."

"Good morning, Miles. Isn't it a beautiful day?"

"That it is, Miss. Where you be wantin' to go today?"

"Everywhere!"

Miles smiled indulgently and chuckled. "Where you want to go first?"

Carrie laughed along with him. "Let's go this way." She glanced around at the hordes of people already clogging the sidewalks and turned east on Eighth Street. She walked briskly, talking steadily while she forged ahead. "I received quite an education last night. I simply asked several of my fellow hoteliers where I should go. They not only gave me suggestions— they told me great stories as well."

The streets were already busy with carts and carriages. They had only covered two blocks when they reached Grace Street. "Did you know Richmond has forty churches, Miles? A lot of them are right here on this road. That's why they named it Grace Street." Carrie laughed. "It seems rather appropriate."

Miles listened intently.

They continued on another block until they reached Broad Street. The hum of activity increased and the noise level deepened with the roar and clamor of trains entering and leaving the Broad Street depot. Carrie was fascinated by the hectic pace of the station. She loved the slow, easy pace of the plantation, but there was something about this that drew her as well. She longed to be a part of all that was going on. She carefully scanned the sea of people milling around the station and then caught herself. Who was she looking for? She blushed when she realized she was searching for Robert. She hoped to find him returning from Charleston. How silly of her to think they might meet in Richmond.

Carrie turned deliberately away from the station and strode briskly in the direction of the river. She tried to control her thoughts about Robert, oblivious of all they passed, until they reached Monumental Episcopalian Church. "Oh, Miles," she cried, fully aware of her surroundings again. "This is a story *you* should know. This church stands where once the Richmond Theatre stood. In 1811, on the night after Christmas, the theater was packed with many prominent Richmonders. During the performance, one of the chandeliers being used as a prop was the cause of a horrible fire." Carrie shuddered as she envisioned it. "I can just imagine the panic as everyone tried to escape. Seventy-two people, including the governor, died in the fire." She paused, staring up at the church. "There were a lot of heroes who helped save people who were trapped that night. One of those heroes was a black man named Gilbert Hunt. When Gilbert got to the fire, there were people jumping out the windows. He heard a man called Dr. McCaw cry out for help. Gilbert ran over and caught the women as McCaw handed them down from the window where he was standing. Together, they saved about a dozen women who would have otherwise died. When Dr. McCaw had to jump for his life, it was Gilbert who rushed forward and saved him from almost certain death because a wall of the theater was about to collapse on him. Isn't that the most thrilling story?"

"I know Gilbert Hunt, Miss Carrie," Miles stated quietly.

Carrie stared at him in amazement. "You know him? You mean, he's still alive?"

"Yessum. He be a blacksmith here in town."

Carrie was eager to know more. "What happened after the fire?"

Miles shrugged. "Some folks wanted him set free for what he done, but nothin' ever happened with dat. Finally he bought hisself his freedom. Paid eight hunerd dollars for it, I hear."

Carrie stared at Miles. She was sure she heard longing in his voice. Was Miles unhappy at Cromwell Plantation? She looked and maybe saw him for the very first time. A man past the prime of his years but still strong and fit. And undoubtedly the best horseman in the area. Did he have dreams? Carrie had no idea where her thoughts were coming from. She had never had these questions until recently. Suddenly an idea popped into her head. "Can I meet him?"

Miles stared at her. "Meet him?"

"Yes," she stated impatiently. "I'd like to meet Gilbert Hunt. How old is he now?"

Miles looked thoughtful. "I reckon he be somewhere's between sixty and seventy. He still be working his smithin' shop."

"I'd like to meet him."

Miles continued to stare at her, shifting from one foot to the other. "I don't knows as that is such a good idea, Miss Carrie."

"Why ever not?" she demanded. She could tell he was uncomfortable, but he almost always did as she wished.

Slowly, he said, "There ain't many white people go down to that part of town much. Specially not white women. I don't know's how Marse Cromwell would feel 'bout me takin' you down there."

Carrie wanted to push the issue but hesitated. She didn't even know why it was important to her. "Do many black people own businesses here in Richmond, Miles?" she asked instead.

"I guess dere be pretty many."

"How many?"

Miles shrugged, his face nonplussed. "I don't rightly know the number, Miss Carrie." He screwed his forehead tightly as he forced himself to think. "I know there are six or seven that own grocery stores. A couple more got themselves a fruit shop. There be right many who got themselves a barber shop. And I hear about a fella who's got himself a right nice livery stable. I guess there be right many."

"How did these people get free, Miles?"

Miles stared at her harder but answered. "Differnt ways I guess. Some people got their freedom when their masters died and done give it to 'em. Some masters give it to 'em while they still be living. Others done bought dere freedom."

"Don't some slaves just run away?"

"I wouldn't be knowing much 'bout dat, Miss Carrie." His voice was casual as he shrugged his big shoulders.

Carrie stared at Miles as sweat broke out on his forehead. Why was there fear in his eyes? She couldn't help but notice he was choosing every word carefully. Had a white person never asked him questions like this before? She wanted to ask him if he wanted to be free, yet, she didn't really want to know. There was nothing she could do about it. Why was she even thinking this way?

The restless stirring in her heart began to irritate her. These were questions she had never considered before. Why was her belief system being challenged? She wanted to run away from the questions and simply accept what she had always believed to be true. If she just closed her ears to the questions, perhaps she could refuse to deal with it. Reluctantly, she accepted the fact that ignoring them wouldn't make them go away, but that didn't help her know what to do with her questions.

Thomas was oblivious to the beautiful spring morning. He took no notice of the bright blooms vying for his attention as he strode through Capitol Square on his way to the Capitol building. He would be early, but he had been too restless to stay in the hotel longer.

"Mr. Cromwell!"

An eager voice broke into Thomas's thoughts. Startled, he looked up. "Robert Borden! What are you doing here, son?"

"I've just returned on the morning train from Charleston, sir."

Thomas was glad to see the younger man but couldn't shake the heaviness of his heart. "Ah, yes, Charleston...Tell me about the convention, Robert. I'd like to hear your perspective."

Robert shook his head. "I'm afraid it will offer you no consolation, sir."

Thomas managed a weak smile. "I still need to know all the truth I can. Whether I like it or not, the truth is always the best thing to deal with."

Robert nodded and asked, "What are you doing here in Richmond, sir?"

"I'm on my way now to a meeting with Governor Letcher. I'm early, though, so I have some time to talk."

"Why don't we sit here, sir? I'll tell you everything I can."

Thomas glanced up at George Washington's statue as they settled on the bench. Surely it was his imagination that the venerable general was wincing as he stared out at the calamity about to befall his beloved country. Thomas sighed. Was there any way to stop the onslaught of black clouds descending on the country this American hero had helped build?

Robert talked at length and then finished his recital of the events in Charleston. "There is still hope for things to turn around in Baltimore." Thomas nodded wearily, though both of them knew there was little hope. The passion ruling the country showed no signs of abating.

Thomas looked at his watch. "I only have a few more minutes, Robert. Are you staying in the city tonight?"

"Yes, sir. Two or three more days at least. I have some business to conduct."

"In that case, we would be honored to have you join us for dinner tonight. Would you be free to come to the Spotswood?"

Robert had latched onto one word. "We?" he asked hopefully.

Thomas smiled. "Carrie is with me." He almost laughed aloud at the look of delight illuminating the younger man's face. It was nice to have something to divert his dark thoughts.

"I see," Robert murmured, obviously struggling to control the broad smile spreading across his face. "I would love to join you for dinner, sir. What time would you like me to be there?"

"Let's make it six o'clock. That will give you and Carrie some time alone later."

"That's...very kind of you, sir," Robert stammered.

Thomas made no attempt to hide his laughter now. He clapped Robert on the back and rose from the bench. "It's time for my appointment. I'll see you later this afternoon." He was still amused when he reached the Capitol building minutes later. The laughter died from his eyes, though, as he entered the impressive, columned bastion of democracy. Was everything this building stood for soon to collapse? Deep worry once more etched lines around his eyes. He had to wait only a few minutes before his audience with Governor Letcher was granted.

"Welcome to the Capitol, Cromwell!" The Governor's greeting was as open and gregarious as the rest of his personality. "To what do I owe the honor of having such a prominent plantation owner visit a mere politician?"

Thomas smiled in response to the lighthearted greeting but was in no mood to play games. He took a seat in the chair opposite Letcher's desk and leaned forward to lock eyes with him. "I've come to discover if we share a like passion to see our country hold together."

The laughter disappeared from Letcher's face. "Ah... I had heard you were a man of reason, but it pays to tread carefully these days." He stood to stare out the window of his office and then swung back around to face Thomas. "Charleston was but an opening statement on the direction our country is taking, Cromwell. There are those of us, however, who would give anything, or do anything, to see the Union remain."

"Then you believe it is in Virginia's best interest to stay within the Union?"

"I do, indeed," Letcher responded fervently.

Thomas leaned forward intently. "I'm here to offer you any help I can, Governor. I don't know that there is anything I can do, but I'll not stand idly by and watch all that I know and love be destroyed."

Letcher regarded him thoughtfully. "It will take a lot of voices to put down the rising calls for secession."

"I know." Thomas frowned "Is there hope for us yet?"

Letcher walked from behind his desk and settled himself in the chair across from Thomas. He crossed his legs and looked down for several moments while his fingers beat out a rhythm on the arm of his chair. Finally, he looked up. "The battle is going to intensify now that Charleston has made such a mockery of our party. The Black Republicans are ecstatic—as well they should be. They are going into their convention with all the confidence a splintered Democratic Party should give them." He paused, deep in thought.

Thomas waited patiently as the governor stared out the window. There were many who said he would never win the governor's race. It had been a tight race indeed. His Whig opponent, Gogin, had been a better speaker and his support had been strong in the eastern part of the state, but it wasn't strong enough to stand up against Letcher's impressive support from the west. The victory margin had been extremely narrow, however, and Thomas knew there were many Virginians that harbored serious doubts about their new governor.

"I'd like to know where you stand on this whole issue, Cromwell," Letcher finally asked.

Thomas nodded. He had expected this. "I believe the secessionists have many valid points, Governor," he said honestly. "They are angry because they feel their way of life is being threatened. I agree with them that the Constitution gives them the right to remove themselves from the Union if that is what they deem best for their states. Our whole country was founded by a revolution to escape oppression. I also believe slavery is indispensable in the South. Without it, our entire lifestyle would disintegrate. But," he paused and looked deep into the Governor's eyes, "having said all that, I believe secession would be disastrous for the South. I believe with all my heart that the North will not sit idly by if the South secedes. And I don't stand with my neighbors who believe it will be a quick, easy war if by some fluke the North tries to bring us back. I think it will be a long, tragic war that will destroy many lives. I also believe war will mean certain emancipation for the slave. Emancipation could well mean anarchy among the millions of slaves we now control. Once that happens, all our property and all the prosperity the South has worked so hard for will disappear. I believe the prosperity we are enjoying now is a result of our Union. We need the North, just as the North needs us."

"I am impressed with your understanding, sir. What do you feel is the answer?" Letcher asked.

Cromwell shrugged. "I was hoping you could tell me, Governor," he replied drily.

Laughter lightened the office for a few moments before Letcher leaned forward in his chair. "We must make our voices louder. The secessionists are winning because their voices are loudest and because the North isn't taking them seriously. Most people in the North simply refuse to believe it might actually happen. They refuse to acknowledge how desperate many of the Southerners are feeling." Letcher paused. "What our country needs is a strong leader. Someone who can soothe the passions and help both sides find ways to compromise." He sighed deeply, his face lined with concern. "I had hopes Stephen Douglas would be that man. Unfortunately, he has made too many enemies at a time when men refuse to see clearly. Truth is accepted only if it is what they already wanted to hear. I hold onto a hope that the party will still unite behind him, but it is a small hope indeed."

"I will talk to as many of my neighbors as I can, Governor."

Letcher looked at him in surprise. "You were once a Whig, Cromwell. I understand your allegiance to the Democratic Party is quite new. You realize, don't you, that this will put you at odds with most of your fellow plantation owners?"

"That is true, Governor, but I'm also a realist. The Whig Party is dying. We have no real strength to affect change. At a time like this, I find it is loyalty to my country, not to a political party, that seems most crucial. As far as my neighbors are concerned, I hope I will always choose to do what I believe is right regardless of whether others join me. I am an American first." His voice rang clearly in the opulent office.

"I wish there were more men like you, Cromwell." Letcher's voice trailed off as he stood to stare out the window once more. "You need to know something, Cromwell."

Thomas waited quietly until the governor turned around. Sunlight pouring through the window illuminated him as he said firmly, "I love the United States. I will do everything within my power to keep it together. But I am first and foremost a Virginian. I will stand with my state."

"I, too, Governor." Thomas rose and held out his hand. Letcher gripped it firmly for a long moment and then walked back to his desk.

"I would like you to come to the Baltimore Convention, Cromwell."

Thomas, thinking their meeting was over, had started toward the door. Slowly, he turned around and looked at Letcher. "Why, Governor?"

"There is going to be a preponderance of fire-eaters at that convention. Their voices will be loud and strident. The more voices for moderation that can be heard, the better."

Thomas nodded. "I will make plans to be there, sir."

Carrie had been walking through the city for almost two hours and was now deep in thought about what her father had said the night before. Suddenly, she was startled out of her reverie by a muted scream. She jerked her head up and looked around sharply. "I heard a scream, Miles. It sounded like a woman! Where did it come from?"

Miles took in his surroundings. "I didn't hear nothin', Miss Carrie," he said nervously. "Why don't we head back into de city? This ain't be such a good place. I don't think the marse would like you bein' here."

Carrie ignored him and scanned the area with her eyes. "I know I heard something, Miles. Someone may need help."

Just then, another scream erupted from the building across the street from her. It wasn't a scream of fear— this deep cry welled from the bottom of a heart being broken. Carrie turned and moved toward the building.

Miles was alarmed. "Miss Carrie! What you be doin'? You can't go in dat building!"

Carrie stopped, surprised by the fear she heard in Miles's voice. "Why not? Someone obviously needs help."

"There ain't be no help you can be givin' dem," he said flatly. He moved in front of her to block her way, his eyes determined.

Carrie stared at her servant. "What are you talking about, Miles? What is in that building? What is going on?"

Miles sighed. "That be an auction building, Miss Carrie."

"An auction building? What do you mean?" She stared at the plain-fronted, three-story building looming in front of her. The large sign on the front said simply, *Jefferson's Auction.* A steady stream of well-dressed men were coming and going as if they had important business behind the double wooden doors that were devoid of paint.

Miles sighed again. "It be a slave auction, miss." His voice was heavy. "That scream you heard was prob'ly a mama having to leave her man or her chillun."

Carrie gazed up at him, caught by the pain in his voice. Then she turned back to examine the building, thinking of the wagon that had rumbled in late at night a few weeks ago. This was where they had come from. She turned and looked for a street sign. "This is

Franklin Street, Miles. This is where you come when you travel to Richmond?"

Miles simply nodded.

Long moments passed while Carrie stared at the building. "I want to go inside," she said suddenly.

Miles looked horrified. "What? What you want to be doin' a thin' like that for?" He shook his head. "I can't do dat, Miss Carrie. The marse would be mad at me, fo sho!" He kept shaking his head. "We need to be movin' on."

"I want to go inside, Miles. You don't have to come with me." Carrie's voice was firm. Her first comment had been purely impulsive, however, the look of horror on Miles's face had cemented the desire. She wanted to know what could cause her friend such terror.

Miles just shook his head helplessly.

"I'm not in any danger if I go in there am I, Miles?" Carrie pressed.

"I don't reckon so," he mumbled.

"Then I'm going," Carrie stated calmly. She turned and walked across the street, dodging carriages and wagons.

Miles followed.

Carrie received many blatantly curious stares as she walked into the building, but no one tried to stop her. As she looked around, she became aware there were no other females. She wasn't afraid, but she was glad for Miles's solid presence beside her. She knew she wouldn't have come if he hadn't accompanied her. Her bluff had paid off.

The inside of the building was even plainer than the outside. The rough plank floor was unadorned except for a high platform erected in the front and a podium behind which stood a well-dressed gentleman. Narrow benches lined the walls and were scattered randomly through the rest of the room. Fashionably dressed men mingled with those attired in rough, plain clothing. Spittoons were in constant use and conversation created a steady hum.

"Alright, gentlemen. We've got a good one here!" Conversation ceased as the auctioneer called for their attention. Carrie focused on the action up front.

Miles shifted uneasily by her side. He clenched his fist and tightened his jaw as the first slave moved onto the platform. Intuitively, Carrie knew he wished to be anywhere but here. She felt compassion, but felt even more strongly that she must stay.

"Bob here will make someone a good field hand," the auctioneer called enthusiastically. "He's never caused his owner any trouble and he's never tried to run away. He has already sired four strong, healthy babies. He's still in his prime, gentlemen." He paused and scanned the room. "Where will the bidding start? Do I hear five hundred dollars?"

The bidding was off and running. When it reached nine hundred dollars, one of the bidders shouted above the din. "I want a closer look!"

The auctioneer nodded amiably. "Not a problem, boys. We sell only prime stock here." He motioned to his assistant, who stepped forward and made a motion to Bob. Without a sound, Bob peeled off his plain cotton shirt. His expression said he knew it would do no good to fight.

Men surged forward when his broad, black back was bared. "Turn around, boy!" one shouted. Wordlessly, Bob complied.

Carrie felt her heart pounding in her chest. Never had she felt such revulsion. This man was being treated like an animal. She looked up at Miles in protest and began to speak, but she stopped when she saw the look of anger and pain etched across his normally pleasant features.

"What did I tell you, gentleman? There are no whip marks on this one. He has never given his master any trouble."

"Let's see him move!" Bob needed little prodding from the auctioneer. It was obvious he had been on the block before. His face set with helpless agony, he began to jump around the stage, bending up and down to show his flexibility. The assistant, holding the whip and watching his actions closely, did not even have to move.

"Alright, gentlemen," the auctioneer yelled, "I have made my point. Who will continue the bidding?" His gavel pounded when the bidding topped out at eleven hundred dollars. "Sold! To Mr. Josiah Compton."

Carrie stared in horror as the slave they called Bob put his shirt back on and stepped down from the block. He made no protest as he was led from the building.

"Now, gentlemen, we have a fine family here for you."

Carrie swung her attention back to the front, repulsed yet fascinated by the drama playing out before her eyes. She wanted to run from the building, but a power stronger than her seemed to be holding her there, forcing her to see. Forcing her to understand.

The auctioneer knew he had his work cut out for him. "Now gentlemen, hear me out on this one. This family's owner has fallen on hard times. That's the only reason he would let go of this fine collection..."

Carrie felt her stomach turn. They were being discussed as if they were no more than animals!

"I promised the man I would do my best to keep this family together. That's why they're all up here. Jessie here is a fine butler. His wife, Hannah, is a great little cook. Their children are still young — just two, four and six. The oldest is already helping in the house. They are all highly intelligent, gentlemen. They've never given a bit of trouble to their master." The auctioneer peered around at the crowd. "Who will start the bidding at four thousand dollars?"

Disbelieving laughter erupted from all over the room.

"Thirty-eight hundred?"

"Who you kidding?" someone yelled mockingly.

The auctioneer plowed on. "Thirty-five hundred?"

Dead silence and hostile gazes met his efforts. Many men turned away to talk with their neighbors.

"Split 'em up! That's the only way you're going to get rid of them. I got my eye on that woman but I don't want the rest of them." The cold words came from a coarsely dressed man with a wad of tobacco set in his cheek. He turned and let loose with a long spit into a handy spittoon.

"Yeah! Split them up!" The chorus rose around the building.

The auctioneer shrugged his shoulders. His expression said he had tried, but was willing to accept the inevitable.

Carrie could feel the tears welling in her eyes as she watched the look of helpless fear and pain consume the small family.

"Who will start the bidding for Jessie at one thousand dollars?" Once more the building filled with shouts and calls. "Sold! For eighteen hundred dollars to Mark Simmons."

The auctioneer's attempt to sell the woman with all her children was met with the same empty silence as before. Shaking his head with frustration, he yelled out. "Who will take the woman with *any* of her children?"

"I'll take the woman with her oldest kid. I don't want any more of them!" A few nods accompanied the shouted statement.

"Alright, gentlemen," the auctioneer said in a defeated tone. "Who will start the bidding at five hundred dollars?"

Carrie watched helplessly as the auction building erupted with bids once more. As she watched, Hannah lifted her dark eyes and met her own squarely. The mute appeal was more than Carrie could stand. She made no effort to brush away the tears flowing down her cheeks. She felt completely powerless to do anything to help this poor woman who was about to lose almost all of her family.

"Sold! For nine hundred and fifty dollars to Mr. Stephen Manning."

Hannah's remaining children were sold individually for three hundred dollars apiece. The whole family was led separately from the bidding room, Hannah crying out as her children reached for her and were jerked away.

Carrie couldn't breathe. She turned and stumbled from the building, fighting against the sickness and dizziness threatening to overcome her. Once outside she leaned against a lamppost and drew deep lungfuls of air. She was dimly aware that there were still tears running down her cheeks. Visions of Hannah being led from the room, crying for her babies, rose up in her mind and threatened to engulf her.

The soft spring air helped her regain control. Finally she became aware of her surroundings. Passersby were staring at her curiously. Miles, with a carefully blank look, was standing motionless nearby.

"I want to leave here, Miles."

He nodded and fell in place beside her as they slowly walked up the street. Gone was the magic of the day. Carrie felt as if she had been delivered a severe kick to her stomach. They were almost to the Capitol building before she found her voice. "Miles... It was—oh, it was horrible! I'm sorry I made you take me in there."

Miles remained silent.

"Miles. How could they separate that family? How could they do that?" She knew she was bordering on tears once more.

Miles shrugged. "It happens, Miss Carrie." His voice was tired.

"Does it happen often?" Carrie's thoughts were coming back into focus, and with them, the barrage of questions she had been trying to force down for weeks.

"Often enough."

"I'm glad my father doesn't do things like that," she said gratefully. "I can never imagine him splitting up a family like that."

Miles stared ahead.

Carrie turned to look at him, realization dawning in her mind. "It happens, doesn't it, Miles? My father sells slaves and splits up families?"

"Ain't my place to be answering questions like that, Miss Carrie."

Carrie stared up at him. Somewhere from deep in her heart she began to realize what an impossible conversation this was for Miles. He may be her lifelong friend, but he was also her slave. He belonged to her daddy. Miles would have to watch every word that came out of his mouth. She didn't know where her sudden understanding was coming from, but it was there. "I'm sorry, Miles. I won't ask you any more questions."

"Thank you, Miss Carrie."

Carrie and her father were seated at the table. Both were unusually quiet, Carrie deep in her thoughts about the auction. For the second time, Thomas checked his watch.

"Have you somewhere to be, Father?"

Thomas looked up. "What?" He looked at the watch in his hand. "No, I don't have to be anywhere."

Carrie watched him closely, wondering what she had said that prompted the spark of laughter in his eyes. "Then why are you looking at your watch?"

"Is there something wrong with a man wanting to know what time it is?"

Carrie, relieved to be distracted from her own heavy thoughts, willingly entered into the game. "There is when I know good and well you are hiding something."

"Think you know me well, do you daughter?"

"I don't *think*. I know. What's the big secret?"

"I'm sorry I'm a few minutes late."

Carrie gasped as the deep voice she had been dreaming of sounded behind her back. She whirled around, a glad smile on her lips. "Robert Borden! What are you doing here?"

Robert looked at her father. "You didn't tell her you invited me to join you for dinner?"

"Guilty," Thomas replied, smiling. Then he turned to Carrie. "I ran into Robert in the Capitol Square this morning. He has plans to be in town for a few days so I asked him to join us."

Carrie was glad to see her friend. "When did you return from Charleston?"

"Just this morning. I ran into your father when I was out for a stroll to stretch my legs after the long train ride." He seemed emboldened by her open welcome. "May I take you for a walk around the city after we have eaten?"

Carrie's quick glance at her father noted his approval. "I'd love to." Maybe Robert could help her sort through the confusion in her heart.

SIXTEEN

"What's wrong wid you, girl? You been jumpy as a spring toad all night." Rose flushed under her mama's scrutiny. She should have known better than to come for dinner tonight. She had never been able to hide things from her mama. She cast in her mind for something to say, but Sarah saved her the trouble.

"Oh, don't even bother to come up with some purty somethin' to say. I know a girl holdin' a secret when I see one." Sarah laughed at the look on Rose's face. She grew serious as she walked over and put a gentle hand on her daughter's shoulder. "My heart be tellin' me you're gonna be doin' somethin' right dangerous. You be careful, girl."

Rose nodded. "I will." She knew it was useless to rebut what her mama was saying. She had never been able to keep secrets from her. "Mama..."

"Shush, Rose. You ain't got to tell me nothin'," Sarah said firmly. "You just be careful. I don't know what I'd do if somethin' was to happen to you." Moving over to the fire, she picked up her Bible. "Let's just sit fer a spell."

Rose nodded gratefully. In truth, that was all she wanted. She needed to sit still and find comfort in quiet. She needed time to listen to her heart and to gain courage for what she was about to do. The shadows lengthened in the tiny cabin, the silence marred only by Sarah rising to throw another log on the fire. The days were warm, almost hot now, but the nights still had a cool edge that welcomed a flickering flame. Rose felt herself relaxing under the spell of her mama's home.

"It be time now, Rose."

Rose started and peered at her Mama. "How do you know it's time for something, Mama?" Had someone told the secret she had hugged so closely for two weeks?

That was impossible. No one knew but herself. It was safer that way.

Sarah just shrugged. "Get on with ya, girl," she said softly. "You don't want to be late. But befores you go, come on over here and hug your old mama."

Rose wrapped her arms around her wordlessly, drawing from the quiet strength and love flowing from her eyes. "I love you, Mama."

"And I love you. Now git on wid you."

Mystified, Rose did as she was told and moved to the door. She looked back to see Sarah bending her head. The sight of her mama praying gave her renewed courage. She stepped out of the cabin and quietly melted into the shadows. When she was sure she was alone, she soundlessly merged into the woods. Once concealed, she began to walk rapidly, *away* from the direction where her students would soon be converging for school.

Rose moved swiftly. It was important she get to the appointed meeting place early. It would give her a better chance of knowing whether the whole arrangement was an elaborate hoax. Her footsteps slowed as she approached the bend of the road coming into Cromwell Plantation. At least she didn't have to worry about Adams. Cromwell was gone and she knew the overseer would be using the time to get rip-roaring drunk. Someone here would pay the next day, but for now she had no fear he would be lurking in the shadows somewhere. She settled herself in a dense thicket of brush and crouched, listening quietly.

Rose had waited maybe twenty minutes when she heard the sound of approaching hoofbeats. She slunk further back into the bushes and peered out to see who was coming. Yes, it was him. Jamison appeared to be alone, but she was in no hurry to reveal herself. She would wait a while longer. If others were with him, they would reveal themselves. She waited for what seemed like an eternity. Then, finally confident he was alone, she stood and stepped from her hiding place into the road.

Jamison looked up and started, almost falling from his saddle.

"Welcome. I am a friend of a friend," Rose said, giving the code he had directed in the note.

Jamison smiled and dismounted. "Hello. I'm glad to see you." He peered closely at Rose. "You're the girl who gave me the note, aren't you?"

Rose nodded. "My name is...."

An upheld hand stopped her. "It's best if I don't know you for now. There's time for that later. Secrecy is of the utmost importance."

Rose nodded. "Everyone is waiting. Follow me." Jamison led his horse a ways into the woods and tied him securely to a branch. Rose answered his unasked question. "I will bring you back to your horse."

Jamison nodded silently and fell in behind her. They followed a trail only Rose could see for about ten minutes. She had taken every possible minute to scope out the area so things would go smoothly. Suddenly, Rose came to a stop and turned to him. "I am leaving you here for now. The others do not know I have someone with me. I wanted to make sure you were really coming before I told them." Her words were spoken in a low whisper. "I shall return for you soon," she said as she turned away.

"I'm sorry I'm late." Rose said as she stepped into the clearing.

"I thought you be not coming." Sadie exclaimed.

Rose held up her hand before anyone else could say anything. "We have company tonight." She smiled as several peered into the darkness behind her. "I asked him to wait a ways back." She took a deep breath. "Mr. Jamison is with me."

Shocked expressions surrounded her.

"You mean, Mr. Jamison of the Underground Railroad?" Jasmine gasped.

"The same," Rose agreed, smiling. "I made contact with him two weeks ago. I didn't want to say anything in case he didn't show up. I'd like to bring him over now."

The faces surrounding her remained stunned, but heads began nodding. All but Moses, who was watching her carefully. "You want me to come with you, Rose?"

She smiled at him gratefully. "No, thank you, Moses. I'll be right back. He's not far."

Jamison looked around at the circle of eager faces peering at him. "You say y'all meet on a regular basis for school?" He was amazed.

"Yessir," Jasmine offered shyly. "Miss Rose be teaching us how to read so that when we be free we's can do somethin' with ourselves."

"And can you read?" Jamison asked the girl.

"Yessir, I sure can." she proclaimed eagerly. "Just in the last couple of weeks all them letters started to come together and make sense to me. I read old Sarah some out of her Bible last night." The pride in the girl's voice was unmistakable.

Jamison smiled warmly in the firelight. "Good for you." He wanted to find out more about each of them, but he knew time was limited. "How many are in your school, Rose?"

"Fifteen, Mr. Jamison. One of them isn't with us tonight. He's with Master Cromwell in Richmond."

"Fifteen. Hmm..."

Rose broke into his thinking. "They might not all be going with you, Mr. Jamison."

"How many?" he asked. "It can be worked out to transport all of them to freedom, Rose. It has been done before."

Rose shrugged. "Just tell everyone what you have to say. Each person will make their own decision."

Jamison nodded, eyeing her closely. He turned to the faces encircling him and smiled again. "I come to you as a conductor of the Underground Railroad. We have helped thousands of slaves make their way to freedom. We do it because we believe all men are created equal. One is not meant to be owned by another. There is a vast network set in place to help us accomplish this. You will not be told everything in advance, but the question you must all ask yourselves is whether you can trust me. You will be putting your life in my hands. Only I will know what the next step is and many times that will change without my knowing it ahead of time. The Underground Railroad has been successful because we have worked in secret." Jamison stopped and looked around. "I will not lie about the dangers involved. There are many. There are some, in spite of our best efforts, who have been caught and returned to captivity."

Jasmine shuddered and wrapped her arms more tightly around her body. Jamison understood. The wrath of owners and overseers when their slaves were captured during an escape attempt was something to be terrified of. He gave her a warm smile and continued. "In spite of the dangers, there is freedom waiting for you. Thousands who once labored under the bondage of slavery are now free. They are free to live their own lives and make their own decisions—free to marry and have children, knowing they will never have to be separated."

"How difficult has the Fugitive Slave Act made your work, Mr. Jamison?"

Jamison stared at Rose. "How do you know about that, Rose?"

Rose shrugged. "I have my sources. I do a lot of reading." She looked around the fire at her friends. "I think it's something you should know about before you make your decision. The Fugitive Slave Act of 1850 makes any federal marshal or other official who does not arrest a runaway slave liable to a fine of one thousand dollars. If you're caught you won't have a trial by jury, and you won't be able to testify on your behalf. Anybody caught helping a runaway slave by providing food or shelter is subject to six months' imprisonment and a one-thousand-dollar fine. Officers who capture a fugitive slave are entitled to a bonus or promotion for their work."

Jamison smiled in admiration but hastened to calm the fresh fear he saw on the faces around him. "The Fugitive Slave Act has made our job more difficult in some ways," he admitted. "But in other ways it has made it easier. So many people were angered by the government's attempts to haul the poor slaves back into servitude even after they had escaped to freedom, that scores of volunteers have been added to the network. You will find many people who, angered by the injustice of the laws, simply ignore them."

Rose nodded, obviously relieved. "What will be the destination of those who decide to escape?"

"Canada," Jamison responded immediately. "It is the safest for now. There are no laws in Canada to return slaves.

"Where is Canada?" Jasmine asked eagerly. "Be it more than a day from here?"

Jamison smiled kindly. Slaves had no idea of geography. How could they? They had lived a life of enforced ignorance. Their masters knew ignorance bred fear and fear bred obedience.

"Yes, Jasmine. It is more than a day from here. In fact, it could take weeks and perhaps months to reach Canada. We never know how long a trip will take. They're all different."

The whole group gasped in surprise. But Rose just watched, and listened.

"How we gonna get there, Mr. Jamison?" Sadie's voice, sharp and clear, rang out in the clearing. She had obviously made her decision.

"I can't tell you that for sure. The plan now is to take you over land. You'll be walking some, riding some, being hidden in wagons... Whatever it takes to move you from one station to the other. All along the way you will find wonderful people who want nothing more than to help you escape to freedom." He smiled at the looks of stunned amazement surrounding him.

"People really do things like that for ole' slaves?" Jasmine asked incredulously.

"You're not '*ole slaves*,'" Jamison said firmly. "You are people. Just as human as I am— with dreams, hopes, and a future meant to be lived in freedom."

The entire group sat up a little straighter as his words pierced the walls they had built around their hearts and minds.

"How many of you will I be carrying to freedom?" Jamison asked.

Rose stepped forward. "When do you plan on the escape happening?"

Jamison shrugged. "That's pretty much up to you. I will take you when you're ready. Once I know a date, I will arrange everything."

Rose nodded. "I need time to talk with my school. Do you mind if I take you back into the woods for a little ways while we discuss this?"

Jamison smiled. "Whatever you say, Rose." He allowed sternness to settle over his features as he looked at the group. "Another thing you have to know. If you decide to go, there is no turning back. You can't decide you're too afraid to make it to freedom and try to return. It is too dangerous for those with you and would jeopardize the safety of all other Underground Railroad passengers."

Sadie voiced the question all of them were silently asking. "What happens if someone tries to come back?"

Jamison smiled sadly. "Let's just say it doesn't happen." He turned to Rose. "I'll return when you're ready. Let's go."

Much murmuring could be heard when Rose stepped back into the clearing.

"Is he a good man, Miss Rose?" Jasmine asked eagerly as soon as she saw her.

Rose sat down quietly. "What do you think, Jasmine?"

The girl didn't hesitate. "I think he be a good man. He has eyes I can trust."

Rose nodded. "What *you* believe is what's important. But for the record, I agree with you. My instincts say he can be trusted." Then she looked around, making eye contact with each student and friend. "This is the chance many of you have been waiting for. Now each of you has to decide what you really want. Escape isn't going to be easy. You heard Mr. Jamison. It could take weeks, maybe months of being a fugitive until you reach Canada. Once you get there, things might be hard." She softened her stern tone and smiled. "But you'll be free. *Free...*" She allowed the word to flow caressingly into the night air. The very sound of it beckoned and called to those who had spent their whole lives being used as objects for someone else's gain.

Jasmine spoke up eagerly. "I be going to get on that Underground Railroad for sho. Ain't nothing goin' to keep *me* from being free."

Sadie, sitting next to her, spoke quietly. "I aim to be on board, too. I'm determined that sometime during my time here on earth, I gonna be free."

Silence fell on the clearing for several minutes. Then a soft voice broke into the stillness. "I reckon I'm going to pass up my ride this time."

Rose said nothing, just waited for Coral to finish speaking. She wasn't surprised. Coral was twenty-three and had spent all of her living years on Cromwell Plantation. As far as Rose knew, she had never been beyond the perimeter of the property.

Jasmine couldn't stand it. "But why, Coral?" she burst out. "Don't you know this is our big chance? There may never be another conductor come our way."

Coral shrugged her ample shoulders. "Being a slave ain't so bad. I got me a warm place to sleep and plenty 'nuff to eat." She paused and looked to Rose for support. "This be my home."

Rose smiled gently. "It's alright, Coral. Everybody has to make their own decision." In truth, she was incapable of understanding the way Coral felt. Rose had lived, dreamed, and hoped for freedom for so long. She couldn't imagine having the chance and giving it up because the old way of life was more comfortable. But her mama had taught her to accept people where they were. Her mama's words rang in her ears just as if she were standing there. *You can't do people's thinkin' and feelin' for dem, Rose. Some folks you ain't neber gonna figure out—you just got to accept them where they be. Dere ain't no way to get inside a person's head and figure out what makes them be the way they be. You just got to accept them.*

Jamison was beginning to worry. It was too dark to see his watch face, but he was sure he had been leaning against this tree for almost an hour. He was not an outdoorsman. The myriad of night noises did nothing but intensify the sweat beading on his brow. Should he walk back to the clearing? Would he find anyone there? He laughed at himself for his doubts. Rose could be trusted. She would not leave him here. He could not explain why he was so confident—he just was. He wiped the sweat from his brow and tried once more to relax.

Earlier, as he had waited out on the inky road for Rose, he had imagined many things. His greatest fear was that someone would betray his activities as an Underground Railroad conductor. He had heard plenty of stories to justify his fear— conductors being run out of their houses, paying high fines to the court, being ostracized by the community. Some conductors had even given their lives to help slaves escape. He knew the risks. He had made the decision to help no matter what, but it didn't stop the cold sweat from running down his back.

Jamison thought through the careful escape plans. He would find out tonight how many of the Cromwell slaves were ready to lay their lives on the line for freedom. He tried to breathe normally as he waited. Tense business situations he could handle, but this... This was totally different. He felt as if he were cast adrift from everything comfortable and thrown into the vast unknown.

His thoughts turned to Rose. She was beautiful as well as intelligent. Her letter to him was articulate and clear. He sincerely hoped she would be part of this group. Instinctively, he knew she would be a good leader.

"You can come back now." Rose emerged from the shadows as she spoke. "I'm sorry you had to wait so long."

Jamison struggled to his feet. "That's quite all right. How many of the slaves will you be bringing with you, Rose?"

Rose closed her eyes briefly, trying to shut out the pain his question had caused. "I won't be one of your passengers, Mr. Jamison."

"What?" Jamison stopped and looked at her in astonishment. "Why not?"

Rose started to shrug nonchalantly and then stopped herself. This was a man who understood the value of freedom. She turned and faced him. Just enough light filtered through the limbs from the waning moon to illuminate them. "There is nothing I would love more than to be free, but I can't be one of your passengers, Mr. Jamison."

"This is your chance, Rose."

Rose nodded. "I know. And I know I may never get another one, but I made a vow a long time ago that I would never leave my mama. Her first children and husband were killed in Africa when they captured her to make her a slave. My daddy was sold when I was less than a month old. I love my mama. She has had too many losses. I won't be another one."

"Bring her with you," Jamison urged.

Rose shook her head sadly. "She is too old. She would never make it. No," she said firmly. "I will stay here with her. Someday I may get another chance at freedom."

Her effort to conceal her grief and regret brought tears to Jamison's eyes. He reached out and laid a hand gently on her arm. "You're a brave girl, Rose. I'm sure another chance will come."

Rose shrugged and forced a smile. "In the meantime, you have a group waiting for you. There are eight of them. Miles may make nine, but I won't know until he returns."

"The big man. Is he coming?" Jamison hoped so. "His size and strength could come in handy."

Rose frowned as she shook her head. "No." She was sure she had not hidden her surprise very well when Moses had simply stated that he wouldn't be takin' the train right now. She knew his dream to be free and how much he wanted to find his mama and sisters. Why was he not going? She didn't understand what was holding him here. Didn't he know he should get away from Adams while he had the chance?

"But..."

"I don't know why, Mr. Jamison. He just said he wouldn't be catching the train right now." Her tone didn't invite questions. "Time is short. We need to go back now."

"Lead the way, Rose," Jamison said, his voice suddenly heavy. "One more question, Rose. Do the others know you're not going to be with them?"

"No," she said fiercely as she whirled to look up at him. "And I don't want them to know. It will only make them more scared. This is their chance. I don't want them to lose it. They'll find out the night I bring them to meet you. Not before."

It didn't take long to firm up the tiny details of the plan that the slaves were allowed to know. Jamison would meet them at the same bend in the road where he had met Rose, two months from today.

Jamison looked surprised. "Two months?"

Rose nodded firmly. "The ones coming with you need more help with their reading and writing. We'll work extra hard for the next two months." She hesitated. "Is that okay? You did say we could set the time didn't you?" Suddenly she was scared her group might miss their chance.

"It's fine, Rose," Jamison assured her.

As usual, Rose and Moses were the last to leave the clearing. The others had waited, talking excitedly while she took Jamison back to his horse, before they dispersed to their cabins. Moses was comfortable in the woods now and didn't need her to lead him back, but he was always still there when the clearing emptied.

"Did you tell Jamison you weren't going with the rest?"

Rose looked up at Moses sharply. "What makes you think I'm not going?"

Moses looked at her steadily. "You're not are you?"

Rose's eyes fell before his discerning gaze. Mutely she shook her head.

"Be it because of your mama?"

"I can't leave her, Moses. I'm all she has. I know she would tell me to go. She would never want me to pass up a chance for freedom." She caught her breath. "I can't leave her. I love her too much. She has lost too much already." Rose couldn't stop the trail of tears running down her face.

Moses took one of her hands gently. "I knew you wouldn't leave your mama, Rose."

Rose gazed into his compassionate face. "I can't," she whispered. She made no protest when Moses wrapped his strong arms gently around her quivering body, and gratefully leaned into his strength. She was amazed at how good it felt. She was used to being the strong one. Suddenly she looked up into his face. "What about you, Moses? Why aren't you going? What about your dream to be free and come back for your family? Why are you giving it up?" She suspected she knew the answer.

Moses tipped her head up so that he could look down into her tear-filled eyes. "I got me some dreams to make come true here, first," he said gently. He took her hand and led her from the clearing.

Rose followed him, her sorrow mixing with a tingly feeling coursing through her body. She was too tired to figure it out. The feel of her small hand engulfed with his giant one was a sensation she wanted to simply enjoy.

SEVENTEEN

"Make me a promise, Carrie."

Carrie looked up at Robert curiously. "And what promise would that be?"

"Promise me we don't have to say one word about politics tonight."

Carrie laughed merrily. "You will get no argument from me on that one, kind sir. I am sick to death of it."

Robert smiled down at her. "I'm glad to hear it. At this moment I am walking in Richmond with the most beautiful girl I know and I'd simply like to be able to enjoy it."

Carrie, blushing wildly, kept her eyes glued to the ground in front of her. She simply didn't know what to say. She had always kept boys at arm's length. There had been too many other things that interested her more. Now, this situation seemed over her head. Desperately, she tried to regain the easy confidence that had come with the decision they would be simply friends. Why would her heart not cooperate with her head? The silence stretched between them.

"I'm sorry. I didn't mean to make you uncomfortable."

The genuine remorse in Robert's voice gave her courage. She looked up quickly and tried to smile naturally. "It's quite alright. I'm sorry. I just didn't know what to say."

Robert smiled gently. "Thank you is appropriate."

Carrie blushed again, but her gaze was steady. "Thank you, Robert."

"Good. Now that we have established that I am with the most beautiful woman I know in the city I love most, we can get on with the night." Robert laughed loudly as

Carrie blushed brighter. "I'm sorry. That was mean." This time his voice held no remorse.

Carrie, gaining confidence, said, "So, tell me how the Convention went."

Robert pulled back in protest. "You promised."

"And your behavior seems to make promises invalid," she retorted.

"You win," Robert sighed. "I have been properly put in my place."

Carrie laughed at the impudent look on his face. She doubted Robert would ever be *put in his place.* She was quite sure he didn't know the meaning of the words. Suddenly, she was enormously glad to be strolling the streets of Richmond with him. "Where are we going?"

"Are you up for a long walk?"

"Why, yes," she responded, her interest immediately piqued.

"I thought we would walk up to Church Hill and see the lights of the city. If we hurry we might even catch the sunset."

Carrie quickened her pace. "I hope you can keep up with me."

Robert said nothing as he lengthened his strides to match her own.

Carrie gave a sigh of happiness as the late afternoon air caressed her. Fragrant flowers lent a perfume that mixed pleasantly with the smell of tobacco permeating the city. The sky was crystal clear, with the exception of a low band of clouds on the horizon that promised a glorious sunset. It seemed as if the whole city was out to celebrate this gorgeous spring day. Activity surrounded the pair as they walked rapidly down Broad Street. Women dressed in every color of the rainbow strolled with their servants close by. Carriages jockeyed for position in the afternoon parade. Horses pranced proudly along, completely ignoring the clanking and clanging of trains at the depot. Elegantly dressed gentlemen ambled along, either deep in conversation or trying to pretend they weren't gawking at the surrounding ladies.

"It's wonderful, isn't it?"

"The city?" Robert asked.

Carrie nodded.

"It is wonderful," he agreed enthusiastically, "but there is nothing like Oak Meadows. I can stand, and even enjoy, all this busyness for a few days, but I'm always ready to get back home to the beautiful peace and quiet. After all the time I spent in Charleston, I will admit I've had my fill."

Carrie nodded thoughtfully. "I've never gotten to stay in the city long enough to know if I would grow tired of it." She grinned up at him. "I'd love the opportunity to find out, however." She stopped abruptly in the middle of the sidewalk and turned to Robert. "I almost forgot. I'm going to have my opportunity soon."

"What do you mean?"

"Why, I'm going to Philadelphia. For a whole month!"

"A month?" Robert echoed, staring at her.

Carrie nodded. "I'm going with my friends Natalie Heyward and Sally Hampton." She continued to walk while she filled him in on all the details she knew. "Robert, this means I can go to the medical school myself. I might actually discover I can attend school there." She knew her face was glowing.

Robert smiled down at her. "That's wonderful, Carrie." Then he paused, looking off as if he was thinking deeply.

"What is it, Robert?"

"You'll be there in July?" She nodded. "I have a very close friend in Philadelphia. A journalist by the name of Matthew Justin. We were at the university together. I'm sure he would be willing to show you around the campus and introduce you to some people."

Carrie beamed. "That would be wonderful." She could hardly believe how fast everything was happening. Less than a month ago she had despaired of ever finding a way to leave the plantation. Now the road seemed to be wide before her. In her happiness, it was easy to ignore the dark clouds descending on the country.

Little more was said as they tackled the Broad Street incline that would take them to Church Hill. The sun dropping lower on the horizon made them increase their pace. Carrie felt a warm glow as she walked rapidly beside Robert. She knew countless people who would frown at their unrefined race up the hill. Let them disapprove. She was having a wonderful time.

Carrie was sweating in a very unfeminine way when they reached the top of the hill. She loved the two and three-story brick homes overlooking the city. Many wealthy people had picked the elegant heights of Church Hill for the view it afforded them of Richmond. She started to turn around, but Robert reached out and took her arm to stop her.

"No fair looking yet. We're not where I'm taking you."

Carrie smiled up into his laughing eyes. "Lead on, sir."

Instead of removing his hand from her arm, Robert reached down for her hand and tucked it firmly into the crook of his arm. "Do you mind?"

Carrie merely shook her head, speechless as she attempted to understand the wild flutter of feelings coursing through her. She concentrated on keeping up with Robert, aware she was not really seeing anything as she stared straight ahead.

"Now you can look."

Robert had stopped. She forced her thoughts to come back and looked up. "Why, it's St. John's Church," she exclaimed. "It's one of my favorite places in the city. Father brought me here several years ago. I've always remembered it." The church was just the way she recalled it—a white clapboard building with tall windows lining the sides of the sanctuary. The stately church was surrounded by a beautiful, though somber, cemetery. Her father had felt it very important that Carrie visit the place where Patrick Henry gave his famous *Give me liberty, or give me death* speech at the beginning of the Revolutionary War.

She was staring up at the church when Robert took her gently by the shoulders and turned her around. "I meant that you can look over the city now. You're about to miss the sunset."

"Oh!" she exclaimed in delight. The band of clouds hanging on the horizon earlier had taken on a life of their own as the sun slowly lowered in the western sky. The fluffy cumulus had exploded into an orchestra of vivid orange and purple hues, catching the waning sunrays and sending them shooting off into a million shafts of glimmering light. The buildings of the city stood out in stark contrast, their manmade grandeur suddenly diminished in the face of such an awesome display of grandeur.

Carrie quietly absorbed the beauty exploding before her. She was aware of Robert by her side but knew no words were necessary. He would know what this display was doing to her. The surety of her knowledge caused her heart to beat even faster. She had never credited any man other than her father with being able to understand her. Right now she quite simply didn't understand herself. She tried to lose herself in the sunset again, standing quietly until the bank of clouds had once more turned dark. Only then did she look at Robert. "Beautiful."

"Beautiful, indeed," Robert murmured.

Carrie blushed when she realized he wasn't speaking of the sunset. "May we sit down for a while?" she asked suddenly. The beauty of the sunset had somehow accentuated the cruel horror of the auction house. She was yearning to talk to Robert about it. Surely he would understand how she felt.

Robert responded by sinking down on the front step of the church.

"Robert?" Carrie's voice was troubled.

Robert turned immediately. "What is it, Carrie?"

Carrie knew by the tone of his voice he understood something was troubling her. She smiled at him gratefully. "I've needed to talk with someone about today…" Her voice faltered. Robert sat quietly and waited. "I went to a slave auction today," she finally stated.

"A slave auction" Robert exclaimed. "How in the world did you end up there?"

Carrie shrugged. "I was walking down Franklin Street with my servant, Miles—"

"He allowed you to go into such a place?" Robert interrupted with flashing eyes. "He shall be flogged!"

Carrie turned to him, outraged. "Nothing of the sort will happen. Miles tried to talk me out of it. I made him go with me." Her anger was mixed with confusion. Why was Robert talking about flogging? Surely he didn't do things like that?

Robert took a deep breath. "I'm sorry." He leaned forward to gaze into her eyes. "Did someone attempt to harm you?"

"No," Carrie said hastily. "Nothing like that happened at all." She shuddered. "It was just so horrible." She could tell Robert was confused.

In halting words, Carrie relived the experience for him. Tears flowed freely down her face when she told of how Hannah had been separated from her husband and all but one of her children. "It was horrible, Robert. It made me feel sick inside. I've been troubled about it ever since." She wiped her eyes, stared off at the darkening outline of the city, and waited for Robert to respond. The silence stretched between them.

Carrie finally looked up. Dismay filled her heart at the uncomprehending look on Robert's features. Nothing was said for long minutes as she stared into his eyes. She had wanted so much for him to understand.

Robert finally broke the uncomfortable silence with a low laugh. "Well, at least you know to stay away from Franklin Street now."

Carrie turned from him in frustration.

Robert shook his head and rubbed his hand over his eyes. "I don't know what to say, Carrie," he admitted.

Carrie turned to him with a pleading look. "You can't possibly think it was okay for the family to be separated like that?"

Robert shrugged. "They're slaves," he said simply.

"But they're people!" Tears came to Carrie's eyes as Hannah's beseeching face filled her mind.

"Not in the way you're thinking."

Carrie turned to Robert, angry, but unsure of the source of her feelings. "Whatever do you mean?" Not even her father had ever said slaves weren't people. She had hoped Robert's years in the North would make him a little more sympathetic.

Robert struggled to explain. "They inhabit bodies the way we do, but they're not people like you and I. They're a lower order of species. Their destiny is to serve those who have greater favor with God."

"Meaning white people."

Robert nodded. "Without our supervision, the slaves of the South would revert back to the primitive way they lived in Africa. For what it is worth, being slaves has raised them to a slightly higher level. They should be grateful."

This was nothing Carrie hadn't heard all her life, yet everything in her was rising up to fight it. "Would you be grateful if you were suddenly ripped away from your wife and children? Sold to the highest bidder?"

Robert shook his head and his tone became condescending. "They're *slaves*, Carrie. They are simply fulfilling their destiny. It is necessary to do what we must—all of us. Destiny is a hard taskmaster, even when quietly and philosophically obeyed. When resisted and denounced it becomes a tyrant that tramples under foot."

"Those are my father's words." Her mind traveled back to the night she had first met Robert.

"And very true ones," Robert said firmly.

Carrie stared into the distance. She couldn't ignore the raging of her heart. "I'm questioning everything I have ever believed," she said slowly. "I don't see slaves as animals to be sold off. I don't believe they are people on a lower order than us..." Her voice trailed off as she envisioned the faces of the Cromwell slaves. She knew the shine of intelligence in their eyes. She knew the abilities they possessed and utilized for her father.

"It's fine to try and make the world into what you want it to be, Carrie," Robert replied, "but it doesn't change reality. The slave is no better than an animal. We need them like we need our horses and the pigs on the plantation. We need them because they serve a purpose. But that's all. Slaves quite simply aren't people."

Carrie turned and stared. She hardly recognized the face twisted with anger, or the voice hardened with hate. She could think of nothing to say. She simply stared and made no attempt to hide the revulsion on her face.

Robert whitened under her gaze. Then he jumped up from his place on the stairs and began to pace back and forth on the sidewalk in front of the church. He swung to face her. "You asked me one time what happened to my father. I'm going to tell you."

Carrie was a little frightened by the desperation in his voice, but she sat quietly and watched him.

Robert turned his back on her and stared over the city. "I was eleven years old when there was a slave revolt in Goochland. A number of slaves from every plantation tried to escape. Some of them got away. Most of them were caught in the swamps, confused and lost. They didn't stand a chance against the dogs and the superior intelligence of the overseers and owners." The contempt in his voice chilled the night air. "Barns were burned and property was destroyed. It was late at night when the leaders of the revolt were captured and brought back. There was only one thing to do with them. Kill them. Make sure they could never lead another revolt."

Robert paused, remembering. "My father didn't know I had followed them into the woods. I was hiding behind some trees so I could see what happened. They brought the ringleader up to the tree where the rope was hanging. He was so big—much bigger than my father. He was also sullen and arrogant, and it made my father angry. I saw him go up to him once they had the rope around his neck. They had broken that nigger's arms..." His voice trailed off as the pain of his memories seemed to engulf him.

Carrie listened with wide eyes, sickened by the thought of that slave standing there with broken arms waiting to die. She was also filled with sorrow at the pain she heard in Robert's voice. She leaned forward to hear his next words delivered in little more than a whisper.

"My father was standing in front of him with a knife when that nigger lunged off the platform. Somehow…" Tears choked his words now. "Somehow, that nigger got the knife and killed my father. Came right down on top of him in the clearing. It took two men to get him off." Sobs racked his body for a long moment. "I never told anyone what I saw. It was bad enough for my mother. Her husband was dead and nothing was going to bring him back." Robert struggled for control, but could not hide the hatred in his voice. "Don't expect me to feel sorry for the niggers. I didn't ask for them to be brought to this country, but they're here. I'll treat them well because financially it makes sense. But I'll never see them as anything but the animals they are."

Carrie stared at his rigid back. She knew she had to say something. "Robert," she began softly, "I'm sorry about your father. That was a horrible thing to happen." She stood and moved next to where he was staring out over the city.

Slowly, Robert emerged from the past and became aware of Carrie beside him. He reached out and took her hand. She left it there, confusion jumbling her mind and heart. Long minutes passed.

"We'd better be getting back, Robert. My father will be worried."

Robert nodded. "Of course," he murmured. Then his voice strengthened. "I'm sorry to have made you listen to that story."

"Hush," Carrie interrupted. "An experience like that cannot be buried forever. I'm glad you told me."

Robert nodded slowly. The magic had flown out of their evening. They turned and headed back the way they had come.

Carrie stared out her hotel window. She had given up on sleep long ago. Her restless thoughts would afford her slumber. She and Robert had walked back to the hotel in virtual silence. Each of them had tried a couple of times to break the silence with casual conversation but had quickly realized the futility of their efforts.

Neither could find escape from the heaviness of their hearts.

Carrie sighed as she relived Robert's story of his father's death. She could only imagine the pain and terror a little boy of eleven would feel. She could clearly see the pain that still engulfed the man. Yet she could find no basis there for hatred of black people. Hatred of the one who had killed his father she could understand. The sweeping hatred of an entire race she could *not* understand. Neither could she accept it. For in acceptance, she would offer unspoken agreement with his beliefs. Where once she would have shrugged it off and gone on about the business of growing up, now she found herself staring into the reality of what it meant to be a woman—a woman who must know her own mind and heart on an issue that could divide her from the ones she loved most.

As she stared out the window, Carrie honestly faced the realization she had come to on the long walk back to the hotel. Her struggle with her beliefs about slavery could well alienate her from the ones she loved. She wasn't sure she loved Robert Borden. She knew her heart had yearned for him when they were apart and he had been the one she most wanted to talk to when she was confused. That it had blown up in her face could not be denied. The bitter reality was that she could not think of one friend who would support the way she was thinking now.

"Carrie?"

Carrie froze when her father tapped lightly on the door. He had been talking with friends when she had come in, and she had made no attempt to talk to him. She just made sure he saw her so he would know she had returned. It was no surprise he was checking on her. He knew her better than anyone. Surely he had seen the confusion and pain etched on her face when she had come in.

"Carrie?" Once again Thomas called her name softly. Then she heard his footsteps move down the hall. She loved her father but knew he wouldn't understand her right now either. Carrie groaned softly as she dropped her head into her hands. Why couldn't she just go on like before? Why did she suddenly have to question all she had ever known? She preferred her earlier years when she just rolled through every day, content simply to be a plantation owner's daughter. Why did she suddenly want more than the plantation could offer? Why couldn't she just be content? It was so easy before.

Carrie sighed again—a deep sigh wrung from the depths of her heart. No matter how much she might want it, she couldn't go back to the way she was before. Even without trying, she knew the effort would be futile. She was on this path whether she wanted it or not. She would just have to see where it would lead.

EIGHTEEN

"Good morning, dear. How are you?" Thomas peered into his daughter's eyes when she opened the door in response to his knock.

Carrie knew he was searching deeper into her heart. She summoned a bright smile. "I feel wonderful, Father! Isn't it a beautiful day? This is our last one here in Richmond. I want to make the most of it."

Thomas returned her smile but couldn't hide the puzzled look on his face.

"I'm starving. Let's go find some breakfast," Carrie said, anxious to escape his knowing eyes. Carrie knew he had come to find out what had been bothering her the night before. She saw him shake his head in confusion before he moved to catch up with her.

Carrie was not really surprised when Robert rose from a chair in the lobby to meet them. "Good morning, Robert," she said gaily. "I hope you had a good night's sleep!" *Careful,* she warned herself. *You don't want to sound too cheerful.*

Robert fell into step beside her. "Slept like a top," he said. "I was hoping you and your father wouldn't mind if I joined you for breakfast."

"Not at all," Carrie responded graciously.

Their early morning cheer was too forced and the confused look on her father's face confirmed it. Well, she was an adult. He didn't have to know everything that was going on between her and Robert. Her mutinous thoughts surprised her. *I will have a chance to talk with him later on the way home*, she thought as she took her place at the table.

Thomas ordered breakfast and turned to Robert. "Did you and your young journalist friend talk much about the upcoming Republican Convention, Robert?"

Robert shook his head. "There seemed to be enough action on the Democratic side to keep us occupied, sir. From all I hear, Seward is sure to be the Republican nominee."

Thomas nodded, his face creased with tension. "I fear that is true."

"Stop it!" Carrie, knowing her voice bordered on hysteria, managed to bring it under control with difficulty, while her father stared at her in surprise. She tried to make her tone light as she repeated her words. "Stop it, you two. Must every waking moment be spent talking politics and what is going on in this country? I'm sick of it." Visions of Louisa floated through her mind, but she pushed them back and forced a cheerful note. "I am in Richmond with the two best looking men I know. I simply refuse to have every minute of my last day here darkened with distressing talk."

Thomas exchanged glances with Robert and acquiesced graciously. "I'm sorry, Carrie. What would you like to talk about? And how would you like to spend the rest of the day?" he asked quietly.

Carrie shrugged, not sure her victory held any meaning for her. Was she not just playing a silly game? Then her body stiffened. So be it! If she was playing a game, it was surely better than the reality surrounding her at every turn. She pushed away the thought that she detested game-playing.

"Mr. Cromwell, didn't you say you wanted to go visit your friend Mr. Lind who lives north of the city?" Robert asked. He smiled broadly when Thomas nodded. "The *John Marshall* is in dock right now. I heard that it is leaving later this morning for Lynchburg. Carrie and I could take a trip on the *John Marshall* and have it drop us off at Lind's landing. All of us could come back in your carriage." He paused. "I also hear there is a new production at Metropolitan Hall tonight. I would be honored if you would accompany me, Carrie."

Carrie smiled with delight. "*The John Marshall*! Isn't that the wonderful packet boat?" Robert nodded. "And Metropolitan Hall? I've always wanted to go there." She turned to her father, excitement gleaming from her eyes. "It sounds like a wonderful plan. What do you think?"

"I agree, Carrie. You'll have a wonderful time on board. I was planning on spending the day with my friend Lind. It's important I do so in order to live up to my agreement with Governor Letcher." He pushed back from the stable and stood. "I should be leaving soon. I'll see you upriver."

The bustling port at the end of Eighth Street teemed with activity. Fashionably dressed passengers arrived at the landing both by carriage and by foot. The ticket office did a steady trade as baggage was passed up to the boat and carefully stowed by the crew.

Carrie almost danced as she made her way down the hill leading to the landing. She had decided to have a good day in spite of the turmoil boiling in her soul. "The *John Marshall*! I've heard so much about it."

Robert merely smiled at her excitement. "I'll be back in a moment with our tickets."

Carrie took the opportunity to look around. The Kanawha Canal was a marvel to her. It had first extended seven miles to afford safe passage around the Richmond Falls. Packet boats now ran daily trips between the capital city and Lynchburg, over one hundred miles away. She closed her eyes and tried to imagine what it had taken to dig such a massive canal for that long of a distance.

"Daydreaming on such a beautiful day?"

Carrie opened her eyes and smiled into Robert's teasing ones. "Not daydreaming. I'm just trying to imagine what it took to create this canal."

"Most of it done by hand, too, with pickaxe and shovel. Germans, Scots and Irish, brought over and hired to do the job, did most of the work. Along with the help of hired-out slaves." Robert turned toward the boat. "I have the tickets. Are you ready to go on board?"

Carrie followed willingly, breathing in deep draughts of fresh air. The day could not have been more perfect. There was nothing to mar the blue flawlessness of the sky. The sun was warm but promised to not be too hot. A light breeze ruffled her hair and made her full skirts sway lightly.

"All aboard!"

Carrie hurried aboard, taking in all the details of the boat. The roof of the packet boat, open to the weather, looked like a garden. At fourteen feet by ninety feet, it provided ample space for the passengers on board. Carrie knew the enclosed lower deck would be the site of supper, and would then be divided into sleeping compartments for men and women during the thirty-three hour trip. Sometime it would be fun to travel all the way to Lynchburg, but she was content for now.

"Will you be up for some dancing later, Miss Cromwell?"

"Dancing?" Carrie echoed, gazing in the direction Robert was indicating. She smiled with delight when she saw several men warming up their banjos and guitars. "How fun!"

The boat moved slowly as it was pushed under the bridge on 7th Street. Once clear of the bridge, horses were hitched to continue its slow travel until the *John Marshall* passed the crowd of boats moored near the edge of the city. Carrie laughed with delight when the horses broke into a trot and the boat responded with a lively jerk. Thrown off balance, she made no protest when Robert reached out to steady her with his hand. She merely smiled at him when he continued to let it rest on her arm. She leaned into the railing and watched as the cutwater threw up its spray. As they rounded Penitentiary Hill, she looked up and caught one last glimpse of the city before it disappeared.

Carrie turned around and noticed most of the men had drifted off into little conversation knots. Robert was watching them with a gleam in his eye. "Want to join them?"

"Not on your life," Robert responded quickly. He took Carrie by the arm and led her to a bench situated on the aft of the boat. "I'll be back with some cold lemonade in just a minute."

Carrie watched while he disappeared down the stairs that led to the lower deck, and then turned her attention to the rest of the passengers. Packet boats were still the preferred mode of travel for most well-bred Richmonders, but her father told her the reliable old boats were soon to be outdone by the railroad. Carrie knew the train was much faster, but it had none of the romanticism of the old boats. She watched as young girls and women gathered around tables for backgammon, all the time well aware of the activities of eligible young men on board. Knots of men lounged against the railing as they debated and argued.

"I tell you, if Seward is elected the whole country will fall into ruin."

Carrie frowned as bits of a conversation floated over to where she was sitting. She smiled with relief when Robert returned with a cold glass of lemonade, and reached for it eagerly. She was determined nothing was going to ruin the magic of her day. Just then, an outburst of music sounded from the foredeck.

"I think that's our signal, Miss Cromwell," Robert said as he reached for her hand and led her to the front of the deck. Minutes later, a rousing version of the Virginia reel turned the deck into a kaleidoscope of changing colors as bright dresses flashed among the figures.

"Enough!" Carrie laughed breathlessly as she grabbed Robert by the hand and led him to the railing after eight straight dances. "It's too warm out here for this."

"Ah, Miss Cromwell, you disappoint me. I thought dancing was in your soul."

"And I've always heard it is quite improper for a young lady to sweat like a horse in the presence of a young gentleman."

The bantering continued between the two as the packet boat forged up the river. Luxuriant green pastures and hills lined the shores. Trees and brush formed a veritable forest in some places and then would thin and disappear as another of the majestic James River plantations would claim its superior position on a passing hill. The sun hit high noon and began its westerly descent as the two talked.

"Lind's Landing!" the captain called.

Carrie started and laughed. "I can't believe we're already here. Look! There's my father with Mr. Lind." She smiled and looked up into Robert's eyes. "Thank you. I had a wonderful time."

Within minutes she was being ushered into the cool confines of Lind's opulent plantation manor. A servant was waiting to take her to a room where she could freshen herself. She had instructions to appear for dinner in thirty minutes.

"No talk of what we discussed this afternoon, Lind." Thomas lit his cigar and sat back in his chair. He hastened to explain when his friend looked at him, puzzled. "Carrie has about had her fill of it for now. Something is bothering her, but I'm blamed if I know what it is. For now, I'm going to give her what she wants." He paused. "We've discussed what I came to talk about anyway."

Lind laughed. "I think you misread my puzzled look. I had no intention of talking politics at the supper table. My wife would have my head. Not to mention that she wouldn't understand a word of it. I don't think women and politics mix. Do you?"

Thomas spoke smoothly, not wishing to offend his host. "Carrie has always had an interest in politics. I have seen no reason to discourage it. Many times she helps me see things more clearly."

The ringing of the dinner bell saved him from further discussion. He didn't expect his older friend to understand.

Carrie enjoyed the meal with the Linds but kept a close eye on the clock. Robert, too, watched the timepiece in his pocket, and after an hour of easy conversation, he pushed back from the table. "I'm sorry to end such a delightful meal, but if we are to make our performance tonight, we must be going."

Carrie flashed him a look of gratitude.

"Oh, are you attending a performance at the Marshall Theatre tonight?"

Robert shook his head and smiled easily at his attractive host. "Not tonight, Mrs. Lind. Our tickets are for Metropolitan Hall."

Carrie almost smiled at the slightly patronizing air she assumed. She was well aware that well-bred Virginians considered the lighter amusement of Metropolitan Hall to be somewhat below their cultured refinement. "I am quite looking forward to it, Mrs. Lind," Carrie interjected as she stood from her place at the table.

"I'm sure you are, dear." Mrs. Lind managed to keep her voice pleasant.

Carrie exchanged a conspiratorial glance with Robert and found herself feeling once again the glow of excitement that being with him brought. He was everything she had ever thought a man would be. Doubt raised its ugly head as a vision of the night before flashed in her head, but she resolutely pushed it away.

Dusk had deepened the shadows of the city. Gaslights flickered and glowed with light as Carrie and Robert rolled down the street in her father's carriage with Miles driving. She listened as Robert played tour guide.

"Metropolitan Hall used to be the First Presbyterian Church. When its congregation moved to a new building, it was bought and turned into a theater."

Carrie was content to sit quietly and listen. She was tired from her day on the river, but looked forward to the night.

"Have you ever been to a panorama?" Robert asked. Her blank look answered his question. "You're in for a treat," he grinned. "It's somewhat like a large painting that is slowly unwound. There is usually wonderful music and a lecture."

The carriage rolled to a stop, and Carrie looked up in appreciation at the smart two-story brick structure with its charming third-story cupola adorning the front. She felt the magic of the day envelope her once again as she glided up the steps at Robert's side. Admiring glances told her they made a dashing couple.

The evening passed in a haze of delight. It was easy to understand why panoramas were so popular— ancient cities, ruins, sea views, moonlight, winter and summer scenes, fire, and volcanic eruptions came to life as the music swelled around them. Lifelike scenes of midnight mass at the Milan Cathedral and Belshazzar's Feast at the court of Babylon highlighted the show. A lively lecture kept them absorbed in what they were seeing. Finally, as the last scene unfurled and the music died, Carrie reluctantly came back to the present.

"What a wonderful day," Carrie murmured as she leaned back against the carriage seat.

Just then a flurry of movement on the sidewalk drew her attention. She looked up in time to see a poorly dressed black man forced from the sidewalk by a large group of commonly dressed white laborers. He stumbled and almost fell into one of the many carriages still clogging the streets at this late hour. Carrie gasped and then breathed a sigh of relief as he regained his balance and stepped back to safety.

"Hey nigger! Don't you know the sidewalks are for white people?" one of them yelled. He stepped down from the sidewalk, his brawny height towering over the slightly built black man.

"Miles! Stop!" Carrie commanded. She sensed Robert turn to her in protest, but he didn't say anything. Carrie watched as the black man kept his eyes resolutely on the ground and began to amble off down the road.

"Hey, you!" the antagonist yelled, moving to block the other man's path. "I ain't done with you yet. You ain't showed me your pass to be out on the streets." He looked up, became aware of his audience, and took on a more swaggering tone. "Let's see the pass, nigger."

Wordlessly, the black man reached into his pockets and pulled out the demanded piece of paper. Slowly, he handed it over and waited while the larger man looked at it.

"This says you're a free man, nigger. That true?" He leered at the black man. "Yeah, well, don't be too sure you're gonna stay that way. Niggers ain't good for nothing but to be slaves." He shoved the piece of paper at him and snarled, "Get going, nigger. And stay out of my way." He watched while the man pocketed his paper and resumed his travel, careful to stay in the streets and away from the offending sidewalk. The white man looked up in triumph at his audience. Carrie fixed him with as withering of a gaze as she could manage. Discomfited the abuser looked down, muttered a curse, and then joined his friends on the sidewalk. "Let's go, boys."

Silence fell on the carriage. Carrie said nothing when Miles quietly moved the horses along without a command from her.

"Is something wrong with my daughter?"

Both Thomas and Robert stared up the steps after Carrie's retreating back. She had thanked Robert very graciously for a wonderful day but had chosen to retire to her room instead of joining the two men for a cup of hot tea.

Robert shrugged helplessly. "Just when I think I have her figured out..."

"Ah." Thomas took the younger man's arm and led him to a secluded table in the almost deserted restaurant. "There is your first mistake, my boy. Some women you may figure out. Not Carrie. She will always surprise you."

Robert nodded. "That's one of the things that intrigues me, sir." He paused for a long moment before he finally looked into Thomas's eyes. "I love your daughter, sir."

Thomas nodded and smiled gently. "It doesn't take a genius to figure that out."

"You don't mind, sir?"

Thomas laughed. "What *I* think doesn't really matter. But no, I don't mind. I think you're a fine young man." He paused. "You have your work cut out for you, though. Carrie is an independent spirit."

Robert nodded. "You don't need to tell me that. It's another one of the things I love about her..."

"But..."

"But we seem to keep butting heads on a single issue." The frustration in Robert's voice was keen. Thomas waited quietly while the younger man searched for the right words. "It's the slavery issue, Mr. Cromwell. I think your daughter is planning on becoming an abolitionist," he said dramatically.

Thomas laughed heartily. "Hardly that, Robert! My Carrie may be questioning some things, but she will ultimately come out on the side of what is right. She will understand that however unpleasant it may be at times, it is our destiny to be in control of the slaves."

"Do you really think so, sir? I have hopes she is just going through a stage." He paused for another long moment. "I hope to make her my wife someday, sir," he blurted, "but she will have to be willing to accept the condition of slavery on my plantation. That is how I have always lived, and I have no intention of changing it now."

Thomas eyed the younger man perceptively. "It could make life as a plantation owner very difficult if your wife was at odds with you over our peculiar institution," he said dryly.

Robert nodded and continued. "She has many dreams, sir. I don't know what will become of my love for her." Then he straightened and said firmly, "She's everything I've ever wanted, Mr. Cromwell."

Thomas heard the slightly desperate tone of his voice, but chose not to comment on that. His heart went out to the handsome young man sitting across from him. Thomas would listen, but he wouldn't interfere. Carrie would make up her own mind. *As she always had*, he thought wryly. He leaned across the table and abruptly changed the topic. "I bought a house today."

Robert blinked at him in surprise. "A house, sir?"

Thomas nodded. "A three-story brick on Church Hill." He answered the unspoken question in Robert's eyes. "I have promised Governor Letcher I will do all I can to help control the secessionism craze sweeping the South. I will do what I can from the plantation, but I'm sure there is going to be an increased need for me to be in Richmond. It made sense for me to buy a house."

Robert waited, watching him closely.

Thomas paused, well aware Robert hadn't bought his story. Finally he shrugged. "If there's trouble... If all this foolishness leads us into a war, I want Carrie and her mother to have a safe place to live. I'm afraid the plantation would not provide that for them."

The two men stared into their cups as they let their thoughts engulf them.

NINETEEN

Abigail met Thomas at the door with a warm kiss. "Welcome home, Thomas."

Thomas returned the kiss and held her close for a long moment.

Carrie watched them and then ran up the stairs to hug her mother. "It was wonderful, Mama! Richmond is even more beautiful than I remembered."

Abigail laughed. "I'm glad you're home. I had no desire to go along on the trip, but I missed you both." She squeezed Thomas's arm "The house seemed empty without your warm laugh, dear." The three walked arm-in-arm into the house while Carrie chattered nonstop about the last several days.

Carrie interrupted her own chatter as they entered the parlor. "Mama, I forgot to tell you the best news! I'm going to Philadelphia."

Abigail settled herself into a high wingback chair, listened intently while Carrie filled her in on the details and then looked at Thomas with raised eyebrows.

Thomas nodded, not saying anything until he had filled his pipe and had smoke curling toward the ceiling. "I spoke with Natalie's mother about it before we left Richmond. Her sister is an upstanding citizen in Philadelphia and has wanted Natalie to visit for years. I daresay they will experience everything Philadelphia has to offer. It's a wonderful opportunity."

"Indeed it is," Abigail said. "Are you sure it's safe?"

"Safe?" Carrie asked, deciding to ignore her father's earlier suggestion that the North might not welcome a wealthy, Southern plantation owner's daughter. "Why wouldn't it be safe, Mama?"

Abigail turned to Thomas. "Ten slaves ran away from the Blackwell Plantation last night." A strident note had crept into her voice. "The slave hunters are already out looking. It's those blamed abolitionists," she cried, fear and rage darkening her eyes. "They're going to turn all our people against us. Why, they might harm Carrie if she goes north. It's quite obvious she is well-to-do. They might target her as a plantation owner's daughter."

Carrie rolled her eyes and disappeared up the stairs to her room. She would let her father handle her mother's latest tantrum. Nothing was going to keep her from making that trip to Philadelphia. Not even if *she* had to run away.

"Welcome home, Miss Carrie."

The mutinous lines on Carrie's face disappeared as Rose moved forward to greet her. The two friends hugged for a moment until Rose stepped back. Carrie sensed, rather than saw, the reserve in her friend. She decided to ignore it. She had plenty of other things to think about.

"How was Richmond, Miss Carrie?" Rose stepped away and began to unload the trunk Sam had already delivered to the room.

"Richmond was wonderful." Carrie's voice lacked the enthusiasm she had greeted her mother with.

Rose looked up with a question in her eye.

Carrie shrugged. "There were many wonderful things, but there were things that troubled me as well." She was so glad to be home with Rose. She desperately needed someone to talk to. "I went to a slave auction, Rose." Rose stiffened and turned back to the trunk as Carrie described it. Her voice broke and tears filled her eyes as she recounted Hannah being separated from her family. "It was horrible, Rose! It almost broke my heart."

Finally, she noticed Rose was working steadily, her back turned. "Rose! Aren't you listening to me?"

Rose nodded. "I'm listening, Miss Carrie."

"Well, then," Carrie said in an exasperated tone, "why don't you turn around and look at me? Don't you have anything to say?"

Long moments passed as silence filled the room. Slowly, Rose turned to face her. Carrie stared at the set, impassive features in her friend's face. "How can you look like that? Don't you care what happened to those slaves?" Carrie cried.

Rose stared hard at her, then dropped her eyes, and shrugged her shoulders helplessly. "I care, Miss Carrie."

Carrie looked at her friend. She couldn't miss the trembling pain in Rose's voice and eyes. Carrie was suddenly furious with herself. "I'm sorry, Rose," she said softly. It was Rose's turn to stare. "I forgot you don't have a father because he was sold." Tears welled in Carrie's eyes. "I'm so sorry. I don't think I understood until now." She continued in a voice barely above a whisper. "I'm sorry you don't have a daddy."

Rose stood still as a statue.

Finally, Carrie looked up. "Is your mama doing okay?" When Rose nodded, she simply said, "I think I'm going to go down and visit her today."

"Mama will be happy to see you," Rose said as she turned back to finish the unpacking.

Carrie slid off Granite and handed the reins to Miles. "He's still wet from our run, but I walked back the last half mile to make sure he is cool."

Miles nodded and smiled. "You always takes good care of him, Miss Carrie. I'll make sure he gets a good groomin' and some grain."

Carrie smiled gratefully and turned toward the quarters. She had hoped her run on Granite after supper would clear her head, but the confusion and heaviness were still there. She was going where she had always gone when she was little and this confused. She was going to Sarah.

Carrie sat rigidly in the hard chair across from Sarah. Once the initial greetings had been taken care of, a deep silence had fallen over the room. Bright sunshine still danced through the open door, but Carrie was unable to enjoy the performance. She knew Sarah wouldn't hurry her, but she was impatient with her own inability to articulate her thoughts.

"Do you miss John?" she finally blurted out, looking up in time to catch the flicker of pain across the lined face.

"Yessum, I miss my John."

Carrie looked sharply into her face. She saw no sign of anger or condemnation on the peaceful features. Just quiet acceptance. "How can you stand having him gone? Knowing he was sold?"

Sarah peered deeply into Carrie's eyes and smiled gently. "You be askin' 'bout my John, but yo' heart be wantin' to know more."

Carrie's lips quirked upward in spite of her turmoil. "You always did know me a little too well."

"If you didn't want somebody to be knowin' you, you wouldn't have come to see old Sarah."

Carrie sighed. "You are right as usual, Sarah. I'm very confused right now."

Sarah nodded and settled back into her chair. "Let's be talkin' 'bout dat confusion, Miss Carrie"

Carrie looked into her caring face. "It's slavery, Sarah. I've been told all my life that it is right. Actually, I never even questioned it, until recently. Now I'm questioning all of it."

Sarah smiled again. "You be pickin' a strange one to come talk to 'bout slavery, Miss Carrie."

Carrie shook her head. "No, I'm not. Don't you see? I need to talk to someone who *is* a slave. Someone who will be honest with me." She paused. "You've always been honest with me, Sarah. Please don't stop now."

Sarah settled back in her chair and stared thoughtfully at Carrie. Finally she began to speak. "I think 'bout my John ever' day. The nights—dey be the longest tho. Don't reckon I'll ever quit wonderin' where he be—what he be doing." She shifted in her chair and leaned forward slightly. "I had to let him go, Miss Carrie. He'll always be in my heart and mind, but I had to let go the longin' or it would have plum killed me."

"How did you let it go, Sarah?"

Sarah closed her eyes briefly. "I done give my John to de Lord, Miss Carrie."

Carrie shook her head impatiently. "But aren't you angry?"

"Not no more."

"But why? What stopped you from being angry?"

Sarah smiled then—a smile of peace and victory. "De Lord done took all my anger, Miss Carrie. He washed me clean in de river." Her face glowed as she told how the Lord had met her while she was trying to take her life in the James River.

Carrie, leaning forward, soaked up every word. There was no denying the peace on the old woman's face, but still Carrie wasn't finding out what she wanted to know. When Sarah finished and sat back, Carrie sighed in frustration. "That's wonderful, Sarah." Carrie knew all about God. That wasn't what she'd come for though.

"There ain't no answers to life without God square in de middle of it, Miss Carrie." Sarah seemed to know what she was thinking.

Carrie shook her head. "Maybe," she said shortly. "What I really want to know is how you feel about slavery deep down inside. Not how you've been able to deal with it, but how you really feel about it."

Sarah turned and looked out the door. The bright sunshine was now a golden glow turning her sordid little cabin into a tiny palace. Slowly, she turned back toward Carrie. "Miss Carrie, ain't nuthin' but the truth gonna satisfy you. I ain't afraid of truth. I be afraid of what it might do to you. I ain't so sure you be ready for the truth just yet."

"I thought you told me the truth sets people free," Carrie responded.

Sarah sighed and smiled slightly. "So I did, Miss Carrie." She closed her eyes and bowed her head for a moment. Then she looked up, her eyes peaceful. "Ain't nothin' more I'd like den to be free, Miss Carrie. Slavery don't just take a person's body. It tries to take their soul—their mind. It tells dem they ain't really a person. They just a thin' to be used by someone else."

"My Father says it is our destiny to own slaves because you can't take care of yourselves if left to be free."

Sarah looked at her. "You figur' dat to be true?"

Carrie shook her head.

"It's true dat some black folk ain't as smart as some white folk, but dats just because dey ain't had the chance to learn." She paused, a quiet twinkle in her eyes. "I know some white folk who ain't nearly as smart as some black folk I know. The color of the skin don't make no difference. It's what be in the head and heart that count."

"Do you think it's wrong for white people to own slaves?"

The silence built between them again. Finally, Sarah looked up. "What I think don't make no difference, Miss Carrie. It's what you think that counts. That be a decision you got to be makin' on your own." Carrie groaned in frustration and Sarah smiled gently. "You got to keep lookin' round you. Ask God to show you the truth. He'll do it." She hesitated, a troubled look on her face. "You know you could be borrowin' trouble for yo' self?"

Carrie sighed and nodded. "I already have, Sarah. I seem to be arguing a lot lately about slavery with the people I love most. I wish I could just let it go. But I can't!" she cried. "I try to push it out of my heart and it runs right back in. I try to pretend it doesn't matter to me, but it does."

Sarah waited until Carrie looked up and met her eyes. "God don't never take you somewhere He can't carry you, Miss Carrie."

"So you think God is doing this?"

"What you be thinkin'?"

Carrie stood up and strode angrily to the door. Then she turned around and stared at the old lady. "Can't you just give me some straight talk, Sarah? Do you always have to answer my questions with questions of your own?"

Sarah smiled. "My answers ain't the ones you goin' to be livin' yo life by. You'll find yo answers if you want them bad 'nuff." She stood and walked over to where

Carrie was brooding by the door. "Look at me, Miss Carrie." Carrie reluctantly looked down into Sarah's luminous eyes. "What would you do if I was to do what you be askin'? If I was to give you my answers?"

Carrie smiled reluctantly. "I'd keep on askin' questions."

"Right. You be wantin' answers, but I know you, girl. If you don't be findin' them answers on your own, they ain't goin' to mean nothing to you."

"Can you tell me just one thing, Sarah?"

"Maybe."

"If the North has their way and all the slaves are freed, how would you feel?"

The smile on Sarah's face was all the answer she needed.

Ike Adams gave a tight-lipped grin as the baying of the hounds in the distance increased and seemed to focus on one spot. "I think we got 'em, boys!"

The men around him murmured in agreement and pressed their sweating, blowing horses to move faster through the thick brush.

"I told Blackwell I wouldn't come back without them niggers. I intend to keep my promise." Abe Manson, Alfred Blackwell's burly, beady-eyed overseer, wet his lips and gave a sour grin to the men surrounding him.

Adams had received word that a slave hunting party was assembling as soon as word of the escape was received. He had been the first one there.

Tension was growing in the South as more and more slaves chose to make the break for freedom. A group of ten field hands from Blackwell had added their number to the statistics. They had been reported missing as soon as the slaves were called out into the tobacco fields. A stoic Blackwell had given Manson permission to do whatever it took to return the fleeing slaves. His eyes had glittered with anger as he told his overseer, "Just get them back here!" and turned to disappear into his mansion.

Manson had solicited a group of ten men from surrounding plantations, rounded up the dogs, and turned them loose. They had immediately picked up the trail. The men, even on horseback, had been hard-pressed to keep up with them as the slaves' route led them through thick brush and deep ravines. All the men were hot, angry, and cursing by the time the hounds announced they had caught their prey.

"Let's finish it, boys!" Manson yelled. Whoops of victory filled the air as the party surged forward, their eyes red with the light of conquest.

Moments later their curses once more rang on the wind as they broke through the woods to discover the hounds milling in the middle of the dirt road leading north.

Manson jumped down to inspect a set of fresh wagon tracks in the dirt. His eyes glittered with rage when he looked up. "It's those damn Yankees and their Underground Railroad again!" He stood, smashed his fist into his palm, and glared toward the North. "Well, it won't be that easy. I told Blackwell I wasn't coming back without them and I meant it. Who will join me?"

Downcast eyes and muttering told the story. They wanted to help but the tobacco was coming on strong and they couldn't leave their plantations for extended periods of time. Shrugged shoulders told Manson he was on his own.

"Get you some slave hunters, Manson," Adams suggested. "They'll get them niggers back."

Manson nodded shortly, wheeled his horse and took off at a rapid canter. The rest of the men turned back to their plantations, torn between anger and fear over who would suffer the next loss.

Jennings, the overseer from a neighboring plantation, edged his gelding up beside Adams. "You done anything about that Moses fellow yet?" Everyone had heard Ike's plans to put the giant nigger in his place.

Adams flushed with anger and turned to stare hard at Jennings. "No. I had my chance and that upstart of a daughter of Cromwell's stopped me," he said tightly.

Jennings's eyes grew wide.

Adams continued, the rage building in his voice. "She got that nigger off the hook once, but my time will come again." He didn't mention Carrie's threat to monitor the condition of all the slaves. He had been working on a plan that would make sure Moses wouldn't be found for a check. In the meantime, he was nursing a growing hatred for Cromwell's beautiful daughter. No one humiliated him and got away with it. He would watch and wait. His chance would come to get even with her without jeopardizing his job.

TWENTY

When Thomas and Robert stepped from the train in Baltimore, palpable tension permeated the salt air and filled the faces of the men around them. There was none of the lighthearted confidence and excitement that had greeted Robert when he reached Charleston almost two months ago. The men gathering here knew there would be no third chance and most of them were already accepting the bitter truth that a split Democratic Party could never beat the Republican candidate, Abraham Lincoln. They were here to do a job. They would do it and then deal with the consequences as they came. There was no other course of action.

This was Robert's first time in Baltimore. He had passed through on the train during his many trips to Philadelphia, but he had never visited the city. He took deep breaths of the soft, salty air and gazed out at the cluster of schooners, their sails furled tightly to their masts, bobbing in the harbor. The bustle of the train station was eclipsed by the organized chaos of the harbor—wagons rolling and men shouting as they transported goods that came in from all over the world. Robert couldn't help thinking what a critical role this port town would play if the worst happened and war came to America.

Robert started when he felt a solid slap on his shoulder. "I had a feeling you wouldn't let this one go by without seeing it for yourself."

Robert spun with a quick smile. "Matthew. I was also quite sure you would be here to record the floundering of this convention."

Both men's smiles faded as the truth of his words about the next few days hit home. Matthew was the first to break the silence. "Who is your friend?"

Robert came to with a shake of his head and turned to Thomas. "Thomas Cromwell, I would like you to meet an old college buddy of mine, Matthew Justin. I hope you'll be able to overlook the fact that he works for one of those Yankee newspapers and get to know him. In spite of his failings, he is a wonderful fellow."

Matthew laughed as he shook Thomas's hand warmly. "Are you a delegate, Cromwell?"

Thomas shook his head with a smile. "Heaven forbid I would have to jump into the middle of *this* fray. No, I simply came to see for myself what these gentlemen are going to do to my future." His face sobered as he spoke.

Matthew nodded with understanding. "If more people would be persuaded to do that, there might be more consideration and careful thought before these men speak for the country as a whole. I think many times they forget there are millions of people whose lives they hold in their hands by their decisions." The three men stood watching the bustle of activity around them. "Enough talk," Matthew said. "I am sure you gentleman have hotel reservations. I have a carriage waiting. May I take you where you're going?"

Once in the carriage, Thomas turned to Matthew. "I assume you were in Chicago for the Republican Convention, Matthew?"

Matthew nodded. "The place was packed with the press. No one wanted to miss *that* show."

"What do you think of this Lincoln fellow?" Thomas asked eagerly.

Matthew shrugged. "I was as surprised as everyone else when Seward lost the nomination. He was the frontrunner one minute, a has-been the next. That Davis fellow who masterminded Lincoln's nomination is a veritable genius. His swaying the Pennsylvania delegation at the last minute assured Lincoln his spot. That," he chuckled, "and his army of a cheering section in the Wigwam—the huge building they used for the convention. You should have heard them. The morning of the nomination vote, Seward formed all his followers into a parade, and with the brass band blaring out what they thought was a victory song, they marched to fill the galleries. The only problem was," he shrugged, "when they got there, there wasn't any room for them. Davis had already filled them up with men who yelled their lungs out for Lincoln. He created a momentum that couldn't be stopped."

"What kind of president will he make?"

Matthew peered at Thomas as they rattled down the street. "Are you already conceding defeat, Mr. Cromwell?" he asked in surprise.

"Young man," Thomas said, "I'm not much into playing games. You know as well as I do that a divided Democratic Party has no hope of beating the Republican nominee. Our one hope lies in a united party standing with Stephen Douglas. Quite frankly, I hold no hope of that. I will do all I can to make it happen, but I hold no confidence that it will."

Matthew sat silently for a few moments, and then Robert repeated Thomas's question. "So, what kind of president do you think Lincoln would make?" He wasn't quite as resigned to the inevitability of the outcome as Thomas was, but he *was* curious about this man, Lincoln. He had come from nowhere. Other than the statistics of a career that had failed over and over, Robert knew nothing about him.

Matthew shrugged. "Lincoln is levelheaded and thoughtful. His debating ability is impressive. He is a man who loves his country."

"What about the slavery issue?" Thomas had raised the question foremost in Robert's mind.

Matthew looked at him squarely, obviously realizing how important his answer was to Thomas. "Lincoln abhors the institution, but as far as I know, he has no plans to coerce the South into any kind of emancipation. I don't believe he plans to interfere with slavery. He is much more interested in how the country can be healed from all the divisions being wrought now."

Robert found no comfort in Matthew's words. Lincoln may have no plans to interfere, but Robert knew the mere existence of a federal administration hostile to slavery spelled eventual doom for the institution, even if the doom could be delayed for years. The heaviness in his heart increased as he felt the clouds dipping deeper over his beloved South.

Thomas frowned heavily and turned to stare at the streets.

Matthew and Robert exchanged troubled looks. Quietly, so as not to break into the older man's thoughts, they talked. "I have a friend coming to Philadelphia in July for a visit. I told her you might show her around the college campus."

Matthew raised his eyebrows. "Her?"

"Her name is Carrie Cromwell." He nodded when Matthew looked in Thomas's direction. "He is her father." Then he continued, his voice lower now because he didn't know if Thomas knew of his daughter's dream. "She is particularly interested in the medical college." He smiled when Matthew raised his eyebrows higher. "Just show her around, buddy. She has dreams."

Matthew nodded. "I'll be happy to be her escort for a while. Is she pretty?" Robert shot him a sharp look. Grinning, Matthew held up his hand. "No need to respond to that. The answer is *yes, and you better stay away from her.* Now that I know how the land lies, I promise to be just like an older brother."

The look on his face told Robert they would pick this conversation up later.

With Thomas embroiled in debate with some of the Virginia delegates, Robert and Matthew were free to stroll the streets of Baltimore. They had been in the city for three days, and still nothing had been done. Any voices of reason were being drowned out by unrelenting passion. Both of their hearts were heavy as they watched the seemingly unstoppable destruction of their country.

The convention was locked on whether or not new delegates added to the Southern delegations in order to obtain Douglas's nomination would be allowed. The Northern delegates had been surprised when the Southern delegates who had walked out of the Charleston convention had arrived in Baltimore.

Decisions would have to be made concerning which delegates would be voting. Nothing would happen until some decision was made. At least not in the Front Street Theatre. On the streets, the collective temper was rising hour by hour.

"Let's stop for the show."

Robert looked in the direction Matthew was pointing just in time to see Yancey take his place on the steps of the Gilmore House. His face twisted with distaste. "I heard enough of him in Charleston."

Matthew took his arm and propelled him forward. "I agree it will be unpleasant, but it's part of my job. I've already heard the Douglas people harping that the only way to show true fidelity to the Democratic cause is to vote for Douglas. It's my job to hear both sides."

Robert relented and allowed himself to be led to the edge of the crowd of agitated listeners. The three days of inactivity had been good for no one. Passions and feelings were building to a crescendo as the days wore on.

Yancey turned to the group and began his usual castigation of the Douglas men. His words built to a fevered pitch until he raised his arms and cried, "The Douglas men are nothing but abolitionists in disguise! They are nothing but selfish men who have buried their heads in the sands of squatter sovereignty and are now showing their abolitionist posteriors!"

Robert looked around him with disgust as the cheers erupted. He was startled when he felt a rough hand descend on his shoulder.

"You with us or not, boy?"

Shaking off the hand, Robert stepped back and viewed his challenger disdainfully as he took in the coarse clothing and the gagging stench of whiskey on his breath.

Not to be thwarted, the man moved forward and pressed his face closer to Robert's. "I'm talking to you, boy! You don't look like you agree with our Mr. Yancey."

"And if I don't?" Robert's voice was clipped.

The drunken man didn't bother with a response. He grinned as if he were delighted with the response, and then his fist shot out and connected with Robert's chin.

Robert, surprised by the attack, staggered back, shook his head to clear the stars, and braced for the next attack, berating himself that he had been caught unaware. He had seen violence erupting all over the city. While he was not looking for a fight, neither would he run from it. He was ready when the other man charged. Stepping aside lightly, he drove his fist deep into the soft belly exposed to him. He gave a satisfied smile when he heard a grunt and felt the other man go limp as he gasped for air. Gazing down for just a moment, he turned and spoke to Matthew. "You ready to move on?" he said cheerfully.

Matthew grinned. "I'd say it's time before anyone else decides to try their luck. I'd hate to see you litter the street with any more drunken men."

Backs straight, they moved on down the street, ignoring the muttering of the mob behind them. Robert found it easy to disregard the throbbing in his hand. It was not so easy to ignore his throbbing heart. It hurt to watch the events unfolding in the country he loved so much.

The two men walked until they found a quiet spot overlooking the harbor and sat down. The dark, moonless night wrapped a blanket of quiet around them. Each man was lost to his own thoughts as the water lapped gently below them.

"You'll live in another country, you know."

Matthew looked over at his friend. "I know, but Robert, don't give up hope yet. There might still be a way to turn this craziness around."

Robert just shook his head. His hopes had dwindled in the last few days. Reality had become his bitter friend.

"Tell me about Carrie," Matthew invited.

Robert managed a slight smile. He knew Matthew was searching for a way to take his mind off the troubles in the country. He also knew his friend, in reality, was no more optimistic than he was. Still, he would play his game. "She is the most beautiful girl I have ever known. But," he hastened to add, "it's not just her beauty on the outside. She is more alive than any girl I have ever met. She fairly glows with life and enthusiasm."

"And she has dreams?"

"Yes. She wants to be a doctor."

Matthew whistled. "Quite an undertaking. Especially for a southern woman."

"She knows."

"And what about you, Robert?" Matthew asked. "How does that fit in with your plans for your plantation? Will she be a plantation wife?"

"She abhors the very idea," Robert admitted ruefully. Then he shrugged. "I love her, Matthew."

"But...?"

"We are on opposite sides of so many things. I want plantation life. She wants nothing more than to be free of it. I believe with all my heart that slavery is right—"

"And she doesn't?"

"I'm not sure she knows *what* she believes," Robert said slowly. "I just know it could tear us apart. Why can't she just see that it's right?" Then he realized who he was talking to. "Sorry. I know you don't share my feelings. I guess I'm talking to the wrong person."

Matthew hesitated for a long moment before he spoke. "Are you sure *you* believe slavery is right?"

Robert looked at him sharply. "Of course I do."

"Then you'll have to figure out a way to deal with it." Matthew would say no more.

Robert gazed out over the water. Why had Matthew's last question bothered him so much? He knew what he believed about slavery, didn't he?

The showdown came at seven o'clock in the evening on Friday, June 22. The theater was packed and a strange silence hovered over the crowd. It didn't take long for the inevitable to occur. With the addition of the pro-Douglas delegates from the South, Douglas could now be nominated.

Thomas's heart sank from where he was watching in the gallery as Delegate Russell of Virginia stood. He knew what was about to happen, but the pill was even more bitter to swallow when he realized it was coming from his own beloved state.

Russell's speech was brief. "It is inconsistent with our convictions to participate longer..." Most of the Virginia delegates rose and quietly left the room amid the turmoil Russell's words had provoked. They were followed by a large number of delegates from other states.

Thomas frowned as he scribbled notes to take back to Letcher. *The Deep South has formalized the decision made earlier in Charleston. It will not go along with Douglas under any circumstances.* Thomas was sure the actions of Charleston would be imitated. The withdrawing states would form their own convention and nominate their own candidate.

He continued to scribble as the bedlam roared around him. *What is the Deep South doing? Instead of bringing a candidate to oppose Douglas; instead of laying issues before the people so they could be enlightened in making a choice; instead of principles discussed, what have we seen? An unrelenting war against the individual brought forth as the favorite of the nation. A war of unscrupulous politicians who want nothing more than to war against their nation.* Heavyhearted, Thomas put down his pen and settled back to see what would happen next in this two-ringed circus.

Thomas shouldered his way out of the crowded theater. All he wanted was fresh air. He had seen enough to make him sick for the rest of his life. He still could not believe a group of self-interested men had bartered away his country. It was just a matter of time now.

"Are you ready to go home now, Robert?" Thomas asked as he joined Robert on the sidewalk. "There is nothing more we can do here now," he said bitterly.

"You're right, sir." Robert hesitated. "I guess I just want to see how it ends."

Thomas nodded reluctantly, wanting nothing more than to go home to the peace of his plantation and enjoy his home for as long as he still had it, but he had to consider Robert as well. "Very well. We'll stay until it's over."

It was over quickly. Douglas received his nomination. So did John C. Breckinridge, nominated unanimously by the withdrawn states that were claiming themselves to be the *real* Democratic Convention, based on sharp pro-slavery issues.

Thomas added to his pages of scribbling. *The Douglas men came to Baltimore blinded by their own optimism and confidence. They did not understand the power and desperation of the South. They were foolish enough to believe the opposition to their plans would quietly subside and disappear. They were, however, met by a spirit more intolerant than their own. At Charleston and Baltimore, the South has taken its stand. It will remain the South, separate and unalterable.*

Thomas sighed and stared out at the scenery unrolling beneath the train wheels. He was heartsick, but glad it was over. The reality was a tragedy, but at least a course had been determined. He was sure the course would lead to nothing but destruction of all he held dear, but still a faint hope persisted that the supposedly unalterable course of events could indeed be changed.

Robert had thrown aside his coat and was sprawled on the seat next to him. Thomas watched him carefully, and leaned over to lay his hand on the younger man's arm. "Are you awake?"

Robert opened his eyes. "Unfortunately."

Thomas smiled slightly. "May I talk to you for a few moments?"

Robert nodded and sat up in his seat. "What is it?"

Thomas struggled with how to express what he was feeling. "A great darkness is about to fall on our country." He paused as he heard the desperation in his own voice.

Robert nodded. "I wish I could close my eyes and forget life for a while. Maybe if I forget it, all of this madness will disappear." He sighed heavily.

"I'm not afraid for myself. I am afraid for my family," Thomas said quietly.

Robert scowled. "I think I am afraid for all of us."

Thomas leaned forward. "If war should come, Virginia will be on the frontlines just because of where we are geographically. If war should come to Cromwell Plantation..." his voice tightened and then he regained control. "Robert, you need to know about—" Suddenly Thomas could not tell the secret he had kept all of his life, even from Abigail. He shook his head and sat back, staring out the window as he tried to pull his thoughts together. He was not old. Why was he suddenly feeling *very* old?

Robert leaned closer.

Thomas took a deep breath and turned back to the boy. "I'm sorry."

"It's quite alright, sir."

Thomas shook his head. "Will you help me take care of my family, Robert?"

"Of course I will, sir."

Thomas fixed him with a steady gaze. "You realize Carrie may never return the feelings you have for her?"

Robert swallowed hard and nodded. "Yes, sir. That doesn't matter, though I will help take care of your family in any way I can."

Thomas stared into his eyes, satisfied with what he saw. "There may come a time when neither of us will be able to defend our homes, but as long as I can..." A long pause followed. "Robert, the next time you come to Cromwell, there is something you must know about." Then he closed his eyes and sat back.

TWENTY-ONE

Carrie hugged herself excitedly as the train pulled into the Philadelphia station. She could hardly believe she was actually here! Her neck was sore from craning to see everything she could on the way up. She had been determined to not miss a thing. Now that she was actually here in Philadelphia, her excitement, if it was even possible, had increased even more. She grabbed her small overnight bag and stepped off the train, instantly mesmerized by the clamor assailing her.

"There's Aunt Abby," Natalie cried.

Carrie spun around and watched the middle-aged woman approaching them. She immediately liked the strong lines of her face and the erect way she carried herself. Taller than many of the men surrounding her, Aunt Abby made no effort to make herself seem smaller. Her confident bearing said she had nothing to feel awkward about. Soft brown hair pulled back into a bun framed a pair of startling, bright gray eyes. Her clothing spoke of her wealth.

"Hello, girls. Welcome to Philadelphia." The voice greeting them was low and melodious, with a hint of humor lurking behind the musical tones.

Carrie felt herself drawn to this woman—a complete stranger to her.

Natalie threw herself into her aunt's arms. "Aunt Abby. It's so wonderful to see you. I can hardly believe I'm here at last!"

Abby laughed as she gave the excited girl a huge hug. "It's wonderful to have you here, Natalie." Then she looked over her head. "Are you going to introduce me to your friends?" she asked in an amused voice.

Natalie pulled back with a laugh. "That would be the proper thing to do, wouldn't it?" She reached out and pulled Sally forward. "This is my best friend, Sally

Hampton. And this is Carrie Cromwell." She reached her other hand out and pulled Carrie into the circle. "She reminds me of you, Aunt Abby."

Abby reached out a hand to both the girls, holding Carrie's for a few moments after she had released Sally's. "Why does she remind you of me, Natalie?"

Carrie looked into her eyes and knew she had found a friend. She didn't know how to explain it. It was just a knowing that settled in her heart with surety. The older woman's warm gray eyes sparkled with life and compassion, and Carrie knew instantly that great wisdom lurked behind the humor.

Natalie laughed. "Because she has crazy ideas like you do. She's not at all like me and Sally. She's always asking questions and always doing things none of the rest of us would even consider."

"Is that true? Well then, Carrie Cromwell, you are most definitely welcome in Philadelphia."

Carrie laughed along with the rest of them. She wasn't offended by Natalie's analysis. She knew it was true. The idea of being like Aunt Abby intrigued her. Suddenly, the most important thing on her mind was to get to know this woman better.

Carrie's chance came two days later.

"Carrie, there's a new art exhibit in town. We're leaving in about thirty minutes."

Carrie groaned and shook her head. "Not another art exhibit, Sally. We haven't stopped for one minute since we've been here."

"Well, of course not, silly. We may never be in Philadelphia again. I intend to make the most of it."

"You and Natalie go ahead, Sally. I'm going to stay here and enjoy the Philadelphia skyline from my chair." To emphasize her statement, Carrie walked over and sat down in the elegant rose-colored chair stationed by the tall window looking out on the street. She gazed for a moment at the clog of carriages before turning back to her friends. "I can think of nothing I would rather do more than sit right here in this chair.

Sally shrugged. "Help yourself. We'll fill you in on all the handsome men you miss."

Carrie had just opened a book she had chosen from the extensive library when Aunt Abby arrived home. She had insisted on all of them calling her Aunt Abby. She would have no formality in her home, she said.

"Carrie, did they abandon you?" Aunt Abby had been out to a meeting and probably anticipated the house being empty when she returned. She stood by the open window and seemed to enjoy the breeze blowing gently through the room. Summer had settled on the city with a vengeance.

"I was abandoned by choice, Aunt Abby. I hate cramming every second with activity. It gives you no time to savor what has already happened."

Abby eyed her closely. "I believe Natalie was right. You and I are much alike." She looked toward the kitchen. "Would you like some lemonade?"

"That sounds wonderful. I'll help you." The two of them moved into the kitchen and quickly squeezed some lemons. Carrie watched while Aunt Abby poured two large glasses of cold lemonade. "You don't have servants?"

Abby looked up. "I have someone who comes in occasionally to cook and clean. I find I am perfectly capable of taking care of most of my work—*all* of it actually if I weren't so lazy at times," she said with a chuckle. "Let's move out to the porch to take advantage of that breeze."

Carrie settled herself onto one of the lounge chairs on the porch, took a moment to savor the breeze, and leaned forward. "Is it very scary being on your own?" she asked.

Abby eyed her with amusement. "Planning on trying it yourself?"

Carrie flushed. "No. Yes. I mean... I don't know." Suddenly embarrassed, she stared at the floor, unsure of what to say next.

Abby leaned forward and put her hand on Carrie's leg. "Tell me about yourself, Carrie. Who are you? What do you want?" Her voice was caring and compassionate.

Carrie looked up and managed a short laugh. "That's the problem. I don't know!" She gazed into Aunt Abby's warm eyes and tried to pull her thoughts together. She very much wanted this woman to know her. "All I know is that I don't fit where I am supposed to belong." She paused and looked up again. Somehow she knew Aunt Abby wasn't going to respond. Not yet. She would just listen for a while.

Carrie took a deep breath and told Aunt Abby of her increasing restlessness on the plantation and how she could not imagine spending her life there. "I feel I'll burst if I have to live that life."

"What is it you want, Carrie?" Abby asked quietly.

"I want to be a doctor," Carrie said firmly. She leaned forward, suddenly nervous. "Do you think I'm quite crazy?"

"Do you?"

Carrie laughed loudly.

"Did I say something funny?"

Carrie shook her head, smiling. "You remind me of one of our slaves. Her name is Sarah. She's always been like another mother to me. She likes to ask questions, too."

"Do you mind questions?"

"Sometimes," Carrie admitted. "But only when I'm afraid of what the answer may be. Then is the best time for questions, though, I suppose."

Aunt Abby smiled gently. "It takes great courage to be honest when the honesty is pointed at yourself. I admire that."

Carrie flushed again, this time with pleasure. "You asked me earlier if I believed I was crazy to want to be a doctor. The answer is no. I fear sometimes it is impossible, but I believe I would be a good doctor. That's one reason I'm here."

"Oh?"

"My friend Robert has made arrangements for an old college buddy of his to show me around the University of Pennsylvania campus, including the medical school.   Abby sat back and studied Carrie for a long moment. "You will face many disappointments and heartaches."

"You sound as if you speak from experience."

Abby shrugged. "Anyone who goes against the conventions of their time will experience heartache. People fear change, Carrie, and they fight the things they are afraid of. You are going against the age-old tradition of the South. Add to that the fear people have of women having dreams and ambitions of their own..." She spread her hands and smiled gently. "That is a recipe for disappointment and heartache."

"I have to do it. It's the only thing that makes any sense to me— no matter how hard it is."

Abby smiled and reached forward to take one of her hands. "I know, Carrie. And that is exactly why you're *going* to do it. We only truly fight to make changes when we believe in those changes with all our heart. You have to want your dream badly enough to hold on through the bad times." Abby looked off into the distance. "When my husband, Charles, died several years ago, it was expected I would return south to my family. I decided otherwise. Philadelphia is my home. My family implored me to return in order to maintain my respectability. The business world here was aghast when I decided to continue with my husband's business. I was quite capable of running it, you know. It's just that it wasn't done. Many people worked against me to make the business fail—men who had been our friends before Charles died. I refused to go away, however, and finally they accepted me. It is still hard at times, but it's worth it." The last quiet words were spoken with a triumphant note.

Carrie looked at her with even greater admiration. "Thank you for telling me that."

Abby laughed suddenly. "My goodness, dear, if we women fighting the tide don't stand with each other, there is surely no hope." She leaned forward and stared intensely into Carrie's eyes. "Tell you what. There are many times you are going to find it difficult to believe in yourself. When you run into those times, try and believe in those who believe in you. *I* believe in you, Carrie. I believe you can make your dreams come true."

Carrie stared into Aunt Abby's eyes, her own filling with tears. "Thank you," she whispered. She leaned forward impulsively and gave the older woman a hug. "I knew you were going to be a friend."

"Aren't you girls ready yet?" Abby called up the stairs. "The dance is going to be over by the time we get there," she teased.

"You don't want us going out looking less than our best, do you Aunt Abby?" Natalie challenged as she floated down the stairs in her light-blue gown.

"I hardly think that is going to happen," Aunt Abby said dryly. "I grew up in the South, remember? I know what a premium is placed on proper appearance." Aunt Abby looked beautiful in a soft-gray gown that swept the floor and matched her eyes. She smiled. "All three of you look lovely. I believe these poor Northern gentlemen are going to be taken off guard."

"I hope so," Sally exclaimed.

All of them laughed. "Do you ever think of anything besides men, Sally Hampton?" Carrie demanded.

"Why, is there anything else to think about?" Sally asked in a bewildered voice. Then she grinned. "I also think about food and clothes."

Groans filled the hallway as the four women walked out onto the porch. A well-appointed carriage waited for them at the bottom of the steps. "Are we really going to be late for the dance, Aunt Abby?" Natalie asked.

Abby shook her head. "I remember what it was like when I was a young lady. I gave you plenty of time to get ready."

They had traveled down the road not more than ten minutes when all traffic came to a halt. Abby craned her neck to identify the problem. "Driver?"

The driver shrugged his broad shoulders. "I should have gone another way, ma'am. I'm sorry. Some other drivers told me the Wide Awakes were in town for a parade. I thought we would be past their route before it began. I'm afraid we're not going anywhere for a while."

"Oh, bother!" Abby exclaimed in an exasperated voice.

"What is it?" Carrie asked. She leaned out to see the parade they were discussing but a sea of carriages blocked her view.

"It's another one of those Republican parades. I'm all for party enthusiasm but I'm afraid we're going to be horribly late for the dance." Abby turned around and looked back at the carriages stacked up behind them. "I'm afraid there's no way to get out of this mess."

Carrie still didn't understand what was happening. "Who are the Wide Awakes?"

Abby rose suddenly, without answering. "If we're not going to make it to the dance on time, the least we can do is see the parade," she stated. "Driver, we'll be back when the parade is over."

The driver nodded complacently, settling back against his seat. "I don't reckon I'll be going anywhere before then, ma'am." He reached under his seat and pulled out a bucket. "I'll just eat the dinner my missus fixed for me. I'll be right here when you get back."

Within minutes Carrie found herself pressed into the massive crowd lining the street. She wondered uneasily if they were all going to be trampled. She stretched herself as tall as she could but could see nothing but a mass of heads blocking her vision. It didn't matter if the parade came—she wouldn't see it anyway.

"Let's go up there." Aunt Abby pointed to the high landing of an office building.

"Do you think it's alright?" Natalie asked with a troubled expression. Carrie knew the crowd was frightening her. She, too, wanted nothing more than to remove herself from the milling bedlam, but she didn't want to get in trouble.

Abby grinned. "It should be. I own the building." With a laugh she led the way up the stairs, pulled out the key that would let them in, and swung open the solid door. All four entered with a sigh of relief. Carrie glanced around the immaculate offices and then followed Abby up the stairs. This lady was a constant source of surprises.

Just as they stepped out onto the landing above the second floor, Carrie heard a sound in the distance. It seemed to have a life of its own as it steadily increased and swallowed the noise of the crowd. Carrie had never heard anything like it. She leaned against the railing and peered down the street. As the sound, still undecipherable, drew closer, a strange glow lit the distance. Breathless, Carrie kept her eyes fixed on the street.

Finally, the sound took a shape and identified itself. Moving toward them were thousands of men dressed in dark oilcloth capes, tramping in military fashion, and holding aloft smoky torches that cast their flickering light on the teeming crowds assembled to meet them. Carrie had seen military parades performed by the Virginia militias but never anything to equal this. What was going on?

Aunt Abby seemed to be reading her mind, for she leaned forward and shouted, "The Wide Awakes are young Republican enthusiasts who march to generate political enthusiasm. They are determined to see Lincoln elected."

Slowly, Carrie turned back to stare at the scene before her. Never had she felt so out of place. As the tramping filled the night and seemed to take on a life of its own, she was thankful for their place high above the masses. Instinct told her a large number of the people assembled below would not be friendly toward three plantation girls from the South. The very thought frightened her. Never had she thought she would need to be afraid in her own country. Her hands trembled on the railing as the clamor of the crowd grew. *Lincoln! Lincoln! Lincoln!*

Once again, she felt the same strange sensation she had experienced in Richmond standing beneath Washington's Monument. Even though dusk had claimed the city, she felt dark clouds lowering to engulf them. She stared down, somehow aware of the blind emotion swirling through the masses—their allegiance seemingly given to whoever made the most noise. It both frightened and fascinated her.

Carrie stood alone at the balcony with Abby. Natalie and Sally, alarmed by the spectacle, had retreated inside. Finally, she turned to the older woman. "They believe in him, don't they?"

Abby shrugged. "They believe in him tonight while the bands are playing and the night is full of the tramping of feet pounding out their message. Will they believe in him tomorrow?" She smiled ruefully. "People believe easily when it doesn't cause them any discomfort. It's when it hurts to believe that believing means something."

Carrie stared at her. Never had she heart a woman talk this way.

Abby interpreted her look. "Natalie was right, Carrie. We are alike in one major way. We question everything that goes on around us. I happen to think it's one of my better traits." She grinned. "If more people had asked questions, I don't think our country would be in the mess it's in right now." She grew more serious. "I think our country is in desperate need of more balance, Carrie. Men need women to help keep the perspective straight and to see an issue from all sides. Women need to be able to vote."

Carrie could think of nothing to say. She had never even considered women having the vote. She opened her mouth but nothing came out.

Abby laughed at her bemused expression. "I'm sorry, dear," she chuckled. "I get carried away sometimes." Her expression changed suddenly. "Not that I don't mean it with all my heart, but I sense you have plenty to deal with already. I don't need to add anything to your load. Do me a favor," she added with a sudden smile. "Don't tell Natalie of my wild ideas. She'll feel compelled to share them back home and my dear family will be convinced they need to come lock me away. There will be a time to let them know how I feel, but it's not now."

Carrie nodded. "Of course," she replied instantly, honored Aunt Abby had entrusted her with a secret. She would never betray her new friend.

Just then the bands stopped playing and the tramping of feet abruptly came to a halt. Carrie returned her attention to the street just in time to see a man climb onto a platform that had been hurriedly put in place.

"Seward," Abby said in response to the question in her eyes. "It took him a while to adjust to the fact he was not going to be the next president, but now he's campaigning like crazy for Lincoln. Whatever else people might say, he is a man committed to his party."

The crowd quieted down enough for Seward's voice to be heard clearly. Carrie listened intently as he went on at great length about Lincoln and why he should be the next president.

When he seemed to be winding down, a question was shouted from the crowd. "What is going to happen if the Southern states secede as they are threatening?"

Seward's smile never dimmed. He waved his hands for renewed attention and delivered his statement with great confidence. "For ten, aye twenty years, these threats have been renewed in the same language and in the same form, about the first day of November every four years, when it happened to come before the day of the presidential election. I do not doubt but that these Southern statesmen and politicians think they are going to dissolve the Union, but I think they are going to do no such thing!"

The crowd roared its approval and once again started its chant. *"Lincoln! Lincoln! Lincoln!"*

"Carrie?"

Carrie turned to see Aunt Abby's staring at her. Only then did she become aware of the tears streaming down her face. "He's wrong you know," Carrie said softly, wiping away her tears, and turning to stare at the crowd below. "The South isn't just threatening this time. If Lincoln is elected, they will secede."

Abby opened her mouth as if to argue and then merely nodded, her eyes suddenly very fatigued.

"My father says the passions of men have destroyed any possibility of reason. He says there is no chance Lincoln will not win, and that when he wins, the South will secede." Carrie's voice trembled. "And then there will be war."

Both Carrie and Aunt Abby turned back to stare as the band broke out into victorious music and the hordes of Wide Awakes resumed their relentless tramping. Abby reached out and took the younger girl's hand. "I wish I could refute what you are saying. I would like to insist reason will save us." She sighed instead. "I'm afraid your father might be right. Passion is now ruling our country."

Natalie and Sally eased out the door and joined them on the balcony. Both girls were frightened but determined to ignore the obvious. "Aunt Abby? The crowd is breaking up. Do you think we can make it to the dance now?" Sally asked.

Aunt Abby turned slowly to look at them, seeming almost surprised to see them there. "The dance?" she asked vaguely. "Oh, yes, the dance!" She shook her head and focused on Natalie and Sally's faces. "Goodness me, we don't want to lose our carriage." Glancing over the balcony, she exclaimed, "Let's go, girls. We must hurry."

The dance, held in the ballroom of a huge mansion set high on a hill overlooking the city skyline, seemed a different world from the smoky torches and the endless tramping of feet. Carrie breathed a sigh of relief when she entered the glowing beauty of the home. Music swirled around her, drowning out the tramping that seemed etched into her mind and heart. It was not long before the three beautiful girls were surrounding by admiring men.

"Good evening, ma'am."

Carrie looked up into the sparkling eyes of the tall red-haired gentleman in front of her. He didn't have the same elegant bearing of many of the men around him, but she liked the sparkle and warmth of his eyes, and the confident way he held his angular frame. "Good evening, sir." She smiled as his eyebrows raised slightly. "Virginia," she said in response to his unspoken question. "Richmond, to be exact."

"Welcome to Philadelphia, Miss....?"

"Cromwell. Carrie Cromwell."

The tall redhead suddenly threw back his head with a hearty laugh. "I *would* have to approach the only girl who is already spoken for!"

Carrie stared at him, wondering vaguely if he was a little mad. Her look only made the man laugh harder. She watched as he forced himself to quit laughing. He was merely chuckling when he extended a hand. "Welcome to Philadelphia, once again, Miss Carrie Cromwell. My name is Matthew Justin."

"Robert's friend!" Carrie gasped. She reddened when she recalled his earlier comment. *The only girl who is already spoken for...* What had Robert told this stranger?

Matthew, aware of her embarrassment, bowed deeply. "May I have this dance, Miss Cromwell?"

Carrie stared up at him and nodded. She knew she should say something, but all she could do was move toward him, her thoughts still on his surprising announcement. He took her lightly in his arms, and they waltzed off to the music. The music and the dancing helped Carrie regain her composure. Finally, she was able to look up and say in a natural voice, "You must think me quite an idiot."

Matthew looked down with a laugh. "Hardly that. You were caught by surprise and I have the distinct feeling I spoke out of turn when I said you were already spoken for."

Carrie flushed again but didn't break eye contact. "As far as I know, I am still a free woman, Mr. Justin," she said calmly. "Robert has told me about you. You are a journalist, I believe?"

Matthew nodded. "That I am. It is probably the only reason I am at this dance. People in high places like to court the press in hopes that anything we may write about them will be more favorable. Country boys from the western hills of Virginia would not likely make it to this grand event otherwise."

Carrie laughed at the dryness of his tone, suddenly aware Philadelphia was full of people she knew she could be friends with. She liked the direct way they spoke, unconcerned about the social protocol and expectations that governed southern society. Then her expression sobered.

"Did I say something to offend you?"

"No, of course not." Carrie forced herself to smile. They continued to dance, but she knew Matthew was hoping for an explanation. She shrugged and tried to speak lightly. "I find it difficult to believe I may soon be at war with people I have discovered I like so much."

Matthew regarded her with serious eyes. "You believe there will be war?"

"I'm afraid so, Mr. Justin."

"Please call me Matthew," he insisted. He waited for her nod before he continued. "Robert told me you were different. He said you see things most women—especially southern women—prefer to ignore. I believe he was right."

Carrie met his eyes squarely. "Ignoring something will not make it go away. I would rather prepare myself than wake up one day realizing all my delusions have been shattered by reality."

"I quite agree, but I made myself a promise tonight," he said firmly. "Just for this one night, I have decided to pretend my world will always remain the same." He smiled down at her. "Will you play my game with me?"

Carrie smiled and dipped into a low curtsy. "I would be honored to play your game, kind sir. I will do my best to abide by your rules."

Matthew threw back his head in a hearty laugh. When the music stopped, he led her over to a small window seat overlooking the city. "Where are you staying, Carrie?"

"With a most wonderful woman. Her name is Abby Livingston."

Matthew nodded with a smile. "I know her well. She is indeed a wonderful woman."

"You know Aunt Abby?"

"I'm afraid he does," an amused voice broke in. Abby stepped up and laid a hand affectionately on Matthew's arm. "This one is special, Matthew. Treat her well."

"Have no fear, Abby. I would have met her tomorrow even if I hadn't had the privilege tonight."

Carrie laughed at her puzzled expression. "This is Robert's old college buddy that I was telling you about."

"I hardly think I'm *old* yet," Matthew protested.

Carrie and Abby laughed, and Abby linked her arm through Matthew's. "What brings you to the top of the hill, Matthew?"

"Instead of down in the streets and gutters where I usually work?" Matthew smiled and bowed deeply. "You are now looking at the new leading political reporter for our fair newspaper."

"Matthew Justin! That's wonderful," Abby exclaimed, giving him a hug. "Congratulations."

Carrie watched the exchange, wondering what it was all about. Abby turned to explain.

"Matthew and I met three years ago when I was fighting the men who tried to destroy my business. I'm afraid they used some rather unscrupulous ways to try and promote their agenda."

"*Rather* unscrupulous?" Matthew laughed and picked up the story. "Those men were sending thugs after this wonderful lady, trying to scare her out of the business district. I happened upon Abby one night when she was being held at knifepoint in an alley. I was able to persuade the gentleman he was in the wrong place."

The look in his eyes told Carrie his *persuasion* had been a little rough.

"After that, Matthew helped me fight my opponents with the paper," Abby continued. "He wrote articles about the attacks being made on me. Not long after, they mysteriously ended. Men who had turned their noses up at me before were suddenly willing to do business with me. I don't know what I would have done if Matthew hadn't come along."

Matthew grinned self-consciously as he regarded Abby with obvious affection. "Carrie, you couldn't find a better friend. If *she* thinks you're special, your estimation has risen even higher in my already admiring eyes." He smiled. "I see another man heading this direction to claim you for the next dance. Shall I pick you up tomorrow morning around ten for our tour of the university?"

Carrie nodded. "That would be wonderful, Matthew. I shall look forward to it."

Matthew grinned down at her and then turned to Abby. "May I have this dance, Mrs. Livingston?"

Carrie was quickly claimed and drawn into another waltz. She released herself to the magic of the evening, allowing all negative thoughts to flee her mind. This was an evening made for dance and laughter.

Then, as the night was drawing to a close, reality reared its ugly head once more.

"My I have this dance, Miss Cromwell?"

Carrie looked up into the icy blue eyes staring down at her. "Well, I—"

Without waiting for an answer, the stranger took her hand and led her onto the dance floor. Carrie swallowed her misgivings and followed without protest. She noticed Matthew watching from across the ballroom.

"I hear you are from Richmond, Virginia, Miss Cromwell."

"Yes." Why did Carrie suddenly feel she was being interrogated? "And you are from Philadelphia, Mr....?" Coolly, she inspected the young man standing before her. His classic, blond good looks were marred by the icy intensity of his eyes and the arrogance of his bearing.

"My apologies, Miss Cromwell. My name is Alex Morning. And yes, I am a Philadelphian." The mocking tone of his voice sharpened suddenly. "I take it you are a plantation owner's daughter."

"And what would make you think that?" Something told Carrie she must tread lightly. All of her mother's fears about what could happen to her in the North suddenly reared their heads to taunt her.

"Come, Miss Cromwell. Surely it is not something you are ashamed of."

Carrie pulled away and came to a standstill. Morning matched her actions, staring down at her with undisguised hostility. "If there is something you want to say to me, then say it, Mr. Morning. I am not interested in games."

A faint light of appreciation lit his features at her directness, but he was not to be deterred. "I simply find it difficult to believe that someone with your obvious intelligence could be a slave owner." The contempt in his voice was obvious. "Of course, intelligence is of no importance if you choose to ignore the truth."

"And just what is the truth, Mr. Morning?" Carrie demanded icily.

"The truth is that you people in the South are subjugating an entire race of people to exploit your own selfish desires. Exploitation that includes beating, torture, and selling loved ones away from each other. It is the work of the Devil."

Carrie pulled away from the venom in his voice, but Morning wasn't done. His voice rose and carried through the ballroom as he continued his attack. "The time is coming soon when God will have his way! The tyranny of the slave master will be ended! The Devil will be defeated!"

His last words ended with a triumphant laugh that caused shivers to course through Carrie's entire body.

"That will be quite enough, Morning." Carrie looked up with relief as Matthew loomed at her side.

"Think our little southern belle can't handle a dose of the truth, Justin? She's going to learn it sooner or later." Morning smiled triumphantly as a few murmured agreements rose on the air.

Carrie was suddenly very frightened. She had heard about mobs attacking people from the South because of slavery. Clutching Matthew's arm, she welcomed the feel of his strong hand engulfing hers. She fought to control her trembling. It would never do to let the stranger sense her fear, or let him know how much his words had pierced her. She struggled to control the tears threatening to overflow. She had wanted so much to leave everything behind for just one magical evening. Were there to be no more magical evenings in America? Suddenly, she felt very tired.

Matthew turned to lead her off the floor but sent one final shot. "Hatred does nothing but beget hatred,

Morning. Your brand of hatred and anger is no different than the emotions that enforce slavery. They both promote violence and misunderstanding." He sent the other man a withering look as his next words rang out loud and clear. "The only way for this country to survive is for people to start thinking with their hearts and minds instead of with that portion of their body they sit on."

Ripples of laughter met his loud proclamation. Morning swore, shoved past them, and strode out of the room.

"I'm afraid you have made a rather nasty enemy, Matthew." Abby's quiet voice sounded next to them. She reached over and took Carrie's icy hand in her own. "I'm so sorry, dear."

Matthew shrugged. "I have no interest in him being a friend, so he might as well be an enemy. I meant every word I said."

"What exactly was that all about?" Carrie murmured, her voice sounding strange to her own ears.

Just then Natalie and Sally hurried over. "Carrie! Are you alright?" Natalie cried, her eyes large with fright.

Carrie nodded, the tears she had controlled until now, brimming in her eyes.

Abby held her hand tighter. "There are people who feel very strongly that slavery is wrong. However wrongly, they feel justified in believing nothing is off limits in their efforts to end it—even harassment of visiting southern young ladies," she said heavily. "I am so sorry you had to endure that, Carrie."

Carrie managed a smile and brushed her tears away. "I'm alright, Aunt Abby. Matthew came to my rescue." She patted Matthew's arm and then removed her hand from Aunt Abby's grip. She was starting to feel more normal. "Thank you very much, Matthew. I hope I haven't caused trouble for you."

Matthew shrugged with a tight grin. "Like I said, Morning is no friend of mine." Then he relaxed and gave a more natural smile. "Besides, I promised Robert I would look out for you. I would hate to have to answer to him if something were to happen to you."

The magic of the evening was shattered for all. After thanking their hosts, the four women headed for their carriage.

"May I accompany you home, ladies?" Matthew appeared at the side of the carriage as the driver picked up the reins.

Carrie didn't miss the look he exchanged with Aunt Abby over their heads. Aunt Abby nodded briskly. "That is very thoughtful of you, Matthew. Thank you for your offer."

Carrie was nervous all the way home. She knew Matthew was afraid there would be repercussions from the evening. She did not breathe normally again until she was safe behind the doors of Aunt Abby's home. Even then, rest did not come easily when she retired to her bedroom. She had so wanted to refute the horrible words Alex Morning had hurled at her. She knew there were many slaves who were never abused and who were cared for by their owners. She also knew the accusations he had poured out like hot acid tonight were, in many cases, true. It was a long time before she drifted off into a restless sleep.

TWENTY-TWO

Carrie walked slowly by Aunt Abby's side, savoring the smells and sights of the marketplace. Just like so many things in Philadelphia, this was a new experience for her. Fruits and vegetables were all grown on Cromwell Plantation. She had always taken the abundance for granted. It was a new experience to see the myriad varieties spread out under the tin roofs of the market, vendors hawking their ware as zealously as Southerners sold tobacco. Elegantly dressed women, along with more commonly dressed house servants, poked and examined the produce until they found what met their discriminating tastes. Huge baskets hung heavily on their arms as the fresh food threatened to overflow. The sun was just beginning to rise over the horizon. The throng of people crowding the aisles had chosen to come early before the searing July heat made staying in the house with a cold glass of lemonade much more appealing than strolling among the market stands.

"I'm glad you came with me, Carrie."

"Oh, so am I, Aunt Abby. This is absolutely fascinating." Then Carrie sighed. "I've had such a wonderful time. It's going to be so hard to go home tomorrow." She knew the hardest thing was going to be leaving Aunt Abby. She had grown to love her deeply. "I can hardly believe it's already been a month."

"I'm going to miss you, Carrie."

Carrie brushed at the tears welling up in her eyes as she turned to the older woman. "I'm going to miss you, too." She paused. "You've become like a mother to me. I love my mother, but..." She shook her head. "She has no idea what to do with a daughter like me, so her goal in life has become to change me so I will fit the mold she has made for me."

"That would seem a plan destined for failure," Aunt Abby observed dryly.

Carrie managed a laugh. "I'm afraid I'm quite a disappointment to her."

Abby looked directly into her eyes. "I'm sure your mother loves you very much. At some point in time she will become comfortable enough with herself to accept you just the way you are. In the meantime, you can be nothing but who God created you to be. Some people will be comfortable with it, others will not. The important thing is that you be comfortable with yourself."

Carrie nodded, knowing she spoke from experience. "Thank you, Aunt Abby. I'll do my best."

A comfortable silence fell between the two women. Abby picked up a head of lettuce and two tomatoes. "I'm done here, Carrie. We'll go home a different way. Since it's your last day here, you might as well squeeze in everything you can."

Heat was already beginning to radiate off the pavement as the two women strolled down the road.

"Did you get what you came to Philadelphia for, Carrie?" Abby asked.

Carrie looked at her quickly. She would not even consider dodging the question. She trusted Aunt Abby. "I think so," she said slowly. "Matthew was wonderful to show me around the school. I know college and medical school are what I want..."

"But...?"

Carrie shook her head firmly. "No buts. I'm just not sure of the timing. I was disappointed when we found no one to talk to at the college— especially another female. Matthew encouraged me, but also warned me it would be difficult." She paused and thought back to the intense longing she had experienced when she was walking the tree-covered sidewalks of the university. Her desire to learn had been fueled by the spirit of those who had gone before. Even though she hadn't seen any other women, she could feel them urging her to join their ranks in breaking the status quo. It had both scared and exhilarated her. "I will talk with my father about it when we get home. I know he will support me and, in the end, he will have mother make a show of supporting me too."

"Your father sounds like a very special man," Abby said thoughtfully. "He is obviously a very wise man—and also a brave one. It is hard to go against tradition. Especially for a man. *Especially* when it is his daughter going against the tradition."

"My father is wonderful."

"But...?"

Carrie laughed. "Does there have to be a but with everything I say?"

Aunt Abby shrugged. "No, but when I hear one I'm going to ask."

Carrie looked at her and smiled. She knew she would never have to worry about Aunt Abby saying what was on her mind. They rounded the corner and started down a long street of brick row houses. The postage stamp yards still fascinated her, but they held no drawing power. She loved city life, but the freedom of her childhood would always demand more space for her restless spirit. She would feel caged in one of these yards.

"Aunt Abby, do you believe slavery is right?" Carrie asked suddenly. She had wanted to ask that question for the entire month. She had let dances, the theater, museums, and luncheons occupy her time, but the thought had never been far from her mind. She had talked to her new friend about endless topics but had always managed to avoid the one most troubling her.

Abby took a deep breath, stopped walking, and turned to gaze steadily into her eyes. "What do you think?"

Carrie shook her head. "Not this time," she said firmly. "I know I have to make my own decision about this, but I really want to know what you think and believe."

Abby took Carrie's arm and led her to a bench underneath a spreading maple tree. Once they were seated, she gazed, deep in thought, at a large brick building across from where they were sitting. Finally, she took a deep breath and spoke. "I am a member of the Philadelphia Abolitionist Society."

Carrie was speechless. She could do nothing more than stare at the woman across from her. Aunt Abby was an abolitionist? Abby waited patiently. Finally Carrie spoke. "Why didn't you tell me?"

"Would it have mattered?"

Carrie pondered the question. *Would* it have mattered? Would it have changed the fact that their hearts had bonded so closely? Would it have kept her from loving this woman who had become like another mother to her? "I don't know," she said slowly. She caught the flash of hurt on Abby's face, reached out a hand, and took the other woman's in it. "It wouldn't have changed how much I've grown to love, admire, and respect you even one iota."

"But...?" Aunt Abby made no attempt to hide the laughter in her eyes when she asked the question that seemed to have become a kind of code between them.

Carrie managed a laugh. "Why didn't you tell me before?" She couldn't hide the hurt in her voice.

Abby paused. "You are struggling with the slavery issue yourself, aren't you?" When Carrie nodded, she continued softly. "How could I expect you to confront how I feel about the issue, when you are running from how *you* feel about it?"

Carrie stared at her, slightly stunned by Aunt Abby's words. "How did you know?"

Aunt Abby laughed gently. "It's an old trick I once used quite often. I recognize it easily. I seemed to always have this absurd hope that if I ignored an unpleasant situation long enough it would go away. I found it usually only became more difficult."

"That's true," Carrie agreed, looking down at the ground. "How long have you been an abolitionist?"

"For ten years."

"You don't talk like Alex Morning."

"Heaven forbid!" Abby exclaimed. "I should certainly hope not."

"But do you feel the way he does?"

Abby paused for a long moment. "Carrie, I hate slavery. I hate what it does to people—both blacks and whites. I believe it means misery and suffering for the black people who are slaves. I believe it means a lowering of the selves God made us to be for the white people. Both are a tragedy. But I don't hate slave owners."

"Why not?"

Abby seemed to struggle for words. "I believe slavery has become a trap for everyone involved in it. A terrible process, with terrible consequences, was put into motion when the very first slave set foot on American soil. We were a people dedicated to the equality and freedom of everyone, yet we chose to deny an entire race of people that for which we founded this country. We have sought to ignore our conscience ever since. The only way white people can continue slavery is by convincing themselves that black people are a lesser people than they are. By doing so, I believe they make *themselves* the lesser people. Black people are in bondage by no choice of their own. White people are in bondage because they choose to follow their own sin and deception."

Carrie fought to make herself listen. Part of her knew Abby was speaking truth, while another part wanted to throw the words back in her face.

Abby smiled sadly. "Carrie, only God can show you the truth about slavery."

"But God says slavery is right!" She couldn't identify why she was supporting something she had grown to abhor.

"Does he?""

"Of course he does. I've heard preachers give sermons on it many times. They say the Bible supports our owning slaves."

Abby spoke softly. "*My* church preaches that slavery is a sin and that the Bible clearly teaches against it." She continued. "Carrie, have you read the Bible for yourself? Do you know what it says?"

"My father says that's what ministers are for. To tell us what the Bible says and then to interpret it." Carrie's voice rose in stubborn defiance. She could not explain why she was close to tears. Blinking her eyes rapidly, she forced them back.

Abby edged closer. "Carrie, listen to what I am about to say." Her voice, though low, was more intense than Carrie had ever heard it. "This has nothing to do with our differing beliefs about slavery. It has everything to do with how you'll make decisions for the rest of your life." Abby waited several moments for Carrie to regain control. "Carrie, the church is made up of people. The ministers who stand and preach the word of God are nothing but people. Yes, many of them have been called by God to serve in that way, but they are still *just people*. And people make mistakes. People, even ministers, form opinions and beliefs based on their own experiences and their own interpretations. How else can you explain two men—both ministers of God—standing in their pulpits delivering vastly different messages about the same issue?"

Carrie leaned forward now, intent on every word coming out of Aunt Abby's mouth. Somehow she knew this was critically important.

Abby continued. "Both men obviously believe what they are saying enough to preach it to whomever will listen. But, Carrie," she said earnestly, "those men are *not* God. Only God holds the real truth. And I believe he will give it to anyone who honestly seeks and asks questions. The Bible says 'all who seek me will find me.' It is good to listen to what people have to say. Listen, and then examine it. Read the Bible yourself and then ask God to show you the truth. That's the only truth you can stand on—the only truth that will not falter when attacked by others around you."

"That's a lot of work."

"Yes," Abby said flatly, her eyes kind, "and that is exactly why most people are merely sheep being led by the person who steps forward claiming to be their shepherd. It's much easier to be blindly led along. They echo sentiments put forth by someone else without knowing God's mind, and certainly without knowing his heart."

"Alex Morning said slavery is of the Devil," Carrie stammered, dismayed by the increased chaos in her heart.

Abby looked into Carrie's eyes. "If something is not of God, then who is it of?" she asked softly. She didn't give Carrie time to answer. "Alex Morning was very wrong that night. I may think some of the things he said were true, but his method did more harm than good. He was every bit as wrong as the thing he was attacking. When people fight something with hate and anger, they close the doors to actual change because they close the doors of the person's heart they are trying to change. Carrie, I believe slavery is wrong, but I also believe many of the methods used to end it are also wrong because they employ hatred."

"Like John Brown?"

Abby nodded vigorously. "Like John Brown. I sympathize with his heart and his desire to see people set free, but hatred and murder are not the ways to accomplish it. In the end he walked away from the love of God and chose his own ways." She paused again, obviously deep in thought. "I wish there were a painless way to end slavery—a painless way for both blacks and whites. I have come to the conclusion that it is not possible. The minute man decided to do away with another man's freedom, the wheels were set in motion that would insure a painful ending for the one who began such a system. The South has grown to depend on slavery. That doesn't change the fact, however, that people's freedom has been stolen from them. Which is more important?"

Carrie felt as if her head were going to burst. Why, oh why, did this issue have to constantly haunt her?

Abby drew closer and leaned over to look into Carrie's downcast eyes. "You say you want to be different. You say you want to go places most women never think of. There is a responsibility that goes with being different—with being a leader. Women—people everywhere—will look up to you for daring to be different. What will they see, Carrie?" she challenged lovingly, yet firmly. "Will they see someone with the courage to stand for truth? Will they see someone who moves beyond what is comfortable in order to do what is right?" Abby stopped and leaned back against the bench. She had said all she was going to say.

Carrie stared at the ground, struggling to bring her rampaging thoughts under control. "I wish I could stay with you longer, Aunt Abby." Her words trailed off into the glimmering heat waves bouncing off the street. She was completely unaware of the sweat beginning to trickle down her face. Carrie had no idea how to put into words what she was feeling, she just knew she didn't want to leave. She both despised and welcomed the challenges Aunt Abby was throwing at her. Slowly, a fire ignited in her heart. A fire to live up to Aunt Abby's standards. But most importantly, a fire to know her own mind--to know her own heart. Suddenly, she truly understood she was the only one who held the answer to all her questions about slavery.

"I would love for you to come back, Carrie," Abby said earnestly. "You could live with me a few months if you would like." She reached out and took her hand. "I have grown to love you deeply."

Carrie stared at her, unable to believe her own ears. But then, suddenly, a steady stream of people began to pour into the building across the street. Carrie's attention was drawn to the oddity of the group. She saw as many blacks as she saw whites. What was going on?

Abby answered her unspoken question. "That is the meeting hall of the Philadelphia Abolitionists. They meet every Thursday morning."

"Is that why you brought me this way?"

"Heavens, no!" Abby laughed. "I thought we would be home by now."

Carrie stared across the street thoughtfully. "Can we go?"

"Go home?"

"No. Go to the meeting."

Now it was Abby's turn to stare at her. Slowly she nodded her head. "If you want to."

Carrie's answer was to stand up and make her way across the road. Heads nodded pleasantly toward Abby as they entered the large room filled with chairs and a podium in the front. The looks directed toward Carrie were curious but not unkind. Carrie had never been to a meeting like this. There were equal parts black and white. There were also equal parts women and men. She wondered if everyone had an equal say.

Carrie was too busy looking around during the opening portion of the meeting to hear much of what was said. Her attention was drawn to the front, however, when a small, plainly dressed woman with a head covering took her place behind the podium. "I have a special guest I would like to introduce," the woman began. "Many of you remember me telling you about Harriet Masters. For those of you who don't, you're in for a real treat. But I'm not going to say anything else. I prefer to let her speak for herself."

Carrie gasped when Harriet took her place behind the podium, and she pulled her hat a little closer down on her face. She was glad Aunt Abby had selected chairs toward the back of the large room. She sensed Aunt Abby looking at her inquisitively, but she refused to return the look.

Harriet gripped the podium and spoke slowly. "My name be Harriet Masters. I don't speak too good, but I got me somethin' to say. First off, I want to say thank you to all you fine folks who helped me get free. I know I ain't all the ways free yet. I stills got to get myself to Canada. I know I only be here in this city of Philadelphia for a while, den I'll be on my way again. Only I know I won't be alone. I got fine folks helping me break away from the misery I was in."

Carrie leaned forward, soaking in every word. Her eyes never left the familiar face.

"I ain't always been a slave. I was born a free girl somewhere's up north. I can't rightly recollect where. I was only a little gal—maybe seven or so—when some slave hunters kidnapped me from my mama and daddy's front yard. I screamed for my mama but it didn't do no good. I never did see them again." Harriet paused to take a deep breath. "I done been livin' as a slave for twenty years now. Some of it was not so bad. Some of it was real bad. I worked out in the fields for my owner. The first overseer weren't so bad. He yelled and hollered a lot but he didn't use the lash too much. But then the new one come. He be a real bad man. He didn't have no problem using the lash. We done worked in the fields sometimes till it be way past dark. The old overseer let us have garden patches and we could even keep some animals for eating. The new one, he made us get rid of our gardens. Then he killed our animals and put the meat in the marse's meat house. As long as the work got done, the marse didn't care nothin' about what be going on with us." Harriet's voice was a mixture of bitterness and sorrow.

Carrie looked quickly around the room. Faces were set in anger. Many women wiped tears from their eyes as they listened to the woeful tale. Carrie battled the sickness rising in her stomach like bile. She wanted to jump up and run from the room. Instead, she turned and leaned farther forward to listen intently.

Harriet continued after a long moment. "Being a slave can be either *real* bad or just bad. Even when I got treated good, all I wanted was to be free. It be hard on the mind and the heart when everythin' around you be telling you that you ain't no more use than an animal. Sooner or later you start wonderin' if it be true. Your spirit be tellin' you that you be somebody. Everythin' else be telling you that you're nothin'." Her voice grew more intense. "The South be full of people like me just wantin' to be free. Most of us have heard somethin' bout the Underground Railroad, but we think it be a dream. We can't believe it be for real—dat people really care 'bout what be happenin' to us." She stopped to wipe a tear running down her cheek. "Why, I thought it be too good to be true when one of yo conductors came and took us away from our plantation. It took us near two months to make it this far. I can't tell you how many mounds of hay I been hid under, nor how many barns I been sleepin' in. The slave hunters done 'most caught us a bunch of times. But the good Lord done been watchin' out for us. We done got this far. I think we be movin' on soon." The tears were flowing in earnest now. "I be a free woman now. I aim to find my mama and daddy somehow. I know somewhere they're still out 'dere wonderin' where their little girl be." Then she took a deep breath and straightened her shoulders. Pride and determination shined from her strong features. "And one day I be goin' back to find my own chillun'. I have three of dem. Fine chillun... They be taken from me when they was little and sent off to be house chillun' for people in the city. They told me we could visit sometime. I ain't seen nothin' of them since they be gone. But someday," she vowed in a strong voice, "my chillun and I will be together again. Someday..." Body erect, Harriet turned and made her way back to her seat.

Carrie was trembling all over.

"We need to go, Carrie."

Carrie started when she felt Aunt Abby's hand on her arm. Nodding wordlessly, she rose to follow her from the room. The searing heat hit them full in the face when they exited the building, but Carrie barely felt it.

"Want to talk about it?" Aunt Abby's voice was deep with concern. "You went white as a sheet the minute Harriet took the podium. Was it too much for you? Was I wrong to take you to the meeting?"

Carrie shook her head, too full of emotion to talk just then. They were several blocks from the building before she regained control of herself. She turned to Aunt Abby. "It was Harriet. She—" Just then her eyes widened in horror and she broke away from Aunt Abby to stride across the street. Several swiftly moving carriages barely missed her.

"Mr. Manson! What a surprise to see you in Philadelphia." Carrie's voice gushed with enthusiasm.

The burly man who was the target of her pursuit pulled up short as Carrie appeared in front of him. The two men accompanying him stopped but didn't bother to hide the impatient looks on their faces. "Hello, Miss Cromwell." He made no attempt to hide his surprise.

Carrie bit her lip. She knew it wasn't proper for a plantation owner's daughter to be familiar with an overseer, but now was no time to worry about protocol. "Why, what a delight to see you here. What brings you here? Do tell me how you like Philadelphia!" Carrie maintained her position in the middle of the sidewalk.

Manson looked at her sharply. "It's nice to see you, Miss Cromwell, but I am in rather a hurry right now." The two men beside him shifted uneasily.

"Why, Mr. Manson, what could be more important than talking to little ol' me?" Carrie almost laughed aloud at the sound of her own petulant voice. "I have *so* missed everyone from home. You're like a breath of fresh air! Do tell me how things are back in Virginia.

The Blackwells? Louisa?" Carrie fought to control her panic. She had to stall them. She was counting on the close friendship between her father and Alfred Blackwell to keep him there.

The two men stared at Manson as he pushed his hat back on his head and sighed heavily. "Miss Cromwell, the truth is that I am not here in Philadelphia on pleasure. It's business. I really must be going." He moved as to walk around Carrie.

Carrie, fighting a desire to laugh, moved forward suddenly and put her hand on his arm. His tanned face blushed crimson. Why, it was rather fun to use her feminine wiles! "Oh, business," she gushed, stretching out the word as long as she could. "I am so fascinated by business, Mr. Manson. Man's ability to handle business is something I so admire. Do tell me what kind of business you're here on."

Manson ignored the two men at his side and settled into a relaxed posture on the sidewalk. "Well, Miss Cromwell. It's quite a long story."

"Oh, I love long stories," Carrie cried, feeling quite triumphant. The men behind Manson ground their teeth in frustration.

Thus encouraged, Manson embarked on his long tale of frustrations and thwarted opportunities as he had sought for weeks to hunt down the Blackwell slaves who had escaped. "There were ten of them, Miss Cromwell. They be mighty valuable to Blackwell. I've had to come and go in the hunt because I still have my responsibilities at the plantation. But we've been told they're here in Philadelphia. Close, as a matter of fact." Suddenly he was all business again. "Good day, Miss Cromwell." He tipped his hat, stepped around her, and disappeared into the crowd.

Carrie looked after him, biting her lip. Had she given Harriet enough time?

"What in the world was that little show of southern seduction all about?"

Carrie started as Aunt Abby's amused voice sounded at her side. "Oh, Aunt Abby," she cried. "I hope I gave her enough time." The despair in her voice was obvious.

"What in the world are you talking about, Carrie?"

Carrie looked around the crowded sidewalks, now aware of people having to sidestep around her. "Can we sit down on this bench for a moment? I know you said we had to be going, but—"

Abby was already seating herself. "Tell me what is going on," she demanded.

Carrie nodded. "It was Harriet. I've known her all my life." She paused and took in Aunt Abby's startled look. "She ran away from Blackwell Plantation. Alfred Blackwell is one of my father's closest friends." She paused as she remembered the tears streaming down Harriet's face. "That man I was talking to is Abe Manson, Blackwell's overseer. They heard the runaway slaves were in Philadelphia. As soon as I saw him I knew what he was here for." Her voice caught. "Do you think I gave them enough time?"

Abby nodded. "You did fine, Carrie. There was just enough time."

Carrie stared at the smile on her face. "How do you—"

Abby took the girl's hand. "When you looked so frightened, and then darted across the street, I knew something was wrong. Then I got a close look at those men and recognized one of them as a slave hunter. I also remembered your reaction when Harriet rose to speak. I couldn't figure out the whole story, but I put two and two together enough to send a passing friend back to the meeting." She smiled warmly. "Harriet and her friends are being taken to a safe place even as we speak."

Carrie fell back with a deep sigh of relief.

Abby squeezed her hand. "Thank you," she said fervently, her voice choked with tears. She looked deeply into Carrie's eyes. "Why did you do it, Carrie?"

Carrie shrugged. She hadn't really stopped to think through any of her actions. There had been no time. "Harriet was so happy to be free, and she's gone through so much already..." Her voice trailed off, then strengthened. "I could never have lived with myself if I hadn't done something to stop them." Silence fell between them for a moment and then Carrie laughed merrily. Her laughter continued as she saw Aunt Abby staring at her with concern. Finally, she sobered enough to speak. "None of my friends would have recognized me today. I hardly recognized myself. I've never been one to utilize feminine wiles." Mirth overcame her again as she gasped, "I'm really quite good at it, you know. It was rather fun."

Abby's laughter rang out with her own, attracting the stares of many passersby. Carrie didn't care. It felt good to laugh after the tension and heavy feelings that had permeated her entire day.

When both women had regained control, Abby leaned over. "I meant what I said earlier, Carrie. I would love for you to return and stay with me for as long as you would like."

Carrie stared at her for a few moments and then nodded firmly. "I am going to talk to my father when I get home. I'm sure he will allow it." Suddenly the most important thing in the world was to come back to Philadelphia and continue to explore the feelings and thoughts exploding through her mind and heart. And she wanted to be with Aunt Abby –an honest woman who would challenge her and allow her to be herself.

Carrie took deep breaths of fresh air as Miles skillfully guided the carriage around new potholes that had sprung up since she'd been gone. "It's so good to be home, Miles." Carrie meant it. Aunt Abby expected her back within a month, but Carrie knew she would never lose her love of the Virginia countryside. This was where a part of her heart would always be. No matter where she went, or what she did, Virginia would always be home.

"It's good to have you home, Miss Carrie." Miles said sincerely.

"How is everything at home, Miles?"

"Everything be fine, miss." He raised the reins and clucked to make the horses go faster.

Carrie nodded and relaxed back against the seat. She had been surprised when her father had not been there to greet her but had been satisfied with Miles's explanation that he was too busy on the plantation. Summer was the busiest time of the year. She knew it could be hard to get away. She watched the countryside slip by as she carefully planned just how she was going to convince her father that her returning to Philadelphia was the best thing. She and Aunt Abby had already made so many plans. Her head spun with the thoughts of all that was waiting for her when she returned. Her fear that Natalie would be upset had been completely unfounded. *Oh, pooh, I'm happy for you. But me? All I want to do is get back to the South where I belong.*

Carrie was ready for a long bath and a good night's sleep by the time the carriage rolled up the driveway. A long talk with Rose and then a good night's sleep. That was all she wanted.

"Welcome home, Carrie."

"Father!" Carrie jumped from the carriage and ran up the stairs to embrace her father. Then she pulled back in alarm. The lines around his eyes were deeper than ever and his eyes were distressed—almost afraid. "Father, what's wrong?"

Thomas hesitated. "Your mother—" He paused and struggled to control his voice. "Your mother is very ill."

Without another word, Carrie turned and ran up the stairs.

TWENTY-THREE

"Mama!" Carrie cried as soon as she reached her parents' bedroom door. She knew without entering the room that her mother was seriously ill. Nothing else could have imprinted the deep fear in her father's eyes.

"Shh..." Rose raised her finger to her lips. "She's finally sleeping," she whispered. She handed the huge peacock feather to another house servant standing close by and walked over to where Carrie stood staring at her mother. The house servant immediately began fanning the sleeping woman.

Carrie allowed Rose to lead her from the room and back down the stairs to where her father was still standing on the porch where she had left him. As soon as she saw him, she broke away from Rose and ran to him. "Father! What is wrong with Mother?" she demanded.

Thomas turned weary eyes to her. "We don't know yet. The doctor has been called, but he hasn't been able to get here. I hear a lot of people are sick."

"How long has she been like this?" Carrie asked sharply.

"Four days."

"*Four days?* And the doctor hasn't been here yet?" Carrie fought to think clearly. She knew her father wasn't good with medical emergencies. He seemed to fall apart when those he loved became ill. That was why she and her mother had always taken care of the medical needs on the plantation. She laid her hand gently on her father's arm.

"How did this start?" she asked Rose.

"Your mama complained of a bad headache a few days ago."

Carrie frowned. For all her genteel southern ways, her mother could endure a great deal of suffering without complaint. She must have been in intense pain to have complained.

"She was helping some of the house servants cut out dresses for some of the children in the quarters," Rose continued, "but she finally laid it down and went up to her room. I was worried about her, so I went to look in on her an hour or so later. She had fallen across the bed without getting under the covers and was burning up with a fever. Later, she started mumbling to herself and thrashing around." Rose had fear in her eyes when she looked up at Carrie. "I've done everything I can, Miss Carrie. All the things I've seen you and your mama do when one of us is sick. I can't get the fever to come down."

Carrie nodded and started back up the stairs. "How soon was the doctor called?"

"We sent Miles to Richmond that very first day," Thomas answered.

Carrie whirled around to stare at her father. "Miles *knew*? He didn't tell me?"

"I didn't want to worry you until you got home."

Carrie groaned. "I could have perhaps found the doctor in Richmond. At least I could have brought back some kind of medicine." She opened her mouth to say more, but the pain in her father's eyes stopped her. She bit back any more words, climbed the stairs, and entered the sick room. She moved closer to her mother's still form and laid a hand on her burning forehead. Her heart sank. "She's had a fever like this for four days?"

Rose nodded silently. "I've tried to get her to drink, but she mostly just thrashes around and knocks it out of my hand. I haven't been able to get much into her." She paused. "Miss Carrie, I'm glad you're home. I'm real worried about your mama."

Carrie turned to Rose with a faint smile. "I'm glad I'm home, too, Rose." She wrapped her arms around her friend and gave her a hug. She needed Rose's strength. Then she straightened and started barking orders.

In short order she had a tub full of chopped ice brought up from the ice house. Buckets of cold water drawn from the well were poured into it. Great strips of sheeting were torn and brought to the room. Only then did Carrie begin to work, ordering everyone but Rose out of the room.

"Your father wants to know if you want his help."

Carrie shook her head firmly at Sam who had suddenly appeared at the door. "Tell him I'll keep him posted." She didn't add that he would just be in the way. Sam nodded and pulled the door shut.

Carrie moved over and pulled all the covers off her mother. The first thing she had to do was bring the fever down. She pulled the soaked nightgown off and directed Rose to drench the sheet strips and wring them out. As Rose passed them to her, she carefully wrapped all parts of her mother's body with the cold cloths. She worked relentlessly, stopping only long enough to wipe the sweat dripping from her forehead. As soon as she finished wrapping her mother's body, she would start all over again, replacing hot cloths with new cold ones. She lost all track of time.

"Are you hungry, Miss Carrie?" Rose asked at some point.

She shook her head impatiently. "We need more ice. Please send Sam to bring more."

The evening wore on as she continued her battle. As darkness fell she imagined that the sheets weren't getting hot quite as fast, but by now she was too tired to really tell. Her movements were automatic. Wrap. Unwrap. Wrap. Unwrap.

It was past midnight when Abigail opened her eyes. "Thomas?" she said weakly.

Carrie spun from where she was kneeling next to the tub. "Mama!" Leaping up, she flew to her mother's side and laid a hand on her forehead. "Your fever has broken," she whispered joyfully, her fatigue forgotten.

Abigail stared at her uncomprehendingly. "I've been sick, haven't I?" She closed her eyes for a moment, and opened them again with effort.

"Yes, Mama. You've been sick," Carrie confirmed. "But you're going to be okay now." She wondered at the truth of her own words. She had seen what a fever like her mother's could do to a person. She had brought it down, but had she done so soon enough?

Her mother spoke again, her words slow and halting. "You're home. I'm glad."

"I'm home," Carrie agreed softly. "You need to drink some water, Mama." She reached out and took the glass Rose was holding out to her. She controlled her shudder when she lifted her mother's shoulders to steady her. How had she become so frail and thin in just four days? Her heart was heavy when she gently lowered her mother back down on the bed. The fever had already done a lot of damage. How much would have to wait to be seen.

"Your father is outside, Carrie. Sam went to get him."

Carrie nodded and went to open the door. "The fever has broken, Father."

Tears filled Thomas's eyes. "I knew everything would be okay as soon as you got home, Carrie."

Carrie said nothing about her misgivings. Words would not change the situation. Only time would tell. "She needs rest, Father."

Thomas nodded. "I'll only stay a few minutes."

Carrie stepped back. "I'm going down to get some fresh air. When I come back I'm going to see if she can drink a little broth. She has lost a lot of strength."

Carrie stayed on the porch just a few minutes, gulping in the cool night air. She could hardly believe she had arrived home that afternoon. She gave one long look north and then turned to re-enter the house.

Rose glanced up at the light still shining from the Cromwell's bedroom before she soundlessly slipped into the woods. Carrie had been home for two days. During that time she had rarely left her mother's side. The fever had tried to creep back several times, but her determined friend had fought it off. Her mother was eating a little, but her tiny frame had begun to look emaciated. She knew Carrie was deeply concerned. Rose shook off her thoughts as she walked quietly through the woods. There were other people who were depending on her. She prayed Carrie would not call for her and find her missing.

"That you, Rose?"

"Yes, Moses," Rose whispered back. She smiled when his towering form appeared by her side. Just his being there made her feel more confident. She waited until they were deep in the woods before she spoke again. "Are the others in place?"

Moses nodded. "They'll be only a few minutes behind us. They're all meetin' in the school ravine. They'll wait there for us."

Rose smiled in the darkness. Moses had been working so hard. He had mastered reading in only a few weeks and devoured everything she could get to him. It wasn't much, but she did the best she could. He also made sure she corrected him on his speech. In only a few months he hardly resembled the defeated man who was brought to Cromwell from the slave auction. Rose had grown to depend on him, but he had never spoken his heart again after the night Jamison had come. She was content in what they had.

Her face grew more serious as the two slowed their pace and crept quietly toward the road. Moses had insisted they come early. *In case it's a trap*, he had said. *I trust Jamison but it never hurts to be careful.* He figured if a trap was going to be laid, it would be done just before the slaves were supposed to meet the wagon on the road. They intended to be there to watch.

They peered out of the bushes, scanning the road and the surrounding forest. Great banks of clouds obscured any moonlight that would betray their actions. Flashes of heat lightning competed with the luminescent flashes of lightning bugs. Rose forced herself not to slap at the mosquitoes leaving their mark on the exposed parts of her body. The night, still simmering with the heat of the day, wrapped itself around her like a wet cloak. She fought to control the nervous pounding of her heart. Finally, she tugged at Moses's arm. They had to go get the others.

Moses nodded. He seemed satisfied. No one was waiting in the murky blackness. If their friends were going to escape, tonight would be the night. He held

Rose's hand as they walked back through the night. He knew the wooded trails as well as she did now.

When they broke into the school clearing, eight sets of frightened, yet determined eyes met them.

Jasmine, carrying nothing but a small bundle of clothing, rose to greet them. "Is everythin' alright?" she asked anxiously. Then she looked closely at Rose. "Where be your other clothes? Mr. Jamison done told us we could bring some extra, didn't he?" she asked with a worried frown.

Rose nodded reassuringly. "Yes, Jasmine." She took a deep breath. "I have something to tell all of you," she said softly. "I...I won't..." she gulped, trying to force the words out. Now that the time had come, the pain of being left behind was almost unbearable. "I won't be coming with you," she finally forced out in a barely discernible whisper.

A shocked silence fell on the group of soon-to-be fugitives. Jasmine was the first to speak. "What you talkin' bout, Miss Rose? What do you mean you ain't comin' with us?"

"Rose can't leave her mama." Miles spoke in a soft voice that expressed admiration and understanding of her pain at the same time.

Rose turned to him with a grateful smile. "Miles is right. My mama needs me. I can't leave her now. But it's alright," she said, summoning a brave smile. "My turn will come sometime."

Sadie's troubled voice broke into the stillness of the night. "You be knowin' this all along, Rose?"

Rose nodded. "I thought it would make it easier for all of you if you thought I was going to escape with you. You're doing the right thing," she said earnestly. "Jamison can be trusted. I will be back here praying and believing for you."

The little group gazed around at each other in concern. They had counted on Rose being with them.

Miles was the first to speak. "So be it," he said firmly. He turned to Rose. "We'll miss you, girl, but I know you're makin' the decision best for you." He turned to the others. "We have to git goin'. This is our chance to be free. We can't do nothin' to mess it up. *We's going to be free!*"

The strength of his words flowed into the rest of the group. Their backs straightened, and one by one, they all nodded.

"You'll always be right smack in the center of our hearts, Rose." Sadie spoke for all of them. "You done taught us how to read and write. Cause of you we can do somethin' wid our lives when we make it to Canada. Thank you."

Rose made no effort to hide the tears running down her face. She hugged each one and then stepped back. "We need to be going," she said firmly. She turned and led the way back down the trail.

"She's better isn't she, Carrie?"

Carrie looked up at her father standing next to the bed where his wife had just drifted back to sleep. "She's better," she agreed. She would not burden her father with her fear.

"The doctor said you worked a miracle bringing her temperature down."

Carrie frowned. "He couldn't tell me what caused it." Actually, the visiting doctor had deeply frustrated her. His examination had been perfunctory and he seemed stymied by his patient's sudden onset of sickness. His manner had been brusque and uncaring. She had tried to justify his behavior by saying he was tired and overworked, but still it had grated on her. Her desire to be a doctor had risen steadily while she watched him work.

Thomas continued to stare down at his wife. "How long before she is back to normal?"

"I don't know, Father." Carrie didn't know what else to say. She knew from all of her reading in the medical journals that a high fever sustained for as long as her mother's could be very serious. She reached out a hand and patted his arm. "I'll do everything I can."

"What did the doctor say to do?"

Carrie shrugged. "Nothing," she admitted flatly. That had been the hardest thing. The doctor had offered no word of hope and given no clear instructions on what she could do to help her mother. He has simply shaken his head, closed his bag, and walked from the room. She had been so glad her father hadn't been there to see it. He still had hope. She was trying to.

Rose could hear the low rumble of a wagon coming down the road when the group had almost reached the edge of the woods. Jamison, if it *was* Jamison, was right on time. She held her finger to her lip and crouched down behind the surrounding brush. Everyone followed her example. Not a sound betrayed their presence.

Slowly, the wagon approached and stopped. Rose peered out into the darkness. She would wait for the signal.

"I am a friend."

Rose sighed with relief and moved out into the road. "Hello, Mr. Jamison."

"Hello, Rose. It's good to see you again." Jamison's voice was calm, but his eyes never stopped moving.

"I have eight people waiting to join you." Rose answered his next question before he asked it. "Adams is off on a drinking binge. It's Saturday night. He won't come near the quarters until Monday morning. Mrs. Cromwell is sick. No one will be missed until Adams raises the alarm."

"Good." Jamison jumped down from the wagon and turned to her. "Have you changed your mind, Rose? It's not too late to join us."

Rose shook her head and managed a smile. "No, Mr. Jamison. I will be staying here."

Jamison frowned slightly and nodded. "I have no way of knowing how long it will take to get them to freedom. It is getting more difficult. As the number of escaping slaves increase, more and more effort is being made to stop it. It took us two months to get a group from Blackwell to Philadelphia. Even then, one of them almost got caught. A young girl managed to delay the slave hunters long enough for us to get her away. They are on their way to Canada now. They should be free soon."

Rose smiled. "I'm glad," she murmured.

Jamison nodded and looked toward the woods. "Let's go, everyone. We have to be at the next station before it starts to get light." He waved his hand at the wagon piled high with sweet-smelling hay. "Everyone under the hay." He waited while the group of slaves filed silently from the woods, and smiled encouragingly at each one of them. "My job is to take you to freedom. Thank you for trusting me. I admire your courage."

The group nodded soberly and began to climb into the wagon. Rose knew now that the moment was here they were overwhelmed with their fears of what could happen, but there was no turning back. They had set their faces to freedom and nothing was going to make them turn away. She and Moses watched them silently.

Jamison climbed into his seat and stared down at them. "If there is some way to let you know they made it, I will." Then he picked up his reins and clucked to his team.

Rose watched as the wagon rumbled down the road. Long after it had disappeared she continued to stand, staring into the blackness.

"Rose?" Moses's gentle voice and soft touch on her shoulder broke the dam. Sobbing, she turned and pressed her face against his massive chest. He said nothing—just held her close and stroked her hair, staring into the darkness as she had done.

"Manson back yet?" Ike Adams tipped his glass back and took another long gulp of whiskey. He grinned as the burning liquid flowed down his throat and numbed his mind.

"Nah," Jennings smirked. "He ain't gonna find them niggers. Blackwell will probably give him the boot. Them slaves were worth thousands of dollars."

"It weren't his fault them niggers got away." Adams protested hotly. "You can't be with them every second." He scowled into his drink. "It's them damn Yankees. They're coming down here and taking our slaves. They need to come down here and fight like real men. Then we'd show 'em." He sounded tough, but the other man's words had awakened an ever-present fear. What would happen to his job if some of the Cromwell slaves managed to escape?

"Manson's had hunters after them slaves for two months now. I heard he even took off for Philadelphia himself something about them slaves maybe being there." Jennings shook his head. "I wouldn't want to be him if he has to come back and tell Blackwell he didn't find them slaves." Dramatically, he pulled an imaginary knife across his throat and grimaced.

Adams jumped up and reached for the whiskey bottle. "It ain't his fault I tell you!"

Jennings shrugged. "Somebody going to carry the blame." He squinted his eyes. "What about the Cromwell niggers, Adams? What you gonna do if some of them get away?"

Adams slammed his glass down on the table. "That ain't gonna happen!" But the fears had started spinning in his brain. Suddenly, there was nothing to do but go to the quarters and satisfy his fears. It didn't matter that it was after midnight. He threw his glass aside and smiled bitterly as he heard the tinkle of glass against the wall. Then he turned and stalked from the house.

Moses and Rose had just reached the wooded edge of the quarters when they heard the sound of a horse galloping in their direction.

"Hurry, Moses. Get back to your cabin." Rose was suddenly very afraid. The sound of a horse could mean nothing but trouble.

Moses hesitated. "You're going to be okay?"

Rose nodded impatiently and gave him a push. "Hurry!"

Moses looked down at her and then turned and sprinted into the darkness.

Moments later, Adams reined in his horse and glared at the dark cabins. He scowled and reached behind his saddle, pulling out the whip he carried when Cromwell wasn't around. He uncoiled it, gave it a mighty crack, and yelled, "All niggers out of the cabins!" The sound of the cracking whip filled the air as slaves stumbled from their beds, sleepy-eyed and confused.

Horrified, Rose watched from her concealed spot. She should go before she was missed in the big house, but her feet were rooted to the ground. What had brought Adams to the quarters on his drinking night? She could do nothing but stare helplessly as Adams slid to the ground and began to inspect the slaves. She breathed a sigh of relief when she saw Moses's massive shape line up with the rest of the men. He had made it back in time. Then she groaned softly. He still had his shoes on. The rest of the sleepy-eyed men standing in line were all barefoot. *God, please!*

Just then, Moses looked down and quickly back up. Adams was at the other end of the line. Moving slowly, so as to not draw any attention, Moses carefully eased a shoe off with one big foot, and pushed it back into the shadows of the cabin. He had just pushed the other shoe back into the protecting darkness when Adams broke into a stream of curses.

Moving quickly now, Adams continued his count. Soon the air was thick with his curses and hollering. Rose watched as he grabbed her mama by the arm. "Where are all the niggers, old woman?"

Sarah shook her head calmly. "I wouldn't be knowing nothin' 'bout that." Adams cursed again and shoved her away. A steadying arm reached out to keep her from falling.

Adams's glazed eyes focused on Moses. He seemed to grip his whip tighter as he stalked up to him. "Where are the niggers?" he demanded.

Moses just shook his head.

His silence only made Adams angrier. Pulling back his arm, he let fly with the whip. It barely missed

Moses's head. Moses closed his eyes briefly, but never flinched.

Rose groaned. What would Adams do to Moses? She knew Moses's heart was with the escaping slaves. The longer Adams stayed there, the farther away they could get.

Somehow that thought must have pierced the befuddled fog of Adams's brain. He cursed loudly, grabbed his whip, and jumped on his horse. "I'm gonna catch them niggers!" he yelled. "And when I do, they're gonna be sorry they were ever born!" He kicked his horse savagely and disappeared down the road.

Rose, wiping tears from her eyes, ran through the woods. She had to get back to the house before they discovered she was gone. She ignored the cruel lash of branches as she flew down the path. She must hurry! Adams was stomping up the stairs when she reached the edge of the clearing. Rose groaned as the pounding of his heavy fist on the door rang through the night. All she could do was watch. She would surely be seen if she tried to cross the yard.

"What in the world is going on?" Thomas Cromwell's angry voice rang out clearly as he threw the massive door open. Carrie watched from the top of the stairs as her father looked with disgust at his overseer's drunken condition. "What is it, Adams?" he asked again impatiently. "My wife is very ill! Your pounding has probably awakened her!"

Adams stared at the angry man. Then he drew himself up to his full height. "Seven of your slaves are missing, Mr. Cromwell."

Thomas stared at him. He leaned his head against the doorjamb for a brief moment and then straightened. "Who is gone, Adams?" he asked sharply.

"Seven of the field hands, sir. Sadie, Jasmine, Molly—"

Thomas held up his hand. "Are they all field hands, Adams?"

"I don't know, sir. I would recommend that you check the house and barn slaves. We need to know who we are going after."

Thomas nodded his head wearily. The strain of worrying about his wife, combined with sleepless nights, had taken its toll. "Sam?" he called sharply. He waited as Sam took what seemed to be much longer than normal to respond to his call.

The old man's face was impassive as he joined them at the door. "Yes, sir?"

"I want you to call all the house and barn slaves. Tell them to line up on the porch."

"Yes sir, Marse Cromwell." Sam turned and disappeared back into the house.

Thomas rubbed his hand over his eyes. He glanced up the stairs and saw Carrie staring down at him, but she made no move to join him. She needed to stay close enough to her mother to hear her call.

Adams fidgeted impatiently.

One by one, the slaves filed onto the porch. Rose was the last one to take her place in line. Carrie, from her place on the landing, noticed the sheen of sweat and her bright eyes.

Thomas looked them over carefully. Suddenly his face tightened. "Where is Miles?"

Carrie leaned into the support of the railing and stared down with wide eyes.

Sam shrugged, his face still impassive. "He weren't in his room over the barn, Marse Cromwell." His tone was expressionless.

Thomas shook his head in disbelief. "Miles ran away?" he asked faintly. Then he straightened. "All of you go back to your quarters," he said sternly. Nothing was said as the porch emptied. Then he turned to Adams. "Gather some men and go after them. They can't be far." He stared at Adams, taking in his drunken state once more. "When was the last time you counted them Adams? How long have they been gone?" he asked sharply.

"Just this afternoon, sir. They can't be far..."

"Unless?" Thomas peered at him.

"Unless the Underground Railroad is helping them. The

Blackwell slaves were taken off in a wagon. They ain't been found yet."

"Well, get on it, man! I can't leave. My wife needs me. Find whoever you can to help you. I'll make sure they're paid. Just bring them back."

Adams nodded, his mean features twisting with pleasure. "Yes, sir! I'll have them niggers back soon!"

Carrie shuddered at the thought of Adams catching the runaway slaves. She knew he would show no mercy.

Thomas watched as his overseer strode down the steps and disappeared into the night on his horse. He stared out into the darkness for a long while. Then he turned, looked up at Carrie, and spoke in a low voice. "I don't trust Adams. I should go after the escaped slaves myself." He glanced up at the glowing window of his bedroom. "I can't leave. I won't leave! Abigail is my life. I have to be here for her if she needs me." His voice caught in pain and then grew fierce. "*All* of my slaves could get up and leave. They mean nothing without her." He turned to glare into the darkness again, his shoulders slumped with fatigue.

Carrie had not moved from her place by the stair railing. It had come to Cromwell Plantation at last. Just as her mother had feared. Slaves had run away. An image of Sadie, tossing with fever because of the cut on her foot, rose before her. Miles laughing up at her as he taught her to ride. Jasmine, as a little girl playing around Sarah until she had to go to the fields. Who else who had been a part of her life for as long as she could remember was now gone? Her heart constricted, yet she felt relief. Harriet's tear-streaked face floated back from Philadelphia to stare her in the eyes. *I just want to be free!* "Carrie…" Her mother's weak voice reached out to call her back into the present. She turned quickly and hurried to her mother's side, breathing a quick prayer that the slaves would make their way to freedom.

Adams, thinking clearly now, knew he needed help. He leaned low over Ginger's neck as she flew down the dark road. Adams was on his way to find Jennings and some of the other men. Jennings had dogs. The slaves couldn't be far. Even if they were in a wagon, men on horses could catch up with them easily.

He pulled up to the same house he had left so abruptly earlier that night, vaulted off Ginger, and ran up the stairs. "We got some niggers to catch!" he cried as soon as he entered the dark room that reeked of alcohol.

Jennings peered up at him with red-rimmed, bleary eyes. "Welcome back, Adams," he slurred. "I saved a bottle for ya." He lifted the almost empty bottle of whiskey, gave a hard laugh, and raised it to his lips.

Before he could drain the remaining drops, Adams cursed and ripped the bottle from his hands. He slammed it on the table and turned back to the men in the room. "Didn't you hear me?" he cried angrily. "We got niggers to catch. Eight of the Cromwell niggers have run away. They can't be far." He grabbed Jennings by the collar and tried to lift him from the chair. "We need your dogs, man! Get up!" But he knew even as he was yelling that his efforts were futile. The room was full of reeling, drunk men. They would be useless to him until they sobered up. Judging by the number of empty whiskey bottles littering the room, that would take some time. Adams cursed and swung his arm through the remaining bottles on the table under the window. Crashing glass and oozing liquid attracted the room's drunken attention as Adams turned and stormed from the room. He would have to go after the slaves himself. He patted his waistline. The hard metal of his pistol reassured him.

Adams knew, even as he tore out onto the porch, that his mission was senseless without the dogs and without help. Why, he couldn't even trace the slaves' escape route without the dogs. They could have gone in any direction through the woods. Common sense told him they would head north eventually, but there was no telling where they would go first. He slammed his fist against the heavy pillar holding the porch and glared helplessly back at the darkened room. He was angry, but he knew he would be no good in the same circumstances. He had been on his way to getting rip-roaring drunk before Jennings's words had sent him flying back to the quarters. He sank down on the steps and tried to force himself to examine all his options.

Just then, with a mighty clap of thunder, the bank of heavy clouds opened up to dump their cargo. Rain poured down from the sky in great sheets as the thunder rumbled and lightning flashed. Adams cursed again and shook his head. He knew the futility of even *trying* to follow the slaves in this weather. The rain would wash away all scent before the dogs would even get a chance to follow it. Slowly, he stood and climbed into his saddle. He couldn't just do nothing. He turned Ginger south, then began to jog through the pouring rain. He was on his way to find some slave hunters.

TWENTY-FOUR

"Miss Carrie! There be a letter here for you."

Carrie looked at her mother to make sure she was still sleeping and then ran lightly down the stairs. "A letter, Sam?" Her heart pounded with excitement. Could it be from Robert? She hadn't heard from him since he had written her a short note in Philadelphia saying he hoped her time with Matthew was beneficial. The note had arrived shortly before she left to come home. There had been no opportunity to think of a reply since then.

"Yes, Miss Carrie," Sam smiled and handed the letter to her. Then he frowned. "You need to get out more, Miss Carrie."

Carrie patted his arm. "I'm fine." He had already commented on her drawn, pale face. She knew he was worried. She had barely left her mother's side since she had gotten home. Rose brought meals up to her, which she would have ignored except for Rose's insistence she eat. Her burden was compounded now by illness down in the quarters. When she felt it was safe, she would slip away from the house to care for the sick slaves.

Her mother had just dropped off to sleep, so Carrie took the letter and carried it out to the front porch. Carrie settled down on the porch swing and allowed her eyes to roam across the expansive lawn. It was nearing the end of August. She could hardly believe she had been home almost a month. She shook her head and tore open the thick envelope she was holding in her hand.

"Aunt Abby!" she exclaimed. With a smile of delight she settled back against the swing.

Dear Carrie,

I received your letter with great dismay. I am so sorry to hear of your mother's illness. I understand your deep concern for her. Please know my prayers are with you and that I anxiously await more news of how she is doing. I am so glad she has you there with her.

My dear, I know your heart is there with your mother. I also know you must grieve your lost opportunity to visit Philadelphia. Please know it is not lost. For whatever reasons it has simply been postponed. You are always welcome here and I look forward to the day when you return. The time to spread your wings will come. God will use what you are going through now to prepare you for what lies ahead.

I am sending you some information I have recently acquired. After careful inquiry, I have discovered the Pennsylvania School of Medicine is not open to women at this time. Don't lose heart, however. There is another institution that would welcome you—the Female Medical College of Pennsylvania. I wish I had time to write the brave stories of women like Dr. Elizabeth Blackwell, Dr. Emily Blackwell, and Dr. Harriet Hunt. Their pioneering efforts have begun to swing the doors of the medical profession open to women. True, it is still a mighty battle, but you have warriors who have gone before. It can be done. I know you have what it takes to add your name to the list of women who have fought for their dreams. From one dreamer to another, live each day as if you are making history. You probably are!

I fear what is happening in our country. As the summer continues, the political battle rages hotter. I am almost certain Lincoln will win. Most Northerners are convinced the South's threats to secede are nothing but empty words. I remember your words on the balcony and I fear you are right.

Circumstances keep us apart for now, but, however slow the mail system, it is still a way to stay connected and in touch. I would love to know what is going on in your life—what you are thinking, feeling. Please feel free to write me.

God Bless You,

Aunt Abby

Carrie raised a hand to wipe the tears from her eyes. She tucked the brochure in her pocket to read later. The arrival of Aunt Abby's letter couldn't have been better timing. Her words were like fresh spring air to her assaulted senses. She had begun to lose sight of the fact that there was a whole world out there. Her very existence centered on her mother's bedside. Today was the first day she had thought about the political situation in the country since she had arrived home. Abby's letter was a hand of friendship reaching out to connect her to someone who believed in her.

Carrie stayed out on the porch for a long time. Gradually, the time alone and the beauty of the day released her from the self-imposed prison she had erected. Slowly, it dawned on her that she had been laboring under the belief that her mother's illness was her fault. If she had been at home being a good plantation owner's daughter like she was supposed to be, she would have been here when her mother had gotten sick. She would have been able to control the fever and it would not have ravaged her mother's body so severely. Abby's words reached across the miles and somehow made her realize it was not her fault. It was no one's fault. It had simply happened. Carrie leaned back with a sigh. She would do everything she could to make her mother well, but she would no longer do it with the burden of guilt.

"Can I get you something, Miss Carrie?"

Carrie looked up with a smile. "Yes, thank you, Sam. Could I please have some cold lemonade? Some bread and cold chicken would be wonderful, as well."

Sam's face almost split with his wide grin. "You got the light back in your eyes, Miss Carrie. I sure be glad to see it. That must have been a real good letter."

Carrie nodded. "It was a good letter from a very good friend," she said softly.

She was still moving gently in the swing when her father climbed heavily up the stairs to join her. She moved over to make room for him.

"I'm glad to see you outside, Carrie. How is your mother?"

"She's resting. Other than that, she is the same. She is still very weak and has very little appetite. It's been days since her fever has been high, but she constantly runs a low fever, and she still says her head hurts."

Thomas sighed. "I know you're doing everything you can."

Carrie nodded. "I'm going to go down and visit Sarah in the quarters. None of the medicines sent from the doctors in town seem to be doing any good."

"You think old Sarah can help?" Her father's tone was skeptical.

Carrie shrugged. "I don't know, but I'm willing to try anything. Slaves know remedies that I've never heard of. Many of them work." She tried to sound hopeful.

Thomas nodded and lapsed into deep thought. His face was creased with deep lines as he stared out over the plantation. Carrie watched Granite grazing in the field. She had not been on him since she had been home. She hadn't even been near him. It wasn't just that she couldn't get away to ride him. Being in the stables reminded her that Miles was no longer there. She missed the man who had taught her so much.

"Adams hasn't found the escaped slaves," her father said abruptly. Carrie remained silent. "Those slaves are worth close to nine thousand dollars." Thomas shook his head. "Slave hunters are on their trail, but they keep missing them," he said bitterly. "I still can't believe Miles ran away. Why, he's lived here all his life. I thought he was happy running the stables. Horses have always been his life. Why would he run away?" His tone reflected his complete bewilderment.

Carrie looked at her father. She had grown to accept that her father honestly thought slavery was the best thing for blacks. She couldn't say she agreed with him, but her love for him had in no way diminished. "Maybe being free was more important to him," she said softly.

Thomas shook his head. "What will freedom do for him?" he protested. "He'll probably never have another horse to care for. He'll live somewhere barely scraping by and be looking over his shoulder for slave hunters the rest of his life."

Carrie said nothing more. She knew it would do no good. She just looked at her father.

"What's wrong with you, Carrie? Did you get hooked up with some of those abolitionists while you were in Philadelphia? You've been different ever since you got home. You don't even seem sorry that Miles and the other slaves are gone," he said angrily.

"I'm sorry you think I seem different, Father," Carrie said softly. "I miss Miles and the others very much. I *am* sorry they are gone." She didn't add that she hoped they wouldn't be caught. She paused, trying to decide how to answer his other questions. Sam saved her.

"Miss Carrie. Your mama be calling you."

"Thank you, Sam." Rising, she breathed a sigh of relief and hurried into the house. Sooner or later she would have to decide completely where she stood, but not now. There was too much else going on.

Jamison opened the front door slightly and peered out into the night. If all was as he hoped, this would be his last night on the road before he passed the slaves off to another conductor in Philadelphia. The last month was beginning to show on him. It had been full of close calls as Adams and his two hired slave hunters dogged their trail. He had managed to stay one step ahead of them, but he was tired and he was sure his business was suffering from his extended absence. He had known the risks when he started, but he would be glad to pass the slaves off to someone else. At the same time, he knew he would miss them. He had grown genuinely fond of his brave, uncomplaining charges—especially Miles. The man was thoughtful and intelligent. Time and time again he had helped put their suffering into perspective for the other slaves. He always ended with, *We gonna be free. Ain't nothing mean more than that!* Many were the times it had bolstered Jamison's spirits as well.

Satisfied no one lurked outside, he shut the door and turned to the only other inhabitant of the house. "I'm moving them tonight."

Cartwright nodded. "You only have thirty more miles. I believe you can make it tonight if you push hard." Anson Cartwright was used to these late-night moves. His house had been a station for the Underground Railroad for ten years. It was secluded enough that people rarely visited. His barn had housed hundreds of slaves making their way to freedom. By day he worked the lumber mill. By night he assisted slaves intent on escaping their tyranny.

Jamison moved over to the table where the other man stood. "Thank you, Cartwright. You've been a godsend." Jamison had planned on being at Cartwright's house for just one night. They had been holed up here for six. Messages had been passed along warning of the presence of hostile men. He was sure they referred to Adams and whomever he had with him. He would not move the slaves until he was sure it was safe and word had come that day saying the men had moved on.

"You realize Adams and his men have probably gone on to Philadelphia, don't you?" Cartwright asked, puffing thoughtfully on a pipe.

Jamison shrugged without a care. "*Getting* them to Philadelphia is my worry. Once I'm there, I'm not concerned. I know that city like the back of my hand. There are countless places to hide runaway slaves. Those country yokels don't stand a chance." He smiled as if he relished the idea of a good contest. Then he sobered. "Goodbye, Cartwright. I hope I see you again sometime." He shook his hand firmly, opened the door, slipped out, and then stopped to listen for several long moments. When nothing but silence met his ears, he headed toward the barn.

Miles was waiting for him just inside the door. Jamison nodded at him. Without a word, Miles disappeared into the shadows. Moments later the other seven fugitives were standing next to him. They all looked worn, but the light of freedom still shone brightly in their eyes. Not once had they thought of turning back.

"The wagon is behind the barn," Jamison whispered.

The fugitives nodded. They knew what to do. Silently, they filed from the barn and took their positions under the hay. The huge mound had served them well. Miles led the horses from the barn and quickly harnessed them to the wagon. Then, he too, crawled under the hay.

Jamison had just taken his place on the seat and picked up the reins when he heard the pounding of hooves coming up the road. He froze on the seat, his mind racing.

Cartwright appeared at his side. "Into the woods. This doesn't sound good."

Jamison vaulted from his seat and ran to the back of the wagon. "Everybody out," he commanded in a low voice. The pounding drew closer as the wagon emptied and he found himself staring into eight sets of frightened eyes. There was no time for explanations. "Follow me." He turned and ran for the woods.

Once they were all concealed, he crept back to see what was happening. Cartwright emerged from the barn when three men rode up on horseback. "Can I help you gentleman?" he asked calmly.

Adams stared down at the fully dressed man.

"Awful late to be out working in your barn," he sneered.

Cartwright stared back at him. "Awful late to be calling on folks," he responded evenly.

Adams cursed and swung from his saddle. His wiry form seemed small next to Cartwright's bulk. "I hear you been hiding some slaves, Cartwright."

Cartwright gave a short laugh. "That can be dangerous business nowadays."

Martin, the older of the two slave hunters, snickered. "*Real* dangerous business, Cartwright. The courts don't think none too highly of your activities. Come to think of it—I don't either." He fingered his pistol meaningfully.

Cartwright's voice hardened. "I wouldn't be making accusations if I were you, mister. You won't find any fugitive slaves on my property and I don't appreciate your tone."

Adams moved around him arrogantly and peered into his barn. "Mind if we look around in your barn?"

"I don't reckon you've got any business in my barn. I suggest you boys just be moving on."

Martin swung from his horse slowly and walked over to Cartwright. With a menacing grin, he raised his pistol suddenly and held it to his head. "It's been a long month for me, mister. I ain't in the mood for no games. I got me eight niggers to catch and then I can go home. You catch my meaning?"

Cartwright shrugged his shoulders. "Go ahead and take a look. You won't be finding anything."

Jamison slunk back further into the shadows as Adams stared toward the woods. He was thankful for the rain that had fallen earlier that evening. Wet sticks didn't crack as easily as dry ones.

Adams emerged from the barn just as Martin walked around the back. "There ain't no slaves in that barn."

"Well looky here!" Martin exclaimed. "What's this wagon doing behind your barn, Cartwright?"

"Just got back from hauling a load of hay," Cartwright responded casually. "I hadn't had time to unhitch the horses and put them away."

"This hay ain't even wet," Martin said in a hard voice.

"I put my wagon in a neighbor's barn during the rain," Cartwright said sarcastically. "How else do you think it stayed dry?"

Martin flushed with anger. "Look, Cartwright. I know you're part of that Underground Railroad. If there are any slaves here I intend to find them. And when I do, you're going to get the same treatment as them. Nigger-lovers don't mean scum to me."

"Like I already said—you won't find any slaves here," Cartwright snapped.

Martin pushed by him and stalked back to the wagon. Pulling out his whip he cracked it over and over into the wagon. Wisps of hay flew through the air as the wicked tip of the instrument slashed through it. Once he had satisfied his curiosity *and* his anger, he turned from the wagon with a scowl.

Adams emerged from the house. "The slaves ain't in here, either." Frustration and anger oozed from his words.

Martin cursed and turned to stare into the dark woods. "They're out there in the woods," he said coldly. He whipped out his pistol and fired several shots into the thick undergrowth. "That should at least make them wet their pants," he said with a harsh laugh. He wheeled on Cartwright. "Be glad we don't have our dogs or I'm pretty sure there would soon be eight caught niggers." He glared at Cartwright, and swung up onto his horse. "I'll be back. One of these days I'm going to catch you with some niggers, and you're going to wish you'd never gotten involved with the Underground Railroad."

Cursing loudly, the three men galloped back down the dark road. Cartwright raised his hand toward the woods and then disappeared into his house.

Jamison had seen enough. Cartwright had done all he could. Using the wagon again was out of the question. Adams was smart enough to wait at the end of the drive until he tried to move the slaves. He turned and moved quietly into the woods. Within minutes, he found the fugitives huddled behind some large oaks. He lowered himself next to them. "We're on our own now," he said firmly. "We'll have to make it to Philadelphia on foot. It isn't that far. It will take us a few days, but we can do it."

The somber eyes looking back at him never wavered. Miles stood. "Let's get to it, then. We's going to be free."

Carrie and Rose made their way down the path to the slave quarters. It was their first time alone together since Carrie had returned from Philadelphia. It was Sunday, and Thomas was stationed by his wife's bed. He knew where to find her if Abigail took a turn for the worse.

"Sarah! It's so good to see you again." Carrie moved forward to give the old woman a hug.

"Welcome, Miss Carrie. You be a sight for sore eyes. How's your mama?"

Carrie frowned. "I'm worried, Sarah. Nothing I do seems to make any difference. She's not getting any worse, but she's not getting any better either."

"You thinkin' that fever done burned the life out of her?"

Carrie smiled slightly. Sarah always knew what she was thinking. She nodded. "I've read about that happening. The fever wears down the body and it just doesn't seem to be able to come back." She paused, "I've come to ask for your help, Sarah."

Sarah watched her closely. "Go on, child."

"I know there are remedies the black people use. Ones I have never heard of. Could they help my mama?" She leaned forward and fixed her eyes on Sarah.

Sarah nodded slowly. "They couldn't hurt none, Miss Carrie. Your mama was awful sick," she said thoughtfully, "but there ain't no way to know unless we try."

"You'll teach me what they are?" Carrie asked hopefully.

"Yessum, Miss Carrie. I'll teach you. You be here tomorrow morning 'fore the sun comes up. And don't wear no fancy clothes. I'd hate for you to ruin them."

Carrie was down at Sarah's cabin as soon as the eastern sky began to glow softly. Sarah was already waiting outside for her. She handed her a coarse cloth bag and moved toward the woods. Carrie followed quietly.

"Rose be with your mama?" Carrie nodded. Satisfied, Sarah continued her plunge into the woods. They walked for several minutes before Sarah stopped and motioned for Carrie to join her on a log. Carrie sat down. She had learned long ago not to question Sarah's ways. She would explain herself when she was good and ready.

"There be some things you need to know before we keep going," she started. "Old Sarah is going to teach you the magic of the plants that grow in the earth. God didn't put his people on the earth without givin' them some ways to take care of what ails them. My mama taught me the magic. Her mama taught her. The magic gets passed down. The plants here be diff'rent din the ones in Africa but they's all got magic. You just got to learn it."

"Who taught you the plants here in Virginia?" Carrie asked.

"You wouldn't be remembering Betsy cuz you was just a little girl when she died," Sarah replied. "She lived here on your daddy's plantation for all her life. She took me under her wing when I's first got here. She knew the magic better din anyone else. She done taught me."

"Does Rose know the magic?"

Sarah frowned and shook her head. "She knows a little, but she seems to think she don't need to know it. She puts a lot of stock in readin' and books. Not that they ain't important," she hastened to add, "but she's letting go of somethin' rich. I always figured God wants us to use whatever we got to use. If we find somethin' new, it don't mean the old ain't good no more. It just means that the new makes the old better. All of it is still good. And sometimes the new ain't as good as the old. If you throw the old out you ain't got nothin'."

Carrie nodded. As usual, the old woman made good sense. "I want to learn the magic, Sarah."

Sarah stared into her eyes. "You got the healin' touch, Miss Carrie. I been watchin' you a long time. You for sho got the healin' touch."

"I want to, Sarah. Oh, how I want to."

"Trust me, girl. You got it." Having delivered her final word, Sarah rose again and began to walk further into the woods.

Carrie followed, gazing around her at the lush undergrowth. Ferns, nestled in the shady nooks of protective trees, waved their fronds in the early morning stillness. Summer wildflowers raised their heads and drank in the early morning dew. "Do you know what all the plants are, Sarah?"

"I be knowin' most of them."

"What kind of tree is this?" Carrie asked as she stopped to tip her head back to get a good look at the tree towering over her.

Sarah moved back to join her. "That be a maple tree," Sarah said with a smile. "It be one of my favorite trees. In the spring, it sends down little whirligigs for the chillun to play with. In the fall, it blazes with a color that makes you ache inside. God done made that tree a real special one."

"I want to learn all the plants, Sarah," Carrie said impulsively, suddenly very glad to be out in the woods away from the confines of the house.

"Good," Sarah said shortly. "That's what we be out here for. By the time we get done out here in these woods you're gonna be knowin' all the growin' things. But you got to know more than just what they be. You gots to know the right time to pick what you be lookin' for. You gots to know how to take care of it. You gots to know what to do with it. You got a passel of learnin' to do, Miss Carrie."

Carrie continued to follow Sarah into the woods. Finally, they broke out into a wild field lush with growth. Sarah walked more slowly and then stopped. Carrie came up beside her.

"This here be the yarrow plant, Miss Carrie. Get a good look at it."

Carrie bent close to examine the plant. The stem was covered with a sort of staircase of blue-green leaves split up into many teeth like a comb. Its flowers were clustered together into little white parasols.

"Sometimes them flowers be pink. The thin' to look for is them leaves. You'll know it ever' time that way. Some of the healers call it thousand-leaf. You got it in your head, girl?"

Carrie nodded. "I think so."

"Good, but just knowin' how to find it ain't gonna do you no good. To most folks it just be a pretty flower. That be because they don't know its magic." Sarah's eyes glowed.

Carrie stared at the plant and waited for her to continue. It certainly didn't look magic.

"This plant here be good for a lot of thin's. We's goin' to take some back for yo mama 'cause it be good to fight that fever she got. Fever be awful hard on the body and the heart. This here little plant be good for the heart, too."

Carrie looked at the yarrow with increased interest. "What do you do with it?"

"Not so fast!" Sarah chided. "You still gots to know what it does."

"It does *more*?"

Sarah nodded. "Them thin's I told you. They just be the extras. The yarrow really shines when it comes to stoppin' bleedin'. It stops bleedin' better than any plant there is. Least ways, any plant *I* know 'bout." She reached out and took hold of the flowering plant. "This plant be too far along for it to do any good. You's got to find the plants that the flowers ain't opened up yet." She scanned the area around her until her face lit up and she moved to a patch a little farther on. "These ones here. They be perfect. See how the flowers be just startin' to open? Now's the time to pick the leaves and the big flower tops."

"How did you learn all this, Sarah?" Carrie asked wonderingly.

Old Sarah shrugged. "The magic just gets passed on," she said simply. She reached forward, snapped the tops off several plants, and picked a large handful of leaves. "Put these in your bag, Miss Carrie. You can learn what to do with them later."

Carrie did as she was directed, enthralled by what she was learning. She did have doubts about the plants actually working, but the medicine the doctors were sending her was doing nothing. She was willing to try anything.

Sarah was already moving away from her, this time looking up. Carrie followed her example, but had no idea what she was looking for. Finally, Sarah came to a halt under a large tree at the edge of the woods. "There!" Triumphantly, she pointed upward.

Carrie stared. "Mistletoe?" she asked in disbelief.

"Ah, you know 'bout mistletoe already?"

Carrie laughed. "I know they hang it from doorways at Christmas and girls wander underneath hoping they will be kissed."

Sarah laughed, too, and then sobered. "Can you get me some?" Her face said she wasn't going to say anymore."

Carrie shrugged, pulled up her skirts and nimbly climbed to the first limb. She had been climbing trees for as long as she could remember. She had decided years ago that she wasn't going to let long skirts keep her from doing what she wanted to. Straining upward, she was able to grasp a large bunch of mistletoe and yank it loose from its grip on the tree. Face flushed, she jumped down from the tree and handed it to Sarah.

Sarah grinned and held it up like a prize. "This here magic plant needs to be picked before any of its white berries pop out on it. Now, Miss Carrie, you listen to me careful on this one. Mistletoe be a magic plant for sure, but only for them who knows how to use it. Too much of this plant be poison to a person. You's has to know how to use it," she repeated. Then she pointed to the leaves. "There ain't no berries here. Them berries—they carry the most poison. You don't *never* want to use them berries."

Carrie nodded quietly, drinking in the words of the older woman. Every part of her mind was alert and keyed in to what she was learning.

Sarah looked at her closely and seemed satisfied she was getting it. "Your mama be having bad headaches. She be havin' dizzy spells, too?" Carrie nodded. "This here mistletoe will help her. Put it in your bag." Then she was off again.

Carrie's head was spinning when they got back to the quarters just before noon. From now on she would take a notebook and pencil out on their expeditions. Never had she tried to cram so much information into her head in such a short amount of time.

"Now we learn what to do with all this," Sarah said.

Carrie shook her head to clear it and watched as the old lady unloaded their treasures out of the bags. Yarrow, mistletoe, onion, mint, poppy, broom, thistle, dandelion, and various other plants came spilling out to pile up on the table.

Sarah looked up. "You be hungry, Miss Carrie?"

Carrie nodded faintly, suddenly aware of how weak and famished she was. She had done no physical exercise since returning from Philadelphia and her legs ached from their hours of tramping through the woods.

Sarah nodded, eyeing her closely. "You go's and get you a good meal and some rest. Check on your mama. Come back tonight. Then old Sarah will show you how to draw the magic out of these here plants."

Carrie smiled weakly. "I think that's a good idea. I'm pretty tired." She stood up slowly.

Sarah, still as fresh as when the morning had started, rose to put a hand on her arm. "You're a good girl to want to help your mama. But you's got to take care of yo'self too, Miss Carrie. It ain't good for you to be cooped up in that house all the time." She frowned. "Tell you what. Ever' other mornin', you meet me here. We'll go out into the woods. Ain't but one way to learn the magic. You got to get out and meet them magic plants.

Carrie smiled at her old friend. "I would like that Sarah. Thank you." She turned toward the door and then swung back. "I'll be back tonight."

Sarah nodded and continued to sort through the plants, crooning to them as if they were precious loved ones.

Rose was standing on the porch when Carrie broke out into the lawn around the house. Carrie sped across the grass. Rose saw the fear on her face and smiled reassuringly. "Your mama is fine. Marse Cromwell came in for a while and wanted to spend some time with her."

Relieved, Carrie dropped down on the front steps.

Rose laughed at her exhausted expression. "Keeping up with my mama is rather a challenge, isn't it?"

Carrie smiled. "She is a remarkable woman. My head is swimming with everything I learned today."

"Do you think those plants are really magic?" Rose asked skeptically.

Carrie shrugged. "I know a lot of people who would turn their nose up at it. I also know medicine doesn't have all the answers. I don't see any reason to throw out all the old just because something new has come along. It's fascinating," she said, "and I love learning it." Briefly she told Rose of Sarah's plan. "I'm going to do it. Will you sit with my mother?"

"Certainly," Rose replied. She looked at Carrie closely. "Go sit on the porch swing. I'm going to bring you something to eat. You look all done in."

Carrie stood slowly. "Thank you. I guess I am a little tired."

"Here." Rose reached into her pocket and pulled out a thin envelope. "This will give you something to do while I get your food." Carrie reached for it, and a wide smile exploded on her face. Rose smiled and disappeared into the house. Once inside, she leaned against the hallway wall and struggled to bring her raging thoughts under control. What she would give to be able to have a relationship like free people. It was obvious Carrie was in love with Robert Borden. At least it was to her. She was sure Carrie didn't know it yet. When she did there would be nothing to keep them apart. They would never have to worry about one of them being sold and never seeing each other again. A noise caused her to straighten and continue her movement down the hall. She had fought her bitter feelings for weeks now. Would there be no end to them?

Carrie settled down on the porch and spread her dress around her. She fingered the envelope, closed her eyes, and allowed the fragrant breeze to wash over her tired body. The smell of fresh-cut hay filled the air with its heavy perfume. She had always loved haying time when the tall grass lay in thick swashes on the ground, drying in the sun, waiting to be piled into huge mounds to provide feed for the animals through the winter months. After several long moments she opened her eyes, refreshed. She smiled and tore into Robert's letter.

> *Dear Carrie,*
> *I am sorry to hear from your father's latest correspondence that your mother is still so ill. I hope daily for her renewed health, and my mother sends her deep concerns and best wishes to her.*

Carrie frowned and put down the letter. Why was her father corresponding with Robert? Her brow cleared when she remembered Robert was helping her father with some of his political business since Thomas was not free to leave the plantation. All of that seemed so far away. The conventions, secession, Lincoln—they all seemed to belong to a different time. A time before her mother consumed every waking hour and thought. She continued reading.

> *I have tried to get away but so much here at Oak Meadows demands my attention. My brother has left to pursue his dreams in Richmond, so I find myself with more to do than I have time for. I will be glad for the harvest. Once again I will have time that is my own.*
> *The real purpose of this letter is to let you know I will be coming to Cromwell the latter part of September. I have some business to conduct with your father, and, of course, I am eager to see you once again. I have not forgotten that you*

promised to give me a tour of Cromwell on horseback. I intend to hold you to your word.
     Sincerely,
     Robert

TWENTY-FIVE

Rose was exhausted as she made her way through the shadowy woods. A full moon cast dancing shadows as the wind blew, caressing her with its soft touch. For the first time since she had started her secret school, she found herself not wanting to go. She was too tired to care right now. The combination of caring for Mistress Cromwell, continuing her regular duties, and fighting the battles raging in her heart had left her physically and emotionally drained. She had nothing left to give others, but she knew her students were counting on her. She had not even gone down to her mama's for dinner. When the day ended she had fallen across her bed, too exhausted even to sleep. She had simply lain there, staring out her tiny window until the moon told her it was time to leave. Her students were already waiting for her when she arrived.

"Rose!" Coral exclaimed. "We thought you wasn't coming."

"*Weren't* coming," Rose corrected. "I'm sorry I'm late." She looked up and her eyes caught Moses's gaze across the flickering firelight. He said nothing, but she knew he was worried about her. Knowing that he cared somehow gave her the energy to do what she had to do. She smiled and settled down next to the fire.

"You done heard anything about Sadie and the others?"

"Have you heard anything," Rose corrected gently. She had become even more adamant about her students speaking correctly. It was necessary to keep up their old way of speaking in the quarters so as to not arouse suspicion, but when they were here she was determined to make them speak correctly. Another chance for freedom could come at any time, and more of them might be ready. If her only connection with freedom was preparing others for a new life, she wanted to do it right.

"Have you heard anything about Sadie and the others, Rose?"

"Good, Coral. But, no, I haven't. A note came from Adams the other day but Sam didn't get to look at it, and Marse Cromwell didn't say anything about it. But we know one thing for certain. As long as Adams is gone, he hasn't found our friends. Every day moves them that much closer to freedom." She tried to make her voice sound confident and strong, but she was finding it more difficult to push beyond her fatigue.

Moses, obviously sensing she was at the end of her rope, leaned forward. "I don't think we need to do any bookwork tonight."

Rose looked at him startled. "What do you mean? That's what a school is for."

"Maybe so," Moses conceded easily, "but I know one teacher who needs a break from teaching."

Rose felt tears sting her eyes, and blinked them back quickly. She stared at Moses wordlessly, not able to think of one thing to say in response to his astute observation.

Moses grinned triumphantly and looked around at the students. He let the silence of the woods wrap itself around them, and then he began to sing. His deep, bass voice rose to mingle with the shadows swaying around them.

> Come down angel, and trouble the water,
> Come down angel, and trouble the water,
> Come down angel, and trouble the water,
> And let God's chilluns go.

The other students smiled and joined in, their voices rising to the heavens in a weave of sorrow and hope. Leaning back and staring into the luminescent moon, they allowed their spirits to soar as song gave them wing.

> Canaan land is the land for me,
> And let God's chillun go,

Canaan land is the land for me,
And let God's chillun go.

There was a wicked man
And let God's chillun go.
He kept them children in Egypt land,
And let God's chillun go.

God did say to Moses one day,
And let God's chillun go.
Say Moses go to Egypt land
And let God's chillun go.

And tell Pharaoh to let my people go
And let God's chillun go.
And Pharaoh would not let them go,
And let God's chillun go.

God did go to Moses's house
And let God's chillun go.
And God did tell him who he was,
And let God's chillun go.

God and Moses walked and talked
And let God's chillun go.
And God did show him who he was
And let God's chillun go.

As the song rolled to an end, voices faded into the night and joined with the chorus of frogs and crickets. Rose smiled at Moses across the clearing and raised her clear soprano to lead them on.

Good Lord, in the mansions above,
Good Lord, in the mansions above,
My Lord, I hope to meet my Jesus
My Lord, in the mansions above.

If you get to heaven before I do
Lord, tell my Jesus I'm a comin' too
To de mansions above

My Lord, I've had many crosses an' trials here below,
My Lord, I hope to meet you
In de mansions above.

All the longings of hearts long held in cruel bondage rose on the wind and joined in the grandeur of the night. The moon shone brighter and the air grew softer as the melodious strains spoke the hearts of the people.

Rose lost all track of time as one song rolled into the next. All she knew was that the pain of her heart found an outlet as her voice rose to pour out her fears and frustrations, just as generations before her had done. Tyranny, torture, and suffering had not been able to stop the singing. Song put hope where there was none. It gave courage when there was none to be found.

Moses finally raised his hand and said in his deep voice. "It's time to head back to the quarters."

Rose came to with a start. A quick look at the moon told her he was right. They must have been singing for hours. The clearing emptied quickly, each student moving with the hope and purpose the singing had renewed in their hearts. Rose looked up into Moses's eyes. "Thank you," she said simply. There was so much more to say, but her heart was too full to find the words.

Moses looked down into her eyes and smiled gently. Then he reached out and enfolded her in his arms. Rose gave a deep sigh and rested her head on his chest. She knew she was safe. Nothing could touch her when she was with Moses. The moon dropped lower on the horizon as they stood there, denying the reality of their bondage. For just this time, they were free to love, and their love knew no bounds.

"Look at me, Rose." Rose leaned back in his arms and raised her eyes to meet his. "I love you," Moses said simply, his deep voice deeper still with emotion. "You hear me, girl. I love you."

Tears sprang to Rose's eyes. "I love you, too, Moses." She did. The vow she had made that she would never marry and stand the chance of her husband being sold flashed into her mind. Suddenly, her vow meant nothing. She had found the man that made the risk worth taking. She could no more imagine life without Moses than she could imagine ever giving up the dream of someday being free. Both of them had become as natural in her mind as breathing.

"I want to marry you, Rose. I want to be your husband."

Rose reached up to touch his face with her hand. "I can't imagine anything that would make me happier."

A joyous smile wreathed Moses's face as he stared down at her. "You'll be my wife?" he whispered incredulously.

Rose nodded, her own smile matching his.

"Glory!" Moses whispered. Then he bent his head until his lips found hers. Rose once again lost all track of time as Moses's gentle kiss claimed every part of her heart, mind and soul. Fatigue dropped away as a new life spread before her. She pushed away any fears of what the future would bring. Now was *here*—here in the clearing where she was giving this man all she was. She would not let what might be mar her newfound joy.

Moses finally lifted his head. "You've got to tell Miss Carrie so that we can plan our wedding time."

Reality brought Rose jarring back to earth. Her lips still thrilled to Moses's gentle kiss, but her heart was once more a raging fire.

Moses pulled back and looked at her closely. "What is it, Rose?" When Rose shook her head, he took her hand and pulled her over to sit on a log. "My mama always said locking things up inside made things turn into a poison that would eat your soul. Seems to me that your mama would say the same thing."

Rose looked at him and sighed. She was afraid the poison was already doing its work. "You've changed," she said suddenly. "Why?"

Moses smiled but was not to be dissuaded. "I'll tell you, Rose. But not until you tell me what's causing the shadow in those pretty eyes."

Rose looked away and stared into the shadows. Slowly, she began to speak. "I do indeed have poison in my heart, Moses." She faltered but stumbled on, determined to be honest. "More than anything in the world I want to be free. I want to follow my dreams. I want to live a life with you that won't include fear we may one day be sold away from each other." Her voice drifted off. Then she looked at him and spoke fiercely. "My heart is burning with hate. I hate Miss Carrie. I hate that she can have everything I want. Every time I see her, my dreams are thrown in my face, mocking me with how silly I am to ever think I can be somebody." Now that she had started, her words flowed like the waters of the mighty James. Nothing could stop them. "I hate being a slave. I hate being afraid. I hate sneaking around in the dark to teach people how to read and write. I want to have a normal school—one where folks can come and not have to hide." Finally, her face contorted and her voice broke with the pain she had been pressing in. "Oh, Moses, the hate is eating my heart."

Moses held her close as the sobs wracked her slender body. He held her and rocked her gently as she huddled close to him. Finally, her tears began to abate and her body grew still. Softly, he began to speak. "You asked me why I had changed. I aim to tell you."

Moses looked off, a faraway look in his eyes. "You know what I was like when I got to Cromwell. I was angry and bitter. I reckon I had every right to be. Anybody would be. I hung on to that hate and anger, knowing I had every right to it. Your mama made me real mad that night in her cabin when she told me the anger would hurt nobody but myself." Moses paused. "She got me to thinking, though. You got a lot of time for thinking when you're standing at the other end of a hoe out in the fields. I thought a lot about my daddy. He had a powerful yearning to be free, but he never hated anyone. I never understood why. I knew my daddy was a strong man, but in this one area I was afraid he was weak. I vowed never to be that way. Then I got to watching Adams real close."

"Adams?" Rose echoed.

"Yep, Ike Adams. The more I watched him, the more I saw the poison eating his soul. He is a man full of hate. It pours out of every part of him. I finally realized I didn't want to be like him. One night, real late, I came out here to the woods by myself."

"When Moses? When did you come?"

Moses cocked his head, thinking. "I reckon it was about a month ago."

"Right after everyone escaped?"

"Yeah, I guess so. Making the decision to stay behind meant I needed to learn how to live here for now." He paused. "Anyway, I came out into the woods by myself and stayed here a long time. I did a lot of thinking about what your mama had said. I realized she was right. My soul is all I truly have. People, black *or* white, can destroy my body, but they can't touch what's inside." Then his huge eyes filled with tears. Rose watched in amazement as one escaped and trickled down his face. "Someone came to me that night." He shook his head in amazement. "I don't reckon I can explain it. I didn't see anyone. I just know someone was here—someone a heap more powerful than me. I know your mama would say it was Jesus. I can't rightly say I know for sure. It was just someone shining a lot of love." His voice trailed away and his face filled with awe as he relived the experience. "I gave everything to whoever was with me that night. They took all my bitterness and hatred, and gave me back strength and determination—determination not to let the poison take my soul. I ain't gonna hate no more, Rose. I have too much living to do to concentrate on hating." His voice rang out with confidence as he turned his shining eyes toward her.

Rose stared up at him. She was glad for Moses, but his words did nothing to calm her own heart. She wanted them to. Oh, how she wanted them to. She looked into his eyes and tried to draw the strength there into her own soul. Finally, she shook her head and laid it on his broad shoulder. "I'm so happy for you, Moses."

Moses put a finger on her trembling lips. "Shh... You're fighting your own battle. I told you why *I* changed. You got to find your own answer." He smiled gently. "Let's go. It's time to get back."

Rose, when she reached the edge of the clearing, lifted her head and kissed Moses, then waited until she saw him disappear into his cabin. Instead of heading for the big house, however, she glided across the clearing to her mama's cabin.

"Mama?" Rose whispered into the darkness from the open cabin door.

"Rose, girl? You be alright?"

Rose moved into the cabin. "Yes, mama. I'm not sure why I'm here," she said slowly.

Sarah rose from her chair by the dark fireplace.

"Mama! You're not in bed?"

Sarah smiled. "I was waiting for you."

Rose gasped. Her eyes had adjusted to the darkness, and just enough moonlight shone in for her to see the soft smile on Sarah's face. She didn't know why she was surprised. Her mama always knew when something was going on with her. Sarah opened her arms and Rose walked right into them. Long minutes passed while her mama held her and stroked her hair. Rose finally slid down on the floor and sat with her head resting on her lap like she had done when she was a small child. She knew her mama would wait for her to talk.

"My insides are all jumbled up." The gentle hand never stopped its steady stroking—it just became a little more tender. Rose blinked back the tears trying to escape. She thought she had already cried herself dry. Now there seemed to be a never-ending fountain. The anger was consumed by her fatigue. She simply felt an overwhelming sadness and emptiness. "Moses asked me to marry him."

"Is that a bad thin'?"

"Oh, no!" she cried. "It's a *wonderful* thing. I love him the way you loved Daddy."

"I still love your daddy," Sarah said softly.

"I know," Rose said. "And I know your heart still feels ripped apart because he was taken from you. I've always been afraid of falling in love—of wanting to marry a man. I didn't want to take the chance of hurting like that."

"Can't run from hurt, Rose. You might miss some hurt, but you'll also miss all the joys of livin'."

Rose sighed and shook her head. "I got poison in my soul, Mama."

"Cause of all the hate there."

Rose didn't even bother to ask how she knew. She just nodded and repeated what she had told Moses in the clearing. Sarah's hand continued its gentle stroking. The connection with her mama's love helped Rose to keep going. "I want to get rid of the hate, but I don't know how. Moses has changed. I want to change too. I just don't know how."

"That ain't true, Rose," Sarah said calmly. "You say you want to change, but you ain't really got to the place where you want to do it."

Rose opened her mouth to protest and then closed it again.

Sarah continued. "You been buildin' up this hate fer a long time. Envy and bitterness are bad bedfellows. They eat your heart and then leave you fer dead. I know. They ate mine for a long time. I said I wanted to change, but I didn't—not really. I'd gotten used to holdin' all that hate inside."

Rose didn't bother to deny what her mama was saying. In the darkness of the cabin, surrounded by her mama's love, she was finally facing the truth.

"You got to hate the hate, girl. You say you want to be free. Having your body free ain't gonna do you no good if your heart ain't free. Your heart got to be free first."

"But how?" Rose cried, closing her eyes. Silence was her only answer. She'd known it would be when she'd asked the question. She already knew the answer. Silence fell on the cabin as Rose fought the biggest battle of her life. All the past hurts reared their ugly heads to shout for justice. Images of Carrie living the life she longed for ran before her eyes. Memories of all the years without her daddy caused pain to sear through her heart. Overlaying all of them was the image of a heart oozing bitterness and hate—pulsating with an evil that would soon cause it to explode and destroying the very life it sought to find. Just when Rose thought she couldn't take any more, a gentle light began to slowly illuminate the whole ugly mess. She knew she had two choices. She could give in to the hate, or reach out for the light and invite it into her life. Her heart pounded harder as she stared at her life. It was her decision. Slowly, in her mind, she reached for the light. As she stretched forth her hand, the light's glow strengthened and brightened. The ugly scenes began to recede into the background. The oozing of the heart slowed. Eagerly now, she reached forth as far as she could. *God, take all the hate. Take all the hurt.* The light glowed with an intensity that hurt her eyes. The past faded from view. Only the heart was left—a glowing, pulsating heart—whole and healthy.

Then the tears came. Rose collapsed on her mother's lap as wrenching sobs consumed her body. The tears in the clearing had been tears of pain. These were healing tears washing her soul of the residue that had built up and cleansing her body of all the poison.

Sarah never stopped the stroking. Finally, Rose pulled back and looked up. The moon shone bright on her face, merely illuminating the glow already there.

Sarah nodded. "I know, girl. I know."

Rose laid her head back on her lap. She knew her mama knew.

Sarah waited several minutes and then began to speak. "You know why I gave you the name Rose?"

Rose shook her head.

"You be named Rose cause I knew your life was gonna be full of thorns. But God told me you would truly be like the rose—the purtiest flower in the whole world. Not only would you survive them thorns, you would thrive right in the middle of dem. Your beauty would shine out to every person that be 'round you."

Rose laughed weakly. "I'm not feeling much like a rose right now."

"Don't matter none how you feel right now," Sarah said firmly. "I'm gonna tell you one of the secrets of living, girl."

Rose sat up straighter. It wasn't often that her mama told things directly. She usually asked questions and let Rose figure it out herself. If she was just going to say it, then it was really important.

Sarah looked down at her tenderly. "You got to bloom where you're planted."

Rose stared up at her. *That was it?*

Sarah smiled gently. "I know you was the one to help all them slaves escape last month."

Rose gasped. "How?"

Sarah shrugged. "God gave me a dream. But that ain't what's important." She paused. "I know you gave up your own chance to be free. And I know you gave it up for me. You knows I would want you to take your chance to be free. And *I* know you wouldn't ever leave your old mama." A tear trickled down her leathery cheeks as she gazed lovingly at her daughter. Her voice cracked, but she continued. "I'm too old to be escapin', Rose. I'm gonna end my life right here." Sarah paused. "For now, that means your life gonna be here on Cromwell Plantation. That leaves you only one thin' to do. You got's to live as hard as you can where you be. You got's to look deep inside and find out all the thin's you got to give the world. Then you got to give it. You can't spend all your days lookin' backward. And you can't spend all your days lookin' forward. It's today that counts, Rose. You's got to bloom where you be planted. God's got you planted here for now."

Rose listened hard. She knew her mama was right.

"Girl, you's already been doin' some bloomin'. That school you have is helpin' to fight the evil people has put us under. Teachin' them folks how to read and write—you letting off a powerful perfume, girl. But nows you can bloom bigger and brighter without that poison eatin' your heart. Use the gifts God done give you, Rose. You give ever'thin' you can. God will make sure them gifts don't go to waste."

Rose nodded and then suddenly stiffened. The sound of wagon wheels rumbled in the distance, growing closer. It could only be one person. She stood and crept to the edge of the door and peered out. Sarah rose to join her. The rumbling grew louder as the wagon appeared as a dark speck against the moonlit glow of the road. Rose strained to see the wagon. Were there people in it? She held her breath and peered out into the night.

Slowly, the wagon drew even with the cabin. Adams was hunched on the front seat, obviously exhausted. But the wagon...the wagon was empty. Adams had returned alone. Her friends were free. Great tears rolled down Rose's face as she watched the wagon disappear into the dark night. On the very edge of the horizon, she could see a faint glimmer of dawn. The night was gone. She must get back to the big house. Sam was probably frantic.

"Them folks wouldn't be free if it weren't for you, Rose," Sarah said quietly. "I'm proud of you, girl." Then she added, "Moses be a fine man. He'll make you a good husband." It was the first thing she had said about Rose's announcement. They had taken care of the important things first.

Rose turned, threw her arms around her mother, and hugged her tightly. "Thank you, Mama," she whispered.

Sarah finally pulled back. "I know you's got to go, girl, but I got one more thin' I want to tell you." Sarah moved back to her chair and sank down. "I had a dream a few nights ago. In that dream I was free. *Free!* Walking the streets of heaven hand-in-hand with my Jesus. There weren't no slave or free there. Everyone be equal." She paused. "Jesus told me somethin', girl." Once again her eyes filled with tears. "He done told me that people be people. As long as we live here on this earth, the sin in people will make them try to dominate, to prove they be better than others. It don't matter none whether it be black, or white, or Indian, or anythin' else. There will always be hatred in people's hearts. We can only do two things. We can fight that evil all we can, and we can fight the hate that be in our own hearts."

Sarah leaned back and closed her eyes. Rose kissed her forehead gently. "I love you, Mama."

TWENTY-SIX

"Do you really think staring out the window is going to make him come faster, Carrie?" Abigail's voice, though weak, was amused.

Carrie turned and smiled at her mother. "I suppose not," she sighed. Robert was coming today. The long-awaited day had finally arrived. In her mind, she had pushed away the things that might divide them and spent the weeks caring for her mother, dreaming of the good times she and Robert had shared. She needed the memories of the good times to keep her going. Then she grinned. "But if wishing *will* make him get here faster, he should be here any minute."

Abigail smiled and then doubled over in a fit of coughing. Carrie frowned and hurried to her mother's side. She had done nothing but grow weaker in the last two months. September had brought some relief from the searing heat, but Abigail's strength had continued to fade. Carrie had done all she knew to do. Medicine didn't work. The herbs didn't work. The love Thomas lavished on his wife didn't work. Daily, Carrie watched the life ebb from her mother's eyes.

Finally, Abigail straightened and lay back against the pillows. Her face was flushed with the effort and her eyes had a glazed look, but she forced herself to speak. "I want you to go out with Robert, Carrie." Carrie opened her mouth to protest that she wouldn't leave her mother's side, but Abigail fluttered her hand to stop her. "I'll be fine. Her voice strained to continue. "You need to be with Robert."

Carrie reached for her hand and pressed it gently. "Don't, Mama. Don't try to talk. I'll do it. I'll go out with Robert." She tried to sound cheerful. "I promised him months ago that I would take him for a tour of the plantation on Granite. I'm going to keep my promise."

Abigail smiled and squeezed Carrie's hand weakly. "That's good," she whispered. "You're a good girl, Carrie." Her voice dropped away as she leaned back and closed her eyes.

Carrie knew her strength had been spent. She freed her hand and once again took up her post at the window. Her gaze alternated between the bed and the road. She and her mother had grown closer over the two months they had battled her illness. She held no illusions that her mother understood her, but they had achieved a peace of sorts.

Carrie straightened and pulled the curtains back to get a better look. A bright smile spread across her face as Robert appeared in the distance. She stayed where she was for a long minute, admiring the way he rode his horse so effortlessly. Snatches of happy memories flitted across the screen of her mind. She turned away and moved to her mother's side. Deep, even breathing convinced her she was sleeping soundly. She tucked the blankets in a little tighter, leaned forward to plant a light kiss on her forehead, and left the room to run lightly down the stairs.

Thomas joined his daughter on the porch just as Robert pulled his horse to a stop. "Welcome once more to Cromwell, Robert!"

"Thank you, sir." Robert vaulted easily off his tall chestnut gelding, then strode up the stairs and gripped the older man's hand firmly. "How are you, sir? And Abigail?"

Thomas frowned. "She is no better I am afraid," he murmured, shaking his head. "We have much to talk about. I'm glad you are here."

"And I'm glad to be here, sir." Eagerly, Robert turned to Carrie. He reached out to take her hand and smiled into her eyes. "Hello, Carrie. It's good to see you again." His eyes told her how very glad.

Carrie's returning smile was tremulous. Now that he was actually here, she realized how much she had missed him. She gazed into his deep brown eyes and drew strength from what she saw there. "Hello, Robert. I'm glad you're here."

"I'll be inside," Thomas said. "We'll talk later." He disappeared through the door.

Robert continued to hold Carrie's hand, smiling down into her eyes. Gently, he led her over to the porch swing. Carrie sank into it gratefully. They sat quietly for a few minutes, simply enjoying the sensation of being together again.

Carrie finally broke the silence. "How is everything at Oak Meadows?" It was a safe topic. As Robert described the wonderful harvest of hay and tobacco, she watched the handsome lines of his face. It was enough to have him there.

"It's everything I hoped it would be, Carrie," he said with a little-boy lilt in his voice. "There is nothing now to keep me from doing all the things I have dreamed about over the years. School is behind me and I am free to make all the improvements and do all the expansions I've wanted to for so long." Robert leaned back and stared out over Cromwell. "One day, Oak Meadows will be as glorious as Cromwell Plantation," he predicted firmly.

Just then Thomas appeared on the porch again. "Dinner is served," he announced.

For the first time in weeks, Carrie found she was actually hungry. Even her early morning jaunts with Sarah hadn't been able to raise much of an appetite in her. Caring for her mother, and the concerns of her heart, had slowly sapped her vitality. She laughed aloud when a rumble burst forth from her stomach. "I'm starving," she exclaimed as they walked into the dining room.

Thomas smiled. "You're going to do my daughter good. I haven't seen this light in her eyes since she came home." Silence reigned as they attacked the huge meal set before them.

When they were done, Thomas pushed his chair back and lit his pipe. "Fill me in on what's happening in the world, Robert. I feel so isolated from everything."

Carrie smiled and settled back to listen. She didn't care that they were getting ready to talk politics. She was already feeling stronger. Energy coursed through her body as the food rushed to all the deprived areas, giving strength and life. Not until this minute did she realize she had been robbing her body of the very things it needed to keep going. Silently she vowed that things were going to change.

Robert settled back in his own chair, accepting the pipe Thomas extended to him. He seemed to be deep in thought as he carefully tamped his tobacco and lit it, sending small puffs of smoke into the air. He gazed at Thomas through the smoke. "I think you know what is happening, sir. Things are playing out just as we suspected." He reached into his pocket and pulled out a sheet of newspaper. "Douglas was in Norfolk at the end of August. I decided to go listen to what he was saying so I could see for myself if there remained anything to hope for."

"And?" Thomas leaned forward.

Carrie found herself leaning forward with him. She fixed her eyes on Robert and waited for him to read the paper he was smoothing out in front of him.

Robert scanned the paper until he found what he wanted. "Douglas seems to be the only one who is trying to make a real campaign. He's going against the popular notion that a candidate stays home and lets his supporters speak for him. He's getting out there himself." There was admiration in his voice. "He is a brave man. A brave man fighting a battle he is doomed to lose however." Discouragement thickened his voice. "When I went to hear him in Norfolk, he was speaking from the steps of City Hall."

Robert looked down at the paper. "Here's some of what he said." Thomas and Carrie settled back to listen. "'I desire no man to vote for me unless he hopes and desires the Union maintained and preserved intact by the faithful execution of every act, every line, and every letter of the written Constitution which our fathers bequeathed to us.'" Robert paused and quit reading for a moment. "He said that sectional parties, whether born in the North or the South are the great evil and curse of this country. That it was time for men who loved the country to see whether they could not find some common principle on which they could stand and defeat both Northern and Southern agitators."

Thomas nodded his head. "He's right, you know."

"Yes," Robert responded, "but the country is in no mood to listen to him. Someone in the audience yelled out and asked him if Lincoln were to be elected, whether secession would not be justified." He began to read again. "'To this I emphatically answer 'No'. The election of a man to the presidency by the American people, in conformity with the Constitution of the United States, would not justify any attempt at dissolving this glorious confederacy.'"

Thomas nodded again. "It would be folly for the South to secede before they have a chance to know Lincoln's intent."

"There was another question thrown at him," Robert said. "Someone asked him where he would stand on Southern secession if the cotton states went ahead and seceded before there was some overt act against their constitutional rights." Once again, he picked up the paper. "Douglas responded: 'It is the duty of the President of the United States, and of all others in authority under him, to enforce the laws of the United States passed by Congress and as the courts expound them: and I, as in duty bound by my oath of fidelity to the Constitution, would do all in my power to aid the government of the United States in maintaining the supremacy of the laws against all resistance to them, come from whatever quarter it might.'"

"I'm not sure if that's courage or insanity," Thomas observed dryly.

"How did the crowd react?" Carrie asked.

Robert grimaced. "Like you'd expect. They went crazy—yelling and hollering. They did not respond kindly to the idea of Douglas suggesting force would be a justified response. Finally, Douglas raised his hands and demanded that the same question be put forth to Breckenridge."

Thomas shook his head, obviously frustrated at being so far from the actions shaping his world. Carrie knew he would not leave his wife until she was better, but the inactivity was grating on his nerves. "Was it?" he asked sharply.

"Yes," Robert responded. "I read about it in another paper. In typical fashion, he veered near the issue and then dodged it. He insisted he had not a thought hostile to the Constitution and the United States, lambasted Lincoln for advancing unconstitutional issues, and then went on about how the truth and the right of the South would win out in the end." He paused. "He was not about to confront it as directly as Douglas did. The crowd cheered and clapped while Douglas just shook his head."

"What is Lincoln saying?" Carrie asked eagerly. She had missed the stimulation of political debate.

"Lincoln is sitting in Springfield, letting his past record speak for itself. He knows victory is his. A recent letter from Matthew said Lincoln can't imagine that anyone really believes he holds any enmity to the South, but he has decided not to be pulled into the fray. He is letting others do his speaking for him."

"Like Seward, who is saying the South won't secede." Carrie smiled at their questioning looks. "I heard him give a speech when I was in Philadelphia."

Robert nodded. "Seward insists the South is just crying 'wolf. He assured the crowds over and over that the threats of the South are only empty words."

Thomas frowned. "His blindness is going to lead straight to the secessionists getting their wish for a new country."

"I'm afraid you're right, sir," Robert agreed heavily.

Silence engulfed the table as all of them contemplated the situation in the country. Finally, Robert shook his head and pushed back from the table. "Nothing is going to happen today," he said firmly, "and your daughter has a promise to keep, Mr. Cromwell."

Thomas looked up, pipe smoke swirling around his head. "What's that?" he asked with a smile.

Carrie rose gracefully. "I promised Robert a tour of the plantation."

Thomas nodded. "Good. I will look out for your mother. Rose is with her now, isn't she?" Carrie nodded. "You two go have a good time. It's a wonderful day for a ride."

It was indeed a wonderful day. A brisk wind the night before had brought in just a touch of the fall that was on its way. Carrie took deep breaths of the fresh air as she and Robert strode to the barn. She could hardly control the skip in her step. Suddenly, she was very glad to be alive.

Granite snorted and bobbed his head when he saw Carrie coming down the aisle. "Miss me, boy?" She laughed as his massive head came down and rubbed against her shoulder. She wrapped her arms around his solid warmth and stood there for several long minutes, pushing away the emptiness she had felt when Miles didn't meet her as he had done all her life. She looked up finally and saw Robert watching her, a broad smile on his face. She flashed a grin at him. "I'll have him ready in a few minutes. I told Charles that I wanted to take care of him myself today. It's been so long." Robert nodded his understanding and headed to the tack room to gather Granite's saddle and bridle.

A short time later they were riding side by side down the dirt road leading to the tobacco field. Carrie took deep breaths of the fresh air, thrilling to the feel of her horse beneath her again. "It's been three months," she said disbelievingly. "I haven't been on Granite for three whole months." Out of the corner of her eye, she saw Robert open his mouth to speak, but suddenly she didn't want to talk. She just wanted to enjoy being free. She leaned forward and urged Granite into a gallop. He responded willingly, as thrilled as his mistress to be together again. Carrie laughed as she heard Robert's startled yell behind her. Then she lost herself to the rush of wind and the pounding of hooves. Finally she pulled Granite down to an easy jog and let Robert catch up.

The two rode in companionable silence through the newly harvested fields of tobacco and eased between the tall rows of corn still waving their tasseled heads in the breeze.

"How big is Cromwell Plantation?"

"Twenty-five hundred acres," Carrie said proudly. "My father has added five hundred since he inherited it from my grandfather."

"What was your grandfather like?" Robert asked.

Carrie frowned. "I don't know. He died when I was very young. My father was already running the plantation. Nobody talks about him much but I get the idea he wasn't much like my father." For the next several minutes she told him stories of her and her father—how he had taught her about the crops, the horror her mother had shown when Thomas said she could have the run of the place on Granite, and the many times she had eluded him in long games of hide-and-seek.

Robert laughed. "Where did you go?"

Carrie turned and stared at him, a wild thought bursting into her mind. Did she really want to do it? Robert stared back. Then she leaned forward and once more urged Granite into a gallop. "Follow me!" she yelled over her shoulder.

Granite knew where they were going as soon as they reached the far end of the northern pasture. He slowed to a ground-eating trot and picked his way through the overgrown area. Undergrowth had covered the barely discernible trail, but he knew the way.

Suddenly, the most important thing in the world to Carrie was to be at her place. The pull on her heart was something she didn't even try to argue with. She was taking Robert to a place she had never shared with anyone, but she just knew she had to go.

Granite finally broke through the woods and emerged into the clearing. Her eyes drank in the beauty. There had been no frosts to color the leaves yet, but the green was softer as summer came to an end. Colorful wildflowers danced in the breeze, and vibrant purple blackberries dotted the edge of the clearing.

Wordlessly, Carrie slid from Granite's back and walked to the edge of the river. She gazed out over the gentle ripples caused by the breeze. Only occasional shadows cast by fluffy white clouds obscuring the sun marred the bright azure water. Tears began to flow down her face, but they were not tears of sorrow- they were tears of release. Her spirit, confined for so long by the sick room and responsibilities, was drinking up the peace of her special place. Gradually, she became aware of Robert by her side and slipped her hand through the crook of his arm. Together, they allowed the river to perform its magic.

"Thank you," Robert said gently, breaking the silence after a long while.

Carrie turned to him with a question in her eyes.

Robert looked down into her face. "You've never brought anyone here before, have you?"

"No," she said simply.

"Thank you," he repeated. "I am quite honored you would share it with me."

Carrie stared into his eyes, realizing she had let this man into a part of her heart that had been reserved just for her. She didn't regret it. She returned his smile steadily. "You're welcome," she said softly. "This has always been my special place. I found it when I was very young." She chuckled. "I'm glad the trees can't talk. They hold all the secrets of my life."

"Talk to me, Carrie. Tell me how you're handling everything. Tell me about your mother."

Carrie frowned slightly as reality edged into her magic place. She sighed. It *was* reality, and it was nice to have someone to talk to about it. She shook her head and turned to stare at the river again. "She's not getting better, Robert," she said slowly. Her father wasn't around to draw hope from her words so she opted for total honesty. "In fact, she gets worse every day. The fever did a lot of damage to her body." She paused and tried to form her thoughts into words. "It's like she has given up. Yes," she nodded and turned to Robert, "she has given up. I don't think she wants to get well. In some ways she is making herself get worse."

"But, why?" Robert questioned. "She has so much to live for."

Carrie nodded, but her lips were pursed in deep thought. This was the first time she had tried to give voice to her rampaging thoughts and feelings. She continued on, almost as if she were speaking to herself. "She doesn't think so. The fever made her very weak. In her weakened condition, she has decided life is too much to handle. In spite of the fact that she tries to hide from it, she knows what is going on in the world. She is afraid everything that she has always known is about to end." She shook her head as she struggled to express herself. "I don't think she even knows it, but she has given up inside. Something inside of her wants to die. That's why she's not getting better."

"Is that really possible?" Robert protested.

Carrie shrugged. "I don't know," she said flatly. "All I know is what I see every day. I believe Mama could get better. I believe she's not because she doesn't want to. She's tired—too tired to fight anymore."

Robert stared at her. "Does your father know this?"

Carrie shook her head adamantly. "It would kill him. He wants so badly for her to get well. I keep hoping his wanting will make her want it herself. I know she loves my father very much, but..." Her voice trailed off in frustration. She had done all she knew to do, but she didn't know how to instill hope.

"You'll make a wonderful doctor someday, Carrie."

Carrie whirled around to stare at Robert. "How can you say that? I can't even make my own mother well. What good will I be as a doctor?"

"I don't think the sign of a good doctor is that they make all their patients well. That's impossible. Your depth of caring, however, will ensure that each of your patients get your best effort. Your father told me about your trips into the woods to gather herbs with Sarah. It means so much to him that you are trying so hard."

"She's my mother."

"Yes, but wouldn't you do the same for anyone if you were their doctor?" Robert gazed down at her tenderly.

Carrie nodded. "Of course."

"Which is exactly why you're going to make a good doctor."

Carrie looked at him, and then turned away, fresh tears gleaming in her eyes.

He took her shoulders and gently turned her back. "What is it?"

Carrie shook her head hopelessly. "I want with all my heart to be a doctor. I believe I have found a way I can make a difference." Then her voice took on a slightly desperate tinge. "How will it ever happen? As long as mother is sick I'll have to stay here on the plantation. Father needs me too much, and I would never even think of leaving him alone. And what if mother gets better? I'm afraid this country is headed straight into a war. All the medical schools for women are in the North. They'll be in a separate country if those blamed fire-eaters have their way." Her voice blazed forth angrily now. "Why can't they see that all of us need each other? Why do they think they have the right to destroy my life and my dreams just to satisfy their own selfish desires?" Robert moved over and enfolded her in his arms. Carrie rested her head on his broad chest and allowed the tears to come. She had been holding so much. Great sobs wracked her body as the tensions and fears of the last three months finally found an outlet.

"I'm sorry," she gulped as she gradually regained control.

Robert put a finger to her lips. "Hush. You have nothing to be sorry for. I'm the one who is sorry that I live so far away. I wish I was closer and could offer more support for you and your father."

Carrie continued to rest her head on his chest. Moving slightly, she allowed her arms to encircle his lean waist. She needed his comfort and strength so badly. They stood that way for a long time. On the river, a stronger breeze was kicking up whitecaps, turning the azure water a steely gray.

"Carrie..." Robert's voice caught and he cleared his throat roughly. "Carrie, I need to tell you something."

Carrie suddenly began to feel uncomfortable. There was something in his voice. She began to pull back so that she could see his face, but his arms tightened to hold her where she was. She waited to see what he would say.

Robert took a deep breath. "Carrie, I've known from the first day I met you that I love you." His voice was strong and confident. "I—"

"Stop." Carrie pushed herself away and reached up a soft hand to touch his lips.

"But why?" Robert protested. "I—"

Again, Carrie raised her hand to stop him. "Give me time," she pleaded softly. "There is so much going on right now. So much to deal with..." Her voice trailed off as she looked up at him in mute appeal. He would be hurt by the suggestion that his love was just one more thing to deal with, but their dreams were so different. They were miles apart on critical issues.

Robert gazed at her. Finally, he nodded. "All right, Carrie. But, someday..."

Carrie smiled in gratitude. "Someday," she agreed.

Robert forced a smile. "If we don't want to be very wet soon, we'd better head back."

Carrie turned and saw the dark bank of clouds scudding their way.

"Oh, my goodness!" She watched, fascinated, as the increasing wind whipped up higher waves on the James and then turned to where Granite waited patiently. In moments they were on their way. When she reached the edge of the clearing, she turned for one final look. This would always be her most favorite place on earth. She hated to think that anything could ever separate her from it.

"Hey, Moses!"

"Yeah, Sam?" Moses turned from where he was mending some boards that had torn away from the well house during a storm the week before.

"Miss Carrie just came down and said her mama be running a mite of fever again. She asked me to bring up a tub of ice from the ice house, but I done pulled somethin' in my back this mornin'. I need you to take it up to her."

Moses nodded and turned away. "I'll have it right there, Sam." Moses smiled slightly. This would be the first time he would see the inside of the big house. Field servants didn't usually have a reason to be there. It only took a few minutes to fill the tub.

Sam chuckled as he opened the backdoor for him. "I wish you was around all the time. You make that heavy tub look light as a baby. Those arms of yours look more like tree trunks."

Moses smiled and headed in the direction Sam pointed. Just as he reached the doorway he saw Mr. Cromwell and Robert, deep in conversation, walk up the stairway.

Moses was close behind them, but they didn't notice.

"Remember what I told you on the train, Robert?"

Robert chuckled. "What I remember is that you *almost* told me something on the train," he said dryly.

Thomas smiled in return and then grew sober. "You'll soon understand why I couldn't say anything. I've decided it's time, though. I may not get another chance, and I want someone else to know the secret."

Moses raised his eyebrows and walked a little quieter. They still hadn't noticed him. At the top of the stairs, he turned the way Sam had told him and carried the tub into Mrs. Cromwell's room.

"Thank you, Sam," Carrie murmured, not looking up from applying cold rags to her mama's head. "I won't need anything else for a while."

Moses turned and left. He could hear the murmur of voices down the hall. Moses turned toward the voices, making no sound as he crept forward. He knew he would be beaten if he were found. He just knew something was pulling him forward—making the risk worth taking. When he was close enough to hear the voices clearly, he cocked his head and listened intently. A startled look, and then an admiring smile appeared on his dark face. He heard the sound of footsteps and glided silently back down the hall. He was in the kitchen before Thomas and Robert emerged from Carrie's room.

Robert's face had a serious, slightly awestruck look. "Thank you for trusting me sir. I will not betray your confidence."

"I have no doubt of that young man, or I wouldn't have told you. I hope you never need to know it, but if you do..."

"I'm sorry to have to leave so soon, sir."

"That was a long way to ride for just one day," Thomas observed.

"It was worth it," Robert stated quietly. He looked up at the room above him where he knew Carrie was with her mother. "I'll be back as soon as I can."

TWENTY-SEVEN

"Cromwell giving you the boot, Adams?"

Ike Adams shot Jennings a withering look. "Not on yer life. He knows he can't run that plantation without me," he boasted. He saw no reason to tell the truth. Thomas Cromwell had not been himself since his wife had taken ill. He had merely frowned and nodded his head when Adams had reported he had experienced no luck finding the slaves. His wife had called out then, and he had turned back into the house without another word.

Adams was a mean man, but he wasn't entirely without feelings. He felt bad that Cromwell's wife was so sick. He also couldn't help being glad it had gotten him through a rough spot. Blackwell had fired Manson when he had returned without his slaves and hired another overseer who he said could control his people. "What happened to Manson?" he asked suddenly.

Jennings shrugged his shoulders and scowled. "Headed farther south. Somewhere in Mississippi, I think."

Adams merely nodded and tipped his whiskey bottle back. He knew he shouldn't be drinking. Losing the Cromwell slaves should have taught him that. But what was a man to do when the whole world was going crazy? Get drunk. Nothing else made any sense.

"Miss Carrie?"

A broad smile spread across Carrie's face as she reached for the thick envelope Sam was holding out to her. She tucked it into her pocket, glanced over at her sleeping mother and ran downstairs. Once outside, she headed straight for the porch swing.

Dear Carrie,
By the time you get this, it should be around the middle of October.

Carrie leaned her head back against the porch and smiled. She could almost see Aunt Abby's calm eyes looking into her own. Their correspondence had become a lifeline for her. And Aunt Abby was right. Today was October the fourteenth. Brisk, cool air had settled onto the land, the fields were all harvested, and the slaves were busy at work mending buildings and tools before they were put away for the winter.

It was so wonderful to get your last letter, though I am sorry to hear your mother is not doing any better. I am praying daily that she will have a renewed desire to live. I also pray for your own strength and courage. I know your head is probably full of questions you want to ask God when you get to heaven...

How right she was! None of the present situation made any sense to Carrie. Daily she watched her mother waste away and she saw the lines of worry and despair deepen on her father's face. She sighed and turned back to her letter.

Don't be afraid to tell God what you think. He's big enough to take it you know. Besides, he already knows what you're thinking and feeling. You are not alone down there. You can always talk to God.

Carrie frowned as she read that part. She would have to think about that later. She had been too tired to think about God much, especially when he seemed so detached from her life.

> Life here in Philadelphia is as busy as usual. I saw Matthew Justin recently. He sends warm greetings to you. He also related an interesting experience he had. At one of his political functions he ran into Dr. Harriet Hunt. I have told you about her and her medical school here in Philadelphia. They had quite an interesting chat and Matthew shared with her about you and your dream. Her response was that she would welcome you jumping into the fray. The water is a little brisk, but just right for those who have a strong heart! I know you despair of your dream, Carrie, but hang on. We can never know, and hardly ever understand, the path God has us walk on our way to our dreams.
>
> My work with the society is keeping me extremely busy. More and more passengers are riding the railroad. I understand our activities are creating quite a stir in the South. That is to be expected, but I find myself greatly troubled that anger over activities such as mine are adding to the South's determination to withdraw from our glorious Union. Yet, I cannot turn away from those who want to be free—who deserve to be free. Daily I fight the battle with my conscience. I can only hope that I am indeed doing God's work.
>
> Thank you for telling me a little about Robert. He sounds like a wonderful young man. You mention an issue that you are afraid will keep you apart. You do not reveal what it is, but my heart holds a pretty good guess. Regardless of what it is, you need to decide whether you can spend the rest of your life with a man who disagrees with you on an issue important to you. You have to ask yourself just how important is it to you. Is it something that could create a wedge that would drive you farther apart? Do not marry thinking that marriage itself will change someone.

God is the only one who can change people when they are ready to be changed. Robert sounds like a very special and unique person. It is much to his credit that he supports your dream of being a doctor. But I wonder...how will you be a plantation wife and a doctor all at the same time? Ask yourself many questions while you are still free to ask them.

I fear this letter is becoming too serious. Alas, the condition of our country seems to warrant such seriousness. One bright spot! Recently, the society received a letter from Harriet Masters and some of the other slaves in her little group. They are alive and well in Canada. All of them have found work and are rejoicing in their freedom.

I look forward to hearing from you soon. Take good care of yourself.

Affectionately,

Aunt Abby

Carrie finished the letter with regret. She always hated it when they came to an end. She would have given anything to be able to sit down and have a long heart-to-heart talk with her friend. The ache to see her again had not diminished with time. She folded the letter slowly, slipped it back into her pocket, and rose to return to her mother's room. She seldom left her alone now. She stopped at the door and looked out over the pastures. Granite was there, his head raised, staring at her. She had not ridden since Robert had been there a month before. She was afraid to leave her mother.

Carrie hurried up the stairs to her mother's room. She was still sleeping peacefully when Carrie settled down on the chair next to the window. She picked up her notebook and once again began to scan the voluminous notes she had taken when she and Sarah had been on their jaunts. She did not want to lose any of the information just because their hunts had stopped. *It be too late in the year for any of the magic plants to still have any healin' powers,* Sarah had stated firmly two weeks ago. Carrie closed her eyes and envisioned the shelves in the root cellar full of old Sarah's magic.

A rustle caused her to open her eyes. Her mother was staring at her with an odd expression on her face. "Hello, daughter," she said softly.

"Hello, Mother." Carrie rose, moved over to the bed and took her hand. They talked very little now. It seemed to take too much of her mother's strength.

"Will you prop me up on the pillows, please?"

Carrie instantly obliged her, glad to see even this tiny bit of interest in life.

Abigail continued to stare at her with that odd expression on her face.

"What is it, Mama? Is there something wrong with how I look?"

Abigail blinked and shook her head. "No. I was just thinking how much I love you. How proud I am of you."

Carrie tried to control the surprise she was sure showed on her face. She supposed she had always known her mother loved her—even when they were completely at odds with each other—but it had not been since she was a little girl that she had heard it come from her lips. She didn't know what to say. "Thank you," she murmured. Then her voice strengthened. "I love you too, Mama."

"I know," Abigail said softly. "I need to tell you something—" A spasm of coughing interrupted her words. It was several minutes before she regained her breath.

"Mama, you need to rest. Let me lay you back down," Carrie urged.

"No." Abigail shook her head with more determination than Carrie had seen in months.

Hope mingled with a vague uneasiness as Carrie stepped back. What had given her mother this new lease on life?

Abigail smiled gently and reached out to take Carrie's hand once more. "I know you're not like me, Carrie. I've tried..." She faltered. "I've tried to turn you into a proper plantation mistress, but I know I have failed." Her words were softened with a smile. "You're different than me, Carrie. That bothered me for a long time. I wanted us to be alike. I wanted you to want the same things I did. I was wrong," she admitted with a wry expression.

Carrie stared at her mother. She couldn't believe what she was hearing.

"What is it you really want, Carrie?"

Carrie hesitated and then decided to speak her heart. "I want to be a doctor."

Abigail nodded and smiled again. "I figured you would want something that impossible."

Carrie laughed. It felt good to have her mother know the truth. She had hidden it for so long. Suddenly, she felt a gentle pressure on her hand and looked down into her mother's eyes.

"Follow your dreams, Carrie. You are special. Don't let anyone steal those dreams from you." Exhausted, Abigail closed her eyes.

"Thank you, Mama," Carrie whispered. She knew she would always carry those words—words she had thought she would never hear—close to her heart. Abigail's eyes fluttered open again. "Robert Borden loves you."

"I know."

"Do you love him, Carrie?" Abigail's voice, though weak, was intense.

Carrie struggled for words to express her feelings. "I love him, Mama, but I'm not sure that is enough." Her mother watched her steadily. "In so many ways he is perfect—everything I have ever dreamed of. But there are things that stand between us."

"Such as?"

"Such as my desire to be a doctor. Robert dreams of turning Oak Meadows into another Cromwell Plantation. You know how I feel about being a proper plantation mistress. Our dreams may be too far apart."

Abigail frowned. "I would think two people who truly love each other could figure out a way to make both their dreams come true. I admit that I don't really understand it—I never wanted anything but what your father wanted—but surely there must be a way."

Carrie shrugged. "There is something else, Mama." She was determined to be honest.

"What is it, dear?"

Carrie hesitated, not sure how to proceed. "There is one very important thing we disagree on." She faltered and then plowed ahead. "Mama, I don't think I believe slavery is right." There, she had said it.

Abigail frowned and shook her head slightly. "I don't understand."

"I'm not sure I do either," Carrie admitted. "All I know is that Robert and I fight every time we get near the subject." Memories of Aunt Abby's letter rose in her mind. "I'm not sure I can spend the rest of my life with someone who believes so differently from me."

Abigail peered into her eyes. "I'm trying to understand." Her face revealed her confusion.

"I know you are," Carrie said helplessly, "but I'm not sure I understand it myself yet. How can I expect you to understand?"

Abigail stared at her intensely. "I just know Robert Borden loves you. The same way your father loves me. I hope you find a way to each other. I want you to have that kind of love."

Carrie nodded, her throat suddenly constricted by the look of love on her mother's face. Tears sprang to her eyes as she leaned down and gave the frail form a gentle hug. "I love you, Mama." When she stood back up, her mother's eyes were closed. She walked quietly back over to the window.

Her mother wasn't done however. "Carrie?"

Carrie spun from the window. "Yes, Mama?"

"Will you do two things for me?" Carrie nodded. "Will you get your father...and then will you promise me you'll go for a long ride on Granite?"

Carrie stared at her, unsure of what to say.

"It's a beautiful day, isn't it?" Abigail smiled. "I want you to enjoy it. You've spent too much time up here with me in this little room. You've been so wonderful. But today...today, I want to know you're outside with Granite." Her voice was strong and firm.

There was a light in her eyes that Carrie hadn't seen in a long time. Suddenly, hope sprang into her weary heart. Maybe her mother had finally turned the corner. Her mind raced as she thought of all the herbs she could use to strengthen her frail body. "Alright, Mama," she assented joyfully. "I'll get Father and then I'll go for a ride." She moved over and planted a gentle kiss on her mother's brow. "Thank you."

"Mr. Borden!"

Robert had just mounted his horse, and now he turned around impatiently. He was on his way to the first drill for the Goochland County cavalry unit he had founded. It had irked him to see all the militia units marching the streets the last time he had been in Richmond. More than anything, he wanted to see the country remain united, but if the worst came, he hadn't changed his mind. He would fight. It had been easy to find eager young men like himself who wanted to be prepared for any contingencies.

"What is it, Jacobs?" he asked tersely as his overseer reined in his blowing horse. Robert looked with disapproval at the horse's heaving sides.

"Two of your slaves are missing, Mr. Borden," he said tautly.

Robert went rigid in his saddle. "What? Are you sure?" he asked tightly.

"I'm sure, Mr. Borden. Two slaves are missing from White Hall down the road, too. Michaels down there thinks they are together. They used to all be from Oak Meadows, but you sold the two men a couple of years back. The two women missing from here are their wives."

"How did they get away?" Robert asked angrily. "Where were you?"

Jacobs flushed but didn't look away. "I was doing my job, Mr. Borden. You told me to take the men and clear off the bottom field. When I got back, they were gone."

Robert cursed and his face twisted with anger. Immediately, he was eleven years old, seeing his father ride off to hunt down the nigger who would kill him. He took a deep breath. "Get the dogs, Jacobs. We're going after them." His voice was deadly calm.

Jacobs stared at him and nodded. "I'll be right back with the hounds, Mr. Borden. Them niggers can't be far."

Robert didn't hear him. He was already planning the chase. He vaulted off his horse and ran into the house. Minutes later he reappeared, patting his waist to make sure his pistol was secure. All thoughts of the Goochland Calvary Unit had fled his mind. Only one thing was important. To catch those slaves and teach them the lesson once and for all that they were no more than animals.

Carrie leaned back against the log in her special place and took deep breaths of the brisk afternoon air. Grateful for its warmth, she hugged her cloak around her body. The vibrant red, orange, and yellow hues of the trees filtered the sunlight and cast a golden glow over the clearing. It was wonderful to be there. Carrie tried to think of the last time she had been alone. Unbidden, memories of her last time there rose in her mind and flashed across her eyes as if it were actually happening. Robert holding her gently... Telling her he loved her... Her stopping him... Carrie shoved the thoughts back firmly. The combination of Aunt Abby's letter and her mother's words had made her realize she could no longer run. The time was now.

She reached into her deep pocket and pulled out a sheaf of papers. She had heard her father talk about these papers many times. She knew they formed the basis for his beliefs about slavery. She had taken them from his office so she could find out for herself what they said. She laid them on the ground next to her and reached into her other pocket to pull out the thick envelopes she had been receiving from Aunt Abby. A Bible followed next. When she was surrounded, she stared out at the river for a long moment and then picked up the first stack.

The Scriptural theory respecting the origin of Slavery, may be stated, in brief, thus: The effect of sin—disobedience to God's laws—upon both individuals and nations, is degradation. A people under this influence, continued through many generations, sink so low in the scale of intelligence and morality as to become incapable of safe and righteous self-government. When, by God's appointment, slavery comes upon them— an appointment at once punitive and remedial; a punishment for sin actually committed, and at the same time a means of saving the sinning people from that utter extermination which must otherwise be their doom, and gradually raising them from the degradation into which they have sunk.

Negroes are condemned to slavery by Noah's curse of Canaan, as recorded in Genesis. But there is hope! Of the remedial operation of slavery, we have a striking illustration in the case of the African race in our own country. In the history of nations, it would be difficult to find an instance in which a people have made more rapid progress upward and onward than the African race has made under the operation of American slavery. That they have not yet as a people, attained a point at which they are capable of safe self-government, is, we believe, conceded by everyone personally acquainted with them, and therefore capable of forming an intelligent opinion. That it may take generations yet, to accomplish the gracious purposes of God in inflicting slavery upon them, is very possible. The work which it has taken ages to do, it often takes ages to undo. But nothing is more certain than that God's plan has operated well thus far.

Carrie laid the paper down and frowned. Memories of her father quoting from this paper still rang clearly in her head. She shook her head and reached for another stack of papers. The sun sunk lower in the sky as her shining ebony head bent in concentration.

> Slavery is authorized by the Almighty himself! The examples are many: Noah's curse of Canaan; Abraham with his bond servants; the Hebrew servants...The treatment of slaves, especially as it regarded the degree of correction which the master might administer, occurs in Exodus. "If a man smite his servant or his maid with a rod and he die under his hand, he shall be surely punished. Notwithstanding if he continue a day or two, he shall not be punished, for he is his money." Here we see that the master was authorized to use corporal correction toward his slaves, within certain limits. When immediate death ensued, he was to be punished as the judges might determine. But for all that came short of this, the loss of his property was held to be a sufficient penalty.

Unbidden, a scene from her childhood floated into Carrie's mind. She had been only six or seven, and spending several days at the Blackwell Plantation. A slave had been found missing just before she returned from a clandestine meeting with her husband at the next plantation. Blackwell had insisted she be made an example of and then turned to walk into his house. Curious, she and Louisa had followed the overseer and the frightened woman. Carrie had never been able to erase from her mind the terrified screams of the woman as the lash had fallen repeatedly on her bare back. She had strained against the bonds that secured her to the whipping post and had begged for mercy, but there had been none. Carrie had run sobbing from the awful scene, but had never been able to rid her mind of the picture. Tears once more clouded her vision as she continued to read.

In the relation of master and slave, there is incomparably more mutual love than can ever be found between the employer and the hireling. And I can readily believe it, for the very reason that it is a relation for life, and the parties, when rightly disposed, must therefore feel a stronger, and deeper interest in each other. Slaves are the happiest laborers in the world. Their wants are all provided for by their master. Their families are sure of a home and maintenance for life. In sickness they are kindly nursed. In old age they are affectionately supported. They are relieved from all anxiety for the future. Their religious privileges are generously accorded to them. Their work is light. Their holidays are numerous. And hence the strong affection which they usually manifest toward their master, and the earnest longing which many, who were persuaded to become fugitives, have been known to express, that they might be able to return. Perhaps a fugitive comes along, who has fled from his master and who in justification of himself, will usually give a very distorted statement of the facts, even if he does not invent them all together. People are easily deceived - their good and kindly hearts believe it all implicitly, without ever remembering the rule about hearing both sides before we form an opinion.

Aunt Abby's strong face and shining, intelligent eyes rose in Carrie's mind. She was not a woman to be easily deceived. Carrie thought of the roomful of people she had watched grieve as Harriet Masters haltingly told her story. Willing to defy the laws that insisted runaway slaves be returned to their owners, they gave of their time and their money. Only a deep belief could motivate such actions. Carrie also knew that a vast number of slaves were treated humanely. For all of her life, she had considered the Cromwell slaves as part of her family. There had been a genuine love given and received. A great many of her father's friends felt the same paternalistic way that he did about their slaves. Surely there was good in that. She shook her head. Was there really an answer to this?

The next few pages rambled on at great length, but Carrie was able to cull the meaning out of the voluminous words.

> The Declaration of Independence states that "all men are created equal; that they are endowed by their Creator with certain unalienable rights; that among these are life, liberty, and the pursuit of happiness." The truth is that men are not created equal... every sensible person must know we are not all equal... a vast diversity among the races of mankind...the highly privileged Anglo-Saxon which now stands at the head... All men are born equal? The proposition is a sheer absurdity. All men are born unequal in body, in mind, and social privileges. Their intellectual facilities are unequal. Their education is unequal. Their associations are unequal. Their opportunities are unequal... Those who take the lead are sovereigns. It is their job and their mission to rule over those less equal. The writers of the Declaration of Independence surely were never referring to the Negro race or to other inferior people. Surely no one could imagine that these men intended to stultify themselves by declaring that the Negro race had rights, which nevertheless they were not ready to give them. They quite simply were not considered.

Carrie's head pounded unmercifully as she plowed on.

> The Negro is happier and better as a slave than as a free man... It is simply true that the Negro is intellectually inferior... Freedom will but

> sink the ex-slave lower into his degradation... He
> will never be fitted for freedom... It is kindness to
> keep the slave in bondage...

Carrie lowered the papers and sighed. Then, with grim determination, she reached for the stack of envelopes from Aunt Abby. The older woman had been sending her little bits of information about the abolitionists in her last letters. *Not an attempt to control your thinking,* she had written, *just more information to throw around in your head as you try to reach a conclusion in your battle.* Carrie had smiled and laid them aside. There had been too much else going on to consider more. Now she was ready. The only way to make an intelligent decision was to consider both sides. She knew most of her friends wouldn't even have bothered. They were content to continue on as they always had—believing the things they had been taught to believe. Her heart had been troubled for a long time, but was there evidence against slavery that would trouble her mind as well?

The sun sank even lower in the sky as Carrie poured over the information, jumping back and forth to her Bible to confirm references. Granite snorted impatiently, but his mistress was too engrossed to hear him. She raised her head occasionally to stare out over the water but then lowered it back to her task. Finally, she leaned back against her log. Deep in thought, she allowed all she had read to filter through her mind.

She had often heard that immediate emancipation would cause social disintegration and economic decline because Negroes would not be able to bear freedom responsibly. This theory had been disproved by an intense study of the emancipation of eight hundred thousand slaves in the West Indies. The free Negroes had actually worked harder because now they were working for themselves.

Another argument she had heard many times was that American slavery was a socially beneficial system and that Negroes fared better as slaves than free men. But a system which allowed such deprivation and violation of human rights and such cruelties could not be called beneficial. One overriding theme that ran throughout the abolitionist's literature was the one that most caught her heart and mind, however.

> Jesus said, Thou shalt love the Lord thy God with all thy heart, and with all they soul, and with all thy mind. This is the first and greatest commandment. And the second is like unto it, Thou shalt love thy neighbor as thyself.

Carrie frowned, deep in thought as she allowed this verse to run over and over through her mind. Jesus had said clearly that a Christian was not to treat others worse than he himself would be treated. The battle raging in her head was relentless, but this time she was going to fight through. She wanted to know the truth. She picked up a single sheet of paper and leaned back to read again the letter from the Quaker John Woolman.

Dear Friends,

> If we continually bear in mind the royal law of doing to others as we would be done by, we shall never think of bereaving our fellow-creatures of that valuable blessing liberty, nor to grow rich by their bondage. To live in ease and plenty by the toil of those whom violence and cruelty have put in our power, is neither consistent with Christianity nor common justice, and we have good reason to believe draws down the displeasure of Heaven; it being a melancholy, but true reflection, that where slave keeping prevails, pure religion and sobriety declines as it evidently tends to harden the heart and render the soul less susceptible of that Holy Spirit of love, meekness, and charity, which is the peculiar character of a true Christian. How then can we, who have been concerned to publish the Gospel of universal love and peace among

mankind, be so inconsistent with ourselves as to purchase such who are prisoners of war, and thereby encourage this unchristian practice.... Let us make their case our own, and consider what we should think, and how we should feel, were we in their circumstances. Remember our blessed Redeemer's positive command "to do unto others as we would have them to do unto us" (Luke 6:31); and that "with what measure we mete, it shall be measured to us again" (Luke 6:38)... "Love one another," says he, "as I have loved you," (John 15:12). How can we be said to love our brethren and bring, or for selfish ends keep them in bondage. If it be for your own private gain, or any motive other than their good, it is much to be reared that the love of God, and the influence of the Holy Spirit is not the prevailing principle in you, and that your hearts are not sufficiently redeemed from the world.

Carrie laid the paper aside and buried her aching head in her hands. Her father would say this letter was the emotional pandering of one who had no understanding of the destiny southern plantation owners had inherited from God. Truly, there was good and bad on both sides. There were many slaves who, emancipated, had floundered in their freedom and not been able to make it. Many more had built wonderful lives for themselves. There were many slaves who were well treated and cared for by their owners. There were many who were abused and treated as nothing but animals and property. Suddenly Sarah's words popped into her head. *Ain't nothin' more I'd like den to be free, Miss Carrie. Slavery don't just take a person's body. It tries to take their soul—their mind. It tells dem they ain't really a person. They just a thin' to be used by someone else.*

She could see Sarah sitting serenely in her straight-back chair, gazing at her with steady eyes. Sarah had been at Cromwell for twenty years. She was well treated, yet all she wanted was to be free.

It's true dat some black folk ain't as smart as some white folk, but dats just because dey ain't had the chance to learn." Then she had added with a quiet twinkle in her eye, *"I know some white folk who ain't nearly as smart as some black folk I know. The color of the skin don't make no difference. It's what be in the head and heart that count.*

Tears filled Carrie's eyes as the battle intensified, knotting her stomach until she felt sick. What was the *truth*? She knew what other people thought, but she desperately needed the truth. They all claimed to base their beliefs on scripture, but they couldn't all be right.

Ask me.

The voice was inaudible, but clear in her heart. Carrie's eyes drifted to the Bible in her lap.

My voice is the only one that counts. The only way to know truth is to know my heart.

Tears filled Carrie's eyes as she rose, turned toward the log, and sank to her knees. Resting her arms on the moss-covered surface, she raised her eyes toward the sky. "God, please. What is the truth?" She buried her head in her hands and sobbed uncontrollably as the confusion of the past six months overwhelmed her.

Gradually she calmed. She had no idea how long she had been there when she finally raised her head. She looked toward the river and was shocked to see the sun dipping below the violet horizon. She jumped up and hurried to Granite. Her mother and father would be frantic if she wasn't home by dark.

"Thank you for being so patient, boy." She gave Granite a big hug, led him to the log, and mounted lightly. With a heart full of peace and resolve, she turned toward home. She had her answer. She sang softly as she allowed Granite to pick his way through the darkening woods. She would deal with the consequences of her decisions later. For now, it was enough to know she had her answer. She knew God's heart.

It was almost dark when Robert stomped onto his front porch.

"You didn't find them?" It was more of a statement than a question.

Robert spun to see his mother gently gliding back and forth on the porch swing.

"No," he said shortly. "I'm sorry. I guess we're another statistic of the Underground Railroad. I sent Jacobs to find some slave hunters, but I don't hold much hope they will find them. Those Yankees have perfected their ability to steal our property." He made no attempt to hide the bitterness in his voice.

"I'm glad you didn't find them," his mother said softly.

"What?" Robert stared at her in disbelief. "How can you say that? Those two women are worth over a thousand dollars each. Do you know how many children they have birthed for us?"

"I don't care about that. What I care about is having my son alive." Her voice broke. "I already lost a husband on a slave hunt." She lowered her head into her hands and began to cry. "I can't lose you, too."

Immediately, Robert was at his mother's side, holding her hand and stroking her bent head. "It's alright, Mama. Everything is alright. Nothing happened to me. Nothing is *going* to happen to me." He continued to stroke her head and talk to her softly until she had regained control. Then his voice hardened, "I'll be back soon, Mama. I'm going down to teach the remaining slaves a lesson. They won't be thinking about running away again soon."

"You've become just like your father."

His mother's voice stopped him. "What?"

"You were just a boy when your father died, but the same hardness and hatred is in your heart. Where did it come from?" she asked helplessly.

Robert stared at her. Then he stalked off the porch.

Carrie continued to think as Granite cantered down the road. It was time to talk to her father. She would not leave the plantation until her mother was well, but it was important her father know how she felt—what she believed. They had always been honest. She didn't want that to change now. She would talk to him tonight.

Thomas was waiting on the porch when she left the barn after handing Granite to Charles. Carrie ran lightly up the stairs. As she drew nearer, she realized her father was standing at rigid attention. Concerned, she slowed her steps. What was wrong? She glanced up and saw the light still burning in her mother's window. She must still be awake. Carrie was glad. She wanted to tell her mother she had her answer. She knew her mother wouldn't understand, but she had hope now that she would accept her.

"Carrie..."

Carrie stopped on the last step and stared at her father, but the shadows hid his face. His hoarse voice hardly sounded like her father.

"Carrie..." Again Thomas's voice drifted off as if he could not force himself to say the words. "Your mother..."

"What, Father? What is it?" Carrie stepped on the porch now and was able to see her father's face. She was shocked by the wild eyes and sharp grief etched there. Immediately she knew. Only one thing could cause that look. With a stifled cry, Carrie turned and ran up the stairs, ignoring her father's startled shout behind her. She turned into the room and came to an abrupt halt, before slowly approaching her mother's bed.

She was beautiful even in death. The ravages of the last months had been erased, leaving the smooth, peaceful face she would always remember. Carrie gently picked up one of her lifeless hands, tears flowing.

"I love you, Mama."

TWENTY-EIGHT

Carrie stood on the steps, watching Sam load the last few things of her father's into the carriage. Thomas, standing rigidly at her side, seemed unaware of the biting November cold. Carrie wrapped her cloak tighter to her body to keep out the invasive wind. She kept her eyes on the carriage to avoid looking at her father. The lines of grief had only deepened in the month since his wife's death. He had seemed to age overnight. Nothing seemed to touch him. She had not been able to reach beyond the wall he had erected to deal with his beloved Abby's death. Carrie, forced to act on her father's behalf, had shoved down her own grief. She had no choice but to remain strong.

A recent letter from Governor Letcher, expressing his sympathies and inviting Thomas to Richmond, had been the only thing to penetrate his lethargy. Carrie, encouraged by the small evidence of interest, had urged him to go. It had not taken long to convince her father to leave Cromwell. He seemed to want nothing more than to escape the constant memories that assaulted him at every turn. He had protested only once at the unfairness of leaving everything in Carrie's hands before he easily acquiesced.

Carrie watched as her father's eyes roamed over the pastures. They had once brought him great joy and satisfaction. Now they symbolized a lifetime of dreams shattered by Abigail's death. He'd told Carrie that if he didn't get away, he was afraid he would succumb to the whirling darkness trying to pull him into its endless depths. Maybe in Richmond he would find relief from the unending agony.

"Sam has everything ready, Father."

Thomas started and focused his eyes on Sam who stood next to the carriage. Charles had just climbed into the driver's seat. Steam rose from the horse's nostrils, only to be whisked away by the wind. Slowly, Thomas turned to look down at his daughter. "Thank you," he murmured. "Thank you, daughter."

Carrie's heart caught at the anguish on his face as he lifted his eyes briefly to his bedroom window. She forced her voice to be strong. "I hope you have a wonderful trip, Father. Everything will be fine here."

"I...I don't know...I don't know when I will be back." Thomas looked down as he spoke.

Carrie's heart sank, but she kept her voice steady. "I know, Father. Come home when you're ready." There had been no talk of when her father would return. She hoped for the best, but was prepared for the worst. Carrie was now the mistress of Cromwell Plantation. "I love you, Father." She kissed him gently on the cheek, took his arm, and led him down the stairs. Oh, how she hated to see her father like this. He had always been such a strong man. Now he resembled nothing more than a broken shell.

Carrie watched as the carriage rolled down the driveway. The wind whipped at her cloak, but she was unaware of the cold now. She had wanted nothing more than to leave Cromwell Plantation. Now she watched as the whistling wind snatched her dreams and carried them above the treetops, far from her reach.

Rose watched Carrie from her bedroom window. She ached for her friend but didn't know what to do for her. Carrie had been unreachable since her mother's death, her only concern to care for her father. Rose knew her friend had buried her own grief in order to survive. As she watched the cold wind whipping at the slender body held in rigid defiance of life, she longed to go and wrap her arms around her.

Rose turned away from the window. Her mama had asked her to come down to the quarters this morning. Carrie wouldn't need her for a while. She reached for her cloak and hurried out into the biting wind.

Moses looked up at the sound of the door slamming, and Rose flashed him a smile. Sam was having trouble with his back again and had asked Moses to do some work at the big house. The labor in the fields was done for the season. All the field hands were doing repair work around the plantation now.

Just to see Moses during the day was enough for Rose's hungry eyes. Soon they would be husband and wife. They still wouldn't be able to live together—she would have to stay in the house—but at least they would be man and wife. Time would take care of the rest.

Rose lowered her head, pressed into the wind, and strode down the dirt road. She would have sung, but the wind would have whipped the words out of her mouth before they could even be formed. She felt sorry for Miss Carrie, but her own life was overflowing with love and joy. There was only a month to go before the day she and Moses had set for their wedding. She hadn't had a chance to tell Miss Carrie yet, but she knew she would soon. The biggest change, however, had occurred in her own heart. She was a new person since the night in her mama's cabin when she had let go of all the hate.

"Well, looky what we got here. A nigger woman!"

Rose, startled, looked up and came to an abrupt halt as Ike Adams stepped from the bushes. She could tell in a single glance that he was drunk. His eyes were red and wild, and his face hung in a loose recklessness. She glanced around quickly. No one was in sight. She fought the panic rising inside and stood quietly before him.

Adams leered and moved closer. "Well, well... A nigger woman...and a right good-looking one at that." He reached out his hand and touched her cheek roughly.

Rose struggled to remain calm. She knew the meanness in this man. If she made him angry there was no telling what he would do. She tried to breathe normally as she continued to look him in the eye. *God, help me.*

"Woman, you ever been with a real man?" Adams slurred. "I be needing me a real woman. What a coincidence that you happened along." He reach out his other hand, grasped her hair roughly, and pulled her toward him.

Rose, horrified, knew what the gleam in his eye meant. She knew Adams felt he was all powerful now that Cromwell was gone. Frantically, she tried to figure out a way to escape what was surely to come. Then Adams's lips found their mark. Gagging, Rose pulled away. She knew immediately that she had made a mistake.

Adams cursed, grabbed her head with both hands, and claimed her lips roughly. He let his cruel lips linger for only a moment before he wrenched away, dropped his hands to her shoulders, and pushed her toward the woods. "Think you're too good for me, nigger? You ain't seen the beginning of what I aim to do to your pretty body. I don't reckon it will be fit for any man when I'm done with it." He gave her a mighty shove that almost sent Rose sprawling, but then lost his own balance and stumbled to his knees.

That was all the chance Rose needed. She would not be raped. She knew there would be punishment, but she would not simply submit to Adams's evil plan. Just as the drunken man reached up to grab her again, she wrenched away and began to run down the road.

Immediately, Adams was up and after her. "I'll catch you, nigger woman!"

Rose gasped as his laugh rang out behind her. Her only hope was to reach the quarters. Maybe the sight of the other slaves would bring him to his senses. She ran blindly, pumping her legs faster, her long skirt and heavy cloak hampering her with every step.

Adams caught up to her and grabbed her shoulder. He dug his fingers in cruelly and wrenched her to a stop. "I told you, you can't get away from me nigger woman. I always get what I want. Right now I want you!"

The venom in his voice made Rose's blood turn to icicles. There was no way to escape this monster. She controlled her desire to scream as he undid the buckle of his belt and slowly pulled it out.

"I reckon you need a lesson in how to treat your overseer, nigger woman." Adams pulled back his arm and gripped the buckle so tight his knuckles whitened. His face contorted with anger as he whipped the belt forward.

Rose saw it coming. She tried to brace herself for it, but nothing could have prepared her for the pain that coursed through her body as the rough leather of his belt cut into the tender flesh of her cheek. Her shrill scream pierced the air. Then she turned to flee again.

Carrie, still standing on the porch, heard a scream rise on the wind and then fade away as the wind whipped it past her. "Rose?" she whispered. It took a moment for the scream to register in her brain. Then she whirled around and stared down the road. She could see nothing, but she knew what she had heard. "Rose!" she cried.

She picked up her skirts and began to run down the stairs. Something stopped her in her tracks, however. She dashed back up the stairs, across the porch, and into the house. A moment later, she reemerged and flew down the road.

Adams was only inches from Rose when she ran into the quarters. Blinded by the tears of fright and pain coursing down her face, she headed for her mama's house. She didn't know what else to do. She had no more than turned in that direction when she felt Adams's fingers clutch her bruised shoulder again. Caught off balance, she pitched forward and slammed into the hard ground.

Sarah, roused by the commotion, peered out of her door and then ran toward her daughter.

"Touch her and she'll get it worse, old nigger!" Adams reached for his horse and grabbed his whip and a piece of rope out of the saddlebag. He whirled and stalked to where Rose huddled on the ground.

Sarah groaned, but stopped when she saw the whip. She had seen what it could do.

Adams, an evil leer on his face, reached down and grabbed Rose by the arm. He jerked her up and shoved her roughly toward the middle of the quarters. "Ain't no whipping post of no use here, but that tree there should do the job. It's good enough for a nigger like you. You'll find there ain't no use in not giving me what I want!" He grabbed her shoulder, pushed her up against the tree, and groped for the neckline of her dress.

Rose knew what was coming. Adams was finally going to let out all that meanness.

"No!"

Adams jerked back in surprise as the strong voice bellowed across the clearing. Whirling around to see who was yelling at him, his evil grin spread wider. "Well if ain't the giant nigger himself. My, my! My day just keeps getting better and better." He fingered his whip and locked eyes with Moses.

"Let her go. She ain't done nothing to you." Moses's voice was low and deadly.

"And how would you know that nigger? Besides, what does it matter to you?" Adams's face lit up as understanding flashed into his sodden brain. "This be your woman, nigger? Well, if that don't make things a sight more interesting." Suddenly, he snarled and pulled the whip back. "Back off nigger, or I'll whip this girl until you won't know who she is. For sure, she won't be the pretty thing you're lusting after now!" He released the whip, allowing it to just graze Rose's shoulder. She cried out and shrank against the tree.

Moses growled and prepared to launch an attack.

"Stop it!" Everyone in the clearing spun around when the shouted command was accompanied by the sharp crack of a rifle. "Drop that whip, Adams!"

Adams face tightened into a mask when he saw Carrie Cromwell's slight figure behind the barrel of her father's gun. "What you think you doing, *Miss* Cromwell? You watch yourself or you gonna hurt someone with that rifle." He gripped the handle of his whip tighter, and began to walk slowly toward her.

Moses was still crouched, his eyes darting back and forth between the two.

Carrie never flinched. Calmly, she stepped toward the overseer. Then, pulling the hammer back on the gun, she took careful aim. "You can be quite certain I know enough about this gun to put a bullet through your useless heart, Adams," she said coldly.

Adams stopped and stared at her. "Your father would tell you to leave this business to me, Miss Cromwell," he snarled.

"My *father* told you from the very beginning that there was to be no abuse of Cromwell people. I also know he told you a few months ago that if you were ever to touch another one of our people that it would be the end for you." She gripped the gun tightly as she spat out the next words. "You're finished, Adams. Get off this property and never come back. I want you and your family out of your house by nightfall." She paused, then continued coldly, "I should just go ahead and put a bullet through your heart, but I feel sorry for your wife and children." She raised the gun. "I could change my mind, though. Get going before I do!"

Adams stared at her in disbelief for only a moment. Blanching white, he rapidly coiled his whip and headed for his horse.

"Drop the whip, Adams. I'll want it in case you ever get it in your mind to come on this property again. It might do you good to see how it feels," Carrie snapped.

Adams, his face white with rage, dropped the whip and vaulted on his horse. "You'll be sorry for this, Miss Carrie Cromwell!" He allowed himself one burning look of hatred before he kicked his horse into a gallop and disappeared down the road.

Sarah and Moses both sprang forward at the same time. Rose huddled against the tree, allowed the tears to flow freely as she sobbed into Moses's shoulder.

Carrie lowered the gun slowly, dropped it, and hurried to Rose's side. It was several long minutes before Rose lifted her face from where she had buried it in Moses's chest.

"He hurt you!" Moses cried, anguish twisting his face as he saw the long ugly welt oozing blood.

Carrie felt sick as she stared at her friend's disfigured face. "I should have killed him," she cried angrily. "I should have killed him while I had the chance."

Rose shook her head. "You did the right thing, Miss Carrie. He didn't hurt me bad. God heard my cry and saved me." She reached up and touched Moses's face tenderly, interpreting his look. "He didn't rape me, Moses," she whispered. Moses nodded his head mutely, his eyes full of rage and sorrow. He groaned, cradled Rose's head in his hands, and stared into her eyes.

It was Sarah who took charge. "We got's to take care of that cut. Carrie, go get what we need," she commanded.

Carrie left the gun laying in the clearing and raced for the root cellar.

Carrie prepared a tray of food and carried it to her room. Rose had protested, but Carrie had insisted she recover from her experience in her own room. Moses and Sarah looked up as she entered the room. "I have enough for everyone," she smiled. Rose stared at her as she laid the tray of chicken and fresh biscuits on the table next to her bed.

"Miss Carrie, I'm feeling much better. I can go back to my room now."

Carrie shook her head firmly. "I'm the doctor. I'll tell you when you can leave." She dropped her pretense of sternness and leaned forward to grab Rose's hand. "I just want to be sure you're alright," she said tenderly. "It makes me sick inside to think what that horrible man almost did to you."

Rose stared as bright tears sprang into Carrie's eyes. "I'm all right, Miss Carrie."

"My name is Carrie, Rose. That's what I want you to call me."

Rose was speechless. She looked to her mama for help.

Sarah regarded Carrie for a long moment. "You been doin' some changin', girl."

Carrie smiled and nodded. "You're right as usual, Sarah." She lowered her eyes for a moment. "My mother's death knocked the life out of me for a while, but I'm going to be okay now." She didn't know how to explain that hearing Rose's scream had torn her out of her pity and moved her back into living.

"Your mama be in a better place, Miss Carrie."

Carrie smiled as Sarah put a warm hand on her shoulder. "I know that, Sarah. I know she's with God. It's just going to take a while to get used to living without her." She took a deep breath and looked at Rose. "Rose, it's been so long since we've really talked. I've been lost in a world of my own. I have a feeling I'm very out of touch with your life."

Rose smiled gently. "You've had a lot to distract you, Miss Carrie. You had your mama to take care of for all those long months, and then your father took her place."

Carrie frowned. "I'm worried about my father. It's as if there is no life left in him."

Sarah reached forward again to take her hand. "Your mama *was* your father's life. It will take him time to make a new one."

Carrie nodded. "I don't think I ever realized how much they loved each other. Mama and I were so different..."

"Your daddy have a big heart, Miss Carrie. He had plenty of love to give the two women in his life. Your daddy gonna be alright. It takes time for the aching to make room for livin' again."

Carrie fixed her eyes on Sarah as she talked, but she didn't miss the tender look Rose shared with Moses. She nodded her head and turned back to Rose. "I have a feeling there is some love being shared in *here*," she said with a smile.

Rose returned her smile. "Moses and I plan on being married next month. If that's alright with you," she hastened to add. "There hasn't been a chance to talk with you until now."

Carrie turned to stare at Moses and liked what she saw—the strong face and steady eyes that returned her gaze evenly. She'd had no opportunity to get to know him since her father had bought him, but the soft look in Rose's eyes when she looked at him, told her he was special. "Of course. I'm happy for both of you," she said warmly.

"I never did get a chance to thank you for saving me from the whip when I was out in the field," Moses said.

Carrie frowned. "It never should have happened. I'm sorry." She looked down and then back up. "Nothing like that will ever happen again. I want to know if Ike Adams ever steps foot on this property again. While my father is gone, I'm in charge of the plantation." She tried to cover her troubled voice with a smile.

"When your daddy be comin' back?" Sarah asked gently.

Carrie shook her head and frowned deeper. "I have no idea." She turned to look at Sarah. "He may never come back, Miss Sarah. There is so much hurt for him here. I found out just before he left that he bought a house in Richmond the last time we were there." Her voice trailed off. "I don't know if he'll ever be able to come back and face the memories," she whispered.

Sarah gazed at her sympathetically. "You can't be runnin' Cromwell Plantation on your own, Miss Carrie. 'Specially without an overseer. There be too much here for any one person—'specially a young girl like you."

Carrie knew she was right but she shook her head stubbornly. "I won't hire another overseer," she declared. A wild idea popped in her head and she fixed Moses with a steady gaze. Moses met her gaze, not flinching. The room was silent as her wild idea took shape and substance, and was then accompanied by the quiet voice she had learned to listen to in the clearing. "Moses, I'd like you to be my overseer." The whole room radiated with a shocked silence.

Moses's eyes grew wide.

Carrie smiled as her assurance grew. She nodded firmly and turned to Sarah. "You said a few minutes ago that I had done some changing. I think I need to tell all of you what has been going on." She paused as she gathered her thoughts. "Ever since the beginning of spring, I've been struggling with slavery. Everything I had ever learned was colliding with what I was seeing myself. I tried to push it away, but everywhere I turned it kept coming back." Briefly, she told them about the slave auction. "It made me sick. Suddenly I realized a whole system was treating other human beings like animals." The three in the room just watched and listened. "My beliefs were challenged even more when I went to Philadelphia. I met a remarkable woman who didn't condemn me for where I was, but simply gave me the opportunities to look at it deeper." She paused again as she remembered. "Then I ended up at an abolitionists' meeting. That's where I heard Harriet Masters speak."

Rose gasped as she heard her friend's name. "From Blackwell?" she whispered.

Carrie nodded. "The slave hunters almost caught her again, but I managed to stall them."

"That was you?" Rose exclaimed. She shook her head and stared wide-eyed at her friend. "I heard through the grapevine that someone had saved her."

Carrie nodded. "I still didn't know entirely where I stood on the whole issue of slavery. I just knew I couldn't live with myself if I didn't help Harriet stay free." Once again, Harriet's shining face as she spoke of being free rose in her mind. "She was so happy to be free!"

Sarah said nothing, but reached over and took Carrie's hand.

Carrie smiled at her and plunged ahead. "When I got home from Philadelphia, I could think of nothing but mama and her being sick. Until I went to my place..." Tears filled her eyes as she relived the experience. "I was determined to find answers. I had listened to so many voices—loud voices—that proclaimed the reasons black people were supposed to be slaves; and equally loud voices that said it was a horrible sin for *anyone* to be in slavery, and condemned all slave holders. The voices were pounding in my head, all demanding that I believe them." She shook her head and looked down. After several long moments, she raised shining eyes. "Then I heard God! He told me, 'My voice is the only one that counts. The only way to know truth is to know my heart.'" She shook her head. "I was there for a long time. It was like God took me into a little bubble and showed me the world from his view. I saw him cry when that family was wrenched apart at the auction. I saw him weep when abolitionists I had met lashed out with hate. I saw him smile when slaves reached freedom in Canada. It's really so simple," she mused. "The Bible says it all in one sentence. *Thou shalt love thy neighbor as thyself.*"

Sarah nodded. "Simple, but it ain't always easy."

"I found that out! Why, I've known that Bible verse all my life, but I had also been taught slavery was right. It's so easy for people to twist things around to fit what they want to believe." She paused, wanting the three in the room to understand her. "The people who say slavery is right say that all people aren't created equal. They say some people will never achieve as much as others—that they were never designed to. They say black people can't learn and are inferior to white people." She smiled as she looked at Rose. "I know that's not true. You never let on, but I knew you learned how to read before I did."

Rose smiled, but said nothing. She was obviously trying to take it all in.

"Anyway, I asked God about that."

"And what did God say, Miss Carrie?" Sarah asked.

Carrie answered slowly. "He told me that all people carry a seed of greatness in them. Not everyone will choose to let it grow, but it's not my place to determine who those people are. All I need to do is love everyone and give them all an equal chance to be who God created them to be. So many people are never given the chance." She paused. "God cries over that." Her voice strengthened as she looked around the room. "I believe slavery is wrong," she stated firmly. "I don't believe God ever meant for people to own each other and steal their ability to be all they were created to be." She struggled to express herself. "The South is my home. My love for it has not diminished, but I must play a part in getting rid of slavery. I have no idea how—"

Sarah broke in again. "God don't never let a desire to do good go unused. When it's time, He'll show you what you is to do."

Carrie frowned. "I wish I could give all of you your freedom. Unfortunately, only my father can do that. But I *can* help you reach freedom." Suddenly it wasn't important for Moses to be the overseer. A bigger picture was taking shape in her mind. Her voice grew excited as she looked at Moses and Rose. "I know people in the Underground Railroad. I can contact them!"

Rose laughed softly in disbelief. "You know people in the Underground Railroad, Miss Carrie?"

Carrie nodded impatiently. "Of course!" Her mind was racing. "I'll write Aunt Abby. She'll tell me the best way to do it." She figured rapidly in her mind. "Why, you can probably be free before you get married!"

"We won't be needing the Underground Railroad, Miss Carrie," Moses stated firmly.

"What?" Something in Moses's voice caught Carrie's attention and she turned to stare at him.

"I said we won't be needing the Underground Railroad. We had our chance to go free. We chose to stay here."

Now it was Carrie's turn to be speechless.

Sarah answered her unspoken questions. "Rose won't leave me, and Moses won't leave Rose. I told them to go..." She shrugged. "I may be a slave, but I'm free inside. I'm too old to be startin' over. The Lord done told me I'm to stay right here for now. I aim to do what he says."

Carrie watched as Moses and Rose exchanged deep, contented looks. She was trying to put the pieces together. "Miles and the other slaves...?"

Rose met her gaze and nodded. "Moses and I helped them escape. The Underground Railroad has already been here."

"I prayed they wouldn't be caught," Carrie murmured. "Have you heard from them?"

Rose shook her head. "No. Jamison said he would contact us when he could, but Adams came back without them. That's a good sign."

"Jamison?" Carrie asked. "The man who was here for dinner?" Rose gasped, then breathed a sigh of relief, when Carrie laughed loudly. "I knew I liked that man!"

Sarah was the one to introduce realism into the room. "Miss Carrie, how you aimin' to run this plantation feelin' the way you do? Don't you know you be setting yourself up against a lot of people, including your daddy? You're lettin' yourself in for a passel of hurt, gal."

Carrie nodded. "I know, Sarah. But it would hurt worse to live a lie. If my actions don't follow my beliefs, they aren't worth much. I'm just going to have to cross all those bridges when I get to them." She paused as the matter of the plantation rose to the front of her mind. "Moses...?"

"Someday—I believe someday soon—we will all be free. But for now we have a job to do. I'll help you do that job the best I can," Moses said firmly. "You're a good woman, Miss Carrie."

Rose looked at him proudly. "He's a leader, Miss Carrie. The other slaves already respect him. He will be a good overseer."

Carrie nodded, her brain working rapidly. "I won't tell my father about Ike Adams. He left me in charge. In charge I am going to be." She turned to Moses. "I want you to let me know anytime the slaves need something. Things are going to be different around here. I may not be able to set them free, but I can make their lives different. And, if any of them want to escape," she continued firmly, "I will not stand in their way. They are free to go."

Moses nodded slowly. "Some will choose to go, Miss Carrie. But many will choose to stay for now. They love you. With Adams gone..." His face tightened with anger as he thought of the overseer.

Rose reached out and touched his hand gently. "I'm alright, Moses. The cut will heal."

Carrie knew in her heart that things weren't over with Adams. He was an evil man and his pride had been battered.

Sarah spoke thoughtfully. "You ain't got to worry 'bout all the slaves runnin' away, Miss Carrie. Lots of them don't care too much 'bout being free. They ain't never been nothin' but slaves. When you don't know nothin' else, where you are can look pretty good.

'Specially with Adams gone. They's people with a seed of greatness, but there ain't nobody ever done nothin' but try to stamp out that seed. It'll take a while before they believe it themselves."

Moses spoke calmly. "We may have to scale back some, Miss Carrie, but we can make it work. We're going into winter—the slow time of the year. We won't have to worry about crops until next year."

Carrie nodded. "We'll all work hard and do the best we can. We'll leave the results to God," she said firmly.

TWENTY-NINE

Carrie smiled at the sight of all the quarters' children dancing around Sarah with excitement. Pigtails flopped, and faces glowed with anticipation of what lay ahead. She herself had shared the same excitement with them years ago when she was little enough to go along for the hunt. She felt a small twinge of envy, but pushed it aside. She could go this year if she wanted to, but she had something more important to do.

"You sure you don't want to be joinin' us, Miss Carrie?"

"I'm sure, Sarah."

Sarah looked at her closely. "You look like a girl with a secret, Miss Carrie."

Carrie laughed, wondering if the old woman would always be able to see into her heart. She shrugged and said simply, "Secrets are meant to be kept secrets, Sarah." Her eyes danced with laughter, but her voice was firm.

Sarah smiled. "Get on with you then, girl. I got a hunt to lead." She turned to the pack of children swarming around her slight figure and raised her voice. "It's time!" Then she led the giggling swarm down the path.

Carrie watched them until they were out of sight. The sun was just beginning to peep over the horizon. She hugged her cloak tightly to her body as wisps of steam rose from her breath. She envisioned Sarah carefully snipping herbs and pulling roots. She would point out late fruits and berries to be brought back and pickled, spiced, or dried. She closed her eyes tightly and could almost hear Sarah's old voice, sweet and true.

"Chillun, we be finding gifts for Jesus like the Wise Men did. They done brung the baby Jesus three gifts—gold, sweet smellin' spices, and bitter herbs. Some of the very herbs we be finding now."

A child clamored, "But Miss Sarah, we ain't be taking these gifts to Jesus. We just be takin' them back home!"

"They be gifts just the same, child. Gifts our friends and loved ones be lookin' forward to all year. I reckon when we give gifts of love, it be like a gift to Jesus."

Carrie had never really understood it until now. She turned and strode rapidly up the path to the barn where Granite was waiting for her. She had a gift for Miss Sarah and Rose that only she could give, but she would have to hurry.

Moses looked over the group of slaves standing before him. Carrie had put him in charge of them only two weeks ago. The number of Cromwell slaves was smaller by ten. A direct contact with Jamison had brought another conductor for the Underground Railroad. Carrie had sent them all off under the cover of night with clothing and food. The rest had not yet acted on Carrie's offer for freedom. The amount of work done by the remaining slaves had been astounding.

Moses looked down at his list and began to call out orders.

"Jed, take three men and clean the barn next to the big house."

"Carmen, take the women and make sure all the gardens are raked good."

"Willy, there's a pile of tools in the tobacco barn that need fixing."

His voice droned on until every person present had a job to do, and they had all turned away to begin their day's work. No one stood over them with a whip. No one yelled orders and made threats. And they knew that once they had finished their assigned work for the day— no matter how long it took—the rest of the day was theirs. Work that been performed slowly and begrudgingly before now disappeared under willing hands.

Carrie rode up just as the last person turned away.

"Everything is being done, Miss Carrie."

Carrie nodded. "I'm quite sure it is. I didn't come to check on you, Moses. You are doing a wonderful job. I've never seen Cromwell Plantation look so good!"

Moses ducked his head shyly. "Thank you, ma'am."

Carrie became all business again. "I came to tell you I will be gone for the day. It may be late when I return."

Moses frowned. "You going on Granite?"

"Yes," she said firmly.

"Alone?" His tone left no doubt how he felt about it.

Carrie smiled. "I am perfectly capable of taking care of myself, Moses." She understood his concern. She also was sure the only way to keep her secret was to not take anyone along. "I'll be careful," she promised solemnly. Moses nodded, but the concern did not leave his face. "Good heavens," Carrie laughed. "You're worse than my father." She turned Granite and broke into a rapid trot, posting smoothly. She didn't have a lot of time. She was going to have to put in a lot of miles.

In just a few minutes she was passing Ike Adams's old home. It stood empty, but there was a feeling of relief about the old house, as if it were glad to no longer be harboring hatred and ill feelings. Carrie had requested the house be fixed up, but Moses had found no one willing to go near the place. There was too much fear that Adams would return to settle the score. After careful questioning, Carrie had discovered that Adams was living in a ramshackle cabin several miles from the plantation, making his living as a slave hunter. She shuddered to think of the treatment an escaping slave would receive from his hands.

She forced her thoughts to more pleasant subjects and pushed Granite into a steady, ground-eating canter. Excitement bubbled within her as she firmed up her plans.

Rose had seen Carrie leave earlier but had received no more information than anyone. Carrie had merely smiled and said she would be back later and not to worry if it was late. Rose had pressed her, but her friend's only response had been more mysterious smiles.

Rose had plenty of other things to occupy her mind. She was getting married in just two days and there was still so much to do. If that wasn't enough to keep her busy, Mr. Cromwell was going to be home in a week, bringing Robert Borden. Then only another week until Christmas. Rose shook her head and busied herself with work.

The house was being transformed before her eyes. So much had been allowed to go undone while Mrs. Cromwell had lain sick in bed, in need of quiet. Now a flurry of activity had erupted in preparation for Christmas. The *big times* were almost upon them. Every window had been washed and polished, every floor scrubbed from top to bottom. Chandeliers had been carefully taken apart and each piece cleaned until they gleamed. Every piece of silver had been polished to a brilliant luster, children holding each piece up to make sure they could see their reflection clearly before they reached for the next one. All the rugs had been rolled up, carefully taken outside, and beaten until not a speck of dust remained. Only then were they reinstalled on glowing floors. Mattresses in every room had been turned, and new ticking had been sewn on the pillows. Already the house was alive with the wonderful smells of baking and holiday preparations.

Rose stopped in her cleaning of Carrie's room and lovingly fingered the white satin dress taking shape on Carrie's bed. The material had been a gift from Carrie for her wedding dress. Never did she think she would wear a dress so grand. It was almost done. A few more hours and she would be ready.

"Daydreaming again, girl?"

Rose looked up at Sam standing in the doorway and smiled. "Did you ever think you'd see me get married, Sam?"

"Shucks, girl. I knew some man was 'ventually goin' to come along that would be good enough for you." His voice was gruff.

"You do like Moses, don't you, Sam?" Rose knew Sam felt it was his job to protect her. He had felt that way ever since she could remember.

Sam nodded, and when he spoke, there was suspicious moisture in his eyes. "Your daddy would be real proud of you, Miss Rose."

Rose frowned slightly and looked down at her beautiful dress. "I wish he could be here to see me, Sam." She shook her head and forced the thought away. "I have so much to be thankful for. I'm not going to allow useless wishing to spoil my wedding."

Sam nodded. "You're goin' to be the most beautiful bride there ever was, Miss Rose."

Rose walked over and gave him a big hug. "Thank you, Sam."

Sarah led her entourage from the woods to find the women from the quarters already waiting for them. The children were still laughing and smiling, but the long hours in the woods had taken the dance from their steps. They went where Sarah directed them and dumped their bags on the ground.

Only then did the waiting women move forward. Sarah smiled as she handed out the treasures. There were big handfuls of cedar moss that would be used to make yellow dye. Bandanas were filled with mounds of walnuts that would yield a deep brown color. The biggest pile of bags was saved until last. Every woman in the quarters would receive an adequate amount of elm, cherry, and red oak. When they were all combined, they produced a deep, vibrant red. Red—the color most coveted. There was just time to make a pretty red dress for the Christmas dance. Or for Rose's wedding.

Laughter and talking filled the air as the women moved back to their cabins. Their work was done for the day. Now they could perform their own preparations for the *big times*.

Moses looked up from his work, but didn't stop. Miss Carrie had asked him to build a cabin to add to those already in the quarters. She had given no reason.

She had just asked him to do it. It had steadily taken shape under his hands. He would hang the door tonight and it would be done. Moses had pushed himself to have it finished because Carrie had promised him a week off with his new bride.

Sarah moved over to watch him quietly. Moses looked up, smiled, and bent back to his work of stuffing the cracks against the winter cold.

"That be a mighty fine cabin, Moses."

Moses nodded. "I'm just building it the way Miss Carrie told me to." He had wondered himself at her requests. None of the other cabins had wood floors or shutters on the windows. "I don't figure it's my place to be asking questions." He frowned. "You reckon she wants it built to put a new overseer in here? Maybe she didn't like the fact that Adams's cabin was so far away. This way, an overseer could keep a better eye on things."

Sarah shrugged. "Reckon time will tell."

It was long after dark when Carrie finally rode, exhausted, up to the house. Charles stepped from the shadows and reached for Granite's reins. "Long day, Miss Carrie? I was getting plum worried about you."

Carrie nodded and gratefully relinquished the reins. "I'm fine, Charles. Thank you for being here. All I want is a hot bath and some food. Take good care of Granite. He has earned whatever you give him."

Charles nodded. "I'll make sure he gets a good hot bran mash and plenty of hay."

Carrie paused on the steps and glanced toward the barn. A slight movement of the curtain in Miles's old room caused her to smile and turn toward the house. "Thank you, Charles." In spite of her exhaustion, her steps were light as she climbed the stairs.

Sam met her at the door. "Miss Carrie! I was worried about you."

Carrie smiled warmly. "Thank you, Sam. I'm fine, though."

Sam reached into his pocket. "A letter from Philadelphia," he said with a smile.

"Aunt Abby!" Carrie reached for the letter and ran up the stairs. A hot bath, and then she would curl up with her letter.

Dear Carrie,

How I wish I could talk to you just now. The difference in our age continues to diminish with our correspondence. I so need to hear the Southern perspective of what is happening in our country right now. Matthew has been such a wonderful help in keeping me abreast. I find I rely on him more and more to help me make sense of the madness.

Now that Lincoln has been elected, the North is slowly realizing the threats of the Southern states were in earnest. There is much scrambling to figure out what to do, but no one seems to be willing to take the lead. Buchanan is still president, but his administration continues on in its *lame duck* ways. There was brief talk of a convention of all the states to find compromises that would heal the rift, but it has now faded into the deepening passions. I talk to no one here who wants war, but there is no leadership stepping forward to stop it. Is our country simply going to ride the tide into war? I fear it is so. Matthew tells me a convention is meeting in South Carolina on December 17 to decide on whether that state will secede. He tells me he has no doubt that it will happen.

My dear, please forgive me for launching into my concerns so quickly. I have not even asked how you are. I know you still grieve for your dear mother. I am equally aware of the enormous burden you must be bearing now that your father has gone to Richmond. I am so proud of who you are and who you are becoming. It takes great courage to do the things you are doing.

Thank you so much for your invitation to come for Christmas. How I would love to do so, but the madness of the country is affecting my business. No one seems to have any idea what is going to happen, so many people are simply waiting to see. The business community is reeling from inactivity. My family has asked me to come home and I feel that is my first duty. I can't help but wonder if they will be in a separate country soon and if I will indeed find myself at war with those I love best. Oh, what a horrible thought!

This letter must be brief, as I find myself overwhelmed with responsibilities right now. Please know that I think of you daily and long for the time when we can see each other again. I still hold hope that you will be able to visit, but more and more that hope is being battered with reality. I can do nothing but pray. That I will do every day. Take good care of yourself.

Affectionately,
Aunt Abby

Carrie put the letter down with a sigh. She had so hoped Aunt Abby would be able to come for Christmas. She gazed into the flames of her fireplace and wondered if the older woman was right. It was so easy, here on the plantation, to forget the momentous decisions and acts taking place in the country that could determine her existence as an American. Her brow furrowed deeply as she considered the ramifications of South Carolina seceding.

It didn't take long for exhaustion to win out over her worry. She tucked the letter in with the rest of the thick bundle in her wooden box and climbed into bed. Snug beneath her comforter and quilts, she lay quietly, listening to the wind in the oaks outside her window. In moments she was sound asleep.

Rose hugged herself with excitement when she crawled from her bed two days later. Today was her wedding day! She could hardly believe it had finally come. A quick look at her wall reassured her. The early morning light was filtering in through her tiny window, causing the white satin of her wedding gown to shimmer and glow. It seemed to beckon her to come. Rose walked over slowly and allowed her hands to run lovingly down the beautiful gown. She closed her eyes and tried to imagine Moses's face when he saw her. What it would be like to be wrapped in his arms...

"Daydreaming never got any bride ready for the big moment."

Rose started violently as Carrie's teasing voice broke into her dreams. "You scared me to death, Miss Carrie! Don't you know to knock before you come into a room?"

Carrie laughed easily and moved in further.

Rose reached out to hug her. She and Carrie were truly best friends now. She still insisted on calling her Miss Carrie because she was afraid she would slip sometime when Carrie's father was home, but the relationship between them was more like sisters.

Rose walked over to her bed and sat down on the edge. "I can't believe it's finally here, Miss Carrie. I'm so excited!"

"But...?"

"But, what? I didn't say but."

"Your words didn't, but your voice did."

Rose shook her head. "You sound like my mama."

"Thank you for the compliment," Carrie replied. "But...?"

Rose smiled, stood, and walked over to her dress. She fingered it for several long moments before she spoke. "Getting married makes me think about my mama and daddy. They loved each other the way I love Moses. I used to swear I would never get married and have to worry about being separated. I don't worry about that now, but even if I did, I would still do it. I love Moses too much. I would have to take the risk. But

I hurt for my mama...and I wonder where my daddy is... I wish he knew I was getting married. I wish he could be here." She stopped as her voice caught in a sob.

Carrie walked over and laid her hand gently on her friend's shoulder. "I wish there was something I could do, Rose. I've thought about your daddy so many times. I wish I knew where he was. I was just a baby when he was sold." Frustration was thick in her voice.

Rose blinked away the tears in her eyes. "I told Sam I wasn't going to waste energy on useless wishful thinking." She took a deep breath and smiled. "I may get to tell my daddy someday, but today? Today I'm just going to think about my Moses!"

Carrie smiled and squeezed her shoulder. "He's a wonderful man, Rose. You are very lucky." The day flew by as the two hurried through the last minute preparations. Carrie had insisted the ceremony take place in the house. The dining room was the only room large enough to accommodate everyone. The table, chairs, and china cabinets had all been moved into another room. Great boughs of fresh greenery were brought in to decorate and candles abounded. Finally, it was ready.

Carrie turned to Rose. "I've had your dress taken up to my room. I'd like you to get ready there. I need to talk to Sarah. I'll be up soon."

"Thank you," Rose said softly.

Carrie found Sarah helping put the last touches on the food. "Sarah, can you do something for me?

"Of course, Miss Carrie. What it be?"

"I put Rose and Moses's wedding gift in the room over the barn where Miles used to live, and I promised Rose I'd help her get ready. Will you go get it for me?"

Sarah nodded. "Where you want me to put it?"

Carrie hesitated. "The library will be fine."

Sarah nodded again and left the house. She walked quickly to escape the biting December air, crossed the yard, and entered the barn. She took deep breaths of the comforting aroma and climbed the stairs to Miles's old room. A scuffling noise just as she reached the door made her draw back in alarm. What was in there? She looked around for a weapon, and then laughed softly. She was being silly. It was probably just a rat. Comforted, she pushed the door open and stepped into the sunny room.

"Hello, Sarah."

Sarah gasped and whirled around. What she saw caused her whole world to spin. She groped for the wall, leaned her weight on her hand and shook her head in disbelief. She was imagining things. "John?" she gasped. She began to shake violently. "Is it really my John?"

Immediately, the man stepped forward and enfolded her slight form in his strong, wiry arms. "Sarah," he whispered. "It's really me, Sarah. After all these years your John has come home."

Sarah began to cry as she wrapped her arms around him and clung desperately. Long minutes passed as they whispered each other's names over and over. Finally, she pulled back and raised her hand to stroke his face. She gazed into his eyes and whispered softly, "You still be as handsome as ever."

"And you still be as beautiful as ever."

They both laughed. Eighteen years had changed them, but their hearts remained the same. The laughter broke through Sarah's disbelief and wonder. "How you get here, John?" There were so many questions.

"Miss Carrie done bring me here."

"Miss Carrie!" Sarah exclaimed.

John smiled, took her hand, and led her over to sit on Miles's old bed. "I been in this room for two days. 'Bout killed me to be so close to you, but Miss Carrie told me it had to be a surprise for you and Rose." He shook his head in wonder. "Rose getting married. I can't believe it!" He paused. "Does she know?"

Sarah shook her head strongly. "I done kept my promise all these years. I ain't never told her and I ain't gonna!" Her tone left no room for argument.

John smiled at her and nodded his head. "You ain't changed none, Sarah. I'm glad," he added lovingly. "I done kept a picture of you in my mind all these years. I don't want you to be different."

Sarah nestled up against him and basked in the feel of his warm solidity. "How long you gonna be able to stay, John?" She hated to ask. She wanted to believe he was here to stay, but she knew better.

"Miss Carrie bought me, Sarah."

Sarah jerked back in surprise. "What?"

John nodded. "That gal went through every paper in her daddy's library until she found the papers on me. I been living 'bout thirty miles from here down the river."

"That close all these years?"

John nodded. "My master didn't hand out no passes. I ain't never been off that plantation in all these eighteen years. I tried to get messages to you, but it never worked. Anyway," he continued, "Miss Carrie found me and bought me off Marse Green. She told me on the way here that I could go free any time I wanted to. You and me could go off and start a new life." Sarah stared at him, trying to take in all he was saying. "Miss Carrie done told me how you feel. That you aim to stay here. I aim to be right here with you."

Great tears rolled down Sarah's face as she stared at her husband. Then joy caught up with the shock and forged ahead. Suddenly, a wide grin spread across her face as it exploded with joy. "My John be home again!" she exclaimed. "Oh, wait until Rose sees you! Miss Carrie done give the best weddin' present there could be." She paused and added softly, "And she done give me my heart back."

John smiled, folded her close in his arms, and lowered his lips to claim hers. "I love you, Sarah."

"And I love you, John."

Nothing more was said for a long time.

Carrie slipped the gown over her friend's head, took her hand, and gently led her over to the full-length mirror. "You're beautiful, Rose."

Rose gazed at herself silently for several long minutes. "I didn't ever think I would wear anything so beautiful, Miss Carrie."

"You're what makes it beautiful, Rose. I've never seen you look so lovely."

Great tears sprang to Rose's eyes. "Thank you," she whispered. Then she spun around. "I'm so sorry, Miss Carrie."

"Sorry? Sorry for what?" Carrie asked in an astonished voice.

"I hated you, Miss Carrie. I hated you because you had everything I wanted and never thought I could have." Haltingly, Rose told Carrie of her struggles and of her battle in her mama's cabin. "God took all that hate, Miss Carrie. It just makes me feel so horrible that I ever felt it."

Carrie smiled and reached for her hand. "If the roles had been reversed, I would have felt the same way," she said firmly. "All that is in the past anyway. Right now, you have a man waiting downstairs for you. Someone who loves you very much." She paused. "In fact there is more than one man waiting for you."

Rose stared at her. "What are you talking about? And why are you wearing that mysterious smile again? What is going on?"

Carrie merely smiled, walked to the door, and swung it open. "Is the bride ready?"

Rose nodded and moved across the room toward the door. "I'm ready."

As she moved to the top of the stairs she caught a glimpse of her mama standing to the side with a strange man. She could hear quiet laughter and voices coming from the dining room chapel. She allowed the magic of the moment to engulf her and floated down the stairs, her satin gown shimmering in the brilliant glow of the chandelier.

Rose glided to the bottom of the stairs and turned to smile at her mama. She stopped, confused. The strange man standing next to her was crying.

Sarah stepped forward then with a glorious smile. She reached for Rose's hand and laid it gently in John's. "I'd like you to meet your father, Rose."

Rose could do nothing but stare.

Carrie came up behind her and put both hands on her shoulders. "I wanted you to have the most special wedding gift ever. I hope you don't mind that I kept it a surprise."

Rose whirled to stare into her eyes and then turned slowly back. A look of disbelieving wonder spread across her face. "Daddy?"

John smiled and opened his arms. "Rose," he whispered.

With a glad cry, Rose melted into his embrace, warm tears running down her cheeks. "Daddy! I can't believe it's you!"

"It's me, baby girl. You didn't think I would miss your weddin' did you?" John smiled and laid his finger gently across her lips as she began to speak. "There be plenty of time for questions later. Right now, you got a right impatient man waitin' for you."

"Does he know?" Rose asked, brushing her tears away as bright happiness flooded her face.

"He knows," Sarah said with a smile. "And he knows your daddy be here to stay!"

Rose turned and threw her arms around Carrie's neck. "Thank you," she whispered. She could think of nothing more to say just then.

Carrie laughed and pushed her gently away. "You're welcome. I'm as happy as you are. Now go in there and get married."

Rose was glowing as she walked down the aisle toward Moses. She wasn't sure how one person was supposed to contain so much happiness. Thoughts of her daddy standing behind her faded as she locked eyes with the man she was going to marry. Strong, quiet love reached out to draw her. Deep contentment and surety filled her as she moved steadily toward the one with whom she would share the rest of her life.

The ceremony was brief and simple. Rose had insisted on only one thing with the minister Carrie had brought in. Long ago the marriage vows had been changed for slave weddings. No longer did they say *'til death do us part*. The new version simply said, *'til we part*. She had insisted the original vow be used. She had simply shaken her head when the minister tried to explain it was that way because slaves were property that could be sold, and the old vows didn't apply to them. *Do it my way or I'll find someone else*, Rose had said. He finally agreed, though his expression had left no doubt as to what he was thinking.

Moses took Rose in his arms and kissed her deeply. Loud cheers and clapping broke out as he raised his head and turned Rose to face their friends and family.

Carrie stepped forward then. "I have one more wedding gift for the newlyweds."

"But, Carrie—"

Carrie held up her hand to stop Rose's protest. "Don't tell me I've already done enough. You're my best friend, and you and Moses are helping me keep Cromwell Plantation running." She turned to Moses. "Did you do a good job on that cabin I asked you to build?" Moses nodded, a wide smile growing on his face. "That's good," Carrie continued. "It's your new home." She turned to Rose. "You won't be staying in this house any longer, Rose. It's only right you should be with your husband."

Rose had lost count of how many times she had been rendered speechless that day.

Moses looked down at Carrie. "You're a good woman, Miss Carrie. We thank you from the bottom of our hearts." His voice was deeper than normal.

Carrie smiled up at him. "You've earned it, Moses. I wish I could give you something better…"

Moses shook his head firmly. "That cabin is just perfect. I never dreamed we would have a home of our own for a long time."

Rose threw her arms around her friend and held on for a long time. "Thank you are mighty little words, Carrie," she whispered into her ear. "You're going to have to look into my heart to see how I feel right now. I don't know how to say it."

Carrie hugged her back tightly. "As long as you're happy, that's all I care about." She moved away and clapped her hands. "I'd say we have a lot of celebrating to do tonight. The barn is ready for the dance."

It was many hours later before Moses was able to take Rose to their new home. Taking her hand he led her to the door of the little cabin. "Welcome home, wife."

Rose smiled into his loving face. "Welcome home, husband," she said tenderly.

Together, hand in hand, they moved into the single room. Someone had already been there. A fire was blazing, casting its cozy warmth into the shadows.

"A bed!" Rose cried. "A real bed!" Wonderingly, she moved toward the four-poster bed tucked into the far corner, its thick mattress covered with several heavy quilts. "Miss Carrie..."

Moses nodded, his own eyes moist. "God is giving us things I never thought I would see on this earth. Miss Carrie is a good woman. I only hope I live long enough to give back to her some of what she has given us."

Rose nodded. "Me too," she murmured.

All talk ceased as Moses turned and gently took her in his arms. He lifted her off the floor easily, carried her to the bed, and laid her down, lowering himself next to her. Rose turned her face toward him, her love shining freely. Moses stared into her eyes, his own dark eyes glowing with love and passion. Rose caught her breath and released herself to the passion rising in her body. "I love you, Moses."

The fire had died down to a glowing bed of embers before any other words were spoken.

THIRTY

Carrie couldn't help the shiver of excitement that coursed through her body as Moses dragged the massive Christmas tree onto the front porch. She was still like a child when it came to Christmas. She loved every minute of it. And her father and Robert were coming home today!

Moses smiled at the look on her face. "Where you want this thing, Miss Carrie?" He lifted the giant cedar easily to rest on his shoulder. "It's the best one I could find."

"It's beautiful, Moses. I think it may be the tallest we've ever had!" She almost danced into the house. "I've cleared a space in the living room for it." She looked over his shoulder and saw Sarah leading an army of women from the quarters, their arms loaded with greenery. She clapped her hands with delight and led Moses into the house.

It didn't take Moses and Sam long to secure the tree on its wooden stand. Once it was standing, Carrie and the house servants went to work. Rose led the team of women who were arranging the greenery. The entire house was transformed as great boughs of cedar, pine, and holly were used to artfully decorate every doorway, mantle, mirror, and picture in the house.

Carrie breathed in deep breaths of the fragrant aroma as she directed the decorating of the massive tree commanding attention next to the grand fireplace. Great trunks full of decorations had been carried down from the attic. Within a short time, the tree was dressed with cotton balls, gilded nuts and berries, paper garlands, colored pieces of glass, and white lace.

"We done finished, Miss Carrie!"

Carrie laughed at the glowing face peeking around the corner. "Bring them in, Jubilee! We're ready for you."

The proud little girl, with red ribbons adorning her black pigtails, led her little army into the room. That the children had been hard at work could not be denied. Great armloads of stringed popcorn were laid reverently on the rug in front of the tree.

"Go on, Jubilee. All of you can put them on the tree."

Jubilee slapped her hand to her mouth, her eyes opening wide. "We ain't never got to put it on the tree 'fore, Miss Carrie."

Carrie smiled gently. The little girl was obviously afraid of the repercussions if it wasn't done to Carrie's standards. She walked over and tilted Jubilee's chin until their eyes met. "You did a wonderful job with the stringing. I know I can trust you with the tree. Moses and Sam will hold you up to reach the high branches."

Jubilee's face broke into a wide grin and excited giggles broke out from the other children. Moses and Sam walked over with huge grins to match. The whole atmosphere was one of joy and happiness. Never had there been a Christmas like this one.

Carrie watched with a smile, her heart content. When the strings of popcorn adorned even the highest reaches of the tree, the women moved forward once more to add burgundy velvet and pink satin ribbons. Their final contribution to the stunning tree was an assortment of miniature toys, dolls, and furniture.

"It's the prettiest tree I've ever seen, Miss Carrie," Rose said, stepping in from the kitchen. "Your daddy will be proud."

Carrie turned to Rose with a sudden frown. "Do you really think so, Rose? Mother always took care of the tree in the past." She hesitated. "Do you think it will remind him too much of her? I want Christmas to be special this year, but I fear it may be too soon for him."

Rose looked thoughtful. "Life is meant to be lived, Miss Carrie. It doesn't do any good to run away from those things that bring memories. My mama always told me that all you can do is make new memories to replace the painful ones. That's all you're trying to do for your father." She paused for a long moment. "You've done the right thing, Miss Carrie. How your father responds is not your responsibility. You have to give him room to find his own way. Just like you have to find your own way."

Carrie turned to look at her friend. "You speak with great wisdom," she teased, but her face sobered and her eyes filled with deep admiration. "Thank you, Rose. I'll try to remember what you just said."

Silently, Carrie stood and stared at the tree. She couldn't help wondering if this was the last Christmas like this one the South would ever know. She was sure her father was bringing bad news, but she was glad there was still room for celebration and joy. Reality had not yet stalked in to rob them of all they held dear.

Carrie was waiting on the porch when the carriage holding her father and Robert rolled up to the house. She rushed down the stairs and was in her father's arms as soon as his feet hit the ground. "Father! I've missed you so much!"

Thomas laughed and held his daughter at arm's length. "You're as beautiful as ever, Carrie. I've missed you, too."

Carrie's throat caught as she looked into his eyes. He looked stronger than when he had left, but there was still that haunted look in his eyes, and she was sure she detected fear when he glanced toward the house. Without another word, Thomas turned away and began to climb the steps. Carrie stared after him, unsure of what to do.

"Leave him be, Carrie. He needs some time to adjust to being back here."

Carrie turned to look into Robert's eyes. "Is he going to be all right?"

Robert shrugged. "He's a different man in Richmond. There are no memories assaulting him at every turn. Being there has been good for him. He grew increasingly tense the closer we came to Cromwell."

"What can I do for him?"

"Everything you're already doing. Love him. Support him." Robert's voice changed, and became deep with a different kind of concern. He took her shoulders and turned her to face him. "Hello, Miss Carrie Cromwell. It's good to see you again. Enough about your father. How are *you* doing?"

The warm concern in his voice caused Carrie to smile. She stared into his dark eyes for a moment and then did what she had been dreaming of for weeks. She melted into his embrace and allowed him to hold her for a long moment. Finally, she pulled away and looked up into his face. "Hello, Robert Borden. It's good to see you again too."

Robert's eyes darkened and he pulled her close to him again. Finally, he loosened his grasp and took her hand. "Ready to go in, Miss Cromwell?"

Carrie, her heart pounding, gazed into his eyes. "Yes, Mr. Borden." What she really wanted to do was beg him to take her away. To make all the misunderstandings disappear between them. To make them of one mind on the issue of slavery. To tear down all the walls that kept them apart. She knew what she believed. She also knew she loved this man.

Once inside they saw Thomas in the living room staring at the Christmas tree. The colored pieces of glass caught the glow of the fire, casting rainbow images that danced through the air, only to be caught by the great boughs of greenery. Carrie moved forward and slipped her arm through his. She said nothing, and he seemed to not notice her presence. Robert remained where he was standing by the door.

"Abigail loved Christmas," Thomas whispered. His face sagged for a moment and then he straightened his shoulders and forced a smile to his lips. He turned his head to look down at Carrie. "The house is beautiful," he said warmly. "Your mother would be very proud of you."

"Thank you, Father. I'm so very glad you're home. I've missed you so much."

Thomas smiled again, wrapped his arm tightly around her shoulders and said, "We have much to talk about. You received my letter saying I could only stay until Christmas Day?"

Carrie nodded. "It's wonderful to have you home for *any* length of time." Secretly, she had been relieved he couldn't stay longer. She didn't know how long she could keep the truth about Ike Adams and the missing slaves from him. If he knew there was no overseer, she was sure he would insist on hiring another one. Determined to run the plantation her own way, she could only hope the whirl of Christmas would keep him from asking too many questions.

Thomas moved to a deep chair and settled down with a sigh. Robert and Carrie both took chairs nearby. A deep silence fell on the room—a peaceful quiet that all of them needed.

"We're expecting another guest in a few days," Thomas suddenly said.

"Oh?" Carrie replied with a lift of her eyebrows. "One of your friends from Richmond?"

Thomas shook his head. "I ran into young Matthew Justin at the train station a few days ago. He is on his way to cover the Secession Convention in South Carolina. He had no plans for Christmas, so I invited him here when he returns."

"That's wonderful," Carrie said warmly. She sincerely liked the straightforward redhead. "I'm glad I'll have the opportunity to return some of the hospitality he showed me in Philadelphia." She turned to Robert. "I'm sure you'll be glad to spend time with your friend."

Robert nodded. "I will also be glad to hear his perspective on the situation in South Carolina. He seems to have a knack for seeing murky affairs a little more clearly than most."

Carrie turned to look at her father. "I hate to bring up politics so soon, Father. I know you've just gotten home, but I feel so out of touch here. What is going on in South Carolina? Are they really going to secede from the Union?"

Thomas nodded his head and sighed deeply. "I'm afraid so, Carrie. They meet tomorrow, you know. One hundred and seventy of South Carolina's best men will meet to determine the destiny of the state, and that of the whole country I fear." He paused, his brow furrowed. "Supposedly the matter is still under consideration, but those men are meeting to vote for secession. I know they want it done peacefully. In their heart of hearts they believe it will turn out all right. They are not prepared to compromise, and they seem to have the kind of courage that keeps forlorn hopes alive beyond rational expectations."

"You don't agree with them?" Carrie asked.

Thomas shrugged his shoulders. "They are convinced the rest of the South will follow them out of the Union. They believe that with such a united front, the United States government will make no effort to stop them."

Robert spoke up then. "I've talked to Matthew. He feels their optimism is wildly overstated. He doesn't believe Lincoln will sit idly by and watch the Union disintegrate."

"What about Buchanan? He *is* still our president," Carrie said.

Thomas grimaced. "Yes, I suppose he is. Buchanan is a good man and a strong Southern supporter, but he has taken no action to reverse the flow of the tide. He seems as bewildered as the rest of the country as to how to stop the course of events sweeping our country into war."

Carrie frowned. "You still believe we are headed for war?"

Thomas stood and walked closer to the fire. He didn't answer for a long time. When he spoke, his voice was heavy and old. "I believe South Carolina is right. The cotton states are determined to leave the Union. They will follow South Carolina's lead. I agree with Matthew that Lincoln will not stand idly by. He is definitely not another Buchanan. The whole country is sitting on a keg of dynamite, and the fuse has already been lit. Each day it grows shorter." He stared down at the fire. "It's just a matter of time before the whole thing explodes."

"Will Virginia secede?" Carrie couldn't stop her explosion of questions now that she had the chance to voice them.

Thomas returned to his chair. "Right now there are still enough reasonable men to keep it from happening. The voices for secession are growing loud, but our voices are still louder. Only time will tell..." His voice trailed off.

Carrie suddenly noticed how tired he looked. She jumped up from her chair, hurried over, and laid her hand on his shoulder. "I'm sorry, Father. I know you are exhausted. We can talk in the morning. I'm sure you could use a good night's sleep."

"I'm tired," Thomas admitted with a small smile. His eyes took on that haunted look as he glanced at the stairs.

Carrie spoke quickly. "I had the blue guest room prepared for you, Father."

Thomas turned to gaze down at her. "Thank you," he said simply. "I will see you in the morning."

Carrie watched as he slowly ascended the stairs. She had known intuitively that he would not want to be in the room he had shared with his wife, but she also knew he would have plenty of other ghosts to fight. She breathed a quiet prayer as she noted his heavy steps.

Robert was sitting quietly in his chair when she returned to the living room. Carrie watched him, undetected in the shadows, for a few moments. The light played on the strong angles of his face and glinted off his dark hair. His eyes were closed as he relaxed in the cozy warmth of the room. His face had an almost little-boy vulnerability to it. Carrie felt a warm surge of love shoot through her. The suddenness of it startled her and caused a deep flush to rise to her cheeks. She was grateful for the obscurity of the shadows.

"Are you going to stand there all night?" Robert opened his eyes with an amused smile. "I'd much rather have you in the room with me."

Carrie laughed at the impish look in his eyes. She moved quickly across the room and sank down into the chair next to him.

"Tell me how you're doing," he invited.

The next hour passed in quiet conversation. Not once did they draw near to dangerous topics. Sam entered the room twice to throw additional logs on the fire, but they barely noticed so completely were they involved in each other.

Carrie covered her mouth as a giant yawn escaped. She glanced at the clock and her eyes opened wide. "My goodness, it's getting late!"

Robert nodded. "I think it's time we called it a night. You need your rest so that you'll be ready for the Christmas dance day after tomorrow."

Carrie nodded. "I haven't danced since our trip down the river on the *John Marshall.*"

Robert snorted. "That was a mere fling. I understand that the ball at Berkeley Plantation is quite the social event around here."

Carrie nodded. "I look forward to it every year. People come all the way from Richmond." She was looking forward to it even more this year because Robert would be her escort.

"Has your father asked about Adams yet?"

Carrie shook her head as Rose twisted her hair into a bun. She had learned how to do it herself, but it was nice to have it done for the dance. "No. He hasn't asked once about things here on the plantation. He seems content to sit in his library and go through the volumes of papers he brought home with him." She frowned. "He did say something yesterday about how good the place looked, but nothing beyond that."

"Does that bother you?"

Carrie shrugged and smiled ruefully. "I guess I'm prideful enough to want him to tell me what a wonderful job I'm doing, but the rational side of me knows that the less interested he is, the easier it will be to keep our secret."

Rose just nodded and kept jabbing pins. Carrie knew her thoughts were back in the quarters with Moses. Rose's being back in the big house was temporary, just to keep up appearances for Father, but surely she longed for Moses. As soon as the bun was secure Carrie spun on her seat to look up at Rose. "We won't be home until very late tonight. No one needs to know you're not snug in your little room."

Rose stared at her for a moment and then a wide smile lit her beautiful face. "Thank you, Miss Carrie."

Carrie shook her head. "There is nothing to thank me for. The three of us are partners in this little charade we are pulling off." She stood, walked over in front of the mirror, and gave a quick twirl, laughing as the red folds of her satin gown swirled around her. She stared into the glinting glass and noticed with satisfaction that the edging of green velvet along the neckline reflected her eyes.

"You look like a woman in love, Miss Carrie."

Carrie caught her breath, turned away from the mirror, and laughed. "I suppose I do, Rose." It was the first time she had admitted it out loud.

Rose looked at her closely. "Is Robert Borden the one you want to spend the rest of your life with?" Her eyes were inscrutable.

Carrie turned back to gaze into the mirror. *Was he?* A deep silence filled the room. When she spoke, it was very slowly. "I know I love him more than any man I've ever known." She paused, troubled. Why wasn't that enough? What was causing her heart to hold back? She sighed deeply. "There are things that may be impossible to make right between us." Images of their past arguments rose up to taunt her. An exploding ember flew from the fire and brought her mind back to the present. She shook her head firmly. "It's Christmas. I'm just going to enjoy it."

"You look beautiful, Miss Carrie. I hope you have a wonderful time at the ball," Rose said warmly.

Carrie could easily push away the uneasiness eating at her heart when she thought of the splendor of the Berkeley Ball.

"Does Marse Cromwell know I be back on his plantation, Sarah?"

Sarah shook her head firmly. "You know he would never allow it, John."

"He be bound to find out sometime."

Sarah shrugged. "I reckon we cross that bridge when we get to it." She was not willing to think more about it. She had lived eighteen long years without the man who had held her heart all that time. She couldn't bear to think of them being separated again.

John wasn't willing to just let it lie. "I won't go back to the Green place, Sarah. They was good to me, but I don't aim to finish up my years without you. I'll run away. Miss Carrie said I could go free anytime." He paused. "Will you go with me if it come to that?"

Sarah stared at him. She knew the question was going to come sometime. She also believed she was going to die here on Cromwell Plantation, but it wouldn't do any harm to make her man feel better. Slowly she nodded. "I'd go with you," she whispered softly. The glad light in his eyes was all she needed to see.

John reached over to take her hand. Together, they watched the flames of the glowing fire, feeling deep peace at being together once again.

Elegantly dressed doormen met the guests from Cromwell as they ascended the stairs of Berkeley Plantation. As the door was opened to receive them, a deep voice rang out.

"Thomas and Carrie Cromwell." After a slight pause, Thomas moved forward with Carrie on his arm. "Mr. Robert Borden." Carrie looked up to smile into Robert's dark eyes. She knew her own were alive with excitement. It took only moments for the three of them to greet their hosts.

Thomas took Carrie's hand from his arm and placed it gently on the suit-clad one Robert extended. "Have fun dancing," he said with a warm smile. He moved away and was soon surrounded by men eager for the latest word from Richmond.

Carrie watched him for a moment. "He and Mother used to love to dance," she murmured. "He seems to care for nothing but politics now."

"Politics is keeping your father alive, Carrie. It has given him something to care about. Something to pour his energy into," Robert responded.

Carrie nodded slowly. "And if the country falls apart? What then? What will my father do?"

Robert frowned, but was quick to answer. "Your father is a Virginian, Carrie. He will fight to the end to save the Union, but he will remain loyal to his state. If Virginia secedes, your father will stand with his state and serve anyway he can." Carrie frowned again, and Robert tilted her face up to meet his eyes. "Miss Carrie Cromwell, I refuse to allow any more talk of this kind. It's Christmas. Virginia has not seceded and the band is playing wonderful music. May I have the honor of this dance?" His voice was firm.

A brilliant smile flashed over Carrie's face as she curtsied deeply. "Why, I would be honored, sir." She let all other thoughts flee her mind as Robert led her to the dance floor and swept her into a waltz. Her whole world was Robert and the feel of his strong arms holding her. Everything else faded into insignificance. It was Christmas. They would celebrate!

Carrie leaned back in Robert's arms as another song drew to a close. She laughed up into his eyes. "Isn't this simply wonderful?" She eyed a clock over his shoulder and gasped. "Why, we've been dancing for almost two hours. Is that possible?"

"Indeed it is. My throat is telling me it's true. Can I get you something to drink?"

Carrie nodded eagerly. "Please." She suddenly realized her throat was parched and dry. Robert led her to a chair on the side of the room and then disappeared. Carrie took the time to absorb her surroundings. Many of her neighbors and friends were at the dance, but she had yet to speak to any of them. She had been dancing from practically the minute she had arrived. She leaned back in her chair and looked around. The entire huge room was dripping with great boughs of greenery. All gas light had been extinguished to give prominence to the hundreds of candles flickering their glowing light on the crowd swaying and talking under their shimmering influence. Stringed music swelled softly in the air, lending its own symphonic magic to the evening.

Carrie looked up with a smile as Robert threaded his way back toward her. She could just see the top of his head as he cut his way through the sea of people. Her smile faded as he emerged from the crowd. Louisa Blackwell, chattering brightly, was smiling up at him. That wasn't what bothered her, however. Robert's eyes, when he glanced up at her, had a stormy look in them. What had Louisa said to him?

"Why, Carrie Cromwell. Isn't it just wonderful to see you again!"

"Good evening, Louisa." Carrie's voice was pleasant, though distant.

Louisa seemed to not notice. She dropped down in the chair Carrie had pulled close for Robert and smiled over at her neighbor. "Aren't you just the one for surprises? Whoever would have thought you would throw that wonderful Ike Adams off your property and insist on running Cromwell Plantation all by your little self."

Carrie ground her teeth and cast around in her head for what to say. She should have known the story would get out. She had greater worries than Louisa Blackwell however. What if someone said something to her father? Her only hope was that the current state of affairs in the country would keep all conversation focused on politics. She forced herself to smile pleasantly. "You make it sound like quite a tremendous endeavor. I am flattered." She almost laughed at the look on Louisa's face. That she had not meant to compliment her was obvious. Louisa opened her mouth to say more, but a sudden commotion at the door stopped her.

Carrie looked up, startled, as the front door, only yards from where she was seated, flew open and a mud-spattered man dressed in a Richmond Militia uniform burst in. He waited for no one's recognition, but called out his message in a ringing voice that penetrated every corner of the room.

"South Carolina has seceded from the Union!" His cry was at once triumphant and desperate.

The great room grew immediately silent as the entire assembly turned to stare at the young messenger. The music stopped and the candles seemed to dim as the news was absorbed.

Thomas was the first to step forward. "Are you sure? There is no mistake?"

The young man shook his head and extended his hand. "Andrew Cooke, sir." He looked around the room and raised his voice once more. "South Carolina has seceded from the Union by a unanimous vote. They are now a sovereign nation."

Carrie closed her eyes as she saw the ruin of all she loved edging closer. That the young messenger was excited about the news was obvious. Soon enough he would realize what it would mean to his life and his dreams.

Band members put down their instruments as knots of people formed all over the room to discuss this dramatic turn of events. Though expected, the reality would have to be absorbed.

Louisa, her mouth still open to speak, apparently forgot all about her attack on Carrie. Now her eyes flashed with a victorious light. "Well, it's about time someone in the South shows the North we aren't going to merely lay down while they walk on us. Look at all the worried faces," she said with a contemptuous toss of her head. "Do people really think the North will try to stop South Carolina? Of course they're not going to send their soft, cowardly men down here! I can only hope Virginia gets over their own cowardice soon. It is so embarrassing to live in a state that shows such little backbone."

Thomas walked up as she was speaking. "It sounds as if you have been influenced by our Mr. Ruffin, Louisa." His voice was pleasant but sad.

Louisa looked up. "Indeed I have, Mr. Cromwell. And I find I agree with him wholeheartedly. I'm sure he is a happy man tonight."

"Undoubtedly," Thomas agreed with a small smile. "He is in Charleston now. I'm sure he is celebrating with the city. It was he who sent the young messenger to deliver the news."

Louisa smiled with delight. "How thoughtful of him. It does make a most wonderful Christmas gift!"

Thomas eyed her sadly. "I know there are many in the room who share your sentiments." He turned to Carrie and Robert. "I am very tired. Would you mind if we go home?"

Carrie rose immediately. "Of course not." She knew how devastated her father was by the news. Even though he had expected it, now he would have to deal with all the ramifications of it. Her heart ached for him—for all of them.

It took only minutes to thank their hosts. Great stars shone down on them as Charles urged the team at a rapid trot down the frozen road. No words were spoken.

Carrie bid her father goodnight as he climbed the stairs and then turned toward Robert. "It was a wonderful evening. Thank you."

Robert smiled but laid his hand on her arm to detain her. When her father disappeared into his room, Robert looked down at her. "Could I talk to you for a few minutes?"

Carrie nodded. She had known it was coming. She sighed and turned to lead the way into the living room. "It's about what Louisa told you," she said as soon as she sat down.

"I know it's not really any of my business," Robert said, "but it did concern me. Are you really running the plantation on your own?"

Carrie hesitated. She knew it would only make matters worse if she were to tell him about the partnership between her, Moses, and Rose. "I did fire Adams," she finally conceded, "but I find the plantation is running quite smoothly."

"Why did you fire him?"

"He was getting ready to beat one of the slaves." Carrie made no attempt to hide her anger.

Robert stared at her and seemed to search for words. "Does your father know?"

Carrie shook her head firmly. "No. And I have no intention of him finding out. He has enough to deal with right now." Her tone left no room for discussion. "I am the mistress of Cromwell Plantation. As long as I am the one left to run it, I will run it the way I see fit."

Robert looked at her with a mixture of admiration and amusement. "I know how strong and independent you are," he said slowly. "I also know the pressures, so I can't help being concerned." He reached for her hand. "If you need help, Carrie, please let me know."

Carrie was grateful for his concern and took the hand he extended to her. "I'm fine," she said softly. "Please don't worry about me. And thank you for not telling Father," she added.

Robert flashed a brief grin. "I hope your father never finds out I knew. He'll probably have me beaten, but I'll play the game your way."

THIRTY-ONE

Early on the morning of the twenty-fourth, the carriage containing Matthew Justin rolled up to the door of Cromwell Plantation. Carrie, Thomas, and Robert were on hand to meet him. Sam took his bags and deposited them in the same room Robert was staying in.

Matthew shook hands warmly with the two men and turned to smile at Carrie. "I had a feeling you came from a place as grand as this. You belong here!"

Carrie smiled, but wished she could tell him how wrong he was. This *grand place* was built on a system she had come to hate. "It's wonderful to see you again, Matthew. Welcome to Cromwell Plantation. And Merry Christmas!" Carrie was determined to make this Christmas as special as she possibly could. No one knew what the next year would bring.

Thomas reached his hand out and laid it on Matthew's shoulder. "Of course you know I am anxious for news from South Carolina."

Matthew nodded. "I'll tell you everything I can, but I'm afraid you won't like it."

"That I'm sure of," Thomas replied grimly. "But I still must know."

Carrie watched the exchange and stepped forward. "You will have until dinner to talk politics. Then it will be Christmas! I will not allow dark talk to ruin the holiday." Her voice was unyielding.

Thomas laughed gently. "Whatever you say, daughter. You're in charge now."

Carrie stared at him. She could think of nothing at all to say as he turned and led Matthew and Robert up the stairs and into the house. With that one statement he had spoken his heart. They had not talked at all about the plantation until then—no mention of when he would want to come back to the home he and his family before him had carved out of the wilderness. Carrie had harbored a faint hope that being here would reawaken the love in his heart for his home, but now she realized her hope was futile. It was many long minutes before she followed them.

Matthew gazed around him as they walked into the house. "This is truly a magnificent place, Mr. Cromwell." He paused. "I must tell you, this is my first time to be invited to a true southern plantation. Cromwell certainly lives up to the reputation they hold."

Thomas shrugged. "It's my home," he said simply. At one time he would have been delighted with Matthew's enthusiasm. Now he had more important things on his mind. He led the way to the group of chairs in front of the fireplace, and settled down in the one nearest the flames. He turned to Matthew eagerly. "Tell me about South Carolina," he urged.

Matthew tore his eyes away from his inspection of the room and took a deep breath. "It was a unanimous vote, Mr. Cromwell. I don't believe there was a single man there who had not already made his mind up about secession before he arrived. They had determined that since there was no common bond of sympathy or interest between the North and the South, all effort to preserve a unity would be fruitless."

"I think I may understand how they feel," Robert said slowly. Thomas looked at him sharply. "I didn't say I agree with it, sir," Robert protested quickly. "I simply said I think I may understand how they feel." He seemed to choose his words carefully. "They feel as if there is no other course of action available to them. They believe secession is legal and they see no other way to preserve the only way of life they know. In their minds, they have been backed into a corner."

Matthew nodded and reached forward to take a sandwich from the tray Sam had delivered to the room. "I believe you're right, Robert. I don't believe they have the right to secede, but neither has enough been done to avoid the inevitability of it. Everyone—including Buchanan who refuses to lead, and Lincoln who refuses to talk about it—has taken a wait and see attitude. The leaders of South Carolina feel they have waited long enough," He turned back to Thomas. "The convention initially met in Columbia but a smallpox epidemic forced them to move it to Charleston. They were greeted there about the way you would expect," he said dryly. "There was a fifteen-gun salute and a huge parade." He frowned. "I did some research while I was there. What I discovered troubled me. There are thirty-three thousand men who have eagerly enlisted in the state's military organizations. That's over twice as many men enlisted in *all* of the United States military. They say they are ready to resist any overture by the federal government to oppose their decision." His voice was deeply troubled.

"The government would be wise not to try any such thing," Robert said sharply.

Matthew looked at him quickly. "I hate that we find ourselves on different sides of this issue, Robert."

The glint left Robert's eyes and his face saddened. "I still have hopes nothing more will come of this. It's not too late for the federal government to make the concessions the South needs and demands."

Matthew shook his head. "There will be no compromising from Lincoln on slavery. He has made himself perfectly clear on it. He will do nothing to touch the institution as it now stands, but he will not even consider slavery in the new states."

Robert scowled. "Then he will carry the blood of a war on his head."

Thomas, deeply troubled as he watched the two men argue, broke in. "No *one* man will carry the responsibility for what may come. Please Matthew, tell me more about the convention."

Matthew nodded and reached into his pocket. "Just before I left last night, a copy of this was put into my hand, and I thought you would like to hear it. It was drawn up by the convention." He scanned the pages of paper. "You can read it at your liberty later, sir. Basically, it says that the benefits the Constitution had been drawn up to secure have been defeated by the actions of the free states of the North." He found the place he was looking for and began to read.

> Those states have assumed the right of deciding upon the propriety of our domestic institutions; and have denied the rights of property established in fifteen of the states and recognized by the Constitution; they have denounced as sinful the institution of slavery; they have permitted the open establishment among them of societies, whose avowed object is to disturb the peace and to eloign the property of the citizens of other states.

He scanned further and picked back up.

> A sectional party avowedly hostile to the South is about to take possession of the government. The guarantees of the Constitution will then no longer exist; the equal rights of the states will be lost. The slave-holding states will no longer have the power of self-government, or self-protection, and the federal government will have become their enemy.

"The federal government will have become their enemy..." Thomas echoed in a disbelieving voice. "I fear there is no turning back from the course that has been set."

Matthew nodded soberly, and handed Thomas another document. "There may be changes to this. I received it last night also. It is a letter to the other Southern states, pleading with them to secede and join in forming a Confederation of Southern States. In it, South Carolina requests only that they be left alone, to work out their own high destiny."

Thomas shook his head. "I still believe there has been no act committed that justifies the actions they are taking."

"Governor Pickens was inaugurated just days before the convention," Matthew replied. "I was there for it. He made it clear that the overt action for which secession was supposed to wait has already been committed—by the Northern people at the ballot box."

"I suppose Charleston went wild when the state seceded," Robert commented.

Matthew nodded. "The streets were wild for two days. Fireworks, parades, bands... It seemed as if every person in Charleston was out on the streets laughing, talking, and cheering secession. You would have been hard-pressed to find anyone who was not thrilled."

Carrie had just walked into the room. "I'm sure there was *someone* there with enough sense not to be excited," she said dryly. "Surely not all of them are too blind to see what will come of this."

Matthew smiled. "I happened to run into one of them. A frail, old gentleman by the name of Petigru. He is a devout Union man and didn't care who knew about it. I overheard him talking to a friend. He said, 'They have this day set a torch to the temple of constitutional liberty, and please God, we shall have no more peace forever.' Then he turned and stalked away."

Thomas smiled too, but the flicker on his lips was brief. All he could do was shake his head slowly as he stared into the flames of the fire.

Carrie had her way. As soon as supper was called on that Christmas Eve of 1860, all political discussion ceased. Thomas was relieved to have a reason to push their dark thoughts away and focus on the holiday celebration.

Excitement was running high in the quarters. Sarah had led her little army of children into the woods again and now every cabin was decorated with greenery, pinecones, gourds, and colorful leaves. Rose was rearranging a great collection of greenery on the table when Moses walked in. He stopped short when he saw her, his eyes widening with delight. "I thought you were at the big house with Miss Carrie."

Rose shook her head. "She didn't want us to be apart on Christmas Eve." Laughter glinted in her eyes. "Are you sorry I'm here?"

Moses chuckled as he moved forward to take her in his arms. "Let me show you how sorry I am." He stepped sideways, playfully dumped her on the bed, and lay down next to her. He looked deeply into her eyes and ran a finger gently down the side of her face. "You're beautiful," he said softly.

Rose melted as she looked in his eyes. "I love you, Moses," she whispered.

Finally, she broke away from his embrace. "I have some cooking to do for tomorrow," she said, laughing as he reached to pull her back. "I promised I would bake some sweet potato pies for the big feast tomorrow."

Moses immediately snatched his hand back. "Sweet potato pie?"

Rose pretended to be hurt. "At least now I know what is most important."

Moses nodded gravely. "I wouldn't want you to break your promise."

"Or miss any pie," Rose snorted.

"That, too," he agreed, grinning.

Just then a rap came at the door, and John stuck his head in. "You 'bout ready for the possum hunt, Moses? It be almost dark."

Moses nodded. "I'll be right there."

"Sarah is 'bout to start her storytelling, Rose."

Rose nodded. "I'll be over soon, Daddy. I wouldn't miss that for the world." She turned to Moses. "Y'all had better bring back some good possums. We've got plenty of people to feed tomorrow."

Suddenly Charles stuck his head in the door. His eyes were wide and frightened. "We got trouble comin'," he stated.

Moses waved him in. "What is it?"

Charles was clearly nervous, shifting from one foot to the other. "Marse Cromwell had me take somethin' over to the Ruffin place. I was in the shadows on the porch waitin' when their overseer rode by with one o' his friends. They was talking 'bout Adams."

"Ike Adams?" Moses asked sharply.

Charles nodded. "They said he knew Marse Cromwell was here. That he be comin' over to demand his job back. He done found out that Marse Cromwell don't know he ain't here no more."

Moses frowned. "Do you know when he's supposed to come?"

Charles nodded again. "He was going to wait 'til dark so's to make sure Marse Cromwell be here."

Moses frowned, deep in thought. "Rose, go collect some of the crackers from the children," he said. He turned to Charles. "Get some rope from the barn. We're going to have a little surprise for Ike Adams." He smiled as he envisioned it.

Rose hurried out to do as he asked. When she returned, Charles was just running up with the rope. Moses turned to her and lifted her face gently. "It may be real late when I get back. I'm going to take five of the field hands. I don't reckon any of us will be back for the dance. Don't worry about me. If all goes as planned, Adams won't even know what happened."

Rose opened her mouth to ask questions, but shut it firmly. There was too little time. "Be careful," was all she said.

Moses nodded, grabbed the things he had requested, and disappeared into the darkness. Rose sank to her knees, praying.

Carrie and the men gathered in front of the Christmas tree as soon as supper was finished. During the afternoon, the house servants had helped her place tiny candles all over the tree. They had also allowed the fire to go out, and Moses had carried in the huge Yule log Carrie had selected.

Thomas smiled when he saw it. "You remembered everything, didn't you?"

Carrie wrapped her arm around his waist. "I want to help you build new memories, Father." Her voice was soft as she gazed into his eyes.

Quick tears sprang into Thomas's eyes, but the haunted look was gone. "Thank you, dear." He took the long wooden match she held out to him, moved forward, struck it on the stone, and knelt to light the massive log. The tinder sputtered and caught, and soon an eager flame was eating at the wood.

The rest of the room stood quietly as the roar of the fire soon permeated the room with its welcome warmth. Only then did Carrie turn toward the Christmas tree. "Will you and Matthew help me, Robert?" She made no attempt to hide the excitement in her voice. The lighting of the Christmas tree was always her favorite time. She held out lit matches to the two men. They were soon bringing life to the multitude of candles adorning the tree.

Matthew was the first to speak as the four gazed at the beautiful tree sending its glow into the room. "My family never had a Christmas tree. I never even heard of one until I was twelve years old. Now I know what I was missing."

Carrie nodded. "It has become my favorite part of Christmas. We owe a lot to Charles Minnegerode."

"Who?"

Carrie laughed. "Have you never heard the story?" She continued on when Matthew shook his head. "He was a German immigrant who introduced the first Christmas tree to a Virginian family in 1842. I'll never forget the first one I saw. We had gone to spend Christmas with some friends in Williamsburg when I was six years old. I thought it was the prettiest thing I had ever seen. We've had one ever since. Why, even the Yankees have trees now," she said teasingly. "President Pierce put one in the White House three years ago and now the tradition is spreading in the North, as well."

Matthew smiled. "I understand why you love it so much."

Carrie watched the tree quietly for a few more minutes, and then moved over to the piano. Soon, melodious strains of Christmas carols rang through the house as their four voices joined in song. Carrie sang joyously as she played, thrilled to see the deep lines on her father's face smooth a little.

Rose finally got off her knees, threw another log on the fire, and quickly finished the sweet potato pies. It would do no good to sit in the cabin and worry all night. She had put it in God's hands. Her mama had always told her it didn't do any good to put things in God's hands if you were going to stand in front of him and keep snatching them back. She laid the pies on the table, threw on her cloak, and hurried to Sarah's cabin. She hadn't missed a storytelling session in her whole life. She didn't want to start now.

Rose swung the door open quietly and smiled when she saw the horde of children sitting cross-legged on the floor in front of the blazing fire. Sarah, dressed in white, rocked gently in her chair beside the flames. Many of the women and older children lined the walls, sitting on chairs they had carried in with them It was a good thing all the men were gone on the possum hunt or with Moses because the tiny cabin was already bulging at the seams. Rose slipped in and sank down with the children.

Sarah was just starting another story. "Who here know 'bout the baby Moses?"

Jubilee clapped her hands in delight. "This be my most favorite story, Miss Sarah!"

Sarah smiled at the excited little girl and leaned forward to fix her intense eyes on all the children. Not a sound could be heard as they held their breath in anticipation. "The baby Moses was a little Jew baby. There was a great king at the time who didn't like Jew babies."

"Like some people don't like nigger babies?" a little voice piped in.

Sarah nodded. "I reckon it shore nuff was like that." She put her finger to her lips for silence and continued. "The great king decided he was going to kill off all the Jew baby boys, but Moses's mama didn't want that to happen to *her* baby. So's she fixed a big basket out of reeds down by the river and put her fine baby boy in that basket. When nobody weren't lookin' she hid her fine baby in the bulrushes down by the river. Then she watched to see what would happen..."

Her words trailed off as the children leaned closer. They all knew the story by heart but that didn't affect the magic of hearing it again. The fire sputtered and crackled.

"What happened, Miss Sarah?" Jubilee asked breathlessly.

Sarah paused for a long moment. "The daughter of that great king done found that baby Moses! She knew he was a Jew baby, but she didn't want no harm to come to him. So you knows what she done?" She hesitated, but didn't wait for an answer. "She took the baby Moses and raised him in the palace, just like he was one of them fine Egyptians."

The children's eyes grew wide as they imagined what that would be like. Why, it would be like living in the big house with Miss Carrie!

Sarah smiled. "Baby Moses never forgot who he be, though. He never forgot he was a Jew baby. And God never forgot. He had a mighty big plan for that little boy. When Moses got bigger, God told him what it was." She leaned closer. "Moses was going to be the one to set all his people free."

"Cause all his people were slaves," a voice said.

"That's right!" Sarah agreed. "All his people were slaves. They done been cryin' out to God for a long time to set them free. They done thought he just hadn't heard them. Or maybe that he didn't care none. But all that time, he was getting Moses big enough to do his job. It weren't no easy job," she said intensely. "The man who were the master— they called him the Pharaoh—didn't want to let all them people go. He liked havin' them as his slaves. They did all his work for him and made him rich."

"Like we do!" The women in the room all nodded their heads as a mutter broke from one of the dark corners. All of them were as enthralled by the story as the children. Every year the hearing of it renewed the hope in their hearts.

Sarah just smiled gently. "Moses didn't want to do what God told him 'cause he was right scared of what would happen. And he didn't think God could use someone like him. God done believed in him a bunch more than he believed in himself. He had to set a whole bush burnin' before Moses said he would do what God told him to." She paused. "God done put that Pharaoh through a lot of hard times. It took a right lot to convince him to let those slaves go. The Bible done call them plagues. Why, their water turned to blood one time!" The children gasped and stared at her with wide eyes. Then Sarah smiled. "God won, though. That Pharaoh finally got tired of being so stubborn and he let all them slaves go." She allowed the room to grow silent and still, then closing her eyes, she began to sing softly.

> Go down Moses
> Way down in Egyptland
> Tell Ol' Pharaoh
> To let my people go

Verse after verse rolled out in her rich, velvety voice. The children, shyly at first, and then enthusiastically, joined in on the chorus. Their hopeful voices exploded from the tiny cabin and mingled with the stars. Some of the women joined in, but most leaned back in their chairs, taking comfort in the knowledge that all God's love hadn't been spent on Israel. Surely a deliverer would be coming soon.

Moses and Jupiter took their position on the side of the road, well hidden by the bushes. The other three field hands were crouched just opposite them on the other side. They were ready. Moses had laid out his carefully thought through plan, the rest had smiled into the darkness, and then they had all taken their positions. If it didn't work... None of them would allow the consequences to form in their mind. It *had* to work.

Moses had no idea how long he had hunkered there in the cold darkness before he finally heard the thud of approaching hoofbeats. His heart pounded as he peered down the dark road. Nervously, he fingered the crackers Rose had gathered from the children. They had asked no questions as to why she was taking the carefully dried pig bladders they had been saving ever since slaughtering time. The look in her eyes had been enough for them to know it was important. Moses leaned as far forward as he could without risking detection.

"It's Adams," Jupiter whispered in his ear.

Moses nodded as the horse drew near enough for him to recognize Adams's mare Ginger. He took a deep breath and blew several strong puffs of air into the cracker he was holding. He knew all the other men were doing the same thing. He held the opening closed tightly between his fingers and stared down the road. All he could do was wait. Sweat broke out on his forehead, but his hands and eyes were steady as he gauged the distance carefully. Slowly, he raised the cracker until it was at eye level.

Adams was sitting on his mare loosely when he drew even with Moses and his band. Moses, as soon as Ginger drew even with him, allowed one massive hand to slam against the blown-up cracker. A loud *pop!* exploded into the still winter night. Four more explosions followed his. Ginger, terrified by the loud, unexpected noises, bolted forward and then reared in protest. Adams, with no warning and no chance to prepare, tumbled backward.

Moses and his men were on Adams before he could even focus his eyes. Dazed from his fall, he made no move as a piece of cloth was wrapped tightly around his eyes and another stuffed roughly into his mouth. His hands were pulled tightly behind him and tied, and his feet were trussed.

Jupiter, who had sprung forward to grab Ginger, stood quietly watching the operation. Not a word would be spoken until they had disposed of Adams. They would take no chance he would recognize them.

Moses stood and stared down at the bound man who was just beginning to show signs of struggle. He had hoped the fall would knock Adams out. He knew the slightest whisper or slip among the men could jeopardize all their lives. The other men waited, knowing what he would have to do next. He grimaced in distaste, but set his face with resolve, pulled his arm back, and aimed a mighty punch at Adams head.

Instantly, Adams's head lolled back and his body went limp. Moses leaned down and rifled his pockets. He was no thief, but part of his scheme was to make the attack look like a robbery. There was precious little money, but what he found he threw into the bushes with a mighty heave. Then he leaned down, threw Adams's unconscious body over his shoulder and walked to where Jupiter was holding Ginger. Unceremoniously, he dumped Adams across the saddle, and used the two remaining pieces of rope to secure him. He took the reins, turned, and began walking rapidly down the road in the direction Ike Adams had come from.

Jupiter opened his mouth as if to say something, but Moses held his finger to his lips. He would take no chances. There would be no words spoken until they had disposed of Adams and made it back to Cromwell safely. Jupiter nodded, and sprinted on ahead so he could watch for approaching riders and signal Moses to hide in the woods with his bounty. There would be no way to explain five slaves and a tied-up overseer.

Rose watched carefully as the men who had returned earlier from the possum hunt filed into the great barn. Her hopes that Moses and the rest of the men he had taken would be with them were quickly dashed. Questioning looks were on many faces, but no one said anything. Ignorance was best when it came to things like this. Music was soon floating from the cracks in the barn. Nobody happening by would think anything was out of order. The *big times* Christmas Eve dance was under way!   In spite of her worries, Rose found herself caught in the spirit of the music. Drums, made from hollowed logs, beat a steady rhythm. Handmade, stringed instruments blended with the two fiddles Carrie had sent down from the big house for the celebration. Lanterns illuminated the cavernous building and the smell of barbecue pervaded the air.

The clapping and stomping got louder and louder as the evening progressed.

Sam danced over to where Rose leaned against the wall, watching the celebration. "Not dancing ain't going to solve nothing, girl. They's gettin' ready to *pat the Juba*. How about one dance with an old man?"

Rose smiled in spite of herself and nodded. "Think you can keep up with me, Sam?" she teased.

Sam grinned, grabbed her hand, and spun her onto the floor. Rose laughed and joined her voice to sing with the rest.

> Juba this and Juba that
> Juba killed a yeller cat
> Juba this and Juba that,
> Hold your partner where you at.

The sun was just beginning to tint the horizon when Moses walked into the cabin. Rose, braiding her hair in front of the warm fire, spun to meet him. "Moses!" she cried as she ran to embrace him.

Moses held her close for a long moment and then pushed her gently away. "You've got to get to the big house. Now ain't the time for questions." His voice was tired, but his eyes were content.

Rose stared up at him. "Everything is alright?" She knew they didn't have time to talk.

Moses nodded and leaned down to brush her lips with his own. "I'll tell you about it later. Merry Christmas, wife."

Rose smiled lovingly and pressed her lips against his, longing to stay home and take care of her exhausted husband. "Merry Christmas, Moses."

THIRTY-TWO

Carrie was up long before the rest of the house. Her father had not once mentioned Ike Adams and the slaves, but she knew today would be different. Would he accept her explanation? A soft noise caused her to look up just as Rose entered the house to slip down the hall. "Rose," she called softly.

Rose started but smiled when she saw only Carrie. "You scared me, Miss Carrie!" She walked over and joined her friend next to the Christmas tree. "You're up mighty early."

Carrie nodded and looked sharply at her friend. "You look exhausted. Is everything all right?"

Rose hesitated. "Ike Adams was on his way here last night to talk to your father."

Carrie waited. She knew there was more to the story.

Rose just shrugged her shoulders. "I don't really know what happened. Moses just had time to tell me everything was all right when he came in this morning."

"Moses! What did he have to do with it?" Suddenly Carrie was frightened. She knew how much Adams hated Moses already. What was going on?

Rose shrugged again and looked around. "Later, Miss Carrie. All I know is that he stopped him," she whispered.

Carrie started as she heard footsteps on the stairs. Rose melted from the room and disappeared into the kitchen. Carrie was left to stare and wonder.

"Merry Christmas, daughter."

Carrie forced a quick smile to her lips, grateful her father was so preoccupied. Before her mother died, she never would have gotten away with the game she was now playing. Her father would have known in an instant she was hiding something. "Merry Christmas, Father."

Thomas gave her a quick hug and then turned to sink into his chair. After his initial greeting, he seemed content to stare into the flames of the fire. Carrie could tell his thoughts had already moved on to Richmond and what was waiting for him when he returned. It was just as well, she thought with a sigh. She sat down in the chair next to the fire and allowed her own thoughts to wonder.

Finally, her father came out of his reverie. "What time will the slaves be here this morning?"

Carrie shook her head. "They won't be, Father." Thomas looked startled—with good reason. The slaves of Cromwell Plantation always came to the big house on Christmas morning. It was as much a tradition as the yule log. Carrie hastened to explain. "I didn't want to share you this year, Father," she said with a smile. "You're home for such a short period of time..." She allowed her voice to drift off sadly, almost laughing at her performance. "I handed out all the clothing and gifts the day before you got here. The slaves seemed very happy. They all sent their best to you."

This strange turn of events seemed to have shaken Thomas from his lethargy. He frowned quickly. "Why didn't you tell me this before?"

Carrie smiled gently. "This is the first time you have mentioned the slaves, Father. I thought you had plenty else to occupy your thoughts."

Thomas stared at her for a brief moment. "I've been selfish haven't I, Carrie? You are carrying all the weight of the plantation yourself." He shook his head slowly as he talked.

Suddenly, Carrie realized just how content she was running the plantation. It was not her dream, but she was suddenly very sure she was where she was supposed to be and doing what she was supposed to do. "You're not being selfish at all, Father." She moved over and knelt next to his chair. "I am quite happy here."

Thomas stared at her as if trying to make himself believe it. "I should at least speak with Ike Adams. Thank heavens you have a competent overseer!"

Carrie controlled the sneer of contempt that almost surfaced. She settled for just shaking her head. "Mr.

Adams has worked very hard this year. I gave him some time off for Christmas. I do believe he has gone to visit family." When Thomas frowned again, she hastened to reassure him. "We're managing fine here, Father. Didn't you say the place looked wonderful?"

Thomas nodded. "You're doing a superb job." Still, his eyes were troubled.

Carrie knew she needed to steer him away from the topic of the plantation. "And *you're* doing a wonderful job, Father. I'm so proud of what you're doing in Richmond. What will happen now that South Carolina has seceded?" She knew she was breaking her own rule of no politics on Christmas, but it was the only sure way she knew to distract her father. It worked. He was still talking when Robert and Matthew descended the stairs.

Breakfast was a casual affair as they settled down around the table to laugh and talk. Everyone ate their share of the grilled chicken, eggs, ham, fish, hominy grits, and biscuits piled high on platters set before them. The rest of the morning passed pleasantly as they played games, sang around the piano, and talked.

Around noon, Robert turned to Carrie. "Could I talk you into a ride? I could use some fresh air and exercise." Carrie quickly agreed, but cast a look at Matthew sitting across the room with her father.

He seemed to read her thoughts as he looked up with a quick smile. "Leave me out of this one, please. I would much rather sit here with your father. My hectic schedule has left me desiring no more than peace and quiet."

Carrie turned to Robert with a smile. "Let's go!"

Christmas Day, 1860, was cold but not bitter. The sun shone brightly and the wind was calm. Carrie was thrilled to get outside and release some of her nervous energy. The strain of keeping up appearances the last few days was beginning to tell on her. She knew the house servants were perfectly capable of putting the finishing touches on their Christmas dinner. And so, without even thinking about it, Carrie headed Granite toward her place. Little was said until she and Robert were standing, side-by-side, on the banks of the James.

"Everything has been wonderful, Carrie."

Carrie turned to him. "I'm so glad. I wanted it to be special." She smiled into his eyes and made no protest when he took her gently in his arms. She stood quietly and absorbed his warmth and strength.

Finally Robert spoke. "Is it time yet, Carrie?"

He said nothing else, but Carrie knew what he meant. *Was it time for him to tell her how he felt?* Carrie longed to say yes. She also knew that saying yes would destroy the magic they were experiencing now. To say yes would mean she would have to face all the things that stood as barriers between them. She knew the courageous thing to do. She could continue to put it off, but sooner or later, she would have to face it. She stood quietly as the battle raged in her heart. Then, knowing she was a coward, she slowly shook her head.

She felt Robert's frustrated sigh, but he said nothing—just held her a little tighter. Carrie hated herself for the game she was playing. Except it wasn't a game. She knew she loved this man. She also knew that as long as they kept a distance they wouldn't have to fight about the issues that had caused so much trouble in the past. She pulled away to look up into his eyes. "Thank you," she said softly.

Robert stared into her face for a long moment and groaned softly. He pulled her close into a tight embrace, lowered his head, and claimed her lips with a gentle, warm kiss.

Carrie knew she should resist, that this kind of closeness would make the game harder to play, but she was powerless to do so. Everything in her responded eagerly. She encircled his neck with her arms and clung to him, her heart pounding. She lost all track of time as his lips exposed all the love in her heart.

Finally he pulled away. They stared at each other, but didn't move from their embrace. Robert's voice was hoarse when he spoke. "I will wait, Miss Carrie Cromwell. I will wait for as long as it takes."

Ike Adams came to slowly, confused and aching. Where was he? What had happened? The last thing he remembered was trotting down the road on his mare, Ginger. Where had he been going? He frowned, trying to remember. Cromwell! He had been on his way to see Thomas Cromwell. He was going to be late! Surging forward, he tried to stand, only to discover he couldn't move. Pain exploded in his head. He moaned and lay back on the ground as he tried to get his bearings.

He forced himself to lie quietly, allowing his head to clear and his eyes to adjust to the dim light of wherever he was. Gradually, he realized his hands and feet were bound with ropes, and he was in some kind of small shack. A tiny beam of light shining through the cracks cast a small bit of illumination as he looked around. Things looked strangely familiar. His brow furrowed as he tried to make sense of it. The pain in his head was abating and he could think more clearly now. He tested the ropes and realized they were loosely tied. It took him only a few minutes to break loose from their confines.

He sat up slowly, knowing quick movement could make him pass out again. When his head had cleared sufficiently, he stood and looked around him, his confusion growing. Why did everything look so familiar? What had happened to him? What time was it? A noise outside caused him to look up sharply. Were they coming back? He eased over to the door and crouched, ready to attack whatever came through the door.

A child's laugh filled the air as the door was thrown open. Ike tensed to spring forward, and then stopped, confused. "Joseph!" he exclaimed. "What you doing here, boy?"

"Daddy?" The slight, eight-year-old boy crept forward, his eyes wide with fear and surprise. "What you doing here, Daddy? How come you didn't come home for Christmas?"

Adams stared at him, trying to make sense of all of it. "What day is it, Joseph?"

"It's Christmas Day, Daddy. We just finished dinner a little while ago. We waited and waited, and then Mommy said you must not be coming." He paused, taking in his father's wild condition. "I saved your Christmas present for you, Daddy."

Adams pushed past him and stalked out into the clearing. "How the hell did I get in my own shed, not more than a hundred feet from my cabin? Who's playing games on me? Somebody is going to pay for this!"

Joseph shrunk back against the shed.

Adams's angry roaring caused Eulalia to hurry out of the ramshackle cabin. "Ike Adams? Where have you been?"

Adams continued to stalk around, growling under his breath.

"Daddy's been in the shed, Mommy," Joseph offered.

Eulalia pulled him to her side in a warm embrace and waited for Ike to explain. "Things not go too good with Cromwell, Ike?"

Ike spun around, glad to have another target for his anger. "I ain't never seen Cromwell," he shouted. He looked down and realized his pockets were all pulled out. He held them out to her. "Somebody done robbed me. Then they brought me back and dumped me in our shed." He didn't need Eulalia's look to tell him how ridiculous his story sounded. He shook his head, but could remember nothing.

Suddenly he whirled around to look at the sun. Its position on the western horizon told him it was late. He knew it was of no use, but still, he had to try. Somehow knowing what he would find, he stalked over to the barn and threw open the door. Just as he expected, Ginger was munching hay contentedly, looking like nothing out of the ordinary had happened at all. Adams groaned. Was he really going crazy? Had he gotten drunk and couldn't even remember it? He moved quickly to grab his saddle and felt a sharp pain shoot through his head. He put a hand to the back of his head and smiled grimly at the large lump he encountered. Someone had attacked him all right. Growling under his breath, he swore and cursed as he planned his vengeance. It took only minutes to saddle and bridle his rested mare.

He said nothing to his watching family—just swung into his saddle and headed for Cromwell at a gallop.

Maybe, just maybe, he would get there in time. His thirst for vengeance increased as he rode. So, too, did his realization that he had no idea what had happened. Who could he vent his anger on?

Robert, obviously not caring who was watching, took Carrie in his arms again before he climbed into the carriage. "I'll see you soon," he promised.

Carrie nodded as she smiled into his eyes. "I hope so." She had already said goodbye to her father and Matthew. She watched now as Robert joined the other two men in the carriage. Charles lifted the reins and the horses moved forward eagerly. Carrie stood silently until they had disappeared around the farthest bend, sighed, and turned to climb the stairs. The sun was just setting on the horizon as she turned to see if she could catch one final glimpse. They were getting a late start back to Richmond, but her father had seemed to sense Robert's reluctance to leave and allowed them to linger over the sumptuous Christmas feast long after they should have been on their way.

Just as Carrie turned to enter the house, she heard the pounding of hoofbeats approaching from the opposite direction. She moved to the edge of the porch. What she saw made her lips tighten with anger.

"I figured he might show up." The deep voice came from just behind her.

Carrie gasped and started violently. "Moses! Where did you come from? You scared me half to death!"

"Sorry, Miss Carrie." Moses continued to stare down the road. "That's Ike Adams, you know."

Carrie nodded shortly. "Go inside the house. I'll handle this." She spoke more sternly when Moses opened his mouth to protest. "Your being here will only make him angrier. Please go inside." When Moses nodded and turned away, she added quietly, "Just don't go far."

Moses looked back with a quick smile and reached for the door. It opened before he could touch it. Rose stepped out onto the porch quickly. "Here, Miss Carrie. You might need this."

Carrie reached for the rifle Rose held out to her. "Thank you." She turned to stare down the road and wait for her unwelcome visitor. Rose and Moses gave her one final look and disappeared into the house. Carrie took comfort in knowing they were just on the other side.

"Good afternoon, Miss Cromwell." Adams seemed determined not to look at the gun she was cradling in her arms. He cast his eyes around, looking for her father's carriage.

Carrie made no attempt to acknowledge his greeting. "I believe I told you never to set foot on Cromwell Plantation again, Mr. Adams." Her voice was cold.

Adams narrowed his eyes in anger. "I have come to see your father, Miss Cromwell."

"My father is not here."

"Did he leave recently?" Adams asked.

Carrie wanted to smile at the pleading whine creeping into his voice. "I don't believe my father's activities are of any interest to you, Mr. Adams." Her voice grew colder. "I don't believe *any* activities on Cromwell Plantation should be of interest to you. It would be best if you left."

Adams stared down the road.

Carrie read his thoughts. Shifting the gun so that the barrel was pointed in his direction, she smiled pleasantly. "I'm not going to say it again, Mr. Adams. I want you off Cromwell Plantation. And I want you to leave by the quickest route—the way you came." Her heart pounded as she wondered whether she would actually shoot the despicable man if he tried to catch her father.

Adams turned to glare up at her. "One of these days, Miss Carrie Cromwell, you're not going to be standing behind the barrel of a gun. You'd best be watching yourself."

"And you'd best be watching *yourself!*" Moses and Sam spoke in unison as they stepped out onto the porch behind Carrie. "You got nothing but enemies around here, Adams," Moses said in a deep, angry voice. "Miss Carrie has plenty of friends."

Adams stared up at the massive black man glaring down at him, cursed loudly, spun, and took off at a gallop.

Carrie stared after him with a deep frown, then she turned and put a hand on Moses's arm. "Thank you. But I'm afraid you may have made even more trouble for yourself."

"Adams ain't nothing *but* trouble, Miss Carrie. It's bound to come sooner or later. I reckon I'm just going to have to deal with it when it comes."

Carrie nodded and sighed. "I suppose you're right, Moses." She smiled. "I like to pretend trouble away sometimes, but I suppose it's better to accept the truth of a situation. At least that way, you know what you're up against and can prepare for it."

She looked up just in time to catch the quick look Sam shot at Moses. "What is it, Sam?"

Sam started, averted his eyes and shook his head. "It ain't nothin', Miss Carrie."

Normally Carrie would have let it go, but something caused her to press the issue. She walked over and looked up at her old friend. "I've known you all my life, Sam. What is going on?" Still, he just shook his head and kept his eyes down. Frustrated, Carrie looked at Moses and Rose. "What is going on around here?" she demanded.

Rose frowned deeply and looked away. Moses did the same. Suddenly, Carrie was frightened. What were they hiding from her? "Rose?"

Rose finally sighed and looked up. "We didn't want to say anything to you, Miss Carrie."

"About what?" Carrie was confused.

"About your Robert," Sam said in a low voice.

"About Robert?" Carrie echoed. Now she was completely confused. "I think we all need to go inside." As soon as they entered the warmth of the house, she turned to them. "I want to know what in the world is going on."

Sam looked at Rose in mute appeal. She studied Carrie closely, and slowly nodded. "Carrie just said it's better to accept the truth of a situation."

Carrie waited quietly, her body tense.

Sam looked down but spoke in a steady voice. "We knows how you feel 'bout beating slaves, Miss Carrie. I done got some news a few weeks back about your Robert."

Carrie listened closely, a sick dread rising in her throat.

Sam cleared his throat and continued. "Back in the fall, your Robert Borden had some of his slaves run off. He done went after them, but they were long gone. He decided he was gonna teach his other slaves to not even think 'bout doin' the same thing. So's he went down to the quarters...." his voice choked and he fell silent.

"Tell me what happened, Sam." Carrie didn't even recognize her own controlled voice.

"He took a whip with him, Miss Carrie. He took three of the slaves—one man, one woman, and a child. He... He..." Sam shook his head as tears welled in his eyes. "The child didn't make it. The other two were still in bed the last I knew."

Carrie gasped as huge tears welled in her eyes. The picture of the slaves flashed in her mind, overlaid with the horror that it was the man she loved who had done such a thing. All she could do was shake her head and groan softly.

"I'm sorry, Miss Carrie."

Carrie dimly realized Rose was speaking to her, but she couldn't reach through the fog that was settling on her heart. With a cry, she jerked away and ran for the stairs.

Moses's voice followed her. "You did the right thing, Sam. Robert Borden has to let go of the hate in his heart if he is going to love Miss Carrie the way she needs to be loved. She had to know the truth."

Carrie sobbed until her pillow was soaked. Then she pulled herself up and walked over to stare out the window into the cloudless sky. How could she have fallen in love with a man who could do what Robert Borden had done? She groaned and bit her lip, tears falling freely again. Why did love have to hurt so much? What was she going to do?

There were no answers—only more questions—as she finally drifted off into a troubled sleep.

THIRTY THREE

Moses mumbled and rolled over, groping for his wife's warmth. Rose leaned over smiling and said softly, "I'll be back soon."

Moses opened his eyes sleepily and took in her dressed condition. He sat up quickly. "What time is it?" The cabin was still swathed in dark shadows. "Where are you going?" His voice quickened with concern. "Is everything okay?"

"Everything is fine," she assured him. "I just need some time to think before a new year starts." Rose had been hoping Moses wouldn't wake up until she had returned because she didn't know how to explain her sudden, deep need to be alone.

Moses looked at her closely and then nodded his head. "You're going looking for answers." He smiled. "I hope you find them." He lay back down under the warm covers. "I'm happy right here. I'll be waiting for you."

Rose smiled, leaned down to kiss him one more time, and slipped out into the frigid morning. The sun was still hiding far beneath the horizon but its glow was already kissing the morning sky. She pulled her cloak tightly around her shoulders and hurried down the road leading to the river. When she found the small path to the water's edge, she pulled up her dress and eased down it carefully, aware a misstep in the dark could send her tumbling into the icy waters. Below her was the large granite boulder she was seeking. She jumped lightly and breathed a sigh of relief when the sturdy rock held her. Eddies of swirling water surrounded her, but she was secure. She drew her knees to her chest and fixed her eyes on the eastern sky.

January 1, 1861 marched onto the world scene with a glory that took her breath away. Great banks of fleecy, cumulous clouds absorbed the morning rays of the sun and exploded into a glorious pageantry of color and light. Radiant shafts pierced the clouds and sent probing fingers of light shooting into the early morning indigo sky. The wind, blowing briskly just moments before, completely abated, leaving the James a glassy mirror to reflect the panorama unfolding above.

Rose caught her breath at the sheer beauty embracing her. "Thank you," she whispered softly. Leaning back, she allowed the glory of the morning to penetrate her heart and mind as she watched God usher in a new year.

Rose had come looking for answers. Or maybe just to ask questions. Her life was so full, so rich. Why wasn't she satisfied? Why did her dreams and longings still eat at her, demanding attention? She was so happy with Moses. She and her daddy had spent long hours together catching up on the years that had been stolen from them. Watching her mama's joy gave her a deep contentment of her own. Still, her heart was restless.

"Am I free to go now, God?" she whispered. "Can Moses and I leave Cromwell to start a life of our own?" Moses supported her dream to go to school and become a teacher. He had listened to her talk for hours about teaching Negro children to become all they could be showing them how to break the bonds of tyranny that had held not only their bodies, but their hearts and minds as well. He wanted her to be a teacher and was willing to do whatever it took for her to become one.

Was it indeed time to go? Her mama wouldn't be alone any more. Her daddy was here to stay. The thought of leaving her mama made her heart ache, but the frustration of merely longing for her dreams was eating at her, too. Then she frowned, thinking of all the children she would leave behind her here. Carrie had allowed her to turn one of the barns into a school. For three hours every day she was teaching the Cromwell children to read and write. Daily, she watched them blossom under the wonder of learning. Could she leave them behind? Wasn't she already a teacher? Why was there such a burning to go north and go to school?

Rose already knew the answer. She, too, wanted to become all she could be. There was so much she wanted to learn. So much she wanted to know about things that were nothing more than mysteries to her now. Her heart was hungry for knowledge. She stared into the morning sky and allowed her frustrations to explode from her in a mighty sigh as the brilliance of the sun drove back the colors and painted the sky a vivid blue. "Aren't I ever going to do anything but ask questions, God? Will I ever get answers?"

Slowly, words her mama had said many times floated gently into her mind. *Askin' questions keeps you comin' to God, Rose girl. You can rest sure he done got all the answers. You can also rest sure he ain't gonna tell you till you need to know. He don't mind the askin' though. As long as we're askin' that means there be somethin' in us that still believes he gonna tell us one day. And he will, Rose girl! When the time be right, he gonna answer all dem questions.* Then Sarah had paused and looked deep into her little girl's eyes. *If we done knew all the answers, there wouldn't be no need to trust God. Wouldn't be no need to get to know him. And that, Rose girl would be the tragedy. Knowin' all the answers without knowing God... Why knowin' em that way wouldn't mean nothin'!*

Rose hadn't understood her mama back then. Now she did. She lowered her eyes to stare into the glassy water spread before her and bowed her head. "I trust you, God. You've brought me this far. Just please keep me going in the direction you want me to go. I don't want to choose my own way and end up somewhere I'm not supposed to be." She closed her eyes and lay back, listening to the water lapping against her rock.

Slowly, the lapping of the water faded away and a picture rose in her mind, a picture so clear it was as if she could reach out and touch it. She was walking briskly down a city street, her arms full of papers and books. People, both black and white, smiled and nodded to her as she hurried along. Soon she came to a simple white building, with a small covered porch for its entrance. She stepped inside and was immediately welcomed by a room full of young, shiny, black faces. They reached into their desks as soon as they saw her, and pulled out stacks of paper and books—plenty enough for everyone. Then they turned to face her as she moved to the front of the room and took her place behind a massive, oak desk. "Good morning, Miss Rose," they said in unison. "Good morning, class," she responded cheerfully.

A fish slapping back against the water after it jumped up for its breakfast broke her from the vision, but not before a voice sounded clearly in her mind.

One year, Rose. You will be free... In one year...

Rose was breathing hard as she bolted straight up and stared out at the water. Had she been dreaming? She shook her head, remembering every detail of what she had seen. The voice still rang in her head—every vibration whispering it was true. But it was the peace more than anything that told her it was more than her imagination. The peace stole into her heart and stilled the restlessness. The peace consumed the questions and left her only with a determination to make the most of the next year.

"One year," she whispered in awe. "One year." Suddenly, she had to be with Moses. She had to tell him what she had seen—what she had heard. She jumped lightly from her rock, climbed the bank, and walked rapidly down the road leading back to the quarters.

Sarah rolled over and looked at John. Then she gazed toward the bed of ashes banking the fire. Normally John would already have the fire roaring by this time of the morning. Sarah smiled and rolled out from under her blankets. After doing it herself for so many years, it certainly hadn't taken her long to become spoiled. No matter, when John woke up this morning it was going to be to a warm cabin. Sarah stirred the ashes until live coals lit the tinder she held out to them. In only a few minutes she had hungry flames licking at the armloads of wood she had dumped into the fireplace. Humming softly, she turned to stir up some cornbread for breakfast.

She smiled at John's sleeping form, but she suddenly felt a vague uneasiness. She stood quietly and watched him. What was wrong? Suddenly she knew—a deep knowing that caused her hands to tremble and her heart to pound. Frightened, she just stood there staring at him, willing him to wake up.

Rose was striding up the path when she saw the smoke rising from her mama and daddy's cabin. She was in a hurry to get home to Moses, but something made her break stride and turn toward the tiny cabin. When a knock on the door produced nothing, she frowned slightly and turned away. A slight sound caused her to turn back and stare at the door.

"Rose girl?"

The voice was so low Rose wasn't sure if she heard it or just imagined it. It was enough to make her push the cabin door open. She stepped inside, and then stopped in confusion. Her mama stood still as a statue beside the table, her hands still covered with cornmeal, staring toward the bed where her husband lay. Rose turned to look at her daddy. He was still sleeping peacefully, just his face showing above the blankets. "Mama? What's wrong, Mama?"

Sarah still stared at the bed. Slowly, she began shaking her head as if trying to force herself to accept what she could not bear to. "John." Her voice was just a whisper, but somehow that single word spoke a lifetime of loving.

"Daddy?" Rose had a sudden urge to run from the cabin. Instead, she stepped over and forced herself to put her hand out and touch her daddy. "Daddy!" she cried, and then collapsed beside the bed with gigantic sobs.

Sarah moved over to wrap her arms around her daughter's shaking shoulders and gently stroked her head. Moses found them that way when he entered the cabin. Sarah looked up at him. "Rose be needin' you now, Moses." She stepped back and allowed Moses to take Rose into his arms.

"How long?" he asked simply.

Sarah shook her head. "The Lord done took him sometime in the night. When I woke up he was already gone."

Rose pulled back from Moses's embrace. "But why?" she cried. "Why would God take him? We just got him back! We just got him back..." Her voice trailed off in a confused whimper.

"Yes," Sarah said. "We got him back. That's the important thin'. All those years, I just prayed God would let me see him again. I never did say for how long," she mused. "This last few weeks been like heaven to me. We done did a lot of loving these last few weeks."

Rose stared at her. "But aren't you angry, Mama?"

Sarah smiled. "Angry? I'll miss my John, sure 'nuff, but it ain't gonna be eighteen years before I see him again. I reckon it won't be long now 'fore there won't be nothin' to keep us apart." She walked over and laid her hand on Rose's head. "God gave us a special gift, Rose. We could have lived our whole life and never seen him again. We done got a real special gift."

Rose tried to hear her mama. She tried to find solace in the fact that her daddy had been restored to her for three glorious weeks. She closed her eyes and remembered the long walks they had taken and the long talks they had shared. Tears continued to roll down her face, but slowly her mama's peace filtered into her own heart.

Rose's daddy had been laid to rest in a shallow grave carved out of the frozen ground. It was four days later before Rose thought to tell Moses about her dream, or vision, or whatever it was, down on the rocks.

Cradled in Moses's arms, Rose stared into the flickering flames of the fire. "One year, Moses. The voice said we would be free in a year." Once again she felt the awe she had experienced that morning on the rock. Suddenly, she realized Moses was frowning. "What's wrong, Moses?"

He spoke reluctantly, "What about your mama?"

"Mama!" Rose gasped as the meaning of Moses's question hit her heart. She had sworn never to leave her mama. With her daddy gone, she was once again all her mama had. She shook her head slowly. "I don't know, Moses. I don't know... I'm just telling you what I heard."

Neither one spoke for a long time as they stared into the flames and pondered what the coming year would bring.

THIRTY-FOUR

The blush of spring kissed Virginia as the month of March claimed the wintry landscape. Red maple buds bulged with the promise of life. Low-hanging willows proudly sported their fresh tendrils of green. Carrie was glad for the robes tucked around her legs. The sun was warm, but the air was still nippy as Charles urged the horses down the road at a rapid trot. She leaned back against the carriage seat and pulled out the two letters that had prompted her sudden trip to Richmond. The first was from her father.

Dear Carrie,

I find I have not much time to write. The political affairs of our country are consuming all my time and energy. Having just returned from Washington, there is too much happening at present for me to make a trip to Cromwell. I miss you, daughter. It would give me great pleasure if you would come to visit your devoted father. I'm sure it would also do you good to get away from the plantation for a while. I will look forward with great anticipation to a positive response.

With deep love,
Father

Carrie smiled as she folded the letter and slipped it back into its envelope. There was a troubled look on her face when she pulled out the second letter.

Dear Carrie,

How I miss you. With activity so slow on the plantation during the winter months, I have found myself often in Richmond. I have become very involved with the militia units Governor Letcher has been so wise to develop. My cavalry unit from Goochland continues to give me many reasons to be proud of them, and I am finding myself in demand in Richmond as our leaders discuss the preparation of Virginia's defense if we have need of it. That we will indeed have need of it becomes more certain in my mind every day.

I long to see you, Carrie. I visited with your father recently and know he feels the same way. I am writing to add to his plea for you to come to Richmond. I long to get away and come visit you, but it seems to be impossible now. Please put two men out of their misery. Come to Richmond soon!

With deep affection,
Robert

Carrie released a heavy sigh as she stared at Robert's letter. Her internal struggle had not lessened since Christmas Day when she had discovered Robert's horrendous actions on his plantation. That his actions were completely legal under Virginia law made not one bit of difference to her. The very thought of it caused loathing in her soul, and her efforts to put it out of her mind had been to no avail. The arrival of the two letters had made her accept the truth. She must face the issue. No longer could she run from it. She had left Cromwell only three days after receiving her letters.

Carrie gazed up at the handsome brick house as Charles stopped the carriage. Overlooking the city from its impressive perch on Church Hill, the three-storied structure was graced by a massive front porch, its small yard surrounded by filigreed ironwork. Stately boxwoods lined the walk and blooming camellias surrounded the porch.

"Carrie!"

"Father!" Carrie jumped from the carriage and ran up the stairs to embrace her father. She was relieved by the strong, steady light in his eyes. Obviously, there were no ghosts here to haunt him. "It's wonderful to see you. I've missed you."

Thomas smiled warmly and kissed her on the cheek. "Thank you for coming. My old heart needed the sight of my beautiful daughter." He took her arm and led her into the house. "I have invited Robert over for dinner at six o'clock. He is quite anxious to see you."

Carrie looked around as she entered the house. "You have quite a beautiful home here," she murmured. The expansive entryway was lined with glorious pictures and a glistening chandelier cast its soft glow. A glance into the rooms off the hallway revealed the same kind of splendor. If possible, it was even fancier than the plantation.

Thomas shrugged. "I bought it as you see it. The previous owner passed away quite suddenly. The one heir didn't want to be bothered with selling off belongings individually." He paused. "I am quite comfortable here." Carrie followed him into the elegant parlor. After they were both seated, he turned to her. "My original intent was to provide a safe haven for you and your mother if war should come and you would have to leave the plantation, but it has served quite well as my residence and base of operations."

"You look better than I have seen you in months."

Thomas smiled slightly. "There are no memories to mock all I spent my life building. I am needed here in Richmond." He held up his hand at Carrie's look of protest. "I'm sure I am also needed at Cromwell, but I find I am still too much of a coward to return."

"You're not a coward, Father."

"Maybe not, though I doubt it. It mocks me daily that it is my daughter who is carrying on for me."

Carrie spoke firmly. "It's simply ridiculous for you to feel that way. I am quite happy on the plantation.

And you are doing what you need to be doing. I am very proud of you."

Thomas watched her closely. "You mean that, don't you?"

"I do."

"But, why? How? All you wanted was to leave the plantation. Why are you now content? Surely you must see why I feel so guilty."

Carrie nodded slowly and searched for the right words to assuage her father's guilt. "I'm not sure I can explain it. For a while I felt like Cromwell Plantation was nothing but a beautiful prison for me. I'm not sure when I realized I was exactly where I was supposed to be. That knowledge changed it from a prison to a glorious challenge." She paused and stared deeply into her father's eyes. "Even if you came back now, I would still stay. I have not given up on my dreams," she smiled broadly, "but dreams are meant to be lived in God's time. It's not time yet."

Thomas stared at her. "You've changed," he said simply.

Carrie laughed. "I prefer to think I've grown up."

Thomas reached out to take her hand. "Thank you." He seemed to want to say more, but didn't know what.

Carrie squeezed his hand lightly. "You're welcome." She changed the subject. "Please tell me what is going on in our country. I get it all in bits and pieces, and weeks after it has happened. How was the peace conference in Washington?"

Thomas frowned and leaned back in his chair. "I'm afraid I can only say it was a dismal failure. I suppose I should take solace in the fact there are still reasonable men from all over our nation who wish to see tragedy averted, but I'm afraid there are not enough of us to make any real difference. It was our own Governor Letcher who called for the conference, but there was not even a consensus of feeling among our own delegates. There are many Virginians eager to ride the wave of secession."

"Is it still seven states?" Carrie asked.

Thomas nodded heavily. "Yes, and not one of those seven states, too busy establishing their own government in Montgomery, bothered to send delegates to the peace conference. They are clearly not interested in a peaceful settlement. They insist they want to dissolve the Union in a peaceful way, but they are simply hoping the North will turn the other way and pretend our glorious Union never existed. Jefferson Davis, the new president for the Confederation of Southern States claims he wants peace, but he also says the South will fight to the death if anyone tries to stop their secession."

"And what does Lincoln say? He's been president for less than two months now."

Thomas grimaced. "I both pity and despise the man," he growled. "I also admire him," he admitted slowly. "He has stepped aboard to captain a sinking ship—one that has seven gaping holes. With no hope of plugging those holes, and with many more waiting to spring a leak if he tries to turn the boat around..." Thomas shook his head. "I would not want to be in his place."

"Was *nothing* accomplished at the convention?" Carrie knew her father and Governor Letcher had gone to Washington with such high hopes. She saw none of it in her father now.

Thomas shrugged. "There was a lot of talk of compromise—of safeguards for slavery." His voice grew firmer. "Safeguards that should be implemented and enforced by all the powers of our government."

"And Lincoln? What did he say?"

Thomas frowned deeply. "Our president said, and I quote, 'As to slavery, it must be content with what it has. The voice of the civilized world is against it; it is opposed to its growth or extension. Freedom is the natural condition of the human race, in which the Almighty intended men to live. Those who fight the purposes of the Almighty will not succeed. They always have been, and they always will be, beaten.'

Carrie sat quietly, quite sure she agreed with their new president.

Thomas's frustration was evident. "I believe the secession movement can be stopped. The seven cotton states who have already seceded know how badly they need the border states and the rest who are content to merely watch right now." He leaned forward as he spoke intensely, his eyes blazing. "Virginia is the key. We must hold back the tide of secession *here.* The South needs us too badly. They need our wealth and they need our industrial strength. Without Virginia their dreams of establishing an independent country are just that— dreams!"

"Will Virginia stand?" Carrie asked quietly.

Thomas slouched back into his chair with a sigh. "We are holding for now. There are still enough men in leadership who are determined to keep the Union intact, but the spirit of the people is changing. Richmond itself is full of citizens who are sounding the cry of secession." He shook his head. "If they only knew they were like a herd of mindless sheep being led to the slaughter. They are content to follow the leader, their noses close to the ground, refusing to look up and see the danger that lurks on the horizon. They are headed straight for a cliff but they won't even know it until they have tumbled over the jagged edge," he said bitterly.

Carrie frowned at the agony she saw on her father's face. His words had stirred deep unrest in her heart. Miles away on the plantation, it was easy to focus on her existence and believe the rest of the world continued as it always had. Here in Richmond, she was forced to acknowledge that all she had ever known tottered on the brink of a steep precipice.

Thomas shook his head again, and forced a smile to his lips. "Enough of such talk. You have just gotten here. How long are you going to stay?"

Carrie shrugged. "I decided not to put a limit on it. The plantation is running smoothly."

Thomas looked at her sharply. "You trust Adams to run things?" Then he smiled sheepishly. "I know I shouldn't be questioning you. I seem to have abdicated my rights."

"Nonsense!" Carrie said sharply. "Cromwell Plantation will always be yours. You have every right to ask questions." *And I have every right to not answer them completely truthfully,* she thought as she replied. "The Cromwell overseer is doing a tremendous job. I will

trust him for as long as I feel the need to be here."
Carrie smiled. "The plantation is doing well, Father. The
crops are going in right on schedule." She had already
decided not to tell him that freedom had lured seven
more of the slaves northward. Nor that she had written
the passes that secured them easy passage on the
trains heading out of Richmond and into Philadelphia.
He also didn't need to know that Aunt Abby was
sending them on their way through her contacts in the
Underground Railroad. Carrie loved and respected her
father, but she had long ago decided to be true to her
heart. She had also decided not to cross bridges until
she was forced to.

Carrie talked quietly for several minutes, detailing
what was going on at Cromwell Plantation, determined
to put her father's mind at ease. Thomas listened, but
Carrie could tell his mind was already focusing on other
things. Abruptly, she ceased talking and stood up. "I
would love to freshen up. Could you please tell me
where my room is?"

Thomas nodded instantly. "Of course, dear. I
should have thought of it sooner, instead of rambling
on." He raised his voice. "Micah!" he called.

"Micah?" Carrie asked with a lift of her eyebrows.

Thomas nodded. "I found it necessary to purchase
several slaves to take care of the operations around the
house. They are quite a good bargain right now, what
with the uncertain state of affairs in our country." His
smile lacked any humor.

Carrie's responding smile covered the groan that
wanted to escape her lips. She leaned forward and
kissed her father lightly. "I'll see you at dinner."

Carrie watched from her window as Robert's
carriage rolled up to the gate. He jumped out and
looked eagerly toward the house. She maintained her
position behind the concealing curtain, suddenly
unwilling to face what lay ahead. The mere sight of his
broad shoulders and handsome face caused a deep
longing to sweep through her, yet overlaying the longing

was the deep loathing and fear of the hatred that controlled his actions. She took a deep breath to steady her nerves and focus her mind, then turned and made her way to the parlor.

Robert rose eagerly as soon as Carrie entered the room. "Carrie!" He strode forward, took her hand and gazed down into her eyes. Carrie smiled, but was aware her smile lacked any real warmth. Robert hesitated and then slowly dropped her hand. "It's good to see you again," he murmured.

"It's good to see you again, too, Robert." Her voice was pleasant but noncommittal. She longed to reach up and touch his suddenly confused face, but there was too much standing between them. She saw her father watching her, but knew he would not say anything. Not until later, anyway.

"Robert and I were just talking about Fort Sumter, Carrie. He tells me he is considering going to Charleston again soon."

Carrie, determined not to make the dinner hour unpleasant, smiled up at Robert. "Why are you going to Charleston?"

Robert frowned slightly. "Surely you are aware of what is going on at Fort Sumter, Carrie."

It was Carrie's turn to frown. Robert's tone was one of a superior talking down to a subordinate. "I am aware that the fort at Sumter is being held by a garrison of United States troops. Has it suddenly become a crime for federal troops to be on American soil?" she asked crisply.

"I'm sorry," Robert said contritely. He reddened and reached out to take her hand. "I have been commanding the militia too much lately. I didn't mean to sound like that."

Carrie hated the tension between them. Still fighting the longing in her heart, she allowed her hand to remain there. "Why don't you fill me in on Fort Sumter? I'm sure I am hopelessly out of date," she said warmly.

Robert gave a relieved sigh and settled down in a chair opposite her father. "Jefferson Davis has just commissioned Beauregard to brigadier general.

Beauregard is on his way now to take over command of all the Southern forces in Charleston."

Carrie gasped. She was indeed hopelessly out of date. The standoff between Major Anderson of Fort Sumter and the state of South Carolina had indeed taken some nasty turns since Anderson had moved his troops to Sumter the day after Christmas. She held her breath as Robert continued.

"Southern men are pouring into the Charleston area. Work is being done around the clock to strengthen the forts surrounding Sumter. Guns and ammunition seized from forts and arsenals taken over in the seceding states, is being used to ring Sumter with incredible fire-power. There are also massive amounts of shot and shell being delivered from Richmond's own Tredegar Iron Works."

"What is Lincoln doing about this?" Carrie demanded.

Robert shrugged. "He's had little time to do anything about anything. He's inherited a huge mess from Buchanan who basically did nothing but send some empty letters back and forth and give poor Anderson no real idea as to what steps he was supposed to take."

Carrie frowned as she tried to remember what little she had read. "I thought Major Anderson is supposed to be pro-slavery?"

Thomas spoke up then. "All reports say he is. After all, his wife is a Georgian. But Anderson is an American through and through. His first allegiance will always be to the flag and the Union it stands for. He is also deeply religious. The reports I hear say that he is desperately trying to figure out how to make this affair end in peace."

Robert snorted. "It is far too late for that! I think the South is merely stalling, sir. I believe they have every intention of firing upon Fort Sumter. As long as the North hesitates and does nothing, they have more time to build their military force. If my reports are correct, Fort Sumter as it is right now would have a devil of a time defending herself. It's just a matter of time." He frowned. "I think that time will be here soon."

"Is that why you're going to Charleston?" Carrie asked. "To fight?" Her voice was deeply troubled. Had it really come to this?

Robert shook his head. "I have no intention of fighting. I don't see this as my war yet. I do believe, though, that South Carolina has the right to not have United States forces on her property."

Carrie found herself protesting. "How can they call Fort Sumter their property? Why, the whole island the fort sits on was created from tons of rocks and granite shipped down from New England. The fort wouldn't even exist if the United States hadn't created it."

Robert nodded. "That's true, but South Carolina believes it is a sovereign nation now and they don't believe another nation has the right to endanger their national security."

Thomas shook his head, his focus on only one thing. "So you believe the war will start soon?"

Robert sighed heavily. "I don't really see any way out of it. No one is really looking for a rational way to solve it. It's probably too late anyhow. No, I'm afraid the die has been cast." He turned back to Carrie to finish answering her question. "Governor Letcher has asked me to go to Charleston. He wants a firsthand report of what happens there, and he wants detailed reports on what military moves the South is taking to support their secession. I am going merely as an observer."

Thomas steered the conversation in a different direction. "Matthew Justin was through town a few days ago and was kind enough to stop in to talk with me."

"And to find out whatever he could about the state of affairs in Virginia," Robert added dryly.

Thomas nodded. "That, too," he admitted easily. "We are still one country," he added firmly. "I will work with whomever is willing to try to stop the madness. Justin is at least trying to report the news impartially. That is more than I can say for many of our newspapers, which are wielding their influence to flame the passions already spreading out of control. I fear there are many editors and newspapermen who will bear a heavy responsibility for what happens in our country." He paused. "Matthew tells me the public tide of Northern opinion is turning entirely against the South."

"Let it!" Robert said heatedly. "If they had let us alone in the first place none of this would be happening."

Thomas nodded calmly. "I agree with you, my boy. There is no reason for *us* to fight."

Robert flushed and smiled sheepishly. "You're right, sir. I'm sorry." He took a deep breath. "I seem to be a little tense lately."

"You, along with the rest of the country," Thomas replied. "At least those people in the country who care enough to understand what is happening. That is what troubles me so much about what Matthew told me. For a long time, most of the people in the North could have cared less what was happening down here. Their lives and property weren't being endangered. If the South wanted to secede, they didn't care. Why, Horace Greeley of the New York Tribune has come out in his paper and urged the president to let us depart in peace." He paused, his brow furrowing deeply. "Fort Sumter has changed all that. They are incensed that the American flag was fired upon when Buchanan made his bungled attempt to send reinforcements to Anderson by that ship, the *Star of the West*. Many of them are calling for the use of force to put down the rebellion." He shook his head. "No. I knew it was coming, but I have still harbored a hope that reasonable men could find a way around war. The South says they want to leave peacefully, but there are many itching for a good battle. The North is the same. I'm afraid our frail humanity is going to give them both what they want. Once they have gotten it, they will soon enough discover there is no painless way to let it go."

Carrie stared at her father, suddenly sure his prophetic words were true.

Carrie was not surprised when Robert led her to the stair step of St. John's Church. Not a word had been spoken since they had left her father's house. Both were aware this was no time for light chatter. She also knew it would not help to put off the inevitable so she spoke as soon as she settled down on the top step. "Robert?"

Robert held up his hand to stop her and turned to her eagerly. "Carrie, I must talk to you."

"Alright." Caught by the urgency in his voice, Carrie forced herself to listen quietly.

Robert reached out and grasped one of her hands. "Carrie, I know you have asked me not to tell you how I feel. I have respected and honored that." He paused, and Carrie tensed. But he didn't seem to notice as he pushed on. "Our country is going to war. I am sure of it. Virginia will secede to fight along with the South. That I am also sure of. My duty is calling me to Charleston right now, but when I return I'm certain I will be offered a commission in the military."

Carrie stared at him as he talked. Things were moving too quickly. She wanted to push back time and pretend life was as it had always been.

Robert was bent on his course and nothing could sway him. He took a deep breath and looked into Carrie's eyes. "Carrie Cromwell, I love you. I have loved you from the very first day. You have owned me from the moment you cut a lock of your hair to give me as a token in the tournament." He smiled as he remembered, his voice softening. "I love you and I want to spend the rest of my life with you. Will you marry me?"

Carrie was speechless.

"I realize war will mean I will be gone—but not for long. The North will give up quickly when they realize there is no hope of defeating superior men dedicated to dying in order to preserve all they know and hold dear. It should only last a month or so."

Her father's dark warning that there would be death and tragedy on both sides flickered through her mind, but Carrie said nothing.

"I know how much you want to be a doctor. I also know you are now happy on the plantation. I have hopes you have given up your dreams of being a doctor and will be happy at Oak Meadows, but if not," he rushed on, "we'll still figure out a way to make your dream come true." He paused, and fixed his eyes on her with a note of desperation in his voice. "All I know is that I love you. Will you marry me?"

Carrie expressed all the pain in her heart in two words. "I can't."

Robert stared at her. "What do you mean you can't?" He didn't wait for an answer. "Is it because of the plantation? It will mean extra work, but we can still run both plantations. And once the craziness has settled down in the country your father will want to return to Cromwell. He can hire another overseer to run things while he is in Richmond for his political work."

Carrie shook her head. "That's not the reason."

Robert looked puzzled. "Is it your dream of being a doctor? Didn't you hear me, Carrie? We'll find a way to work it out. There is a medical school right here in Richmond, you know."

If Carrie wasn't so consumed with pain, she would have laughed at the idea of a southern medical school being willing to accept her as a student. Why, it was still almost impossible in the North where thinking was a little more progressive. She was in no mood to be amused, however. She pulled her hand back, pushed herself up from the stairs, and stood, staring out over the city.

Robert finally seemed to realize something else as going on as he stood beside her. "Why can't you, Carrie?" His voice was quiet. "Is it because you don't love me?"

Carrie turned to look at him. "I do love you, Robert Borden. I've known that for a very long time. But I can't marry you."

Robert looked like he wanted to cry out, but he remained silent.

Carrie stared into his eyes for a long moment and then turned to look back over the city glimmering below. Her voice was low as she spoke. "I could never marry someone whose heart carries so much hatred."

Robert stared at her. "What are you talking about?" He seemed genuinely confused.

Carrie kept her eyes and voice steady. "You have carried hatred in your heart from the day your father was killed. You took a hatred for one man and you have turned it toward a whole race of people. I believe slavery is wrong, Robert. When two people are married, there are differences, yes, but on an issue that involves so much of who they are as people, they must be united. You and I are far apart on this. Our marriage would never be what we both want it to be."

Robert's face flushed with a mixture of anger and confusion. "You would let niggers keep us apart?" His voice was disbelieving.

Carrie shook her head. "Slavery is *wrong*, Robert. God created all people with a special purpose. He loves us all equally."

Robert broke in. "If you want to talk about God, fine. Let's talk about God—and the Bible, too, while we're at it. The Bible clearly sanctions slavery."

"Where?"

Robert stared at her. "Where?" he echoed.

"Yes," Carrie said calmly. "Where? Where does the Bible say it?"

Robert glared at her angrily. "That's not my job to know that. It's a minister's."

"So you believe it simply because a minister says it's true?"

"That's a good enough reason for me. They should know what they're talking about."

Carrie nodded. "What about ministers in the North who believe slavery is wrong? Ministers who use the *Bible* to prove it's wrong?" She paused, taking compassion on his confused anger. "Robert, I felt the same way you did. Slavery *had* to be right because it was what I had always been taught. I know your feelings are compounded because of what happened to your father. But that doesn't make slavery right! It just means people can find a way to justify anything they want to believe. It most certainly doesn't make it right!"

"And what makes you think you know what's right or wrong?"

Carrie flinched under the heavy sarcasm in his voice, but she was determined to press through. Long hours alone with her troubled thoughts had convinced her Robert was not an evil person—he was a person who needed hate cleansed from his heart. She didn't really expect her words to do the job, but she had to try. She took a deep breath and tried to explain. "I went alone to my place to have it out with God. I so needed to know the truth." As best as she could, she relived that day for him. "I believe I heard God that day. I believe I saw his heart. I don't believe people are supposed to own each other. Love is supposed to be the greatest law, and the determiner of how we treat one another."

"But the Bible says blacks are inferior! The laws that apply to us simply don't apply to them."

"No, it doesn't!" Carrie said firmly. "That is simply a lie we have created to make ourselves feel better about exploiting an entire race of people for our own gain." She pressed on. "Slavery in ancient times was not based on color. If ancient slavery makes the institution right, then it means slavery is acceptable for white people. Under that reasoning, there is no reason someone might not make a slave of you! How would you feel about it then?"

"That's ridiculous!" Robert snorted.

"Is it?" Carrie questioned gently. "You are no more deserving of slavery than the millions of people we are controlling now."

"You own slaves yourself, Carrie!"

Carrie shook her head decisively. "I own not a single slave, Robert. They all belong to my father. If I had my way, I would let every single one of them go." She saw no reason to tell him she had already granted freedom to seventeen of the Cromwell slaves and that the rest were free to leave.

"And what about Cromwell Plantation *then*?"

Carrie shrugged. She knew Robert was thinking of Oak Meadows and trying to envision it with no slaves. "Prosperity founded on another man's subjugation is not a thing I desire. The South is full of people who will never own a slave. They are supporting themselves by their own labor. I find that preferable."

Robert, completely nonplussed, gazed at her angrily. "So you're saying that if I want you as my wife, I must get rid of all my slaves?"

arrie shook her head. "You could get rid of all your slaves, and it would make no difference at all."

"What then?" Robert cried. "What is it that you want from me?"

"It's not what I want *from* you, Robert. It's what I want *for* you. You are a prisoner of your own hatred. Your hate doesn't come from your actions. It is your actions that spring from your hate." She paused, her eyes pleading with him. "Ask God to show you the truth, Robert. If you're right, there is nothing to be afraid of."

Robert turned to stare out over the city. Carrie watched the struggle on his face—fear mixed with anger in a battle for dominance. His anger won. Carrie knew the memories of his father haunted him.

Whirling, he cried out. "There is nothing that will make me believe a nigger is my equal. It was a nigger who killed my daddy!"

"And it was a white man who killed the little boy on Oak Meadows Plantation."

Robert stared down at her. "What are you talking about?"

"I know, Robert," Carrie said. "I know you beat three of your slaves after some of them ran away. I know the little boy died." She took a deep breath. "I know you murdered a child."

Robert looked at her wildly. "They are my people! I can do with them what I want."

Carrie shook her head. When she spoke, her voice was oddly quiet. "They, just like you and I, are *God's* people. And he wept when you destroyed one of them." She stood up. "I would like to go home now." She turned and began to walk down the street.

Robert followed, but not a word passed between them. Carrie nodded her head when she reached her front door, looked at him deeply for a moment, and moved into the house.

Carrie said not a word to her father, who looked up from his paper as she entered the hallway. He merely watched her as she heavily climbed the stairs. Only when Carrie reached her room did she allow the avalanche of tears to consume her. She had done what she knew she must. She also knew the pain would never go away.

Robert left for Charleston on the first train the next morning.

THIRTY-FIVE

Robert strolled slowly along the Battery of Charleston, watching the parade of people jostle by. That Charleston was a city preparing for war, no sensible person could deny. Proud militia units, sporting the bright colors of their identifying uniforms, strutted around him like proud peacocks all too willing to preen their glory. Women, eager to be a part of the wondrous events happening in their own fair city, flocked to the streets every day. They peered into the harbor with eyeglasses, hoping to catch sight of the shot that would finally end their waiting and escort them into the glory Southern politicians promised so freely and easily. Drums rolling and parades snaking through the streets had become a daily occurrence.

Robert watched all of it, as he had been doing for several weeks, before he moved to lean on one of the railings and peer out to sea. He had completed what he had been sent to do. Stacked neatly in his hotel room were thick sheaves of documents accounting for and describing the military operations that had turned Charleston into a bedlam of activity. He heaved a heavy sigh, rested his chin in his hand, and stared out at Fort Sumter — the unseeming cause of the entire furor surrounding him. He was ready to go home.

"You don't look too excited to be here, young man."

Robert started and turned. "Excuse me?" The man standing before him had a shock of white hair tumbling down over vivid blue eyes that regarded him sharply.

"I said you don't look too excited to be here."

Robert shrugged. He didn't sense any judgment coming from the man, and his observation was certainly not inaccurate. "I've been here long enough."

"You mean to say you're not enthralled by all the chaos exploding in your fair city?"

"It's not my city. I'm just visiting."

"You and a few thousand others," the older man snorted. "You with one of the militia units sent to fire on that paltry number of soldiers trapped out in our harbor?"

Robert shook his head and eyed the other man closely. "Your name is?"

"The name is Crawford, son. Dr. Adam Crawford. I've lived in this city all my life."

Robert took the hand extended to him, drawn to the direct, open manner. "My name is Robert Borden. Virginia is my home—a plantation close to Richmond."

"Lured by the smell of blood are you?"

Robert was aware he was being baited—tested for some reason—but he had no idea why. He opted for honesty. He had no idea who this man was, and he had no reason to play games with him. "No, sir. I'm down here at the request of the governor to evaluate and report on the military fortifications of the city. I am done. I plan on returning home soon."

Crawford barked a laugh. "I wouldn't leave now, boy. You'll miss the best part of the show!"

Robert stared at him, beginning to wonder if the man might be a little crazy. The steady shine of his eyes reassured him. "Why do you say that, sir?"

"There are lots of people down here on the Battery watching the peripheral parts of this crisis. They count the number of troops coming into our city. They keep track of every gun and cannon being added to the arsenal of power surrounding Fort Sumter. Me? I spend my time looking at the inner guts of what is going on. That's where all the real action is. What you're looking at is no more than an outward show of what's going on behind the scenes." Crawford paused and stared out at Sumter. "The waiting will soon be over, boy. The South can't afford to let Fort Sumter continue to defy them." He snorted. "Up until now it's been like a little hangnail. It was irritating, but it could be dealt with. The South has stalled, using Buchanan's indecision to help them reach the place they want to be. With Lincoln in office, the hangnail has suddenly become a serious infection."

"So they've got to get rid of the infection," Robert observed.

"Sure they do! But it's more than that. All the states who jumped so fast to form this Confederacy of the Southern States figured all the other states would jump on board as soon as they sounded the call. It's not happening quite the way they figured. People follow passion, Robert. Always have and always will. President Davis and our leaders know that. They know it's time to give the people some passion—something to rally behind." He paused, and then continued, his voice grim. "They know it's time to give them some blood."

Robert frowned. "You sound as if you think they're wrong." He wasn't sure why it bothered him. He wasn't even sure it did. And he had no idea why this total stranger was talking to him. He stared at Crawford. "A lot of people around here wouldn't take kindly to what you're saying."

Crawford laughed heartily. "My boy, I reached the point, years ago, when I quit basing what I believe on what other people think. People have been frowning at me ever since." He paused. "I have to live with myself, Robert. Other people have to live with themselves."

"Do you think the war is wrong, sir?" Suddenly Robert was eager to talk with this man.

Crawford shrugged. "It's not a war yet, my boy." He sighed heavily. "It's just a matter of time, though, I know." He shook his head sadly. "Can any war be right? Especially when the sheep being sent off to fight the battle have no real idea of what is going on."

"I don't understand, sir."

Crawford smiled slightly. "Robert, the South has attracted the young and the poor to their radical banner with lies. I suppose there is no other way to induce people to jump into the tragedy of war. They have been told the act of secession will produce no opposition of a serious nature, that not a drop of blood will be spilled. They have been told no one's property will be destroyed. They have been promised unbroken prosperity—even greater prosperity because cotton will control all of Europe." He sighed heavily. "People believe what they want to believe. They also believe what people in leadership tell them. That is their first mistake."

Robert searched for the right response. "I take it you don't believe all this, Mr. Crawford."

Crawford turned to stare out at Sumter again. "Robert, I know there are close to seven thousand men crowding the city of Charleston who have only one reason for being here—to commit an act of war against one hundred twenty-eight poorly armed Union soldiers sitting in that fort. Someday people will probably call this a battle, but I think that is a mockery of the term. Those men are nothing but sitting ducks. Our new government is going to use them to rally the Southern people." He paused, searching for the right words. "I don't believe most people understand it..." He laughed shortly. "But whoever waited for the common man when a great move was to be made? Our leaders have decided to make the move and simply force them to follow. They believe this is the way of all revolutions and all great achievements. If they wait until the mind of everybody is made up they will wait forever and never do anything."

Robert stared at the older man. Crawford spoke as if he were merely reporting facts. There was very little emotion in his voice. "But, sir," he protested, "that is simply manipulation. Surely you cannot agree with it!" Robert could not even identify the source of his own unrest. Suddenly the whole picture had taken on a different hue. He felt vaguely certain he was one of the sheep Crawford was alluding to.

Crawford suddenly turned to look deep into his eyes. "As long as there are people willing to be manipulated and controlled, there will be people eager to step forward and accept the position." He glanced down at his watch before straightening. "I have an appointment, Mr. Robert Borden. It was a pleasure to meet you." He reached out and shook Robert's hand firmly. "I'm sure you're wondering why I have bored you with all my talk." Robert opened his mouth to protest, but Crawford gave him no opportunity. "I can't stop the madness going on around me, young man." He hesitated slightly. "But if I can reach out and cause even one person to stop and think—even if all they all do is look back after this horrible war is over and say one old man in Charleston knew what was really coming—then I can sleep at the end of each day." He laughed shortly. "You just happened to be the lucky one today." He turned and disappeared into the crowd as quickly as he had appeared.

Robert stared after him for several long moments and then resumed his position on the railing. The old man had given him a lot to think about.

Two nights later, Robert was jolted from his bed by a deep blast in the distance. The first was followed by yet another, and then another. It took a moment for reality to seep into his fogged mind. When it did, he jumped from his bed, slipped into his clothes and took off for the harbor at a wild run. It was 4:30 a.m. on the twelfth of April. The Battle of Fort Sumter had just begun.

The streets of Charleston were full of people—men, women and children—racing down to find the best seats for the show. Five thousand people crowded the cobblestone roads and filled every rooftop with a view of the battle. Excited calls and cries of joy filled the night. Finally the standoff had been ended. Action had been taken! The honor of the glorious South could no longer be trampled on.

"Now the North will see that there will be terrible consequences to pay if they don't leave us be!"

Robert turned to look at the well-dressed man yelling into his ear. This was the first attention he had paid to the throngs pressed against the Battery railing. He nodded. "Once they get a taste of it, this whole thing will be over before it starts!" he yelled back. "This war will be so short most people won't even know it happened." Robert smiled as a thrill coursed through his tense body. Crawford's words had caused him to think deeply for two days as he had waited for the old man's predictions to come true, and he had started to harbor serious doubts. The whoosh, boom, and mighty explosions caused by the battle raging around him made all doubts flee his mind. The mighty South would not be controlled. Victory would be theirs—by right *and* by might.

THIRTY-SIX

Carrie started violently as the front door closed with a slam. She laid her book down hastily and jumped up to meet her father who was striding into the library. "Father! What is wrong?"

"It's started," Thomas said sternly. "The war has started. Fort Sumter has been fired upon." His last words were spoken wearily, as if the force of emotions he had been assailed with had drained his energy.

Carrie stared at him for several long moments and then moved forward to take his arm. "You look tired. Please sit down and tell me what has happened."

Thomas nodded absently. "Of course." He sank down into a chair and turned to face her. "I thought you should know at once. I have to leave soon to head back to the capitol but I wanted you to know. The telegram just came into the governor. Sumter was attacked at 4:30 this morning after Anderson refused to surrender the fort to the Southern government." He rubbed his face as he spoke. "It was hours before Sumter even fired back. Our report says the skies over Charleston looked like a giant fireworks display as all points surrounding Sumter opened fire."

"The war has started..." Carrie said, sick with disbelief. "Will Virginia secede now?"

"Most of the city of Richmond has *already* seceded," Thomas said bitterly. "Just eight days ago our convention voted down secession but the people may have their way yet. You should see the city. Practically all business has been suspended and the streets are full of knots of people talking of nothing but Sumter. No," he said, shaking his head, "I had hopes this madness would spend itself out in angry words and futile actions of defiance, but the spark has finally reached the keg of dynamite. The whole thing has blown up. Our whole country is full of one dynamite keg after another. Now that one has blown..." His voice dropped to a whisper. "Now that one has blown it won't end until all of them have exploded and burned out. We're in for a long war, Carrie."

Carrie was holding onto something she had heard Robert and others say. "Surely the war will not be long," she protested. "Once the North realizes the South is going to stand and fight, surely they will decide just to let us go. We may be an independent country but all of us can still live in peace!"

Her father stared at her. "Do you really believe that? Do you think the North is full of soft, yellow-bellied cowards who won't fight?"

Visions of the vibrant young men she had danced and talked with in Philadelphia filled her mind. Thoughts of Matthew Justin, his eyes steady and strong, rose to taunt her. The great meeting hall full of people willing to risk everything to help runaway slaves showed her the truth. Carrie settled back with a heavy sigh. "We are indeed in for a long and terrible fight, Father."

Carrie was finishing up a letter to Aunt Abby when she heard a mighty cry raised in the street outside her window.

"Sumter has fallen! Sumter has fallen!"

Carrie hurried to the window and looked out. Even here on Church Hill, the streets were filling as people poured out of their houses in response to the news. She watched silently for a few minutes. In spite of her repulsion at the thought of war, she felt drawn to the excitement exploding in the streets. Her curiosity demanded to know what was happening. "Micah?" She reached for her cloak and hurried to the front door."

"Yes, Miss Cromwell?"

Carrie turned to look briefly at the tall, stooped butler who had taken charge of her father's home. His dark face was set in impassive lines as if he were completely unaware of the chaos reigning in the street just outside the house. She spoke quickly. "If my father returns home, tell him I've gone out for a while. I shouldn't be gone too long."

A brief flicker of concern crossed Micah's face. "I am to tell him you went alone, Miss Carrie?" he asked carefully.

Carrie smiled. "I am perfectly capable of taking care of myself," she responded cheerfully. Then, more firmly, she said, "Tell him what you want. I will be back later." She opened the door, hurried across the porch, and down the steps. Without even thinking, she joined the flow of people streaming down the hill toward the city. She listened quietly as excited talk flowed around her.

"Maybe now our Governor will quit rolling over to play dead. Surely our glorious victory will show him the worthiness of the Southern cause!"

"It's just a matter of time now until the convention votes to secede!"

"I heard Sumter was consumed by flames at the end! Our boys really gave it to those Yankees!"

Carrie stared at the immaculately dressed woman who yelled those words as the mob surged down the crowded streets. The woman's face, under her perfectly appointed hat, was flushed with pride and anger, her eyes glowing with an oddly wild light. Carrie suppressed a shudder and hurried on.

Once on Broad Street, the crowded madness continued, but the voices were slightly more balanced. Jubilant cries that Sumter had fallen were absorbed by knots of citizens wearing worried looks and discussing whether the convention would hold the line for their state. Carrie took slight hope that voices of reason might yet prevail. Try as she might, she could not imagine not being a part of the United States. She stopped long enough to listen to one conversation among a group of serious-faced businessmen.

"The streets are wild, but there are many more people hiding behind their doors, wondering what will be the outcome of this latest act," one man observed.

Another man, older than the first, looked worried. "The whole issue has changed now, I'm afraid. This whole fight used to be about slavery. There were people who didn't own slaves and didn't care about slavery enough to secede from the Union. If the cotton states want it so badly, let them go."

Another man interrupted. "You're right. Now the issue has changed. The question has become whether states have the right to secede or not. Does the Government have the right to force them to stay in the Union? If we really do have a war, there is no way I am going to fight against my sister states of the South!"

Carrie watched closely as the faces lost their worried looks and adopted dark scowls that spoke louder than any words. Suddenly, a mighty surge of people captured her attention. Knocked off balance by a large woman bustling by, Carrie grabbed onto a lamppost and craned her neck, slightly frightened, to see where they were going. The mob grew larger as it swept down the street. Once again, curiosity compelled her to follow.

Twenty minutes later, the mob, now thousands of citizens, converged on the Tredegar Iron Works. The sun sparkled brightly on the waters of the James River as the crowd of people surrounded the building and began their earlier chant. "Sumter has fallen! Sumter has fallen!" As Carrie watched, the Stars and Bars of the Confederate States was raised above the Iron Works to the accompaniment of cannon fire and the *Marseillaise*. As soon as the flag fluttered above the inflamed crowd, a mighty roar of approval rose to meet it. When the shouting finally died down, the speeches began.

Carrie wanted to run away from the raw display of emotion, but somehow it held her. She would never agree to this war—never agree to fight to maintain a way of life she no longer believed in. But these were her people. Her friends and neighbors. Fellow Virginians who were suddenly willing to fight a war over something most of them had no part in. She was both appalled and intrigued.

"Virginia will secede! The Yankee tyranny is over!"

Carrie swung her attention back to the hastily erected platform. Suddenly, all she wanted was to be with her father. In the face of such mindless passion, she desperately needed his thoughtful thinking and careful words. She pushed her way out of the crowd and fought her way to the edge. She looked back only once at the flag fluttering brightly above the Iron Works, and hurried up the hill toward the capitol.

She was almost to the Capitol building when she saw her father's figure emerge from the columned porch. "Father!" she called loudly.

Thomas turned. "Carrie! What are you doing here?" His face was at once both grim and concerned. "Are you alone?" he asked, looking around.

"Yes," Carrie said impatiently. This was no time to worry about protocol. "Father, the whole city is going crazy. I just saw the Confederate flag raised over the Iron Works. And I just heard our Attorney General Tucker say Virginia will secede. Is it true? Have we really seceded?"

Thomas shook his head firmly. "We have *not* seceded! Virginia is still a part of the Union!" A sudden roar of voices caused him to turn and stare down the street. His face paled. "Letcher said they would be here next."

Carrie turned to follow his gaze. "They must be coming from the Iron Works!" she said as the mob surged down the road toward the Capitol.

Thomas nodded, and took her arm. "I don't think they mean any harm, but I don't want you out here alone with them. Come inside with me."

Carrie shook off his hand. "I want to stay out here, Father. This is no time to hide." Somehow, Carrie knew that in the future she would be casting her lot with these impassioned people. She couldn't explain it—she just knew she needed to stay where she was.

Thomas sighed. "Very well," he agreed heavily. "We'll see what the governor has to say from here."

Within moments they were thronged by the milling crowd of people. Fortunately, they were all in good humor. The speeches and excitement down at the Iron Works had reassured them. They simply wanted to see their governor.

"Letcher! Letcher! Letcher!"

The columned porch of the Capitol building remained empty as the chants filled the afternoon air.

"Hoist the flag, boys!" The mighty cry was given by a man standing just a few feet away from Carrie. As if waiting for their signal, two young boys suddenly sprinted from the crowd and headed for the flagpole atop the Capitol. No one stopped them as they raced in and began a swift climb up the stairs that would take them to the roof. The whole crowd cheered them mightily as they appeared on the roof and began to climb the lightning rod that held the Stars and Stripes.

"Father!" Carrie gasped and reached out to grab his arm as she saw the clamps holding the rod began to let go. The pole swayed precariously under the weight of the agile youth. "He's going to fall!" she cried. Staring upward, she groaned as the boy fell and began to roll down the slope of the building. Carrie wanted to close her eyes and turn away, but she was hypnotized by the drama playing out before her eyes.

Suddenly she noticed the other boy flash to lodge himself in the gutter of the building. She shared the tension in his body as he braced himself for the impact. Every fiber in her body strained to help him. "Stop him," she whispered.

"He's got him!" A mighty cheer rang out from the crowd as the other boy stopped his friend's fall. Triumphantly, the two boys turned to the cheering crowd with grinning faces and upraised arms.

Carrie slumped against her father in relief.

Thomas shook his head gravely. "That's just the beginning. There won't always be someone around to save young men caught in their passions."

A young man Carrie's age overheard him. He turned to stare at the older man with the weary eyes. "Don't worry, old man!" he cried. "Let those Yankees come down and try to do something. They'll be running back to their mamas with their tails tucked between their legs." He turned back to cheer as a mighty roar rose from the crowd.

Carrie looked upward. The two boys had accomplished their mission—the Stars and Bars waved proudly in place of the Stars and Stripes. Wild cheering continued as the sun caught the fluttering fabric and sent radiant gleams across the city. Strains of *Dixie*, the new song of the South, mingled with the cheers.

Governor Letcher finally appeared on the porch.

"Letcher! Letcher! Letcher!"

Governor Letcher smiled briefly and lifted his arms to ask for quiet. Only when the crowd had settled down did he speak. His speech was brief and direct. He pledged to do his constitutional duty. His only concession to the spirit of the hour was that he would defend Virginia's honor. He looked up at the flag fluttering high above his head. "I will remind all of you that Virginia has *not* seceded yet. We are still a part of the United States." For a moment he looked out at the exuberant crowd and his eyes caught those of Thomas Cromwell. The two men exchanged a deep look of understanding before the governor looked away. "Goodnight." With those final words, Letcher turned and disappeared into the building.

Carrie knew the crowd had been undaunted by Letcher's mild rebuff. Why, the governor had promised to defend Virginia's honor and there was only one way to do that. It was just a matter of time. Virginia would secede. Other men hurried forward to take the steps of the Capitol and deliver their fiery speeches.

Carrie and her father watched for a long while. As they finally walked away, a shout rose from the crowd to show their approval of a proposed resolution: that we rejoice with high, exultant, heartfelt joy at the triumph of the Southern Confederacy over the accursed government at Washington in the capture of Fort Sumter.

Thomas returned to the Capitol building, leaving Carrie to wander the streets, though he made her promise to be careful and to return home soon. She knew he was worried, but she had to share in this experience. Darkness heightened the enthusiasm spilling over in the crowded streets. It seemed to Carrie that most of the city's population thronged the riotous streets. Bonfires crackled on street corners. Torches and illuminated buildings cast glowing light on the profuse display of Confederate flags draped over windowsills and hanging from doorways. Bells pealed and fireworks exploded as bands played the latest Southern tunes. Speeches erupted where ever there were enough people to listen. Never had Carrie seen such a wild demonstration of emotion and joy.

The people of the South were, for the moment, celebrating. Concealed by the blanket of night and the blindness of their eyes, they could not see the dark, ominous clouds envelope the city. Clouds which had lingered on the horizon shouting out their warning to any who would listen now converged and settled, knowing the passions that had called them could not now send them away. The course was set. There was no turning back.

Carrie was still up when her father entered the house long after midnight. He said nothing, just dropped wearily in his chair. Carrie sat quietly.

Finally Thomas spoke. "Letcher has called out the Public Guard to secure the property and buildings belonging to the United States." He paused. "He also had the Confederate flag taken down. He replaced it with the Virginia flag."

"Not the United States flag?" Carrie questioned, leaning forward.

Thomas shook his head. "Letcher knows Sumter has given the secessionist the final voice, but he is determined that order and legality will prevail. He has also sent commissioners to Washington to seek some kind of guarantees from Lincoln. He is still searching for some way out of this mess, but I believe he knows the inevitable is coming."

Thomas turned to stare into the fire Micah had laid to ward off the late evening chill. "I think you need to have your things moved to Richmond, Carrie." His voice was grave.

Carrie stared at him. "What?" she said in disbelief. "Why?" She was not at all prepared for this turn of events.

Thomas swung around to look at her. "War is coming. I know it. I've told you before it won't be the easy war everyone is talking about. There will be much tragedy and death on either side." It was obvious he had thought this through long before now. "Letcher has already asked me to stay here to help settle all the ramifications of what is coming. I will not return home until after the war." He leaned forward and spoke intensely. "I don't want you on the plantation, Carrie. I would do nothing but worry about you. There is no telling what is going to happen. If the war doesn't actually reach there, you will soon not be safe with the slaves. The spirit of rebellion is going to affect them as well." He paused. "I am sending a letter back with you to Ike Adams. I have asked him to take on the job of completely overseeing the plantation until this is all over." His voice was firm. "I want you to come to Richmond and live, Carrie."

Carrie gazed at him for several long moments. When she finally spoke, her voice was quiet, but equally firm. "I can't do that, Father."

Thomas didn't look surprised, but he shook his head firmly. "I am not asking you, Carrie. I'm telling you this time. I want you in Richmond."

Carrie took a deep breath. "Father, you left me on the plantation six months ago because it was what you had to do. I have never begrudged you that." She paused, not wanting her words to hurt him. "I have always been independent, but leaving me on my own out there made me even more so." She smiled slightly at the look of pain that flickered across her father's face. "It's not a bad thing, Father. I rather like being independent. It's other people who seem to have a hard time with it." She paused again, searching for the right words. "It's more than that, though. At one time all I wanted was to leave Cromwell and move to Richmond. I would have jumped at the opportunity you are giving me. It's different now," she said slowly. "My place is on the plantation for now. I believe that's where I'm supposed to be. I have to go back, and you need to let me do what I have to do."

Thomas looked at her for several long minutes. Not a sound stirred the quiet of the room except the occasional crack of an ember. Finally he nodded. "As usual, I'm going to let you have your way." He smiled faintly, as if determined to face defeat gracefully. "It's different this time, though. I'm not giving in to a strong-willed daughter. I am accepting the beliefs of a strong woman who knows what she wants. I will still worry about you, but it seems we have two different jobs to do."

Carrie moved forward and sank down at his feet, laying her head on his knee like she had done as a child. She smiled up at him. "Thank you, Father."

Two days later, Thomas strode into the house, his whole body held in stern lines. "Lincoln has gone too far!" he proclaimed as soon as he entered the house.

Carrie had just returned from a walk in the city. She laid aside her hat and walked over to look up into her Father's face. "What has happened?"

"Lincoln has requested Virginia to commission eight thousand men to form an army of seventy-five thousand to put down the Southern rebellion."

Carrie gasped. "He wants Virginian's to fight against the South? They will never do that!"

"You're so right," Thomas said grimly. "Lincoln has gone too far this time. The convention is meeting tomorrow. I am sure the vote will be for secession. However strongly most of us feel about the Union, we are Virginians and Southerners first. We will never fight against those we are so closely linked with. Lincoln's choice to use force is a grave mistake." He shook his head. "I knew it was coming. Still," he sighed, "it breaks my heart. What this country had was glorious..." His voice trailed off as he gazed absently out the window at the profusion of flowers heralding spring. Carrie joined him next to the window, linking her arm with his. Together, they stared into the future.

Carrie could sense the dark clouds settling over her beloved country. Their time had come. She thought about all she had learned in the past year and accepted the reality that from the very first moment slavery had been permitted in a country founded on freedom, the threatening clouds presence had been permitted. They had long boiled on the horizon, but now, fed by passion and greed, they were at full strength and intent on devouring everything in their path.

Carrie shuddered and edged closer to her father. Neither spoke as she allowed her thoughts to roam. One year ago, she had made the decision to live her life honestly—letting no one else's opinion form who she would be. It had been a year of massive personal change, challenges, and radical actions. There was not a single one she regretted, but never had she felt so alone, nor so completely fulfilled.

War had come. She would face it.

Carrie had just settled into the carriage seat when she saw her father hurrying up the street. "Father," she said as he drew near enough, "we said our goodbyes this morning."

Thomas reached into his pocket and pulled out an envelope. "I thought you might want this before you leave," he said, handing it to her.

Carrie looked down at the familiar handwriting. "Robert," she said softly. She thought of waiting until she was alone to open the letter, but her impatience and curiosity won out. It took only a moment to break the seal and pull out the single sheet of linen paper.

Dear Carrie,

Virginia is now a part of the Confederacy. As expected, I have been offered a commission as an officer in the new army. I am now Lieutenant Robert Borden. I suddenly realize I find no great thrill in the honor bestowed on me. The reality that I may be fighting friends I spent years in college with has settled upon my heart.

Carrie, I am doing what you asked. I am trying to find out the truth. You are not the only one to challenge me recently. For me, there are now two battles. One for my country, the other to

determine my own beliefs. Please pray for me. I love you, Carrie. I will return.
    Love,
    Robert

Carrie smiled as she refolded the letter. Was there hope after all?

Thomas looked at her closely, then reached into the carriage to give her a big hug, holding her tight for a long moment. "I love you." He paused, and Carrie looked at him expectantly. "Promise me something, Carrie," he continued hoarsely. "Promise me you will leave the plantation if it becomes too dangerous." Sudden tears sprang into his eyes. "I've lost one of the two women in my life. I can't bear the thought of losing the other as well."

"I promise," Carrie whispered. She brushed back her tears and kissed her father on his cheek. "I promise..."

The End

Read the first 2 Chapters of Book # 2 – On To Richmond – starting on the next page!

On To Richmond

ONE

MAY 1861

Carrie Cromwell frowned as she stared out over the raging, turbulent waters of the James River. Four days of steady rain had transformed the usually placid river into a furious monster tearing at its confining banks. Torrents of water sweeping down from the western Appalachian Mountains would soon enable the river to succeed in its quest to top the banks and seek its claim on the surrounding farmland. Massive tree trunks swept by like weightless match sticks, their solid darkness almost matching the muddy swirl of the water.

Carrie lifted her eyes from the river to gaze up into the brilliant blue sky. The rain had ended just the night before, leaving the air crystal clear and deliciously fresh. She allowed herself to stare up into it for just a moment before she turned her eyes back to the river. It more closely matched her thoughts.

"Are you going to tell me about the letter you got from your Father? Or are you just going to continue stewing about it?"

Carrie managed a slight smile as she turned to look at Rose. "How did you know?" Then she laughed. "Don't even bother to answer that question. I should know by now that you know me almost as well as I know myself."

Carrie lapsed into brooding silence again, knowing Rose would give her all the time she needed to answer her question. Granite, her towering grey Thoroughbred gelding, moved under her restlessly as the waters of the river won their fight with the muddy banks and began to edge slowly toward where the two friends watched from astride their horses. Finally, she reached deep into the pocket of the navy blue dress she wore and pulled out a thick envelope.

"This letter from Father came just this morning."

Rose nodded. "I saw the man who delivered it." She paused, and then asked carefully. "Is it bad news?"

Carrie managed a slight laugh. "Is there anything *but* bad news in our country right now? Fort Sumter has fallen. Virginia has seceded. The war has begun..." She shook her head. It would not do to let her thoughts go where they wanted to. She knew the thoughts would come - later - when it was dark and there was no flurry of activity to block them out. But for now she would concentrate on what was at hand. She raised her hand and stuffed an errant, wavy black strand of hair back into her long braid. In a hurry to get to the river, she hadn't even bothered to shape it into a bun. Now the silky strands sought to escape the confines of the thick braid as the breeze teased her hair into rebellion.

A frown creased her brow again as she stared down at the letter in her hand. "Father has been asked by Governor Letcher to take a high position in the Virginia state government."

"Surely you expected that. Your father has been working with the Governor since he left in November."

Carrie frowned again as memories of her father's hopelessness after the death of his beloved wife, Abigail, swept through her mind. She missed her mother, too, but they had grown close only in the last month of her life so her death hadn't left the same gaping hole. She nodded as Rose's words penetrated her thoughts. "Yes, of course I expected it..."

"Then what is troubling you so much?" Rose demanded.

Carrie almost smiled at the impatience in her friend's voice. The freedom they experienced in their friendship was wonderful. A year ago, things had been very different. Rose had still been her best friend, but the reality of Rose being her personal slave, while she lived the luxurious life of a wealthy plantation owner's daughter, had put an impenetrable barrier of protocol between them. The past year had blown those barriers away. Now they were like sisters.

Carrie struggled to express her feelings. "Everything is so different now..." she began haltingly. "It was exciting to think of Father standing close to the helm of Virginia when we were still part of the Union and everyone was fighting so hard to keep it that way. But now..." She paused and stared out at the rampaging river as she tried to force her turbulent thoughts into some form of order. "Father believed so much in keeping the Union together. Now he has flung himself into the struggle for Southern independence. I guess that's what is hard. He is fighting just as hard to defend what he didn't believe in, as he fought to keep it from happening." She shook her head slowly. "I still can't believe it's true. Virginia is no longer a part of the United States. I am no longer a United States citizen."

"What else did your father say, Carrie?" Rose's voice was now gentle, as if she sensed the deep turmoil boiling in her friend.

Carrie shook her head more firmly. "I'm sorry." Her short laugh held no humor. "I realize I'm not being very communicative today. Let me try this again." She gazed down at the letter she held in her hand, and searched for the right place. "Here it is..." She straightened in the saddle to read her father's words, bracing herself to accept the truth of what she read.

Dearest Daughter,

I have grand news for you. Our fair capitol of Richmond is being chosen for a high honor. The decision is being made, even as I write this letter, to place the seat of our wonderful Confederacy right here in Richmond.

Rose looked at Carrie in surprise. "I thought the Confederate Capitol was in Montgomery, Alabama."

Carrie shrugged. "It was." She put down the letter and tried to explain what her father had written without having to decipher his handwriting again. "It seems Alexander Stephens, the Vice-President of the Confederacy, arrived in Richmond just a few days after the Convention voted to secede. He was impressed by Richmond's beauty, but it was much more than that that caused him to make his recommendation for Richmond to become the Capitol. He is well aware of Richmond's economic wealth and the potential for growth."

Carrie paused as she tried to remember what else her father had said. "Tredegar Iron Works played a big role in his decision. That, along with the other iron companies in Richmond. Stephens said the Confederate government's war-waging capacity would have suffered a staggering blow if Virginia hadn't seceded. They're counting on Richmond for cannons, ammunitions, boats and other things." She looked out over the river again as she tried to erase the image of Southern cannons pointed toward her friends from the North. "My father said something about Richmond being strategic in a military sense but I'm not sure what he meant. He may write more about it later."

"Do you want the South to win the war?" Rose asked bluntly.

Carrie turned to stare into her eyes. "You do manage to cut through to the quick of an issue, don't you?"

Rose merely shrugged and returned Carrie's look.

Carrie swung her gaze back to the river. It matched her emotions now even more than it had a few moments ago – her feelings as tossed and jumbled as the muddy cauldron. Finally, she turned back to Rose. "I don't know," she stated flatly. "I think this whole war is stupid. I think people should have had enough sense to keep it from ever happening. But now that it's here? I just don't know, Rose." She smiled slightly. "Does that make me bad?"

Rose sat quietly.

"You're not going to say anything, are you?" Carrie demanded.

Rose shook her head.

Carrie managed a brief laugh and then forced herself to look deep into her heart. Rose's question had made her realize what was really eating at her heart and mind. She was living in a nation at war. Where was her allegiance? Did she have one? Did it make her a traitor to her beloved South if she couldn't enter the conflict wholeheartedly? How could she support a war that was being fought largely over the continuation of slavery - an institution she despised? But how could she *not* fight to keep her homeland from being destroyed? What about Robert...? The turbulence of her thoughts once again threatened to overwhelm her, just as the river was overwhelming the defeated banks it was now creeping over. "I don't know. I simply don't know..." she murmured.

Her troubled thoughts demanded an outlet. She shook her head and cried, "Beat you back to the house!" Spinning Granite on his haunches, she launched him into a ground-swallowing gallop. She knew Rose, on the much smaller mare, Maple, wouldn't stand a chance but she didn't care. She had to release her spinning thoughts. She leaned low over Granite's neck and allowed the fresh air to envelope her. Granite pulled at the reins and she gave him what he wanted. The big Thoroughbred flattened himself to the ground as he flew down the road leading back to the Cromwell Plantation house.

Carrie moved as one with the horse she had owned since childhood. As they flashed through the afternoon sun, flying in and out of pockets of shade, she slowly felt herself relax. She could almost feel the cobwebs floating out of her mind. She didn't have to have any answers yet. Her heart was demanding one, but life wasn't yet demanding one. She knew that for now she was supposed to stay on the plantation, doing what she had been doing since her father had left to go to Richmond. When the time came that she needed to know her heart and mind more clearly, she would know what she was supposed to do. She would simply have to believe that.

As the realization of that truth sank through, she gave a glad laugh and pulled Granite down to a slow canter. Only then did she think of Rose. She glanced back but could catch no glimpse of her friend. She pulled Granite down to a walk and turned him around to stare in the direction she had come from. Nothing. Concern replaced the glad smile with deep lines of worry. Had Rose fallen off? Was something wrong? She had taught her friend how to ride several months ago, but Rose still wasn't entirely confident on a horse. Berating herself for dashing off in a wild run, Carrie urged Granite into a gallop and sped back down the road.

She was halfway to the river before she caught sight of Rose trotting Maple calmly down the road. "Are you all right?" she cried. "What happened?"

Rose laughed softly. "I'm fine. I didn't have any inside bombs to diffuse. Maple and I are simply enjoying the afternoon. She agreed with me that it was silly to go racing after a horse we could never catch."

Carrie laughed at the amused expression on Rose's face and swung Granite alongside to trot with them.

"Are you feeling better after your mad run?"

Carrie nodded. "It always helps," she said simply.

Rose smiled and fell into a short silence. Then she looked up. "What did your father say about the plantation?"

Carrie frowned at her question "I don't know how long we can keep up our little game. Father asked about Ike Adams again. He was concerned that Adams would have to leave the plantation as overseer."

"Why?"

"It seems Virginia is even more nervous about her slave population now that the war has started. They're afraid more and more slaves will try to escape and head north to join up with the Union. The Confederacy is already calling for huge numbers of volunteers to join the army. In addition to that, the Virginia government is calling for more men to join the state militia to keep down any slave uprisings and to bring back slaves who are trying to escape. Father asked in his letter whether Adams was talking about joining the militia and leaving the plantation. He said something about the government making overseers exempt from military service."

"So they can keep all the slaves under control," Rose stated in a hard voice.

"There are a lot of people who are afraid the slaves are going to rebel more and more now that the war has started. They're frightened of losing control."

Rose merely nodded, her contemptuous look speaking her heart. Then she turned back to the subject they had started with. "He's going to find out sooner or later, Carrie."

Carrie nodded impatiently. "I know. I know." She couldn't believe they had pulled off their deception for this long. Her father was working in Richmond, secure in the supposed knowledge that Cromwell Plantation was being managed under the capable hands of his overseer, Ike Adams. He had no idea that Carrie had thrown him off the plantation seven months earlier for attempting to rape Rose. Since that time Carrie had been running the plantation with only the aid of Rose's husband, Moses, whom she had appointed as the overseer.

"I still can't believe someone hasn't told him. It seems like everyone locally knows about it," Rose said.

"Father is so caught up in his work he isn't aware of anything else." There was no bitterness in Carrie's voice. She had long ago accepted she was right where she was supposed to be. She hated the deception but believed it was necessary. Yet more and more the necessity of lying to her father was eating at her. Their relationship had always been built on trust. Would he ever forgive her when he discovered the truth - which of course he would someday? How much longer could she live with herself - knowing she was lying to her beloved father? The plantation was still running smoothly. Isn't that what really counted? She shook her head to push away her disquieting thoughts. Pulling Granite back down to a walk, she reached into her pocket to pull out the letter again. "Let me read you what else he wrote."

Sunday morning, April 21, dawned warm and balmy. The churches of the city were unusually full. The final prayers were just being said by our minister when the bell on the Square began to toll. In an instant all was confusion. Soon the streets were full of shouting that the Yankee gunbout, Pawnee, was steaming up the James to shell the city! Military companies joined together, the artillery was called out, and women and children streamed to the river to watch the battle for the defense of our city.

I, of course, had to go rapidly to the Capitol to confer with the Governor. Word reached us shortly that it had been nothing but a false alarm. Indeed, it was almost laughable. There was no boat coming up the river. Even if there had been, her heavy draught would not have permitted passage to the city. Richmond citizens, relieved there was no attack, were able to laugh at their gullibility and resume their Sunday routine.

It was not treated so lightly in the Capitol building. We are all relieved that Colonel Robert E. Lee arrives tomorrow to take over the command of Virginia's troops. The Pawnee Scare, as we are all now calling it, simply demonstrated the chaotic unpreparedness of Richmond's defenses. It may have been a good joke on the city, but it also revealed a very uncomical state of unreadiness. We have much work to do to be ready to defend our city from the attacks that will surely come from the North.

"When does he think the North will attack?" Rose asked.

Carrie shrugged, folded the letter and stuffed it in her pocket. "I don't know. He ends the letter there with an apology that he can't write more because of time." Something in Rose's voice had caught her attention. She turned to look at her friend. "Who do *you* want to win the war, Rose?" She had been so busy thinking of her own answer to that question that she hadn't bothered to think how Rose would answer it.

Rose met her eyes squarely. "The South is fighting to preserve its right to slavery, Carrie. I know there are many other issues at stake, but wouldn't you agree that is a major one?"

Carrie nodded, knowing where Rose was headed.

Rose smiled slightly. "Surely you don't think I would support a war that would leave my people even one second longer in bondage and misery. I have no idea what the outcome of all this will be, but I can only pray for freedom for my people. Freedom to learn without having to hide in the woods in a secret school. Freedom to live their lives the way they desire. Freedom to marry and never worry they will be sold away from each other. Freedom to know their children will not disappear one day - sold to the highest bidder." Rose paused. "I'm not sure what will happen to the slavery system if the North wins. Maybe nothing. But I *am* sure what will happen if the South wins."

Carrie nodded. "I understand." She knew most of her friends and family were ardently opposed to the beliefs she now held, but she was comfortable with what she believed. There would be times when her position would cause her heartache but she knew she had to be true to herself.

The look Rose directed her way was a mixture of appreciation and compassion. Carrie knew what she was thinking. *Robert...* They had not talked about him since Carrie had returned from Richmond a month ago. Rose didn't know about... Carrie shook her head firmly and reined her thoughts back in. Now was not the time.

"Tell me how your school is going." Rose would know what game she was playing.

Rose played the game well, launching easily into a newer, safer subject. "The school is going wonderfully! Every child on this plantation can now read a little and write their name. There are some who struggle to do that. Others are going almost faster than I can keep up with." Rose paused, her eyes glowing with excitement. "Oh, Carrie, there is nothing more exciting than seeing a child struggle to read and suddenly get it. It's just like a light goes off in their head. I can see it because it lights up their eyes! Suddenly all those shapes make sense and a whole new world is open to them!"

Carrie smiled as she watched her friend's face. "Someday you'll have your own school, Rose. You'll be free. Then you can be the teacher you've always dreamed of being."

Rose frowned. "That's all I've ever wanted." Then she paused. "I'm in no hurry, though. The only way I can have my dream is for Mama to die. I can't even stand to think that way."

Carrie nodded, unable to imagine Cromwell Plantation without Rose's mama, Sarah. Sarah had been a part of her life since she'd been born. She had been more like a mama to her than her own mother had been. Rose adored her mama, and had vowed to never escape the plantation as long as she was alive.

"I'm content for right now," Rose continued. "Moses and I have that wonderful new cabin you gave us. The plantation children are growing and learning, and I still get to teach the adults. So many of them, especially Opal, are learning so fast."

When Rose fell silent, Carrie knew she was thinking about the group of eight slaves she had helped escape through the Underground Railroad 10 months earlier. Opal could have been part of that group, but she had chosen to stay on the plantation, too afraid to leave the security she had always known. It was many months later before Carrie discovered the whole story. "She would make a different decision now, wouldn't she?" Carrie asked quietly.

Rose shrugged. "I think so. She knows she can leave, though. I just don't think she has anything to go to. And all the slaves are happy now. They have plenty of free time. They are working hard because they want to. You've given them plenty of land to plant their gardens and their livestock is thriving. The ones who are left simply don't want to leave." She paused. "Freedom is more important to some of us than others. Some people can think of nothing but freedom. Others concentrate on security and safety because that's what is most important to them. I think all the slaves with a yearning for freedom are gone. The ones who are still here are here because they want to be."

Carrie nodded and then started in the saddle. A far off call had caught her attention. Straining her eyes, she looked off to the west. It took a moment for her eyes to focus. "It's Moses," she said suddenly. "I wonder if something is wrong."

It took only a couple of minutes for Moses to canter up to where they waited for him on the road. The towering black man rode his large gelding easily. He had learned to ride when Rose did, but it had come naturally to him. Now he looked as if he had spent all of his life in the saddle.

Carrie admired his grace for a moment and then spoke quickly. "Is something wrong, Moses?"

"Not a thing," he grinned. "I just saw my beautiful wife and my favorite plantation owner's daughter, and thought you might like to take a look at the fields. It's been a while since you've ridden the fields, Carrie."

"I trust what you're doing."

Moses nodded easily. "I know that. But you've been doing all your work inside lately. You haven't been doing what you love. I'd like to show you what we've been doing."

Carrie hesitated, and then agreed with a smile. "You're right. I've been too chained to papers and reports lately. Not to mention nursing sick people down in the Quarters. I certainly will be glad when this latest illness goes away. Two more of the children came down with it yesterday. It's not too serious, but they will be miserable for a few days." Her face creased with a frown as she thought about them.

Moses interpreted her look. "Sarah will take care of them till you get back, Carrie." His tone was gentle, but firm.

Carrie gazed at him for a moment and then smiled again. "Lead the way, overseer. We're all yours."

Carrie allowed thoughts of everything else to flow from her mind as the three trotted easily down the road. She was thankful for the raised roads her father had so carefully built. The hot sun had already almost dried the well-drained surface, while the fields still had standing puddles from the massive rains. Stretched out on each side were luxuriant fields of green.

Moses pointed proudly to his right. "The tobacco is coming in fine. Even with fewer hands to work it, we're still on target with what they did last year. This last rain is going to help us a lot. The ground was getting pretty dry. These soaking rains will put all the moisture back in the soil. We should have a bumper crop this year."

Carrie smiled as she looked over the fields. She knew her father would be proud of the way they looked. She also knew he would be shocked if he knew they had been completely supervised by one of his own slaves. Her father was convinced blacks were intellectually incapable of being in charge of themselves and of their destiny. If he could only see what Moses and the rest had done, maybe it would change his mind. Not that she held much hope of that. She and her father had argued about slavery before. They clearly stood on opposite sides of the fence. He and Robert were in agreement on that issue. Robert... Once again the thoughts she fought so hard to control flooded her mind. His handsome face and flashing dark eyes, surrounded by a shock of wavy, dark hair rose before her.

Granite, startled momentarily by a rabbit bolting from the brush lining the fields, shied slightly and snorted his disdain for the furry little creature as he once again picked up his steady trot. It was enough to jolt Carrie from her errant thoughts.

The three friends rode in silence for a long while. It was Moses who broke the silence. "It doesn't seem possible there is a war going on. Life is going on around here just like always."

Once again a frown creased Carrie's face. "I hope the war doesn't touch us here." She paused. "I don't know how realistic that is, though." For just a moment she could see swarms of soldiers flooding the fields of Cromwell Plantation. She shook her head to push away the vision. "My father said in his letter that men from all over the South are pouring into Richmond to train as soldiers. Lee has started up a training camp at the Fairgrounds. With Washington less than a hundred miles away, there are sure to be attempts to take Richmond. He said the people seem to be actually eager for a fight." She shuddered as she thought of the death and destruction on both sides. "They seem to think one good beating from the South will make the North tuck their tails between their legs and flee back to their homes."

"You disagree?" Rose asked.

"I think too many people are still seeing it as a game. When Southern boys are killed and the wounded start pouring in, I believe reality will set in. And no, I don't believe the North is full of the cowards they think it is. I know many of them. They, too, are going to fight for what they believe in."

Moses nodded. "It's going to be a long war, I think."

Something in his voice caused Carrie to turn and stare at him, questioning him with her eyes.

He met her gaze without flinching. He squared his shoulders and spoke evenly. "I don't have anything against you, Carrie. You're one of the finest women I know. But I got a big problem with all the folks who done been keepin' my people in bondage for so long. I done seen too much misery to forget it."

Carrie watched him with compassion. It was at times like this when Moses slipped back into the slave dialect he had spoken all his life. He had learned to read and write quickly under Rose's tutelage, and he had worked hard to improve his speech so he would be ready to go out into the world when his opportunity for freedom came. But when his great heart became aroused about something he was passionate about, he could still slip back into his old speech.

"You know what we're doing with the tobacco right now, Carrie?"

Carrie was surprised by his sudden question. What did this have to do with what they were talking about? She furrowed her brow and tried to pull her thoughts back to the cultivation of tobacco. Finally she nodded. "You should be pruning and worming right now."

Moses nodded. "That's right." He paused for a long moment and then continued. "Raising tobacco is the same everywhere. You always got to do the worming or those big, green worms will wipe out an entire crop."

Carrie watched him closely. Where was he going with this? He knew that she was as informed about farming techniques as he was. Her father, lacking a son to train on the plantation, had imparted all of his knowledge to her. She had even spent some time helping with the worming. She remembered her disgust at having to crush the worms one by one so their voracious appetites wouldn't obliterate a crop.

"My little sister was working the fields one day when the worming was being done." Moses face had gone expressionless and his voice was flat.

Carrie's face softened. She knew he was reliving the pain of his life on the plantation he had come from the year before. She also knew how his heart ached for his family that had been sold away from each other at the auction house in Richmond.

"June was just a little thing then. Not even six years old. She had been in the hot sun all day long and she wasn't feeling too good. She finally got too tired to kill the worms. Instead of crushing them in her hands, she just dropped them in the field and moved on to the next one. She didn't have no idea she was being watched..." His voice trailed off and then picked up the story. "I turned around just in time to see the overseer grab her and spin her around. First he slapped her across the face..." Moses' voice roughened as he remembered. "Then he reached down and grabbed a whole handful of them worms and stuffed them in her mouth. June was a gagging and a choking while he just stood there and laughed."

A deep silence fell on the three as they all experienced the humiliation and pain of Moses' story.

Finally Moses spoke again, his voice once more under control. "I don't know for sure what will happen to slavery if the North wins this war. But I do know for sure what will happen if they don't." Moses took a deep breath and straightened his broad shoulders a little more. "I aim to do whatever I can to help the North if the opportunity ever comes. Right now I ain't got no idea what that is..." He paused for a long moment. "But I'll know when the time comes." His gaze swung out over the fields as his voice dropped to a rough whisper. "Yep. I'll know when the time comes."

Carrie watched him, not in surprise or shock, but in sorrow. Sorrow that it had come to this. Americans fighting Americans. Her heart grew heavy as she, too, allowed her eyes to roam the land that was her home.

The clouds that had descended upon America with the fall of Fort Sumter had intensified in their darkness. Carrie shuddered. Brothers were preparing to fight brothers. Men everywhere were leaving their families and homes to fight in a war they little understood. Friends, divided by loyalties and geography, were taking up arms to destroy friends. Families were being ripped apart by differing allegiances. Carrie knew that dark angels of death waited in the wings while the clouds moved ever lower to meet the darkness of men's hearts.

Cool air had moved in to claim the night. Carrie sighed with relief as a welcoming breeze flowed through her curtains and swept underneath the canopy bed where she lay. As usual, she was exhausted. The days began early and ended late, full of frenetic activity as she worked to keep a huge plantation running smoothly.

She lay back against her mound of pillows and allowed the refreshing air to caress her tired body. Gradually she felt herself begin to relax. She knew what would come next, but she also knew there was no way to fight it. She had tried for the last five weeks to control her thoughts - to no avail. She would let them run their course, until she fell into a deep sleep of exhaustion.

Unbidden, thoughts of Robert Borden flooded her mind. His handsome face smiling down at her as they swirled and dipped around the dance floor. His enchanting laugh as they cruised up the James River on the packet boat, the *John Marshall*. His angry look when she tried to talk to him about slavery. And finally, the look of hatred on his face as he told her of watching his father die at the hand of a slave.

Carrie's emotions swirled with the pictures racing through her mind. She loved Robert Borden. She would not deny that. But the love brought her no joy. It brought nothing but pain.

The pictures in her mind faded away as the most vivid one took their place. The look of confusion, pain and anger on Robert's face the day she had told him, five weeks before in Richmond that she could not marry him because they held such different views on slavery and on the value of a people God held as his own. Her heart had broken that day just as surely as his had. There had been a short note the day she had left Richmond that had given her a brief flicker of hope, but nothing since then.

In the lucid light of day, Carrie knew she had done the right thing. She could never join her life with someone who held such hatred and anger in his heart. But at night... At night she remembered all the wonderful things about Robert. The way they laughed and talked so easily. The feel of his arms holding her. The memory of the one kiss they had shared. The kiss that held so much promise... A promise that had been swept away by the reality of their differences.

Once again the questions tortured her. Had she done the right thing? Had she thrown away her only love? Where was he? Would he be going into battle soon? Would she ever see him again? Carrie tossed and turned as the answerless questions stormed through her.

Gradually, fatigue won the battle over her mind. As a new moon lifted its shiny sliver to glimmer a faint light down on the boiling rampage of the James River, Carrie slipped into an exhausted slumber.

CHAPTER TWO

Laughter rang out in the still evening air. Carrie smiled and walked faster in the direction of the Quarters. She was ready to have some fun. Buried under mounds of papers and receipts all day, she had just a few minutes ago pushed herself back from her father's desk. There was still correspondence to take care of but she had determinedly turned her back on it. There would always be too much to do. She was learning that she had to set limits somewhere. Sarah had invited her down for dinner a week ago and nothing would make her miss it.

Carrie's smile widened as she broke out into the clearing surrounded by the slave cabins. It looked as if most of the plantation's children were there, playing a rousing game of chase. Shrieks of laughter and shouts of triumph or defeat filled the air as lithe bodies darted in and out of the shadows, and around the bushes and trees bordering the edge of the clearing. Carrie paused for a long moment and watched the activity and listened to the happy sounds.

Suddenly one of the children, a young girl named Hannah, spied her and dashed over to where she was standing. As if remembering her manners, she came to an abrupt standstill. She quickly smoothed her faded red dress and patted at her tight braids before she grinned up at her. "Howdy, Miss Carrie."

"Hello, Hannah. Sounds like y'all are having a fine time."

"Oh, yessum! We be having a passell of fun!"

Carrie laughed at the excited pleasure in Hannah's eyes. This little girl with her glowing ebony skin, and wide grin had always been one of her favorites. Her

Mama and daddy worked as field hands. Hannah had been born on the plantation.

Hannah's clear eyes suddenly clouded over. "Miss Carrie?"

"Yes, Hannah?" Carrie stooped down so that she would be more on the level of the small child. She knew what she was going to ask.

"How be Jubal? Is he going to be all right?"

Carrie patted Hannah reassuringly on the shoulder. "Jubal is going to be just fine," she said firmly. "I checked on him this morning. His fever is going down and he is starting to eat a little bit of food. I predict he'll be playing with you again in a few days."

Hannah looked up into her eyes for a few moments and then nodded as if satisfied. "That good," she said shortly. Then she turned and dashed back into the wild game.

Carrie laughed and watched her for a few minutes. Jubal was Hannah's older brother. Somehow the little girl had missed the latest sickness being passed around among the Quarter's children. They weren't sick very often, but when something hit they all seemed to share it.

"Miss Carrie!"

Glancing up at the sound of her voice, Carrie moved in the direction of the cabin on the far end of the clearing. It was small, but it was much larger than the other small cabins that housed the Cromwell Plantation slaves. Carrie had asked Moses to build it during the month of December, not telling him the purpose for it. He and Rose had been shocked to discover it was Carrie's wedding gift to them. "Hello, Sarah. How are you tonight?"

"Ain't got no reason to be complainin', and I done got me a heap of reasons to be thankful. I reckon that makes me be doin' just fine, Miss Carrie. It sure be good to see you, girl. I was afraid you weren't goin' to make it here."

Carrie leaned down to give the tiny, wrinkled woman a gentle hug. "I wouldn't miss one of your dinners for anything, Sarah. Even Annie didn't say anything when I told her I wouldn't be eating at the house tonight."

"Humph! That woman better not say nothin'. She knows I done taught her everythin' bout cookin' she knows!"

Carrie laughed loudly. She could feel her spirits lifting as she entered the cabin Rose and Moses called home. Sarah had insisted she fix dinner there tonight so all of them would have more room. She sniffed appreciatively as she entered the room. "Sweet potato pie! My favorite! I was hoping we would have some tonight."

Sarah smiled and settled down in the rocker next to the front door. "It will be ready right soon. I picked fresh greens today and found a mess of new potatoes that be roasting on the coals. I even had Moses bring me a slab of ham."

Carrie glanced over at the table. "Are those biscuits I see there?" she asked hopefully, feeling like a small girl again. There was never a week that had passed by without her coming down to the Quarters for some of Sarah's biscuits slathered with butter.

Sarah snorted. "You know without askin' what them be, chile. You think ole Sarah gonna be fixin' you a meal without biscuits?"

Carrie just smiled and settled back in another chair. "How are my patients?"

"They goin' to be right as rain in a few days, Miss Carrie."

"Do I have time to check in on them?"

"You down here to eat, not play doctor!" Sarah's voice was stern, but her bright eyes glowed with approval.

Carrie stood and leaned down to kiss her leathery,

ebony forehead. "It won't take me long. I'll be able to relax better when I see how they're doing for myself."

Sarah smiled. "You gonna be one cracker jack doctor one o' these days, girl. You mark my words."

Carrie smiled as she tried to push down the feelings of frustration at Sarah's words. She really was content here on the plantation - at least most of the time. She knew she was where she was supposed to be. But the vision of her dream continued to dance before her almost daily. More than anything in the world she wanted to be a doctor. Her mother's death and the beginning of the war seemed to have dashed all hopes of it ever happening, but still she dreamed - still she hoped. Still she clung to the belief she would someday be able to leave the plantation. There had to still be a chance for her to follow her dreams.

The sun was just dipping below the tops of the towering oaks surrounding the clearing when she approached the tiny cabin she used as an infirmary. Having Sarah always in the Quarters was a wonderful blessing. For several years she had been the Quarters' mammy. Someone had to be responsible for the children who were too young to work in the fields. They all adored the tiny, old woman with the big heart who gave them so many hugs.

"Good evening, Jubal." Carrie said lightly as she entered the darkening cabin. "How are you feeling?"

Jubal, a strapping lad of eleven with an easy grin, lifted himself up on one arm and looked at her. "I be feelin' right much better, Miss Carrie. That stuff you done gave me was like some kind of magic!"

"I feel that way about it sometimes myself, Jubal," she laughingly agreed. "That magic is called Yarrow."

Jubal nodded. "Miss Sarah was tellin' me bout it. Said y'all fetched it from out in the woods." He shook his head in wonder. "'Magine that! An old weed keepin' me from bein' sick."

Carrie laughed again. "I used to think they were old weeds myself. That is, until Sarah taught me how to use their magic. There are still regular medicines I use, but sometimes the 'magical herbs' – that's what I call them - work better than anything else. Yarrow works well at bringing down fevers. That - combined with the ice baths Sarah gave you this morning - seemed to have done the trick." She looked with satisfaction at the renewed shine in his eyes as she placed a hand on his forehead.

Then she turned to the other bed. "And how is our other patient doing tonight, Adam?" She reached her hand out and laid it on his forehead. "Still fighting with that fever are you?" His thin face was hot and drawn.

Adam, a wiry little seven year old, nodded wearily. His attempt at a smile failed miserably. "I reckon so, Miss Carrie," he whispered.

Smiling gently, she sat down on the edge of his rough bed. "You've only been sick for today, Adam. It seems to take a couple of days for the worst part of this to pass. I predict you'll be feeling better tomorrow."

Adam nodded again but just watched her with his dark eyes. It was obvious it took too much effort to say anything. Carrie moved over to the table she had set up next to the window and reached for the bottle of dried leaves she had left there from earlier in the morning. Taking a precise amount she mixed two small glasses with the water Moses had drawn for her from the well earlier. Then she handed them to her two young patients. "Drink all of this down. It will make you feel better."

Jubal and Adam nodded solemnly and drained the liquid without a murmur of complaint. Carrie patted them both on their heads and then moved toward the door. "I have to go now. Jubal, your Mama will be over in just a little while to spend the night with you two. She knows to come get me if I'm needed." She fixed a warm smile on her littlest patient. "Adam, try to get a good night's sleep. You'll feel much better in the morning."

"Yessum, Miss Carrie."

Rose was just walking up to the cabin when Carrie emerged into the waning light. "Mama sent me over to get you. She said if you want hot biscuits you better stop doctoring and start thinking about eating!"

Carrie laughed and lengthened her stride. "I'm ready to think about nothing *but* eating!"

Sarah was just setting her pan full of biscuits on the table when Rose and Carrie burst through the door laughing and out of breath.

Sarah looked at them with a smile of satisfaction. "That's the way life's done meant to be lived! The good Lord done made us to laugh. There be plenty of times when the heart be too heavy to laugh, so's you got to take advantage of them times when you *can* laugh. It done makes the soul strong for dem times when you can't."

Carrie took her place at the table set next to the window overlooking the Quarters. All of the children had been called in to eat their own suppers, so for a few minutes peace reigned. A chorus of frogs and crickets had come out to herald the arrival of night. The first fireflies were flashing their magical lights through the thick underbrush of the surrounding woods, an occasional one darting into the clearing as if it dared one of the children to try and capture it's mystic incandescence. Carrie could feel herself relaxing.

Sarah had just turned toward the table with the first plate full of food when Moses strode through the door, his massive body blocking all light from the waning dusk. A single candle flickering on the table shed cast a tiny circle of light. Rose stood to meet him with a kiss and then moved over to light the lantern. Soon the room was filled with a warm glow that turned the rustic cabin into a warm, comforting palace.

Moses gave a sigh of contentment as he settled down in front of the huge plate of food Sarah placed in front of him. "Looks great! And I already know how it's going to taste."

Sarah smiled and moved back to fill the next plate. Within moments the table was almost groaning under the huge plates of food she had placed in front of all of them. Carrie had learned long ago not to complain at the amount of food put in front of her. She always managed to clean it up. And she always felt like she was waddling home. But she was always happy.

After a brief blessing, there was silence for a long while. Finally Moses pushed back from the table, patted his stomach, and said, "You outdid yourself that time, Sarah. Thank you."

Sarah smiled softly at her son-in-law. "Does a heart good to see her cookin' eaten. I hope you done saved some room for some sweet potato pie."

"Since when do you need room for your sweet potato pie? There will never be a time in my life that I won't find some extra space for that!" Moses laughed.

Just then there was a timid knock at the door.

"It's open," Moses called.

No one was surprised that someone was at the door. Moses had become the undisputed leader of the Quarters, Rose was revered by all as the teacher, and Sarah was who everyone came to when there was a need. There was hardly a night they got through dinner without someone coming by.

The door opened to admit a dark skinned woman of average height. Her dress that had once fit her loosely now seemed to clutch at her mid-section.

"Opal! You're here just in time to have some pie," Sarah said warmly.

"Oh, no!" Opal protested. "I didn't come to disturb your dinner." She clutched tighter at a piece of paper she held in her hand. "I can come back later."

"Nonsense," Rose said firmly, rising to pull another rung ladder chair forward. "We were just finishing. And you will too have a piece of pie," she added firmly. "You know how much you love it."

Opal smiled then. "Well, if you insist. Sarah, you do make the best pie in Virginia."

Sarah snorted, but smiled with pleasure. She stood and moved toward the table where the pie waited. "Get on with you, girl!"

Rose turned to Opal again. "What do you have there, Opal?"

Carrie was surprised when Opal turned to her eagerly.

"It was you I came to see, Miss Carrie."

"What can I do for you?" Carrie asked immediately. She had never seen Opal so agitated. Or maybe she was just excited. There was a light in her eyes she had never seen and her ample body seemed to be trying to control a quiver.

Opal looked down at the paper she had in her hand. "My cousin up in Richmond sent me this letter. Sam done brung it to me today. She gave it to him when he was there last week."

"Sam *brought* it to me today," Rose corrected gently.

Carrie almost laughed. Rose was always the teacher. Then she turned her attention back to Opal. "What did the letter say?"

Opal took a deep breath as if she were gathering all her courage. Then she looked Carrie straight in the eye. "You remember telling us slaves that if we wanted to be free we could be?"

"I do," Carrie responded immediately.

"Did you mean it?"

"Of course she meant it," Moses interrupted. "You know that. You know that twelve of the Cromwell people have left in the past few months. What are you asking a question like that for?"

Opal looked down at the ground. "I'm sorry. I didn't mean to say it like that."

Carrie hastened to ease her embarrassment. "That's all right, Opal. I can tell you're very excited about something. What is it?" she asked gently.

Opal seemed to gain renewed courage from her words. "Like I said, I got this letter from my cousin. She's free, and living in Richmond. Seems like they need extra people at the Tredegar Iron Works and at the State Armory. She told me slaves are coming in from the country - hired out by their owners to work there." Opal paused and then looked at Carrie. "I want to go to Richmond to work, Miss Carrie. I'll send you back the money I make. And maybe," she hesitated and then continued, "maybe, I can earn enough extra to pay for my freedom."

"You don't have to pay for your freedom," Carrie protested. "I've already told you you can go free when you want."

"Your father know he's losing a lot of his slaves?"

"Well," Carrie hesitated and then just decided to be honest. "No, he doesn't."

"What's he gonna do when he finds out?"

"I have no idea," Carrie confessed. "I'm sure he won't be happy, however." Then she added, "That's not what's important, though. I don't believe slavery is right and I happen to be the one in charge of Cromwell Plantation. How my father reacts is my problem, not yours."

Opal shook her head firmly. "I don't aim to be causing no problems for you, Miss Carrie. I done already know that your father don't know about what you're doing." She smiled. "I think it's wonderful." Then she continued, "My running away to freedom won't help anyone. 'Cause it's to Richmond I intend to run. Somebody there will see me - maybe say something to your Daddy. Then that would ruin everything here for everyone else. I ain't gonna do that."

Carrie looked at her more closely. What she said made sense. It was obvious Opal had thought through this. "Let me get this straight. You want me to hire you out to work at the Armory or the iron works. Where are you planning on living?"

"My cousin has a place down at the bottom of Shockhoe Hill. She said they have room for me. She and her husband have four children, but they want me to come."

"And you want to go?"

Opal nodded firmly. "Yes, Miss Carrie. I want to go."

Carrie looked at her closely. There was a set look of determination on her face and a shine in her eyes that spoke of something more than Opal was saying. She opened her mouth to press her further and then shut it. She had offered any of her slaves freedom. Opal was turning down freedom to protect the rest of the slaves and was willing to be hired out. She would ask her no questions. Slowly she nodded. "I will arrange for you to be taken to Richmond, Opal. Sam is going into town next week. You can go with him then."

Opal's face lit with a glorious smile as a sigh of relief exploded from her lips. "Oh, thank you, Miss Carrie."

"You're welcome," Carrie said softly. "And just remember, Opal, your freedom is yours when you want it."

Carrie sighed as she ran the ivory handled brush repeatedly through her long, black hair. It still felt better when it was done for her, but she had determined months ago to take care of herself. It was hard to even imagine that she had once had everything done for her. Her baths drawn, her clothes selected and laid out, her hair brushed and arranged. At one time, Rose had done it all for her. Carrie's time in Philadelphia with Aunt Abby had changed all of that. Wealthy enough to pay for any services she desired, Aunt Abby chose to care for herself.

Carrie's face grew sad at the thought of Aunt Abby. She missed her terribly. Most of the time it seemed as if she actually were *her* aunt, and not the aunt of one of her close friends. The month she had spent in her home the summer before was one of the most special memories of her life. The two had connected on a deep level, attracted by the honesty and independence they found in each other. The years difference between them had melted away as they spent hours in heart-to-heart conversation. Carrie allowed her mind to wander and imagine what she would be doing right now if she had been free to accept Aunt Abby's invitation to come and spend several months with her, pursuing her dream of becoming a doctor. Her mother's illness and subsequent death had aborted all those plans. Carrie had become the mistress of Cromwell Plantation. How many times she had longed to walk away from her responsibility and follow her dream. There had been time before the war had started to simply tell her father he must hire a new overseer - then she could have moved to Philadelphia and started her education. Knowing she was where she was supposed to be sometimes did nothing to ease the pain of her situation.

She had struggled earlier when she had walked home from the Quarters. She was excited Opal was going to have a new beginning in Richmond. She had had to fight a creeping bitterness that nothing new was on the horizon for her. Only laughing at herself had finally helped her to gain perspective. How could she be jealous of a slave? Opal, no matter what she did in Richmond, would know she was a slave. Carrie had to keep reminding herself she had options. She could leave the plantation any time she wanted to. She knew her father would understand. It was her choice that kept her here.

She could either make the best of it, or continue to grumble.

Reaching into her dressing table drawer, Carrie pulled out a thick sheaf of letters. Turning the lantern up a little brighter, she flipped page after page of letters Aunt Abby had sent her. Their correspondence had been a saving grace for her as she had struggled to fulfill her responsibilities and duties on the plantation. Now even that had been taken away. Lincoln had ordered all mail service halted between the warring states.

Now, more than ever, Carrie yearned for a good long talk with her friend. Was she making the right decisions? Carrie knew Aunt Abby would give her no answers. But she would ask all the right questions so that Carrie could examine her heart clearly and know what she really believed, what she really wanted, and what would be the best course of action. Sometimes it was so difficult to see a situation clearly when you were immersed in it. You could so easily lose sight of the goal when the surrounding problems pressed in so tightly they obscured your view.

Oh, God......

It was sometime later when Carrie lifted her head, sensing the peace that she could find only in talking with God. Her reflection from the huge, ornately gilded mirror on her wall flickered back at her. Slowly she began to run the brush through her hair once again. She would take one day at a time. She would do the best she could. She could do no more. And no more was expected of her. Carrie's heart would almost fail her at times when she tried to look far into the future. But one day at a time. Most of the time she was sure she could make it through just one more day.

Gazing more deeply into the mirror, Carrie smiled at her reflection. As the soft breeze swirled around her, once more she tried to fathom the secrets and mysteries hidden in the mirror. She had sensed them there ever since she had been a young girl. She would spend hours staring into its clear depths, trying to imagine what secrets her great-great-grandmother had bestowed upon the mirror, and whether she, her great-great-granddaughter, would be found worthy to know the secrets.

Carrie knew the heritage the mirror had bequeathed to her. She knew that it stood as a six foot tall, gilded symbol of courage and determination - and the will to carve the life you wanted out of impossible circumstances. It had stood as a challenge before her all of her life. Each night it spoke to her - urging her on to be all she could be - to not give in to the circumstances of life.

Tonight it spoke to her once again. But in a different way. The mirror issued the same challenge as always, but then as she stared into it, it seemed to offer back the courage she would need to meet those challenges. The flickering lantern light, tossed about the room by the billowing of her long drapes, seemed to sink deep into the mirror and then come shooting back out at her, offering more radiance on its way out then on its way into the depths. Carrie sat quietly, absorbing the strength and courage it was offering her tonight.

She felt awed, sensing she had discovered one of the secrets of the mirror. If she could see herself reflected in the mirror and feel comfortable and confident about the condition of her heart, then the mirror would reach out and give her the strength necessary to follow the dictates of her heart.

Smiling softly, Carrie reached over to lower the wick on the lantern. Moving over to her bed, she slid gratefully under the covers. She sighed as the soft warmth of the bed welcomed and cradled her tired body. Just as she rolled over to bury her head in her pillows, a burst of song reached across the night and crept through her window. Carrie sat up to hear more clearly. She knew it was from the Quarters. On certain nights, when the breeze blew just right, the sounds of the Cromwell Plantation people singing, would rise to her window. Closing her eyes, she listened closely.

> *Swing low, sweet chariot*
> *Coming for to carry me home*
> *Swing low*
> *Sweet chariot*
> *Coming for to carry me home.*
> *I looked over Jordan*
> *And what did I see*
> *Coming for to carry me home*
> *A band of angels coming after me*
> *Coming for to carry me home.*

Carrie smiled and snuggled deep into her covers. No unbidden thoughts would bother her tonight.

****

To purchase either the E-book or Print version of On To Richmond visit:
www.DiscoverTheBregdanChronicles.com

The Bregdan Chronicles

Storm Clouds Rolling In
1860 – 1861

On To Richmond
1861 – 1862

The Bregdan Principle

Every life that has been lived
until today is a part of the woven
braid of life.
It takes every person's story to
create history.
Your life will help determine the
course of history.
You may think you don't have
much of an impact.
You do.
Every action you take will reflect
in someone else's life.
Someone else's decisions.
Someone else's future.
Both good and bad.

****

For notice of new book releases, or to receive my
Blogs and newsletters, go to:
www.BregdanChronicles.net

Spring Will Come
1862 – 1863

Dark Chaos
1863 – 1864

**The Last Long Night
1864 – 1865**

**Carried Forward By Hope
May 1865 – December 1865**

**Glimmers of Change
1866**

Other Books by Ginny Dye

<u>PepperCrest High Series – Teen Fiction</u>

Time For A Second Chance
It's Really A Matter of Trust
A Lost & Found Friend
Time For A Change of Heart

<u>When I Dream Series</u>

When I Dream, I Dream of Horses
When I Dream, I Dream of Puppies
When I Dream, I Dream of Snow
When I Dream, I Dream of Kittens
When I Dream, I Dream of Elephants
When I Dream, I Dream of the Ocean

<u>Fly To Your Dreams Series</u>

Dream Dragon
Born To Fly
Little Heart

101+ Ways to Promote Your Business
Opportunity

If You Want To Be A Success, Learn From 100+
People Who Already Are!

All titles by Ginny Dye
<u>www.AVoiceInTheWorld.com</u>

__Author Biography__

Who am I? Just a normal person who happens to love to write. If I could do it all anonymously, I would. In fact, I did the first go round. I wrote under a pen name. On the off chance I would ever become famous - I didn't want to be! I don't like the limelight. I don't like living in a fishbowl. I especially don't like thinking I have to look good everywhere I go, just in case someone recognizes me! I finally decided none of that matters. If you don't

like me in overalls and a baseball cap, too bad. If you don't like my haircut or think I should do something different than what I'm doing, too bad. I'll write books that you will hopefully like, and we'll both let that be enough! :) Fair?

But let's see what you might want to know. I spent many years as a Wanderer. My dream when I graduated from college was to experience the United States. I grew up in the South. There are many things I love about it but I wanted to live in other places. So I did. I moved 42 times, traveled extensively in 49 of the 50 states, and had more experiences than I will ever be able to recount. The only state I haven't been in is Alaska, simply because I refuse to visit such a vast, fabulous place until I have at least a month.

Along the way I had glorious adventures. I've canoed through the Everglade Swamps, snorkled in the Florida Keys and windsurfed in the Gulf of Mexico. I've white-water rafted down the New River and Bungee jumped in the Wisconsin Dells. I've visited every National Park (in the off-season when there is more freedom!) and many of the State Parks. I've hiked thousands of miles of mountain trails and biked through Arizona deserts. I've canoed and biked through Upstate New York and Vermont, and polished off as much lobster as possible on the Maine Coast.

I had a glorious time and never thought I would find a place that would hold me until I came to the Pacific Northwest. I'd been here less than 2 weeks, and I knew I would never leave. My heart is so at home here with the towering firs, sparkling waters, soaring mountains and rocky beaches. I love the eagles & whales. In 5 minutes I can be hiking on 150 miles of trails in the mountains around my home, or gliding across the lake in my rowing shell. I love it!

Have you figured out I'm kind of an outdoors gal? If it can be done outdoors, I love it! Hiking, biking, windsurfing, rock-climbing, roller-blading, snow-shoeing, skiing, rowing, canoeing, softball, tennis... the list could go on and on. I love to have fun and I love to stretch my body. This should give you a pretty good idea of what I do in my free time.

When I'm not writing or playing, I'm building I Am A Voice In The World - a fabulous organization I founded in 2001 - along with 60 amazing people who poured their lives into creating resources to empower people to make a difference with their lives.

What else? I love to read, cook, sit for hours in solitude on my mountain, and also hang out with friends. I love barbeques and block parties. Basically - I just love LIFE!

I'm so glad you're part of my world!

Ginny

And could you do one final thing for me? I want to be able to share the Bregdan Chronicles with as many people as I can – and the more readers I have, the more books I can write!

If you are on Facebook or Twitter will you share the post/tweet I have below with all your friends and followers? I will so appreciate it!

I just finished reading Storm Clouds Rolling In. Loved it, and have to share it! www.DiscoverTheBregdanChronicles.com

47397337R00291

Made in the USA
Charleston, SC
08 October 2015